THE
LAZARUS CHARTER

The Lazarus Charter

Published by The Conrad Press in the United Kingdom 2020

Tel: +44(0)1227 472 874
www.theconradpress.com
info@theconradpress.com

ISBN 978-1-913567-01-9

Typesetting and Cover Design by: Charlotte Mouncey, www.bookstyle.co.uk

The Conrad Press logo was designed by Maria Priestley.

THE
LAZARUS CHARTER

TONY BASSETT

This book is dedicated to the memory of British mother of three Dawn Sturgess from Wiltshire, who died, aged 44, on July 8th, 2018 from Novichok poisoning. And to the memory of Alexander Litvinenko, a British naturalised Russian defector who died in London, also aged 44, on November 23, 2006 from polonium poisoning. May they never be forgotten.

'This may be the time to say one or two things to the person responsible for my present condition. You may succeed in silencing me but that silence comes at a price. You have shown yourself to be as barbaric and ruthless as your most hostile critics have claimed. You have shown yourself to have no respect for life, liberty or any civilised value. You have shown yourself to be unworthy of your office, to be unworthy of the trust of civilised men and women. You may succeed in silencing one man but the howl of protest from around the world will reverberate, Mr Putin, in your ears for the rest of your life. May God forgive you for what you have done, not only to me but to beloved Russia and its people.'

The last words of former Russian agent Alexander Litvinenko (1962-2006) before his death.

1

That May afternoon when I saw the dead man's face in the window, I had been daydreaming about a cycling holiday I was planning to take in the summer.

It was only by chance I even noticed the face was there.

I had heard a distant rumble. The noise grew louder. The approaching London Underground train slid into the platform at Euston Square station. Brakes screeched. Passengers prepared to shuffle off the train.

It was then by chance I glanced up and saw the man briefly through a carriage window. He was wearing the same brown leather coat he always wore.

And once I'd seen him, I couldn't tear my eyes away, even though I had only seen him for about two seconds.

It was a face I knew so well. But it was the face of a man who shouldn't have been there. Who couldn't have been there.

My heart pounded as though it would burst from my chest.

'Good God! Good God!' I murmured.

I leapt up and paced along the underground platform, straining for a clearer view as the train drew to a halt.

Could I have been mistaken? I nearly collided with a child's pushchair.

'Mind where you're going!' yelled the irate mother as I mumbled apologies.

The double doors slid open. Two young men in T-shirts and faded blue denims were at the front, ready to alight. They were joined by two businessmen in pale summer suits, clasping newspapers and rapt in conversation. Then came a woman in a black cloak and hijab.

Behind them all I saw the man I knew.

Abruptly, inexplicably, he turned his head to the right and, for a second, our eyes appeared to meet. I felt a sudden intake of breath at the sight of the slim features with kind eyes and a grey goatee beard.

Then he turned away without the slightest hint of recognition and I saw him slip a pair of dark glasses on as he left the train and mingled with all the departing passengers.

I had no idea if he'd recognised me and pretended he hadn't, or if he simply hadn't noticed me at all.

His greying hair was cut much shorter than I remembered. He set off up the platform, in a direction away from me, at a furious rate, marching towards the exit. Full of energy, he seemed. Full of life.

I tried to track his progress beneath the fluorescent lighting but I could only catch brief glimpses of him striding along like someone late for an appointment. He was darting in and out of the shadows, leaving other passengers trailing in his wake. The double doors of the red underground train closed again, and a moment later the train moved away.

I didn't know what to do. I just stayed where I was while the clattering carriages disappeared into the black void. Then, on impulse, I belatedly raced up the stairs in an effort to catch up with him. A quest for an explanation. A quest for certainty.

I didn't question the logic – running after a man who shouldn't have been stepping off the Tube on a Wednesday afternoon just after four pm. Tightly clutching my folder of documents in my right hand, I just ran.

While a male voice blared out through the loud speakers: 'A good service is operating on all lines,' I hurried towards the concourse, rounded a corner and nearly careered into two indignant travellers. They were slim, young women in short-sleeved summer tops and jeans, struggling with heavy cases.

'Look out!' one of them cried while the other cursed me beneath her breath.

'I'm so sorry,' I called out as I ran towards the barrier and swiped my Oyster card. My eyes scanned the dark walkways, anxious to make out any sign of the figure I'd seen. It was the start of rush-hour and the concourse was bustling with people. But I refused to concede.

I ran around like a mother who'd lost her child, staring like a maniac into strangers' faces. Where was the man? Had he left by the northern or southern exit? Where was my friend? I gambled he had taken the southern exit and bounded up around twenty-five steps to find myself in Gower Street, close to the Euston Road. Fast-moving traffic thundered by. The air reeked of petrol fumes. But I must have lingered too long on the platform. There was no sign of him.

Doubts crept in. Maybe it wasn't my friend at all. Perhaps a man with similar facial features had drifted into my line of sight. Perhaps he was a lookalike, a double, a ringer.

I desperately wanted to find him, so I could prove this was the case. I ventured out onto the pavement running beside the dual carriageway.

But though I gazed up and down the road several times in the chill air on this first day of May, my friend – or his doppelganger – was nowhere to be seen. There was just an old woman with a mauve headscarf crouched on the ground beside the top step with a sign which read: I'm hungry. Thank you. I guessed he had probably taken the northern exit and had disappeared into the crowds on the other side of the main road.

Tossing a pound coin into the poor woman's tin I murmured 'Good luck!', then I reluctantly retraced my steps, passing through the barrier and walking thoughtfully back to the scene of my apparition.

The brown wooden bench was now occupied by a smartly-dressed, middle-aged couple, who peered at me suspiciously as I was perspiring and breathing heavily. A westbound Circle Line train drew in. The couple rose and approached the train, but I was too shaken to join them. Other waiting passengers boarded and the train moved off with a shrieking sound. Alone now, I stared vacantly along the line at the departing carriages and resumed my place on the bench.

I knew I needed to calm down and settle my emotions. But, as I watched for another train, so many thoughts were swirling through my head.

Did Gus have a twin brother he had never mentioned, perhaps because of some unspoken, cataclysmic family rift? The idea of a secret sibling was implausible.

The man on the train had black jeans and a brown, leather mid-length coat – exactly the kind Gus wore. Would an imitator have been so familiar with his fashion? So the doppelganger option was unlikely.

Had I been mistaken? Many folk in London, it is often suggested, look the same. Yet the face on the train had been so striking, the image so vivid and the man's demeanour so typical of Gus. Like my friend, he was extremely tall and towered over the other travellers. But the most compelling clue had been the brown coat. He always wore it. So I doubted I'd been mistaken.

Was it possible I had forgotten precisely what he looked like? I hadn't actually seen Gus in person for six months, so was I muddled? But no one had challenged my powers of recollection before, so I discounted having a memory lapse.

Lastly, had I fallen victim to some mysterious supernatural force? Something that had wrenched me from my normal humdrum world and propelled me into some time warp where the rules of logic no longer applied? Unlikely as it seemed, this made as much sense as anything else.

My mind kept racing as I stared across at the posters advertising West End shows. They added flashes of colour to the grey walls of the increasingly busy station. Another train clattered in. I resolved to catch it. I looked up, my eyes following the ways of fellow-travellers as they jostled towards the doors. I stepped towards the nearest carriage.

Someone ahead pressed the entry button. I climbed on and sat down, now ready for my journey to Baker Street to meet some friends.

Memories flooded back like long-forgotten film clips of happy days spent in Gus's company, of sharing convivial drinks, lavish restaurant meals and late-night conversations. Of attending lectures together, of flirting with women together and of supporting each other in times of crisis.

Then I was transported back to the present, where, as if in

a scene from a horror movie, his lofty figure rose from his seat and strolled off the Tube.

My brain told me that's what I'd seen. But here's the thing. He'd not just risen from his train seat on that fateful May afternoon. He'd risen from the dead.

You see, it was only a little after five weeks since I'd been to his funeral...

2

Monday, March the twenty-fifth.

'Bob! Over here!' cried a voice I recognised as Anne and I trudged up the country lane towards St Peter's Church. My close friend Tristan Barnes was waiting for us by the lych-gate in a long, dark-green coat. We allowed a small black van to pass by and then crossed over.

'You found somewhere to park then?' he asked.

'We were lucky,' I said. 'We took the last space by the duck pond – next to those Georgian cottages.' I clasped his hand warmly and looked up at the grey church, rising proudly on the hillside among the trees. He bent down to kiss my blonde-haired wife on both cheeks.

'Such a sad day,' he muttered. 'Poor old Gus. What a terrible way to die.' We could only nod our heads in agreement. Then we followed him up the steep pathway through the churchyard.

During our earlier journey from the pub where we had stayed overnight, I had been reminiscing. I had recalled the antics and practical jokes our group of friends had engaged in while at university fifteen years before.

But the sight of Tristan brought me back to reality.

We had come to the quiet, eternally peaceful Gloucestershire village of Hanbury St Peter to bury our much-loved colleague, Professor Gus Morley, whose life had been snatched away at the age of forty-seven.

It had felt like the first day of summer as we climbed the gentle slope to the church.

The sun shone down from a bright blue sky as if the land had finally woken from its long winter slumber. The aroma of freshly-mown grass wafted past us on the soft breeze.

A lone bell sounded its mournful note from the top of the building's fifteenth century west tower while a Union flag fluttered at half-mast.

In silence, we crossed the field of gravestones arranged haphazardly around. Here and there, rows of scented daffodil blooms and clusters of primroses adorned the grass beside the path.

Just as the pallbearers brought in from the hearse Gus's coffin, decked with red and white flowers, the three of us crept through the arched door and squeezed into a pew at the back with other latecomers.

I noticed a cold, musty smell as a churchwarden handed out the order of service. The nave of the country church was packed with mourners.

At the front sat the proud widow, Claudia, her two children and all the relatives, their heads bowed.

As we made ourselves as comfortable as we could, I whispered to Tristan: 'Was it Claudia's idea to have a burial and not a cremation?'

'Yes, there were long discussions,' he murmured. 'But she was insistent on a burial. Family tradition or something.' One of the Gloucestershire MPs gave an address, commending Gus for the brilliance of his scientific research work and his success in reaching the heights of his profession.

The only moment of levity came when the officiating vicar

mistakenly referred to our dear friend by the wrong name, saying: 'Nigel possessed one of the sharpest brains of his generation.' A peal of gentle laughter echoed round the nave.

He quickly apologised and went on: 'The inspirational work of Augustus Erskine Morley will never be forgotten. He has been taken to the Lord in the prime of his life.'

I smiled, recalling a less inspiring Gus who, as a student, organised a football match in our communal lounge. While he attempted to score a goal, the ball struck a light fitting, blowing electrical fuses throughout the house.

After the final hymn, 'Abide With Me,' the pallbearers raised the coffin to their shoulders and walked slowly back down the aisle towards the main door. Claudia clutched the arm of her fifteen-year-old son James, while his sister, Sophie, fourteen, strolled bravely behind holding the hand of an aging relation. With their heads bowed, they led the mourners in a dignified procession out of the church.

Once the committal ceremony had ended, a tearful Anne queued with me and Tristan to cast soil onto the coffin in the open grave.

Each handful of earth struck the lid with a thud like drumbeats signalling to the next world: 'Look out! Here comes Gus!'

Our mood lightened only slightly as we entered the driveway of our late friend's imposing eight-bedroom house for the wake.

We walked past two Bentleys, several large Mercedes, two Jaguars, a Bentley and a Morgan sports car, parked randomly on the edge of the gravel drive.

Bright yellow daffodils, those heralds of spring, nodded their heads in the breeze as we approached the door. In turn, we paid respects to Gus's grieving widow, who was slim, about five feet seven inches tall and with dark, medium-length hair. She waited, solemn and alone, at the pillared entrance porch, greeting mourners in a black, wide-brim hat with a veil and a close-fitting black dress.

'We're so sorry for your loss, Claudia,' I mumbled, bending to kiss her cheek as she drew back the veil. I noticed her eyes were red. 'If there's anything we can do at any time . . . '

They were words, I was sure, she would have heard many times that morning, and in the interval following Gus's death. Anne hugged her.

'Please let me know if there's anything you need at all,' my wife whispered. 'James and Sophie are my god-children, after all, so if there's anything the family need at all, please don't hesitate.'

'Thank you – both of you,' thirty-nine-year-old Claudia mumbled in reply. Although she'd had two months to recover after the death, her face still had the haunted look of someone whose loss was fresh.

We passed through the vaulted reception hall and were greeted by the smell of coffee and freshly-baked bread. Then we stepped into the drawing room – a grand chamber with a polished wooden floor and tall sash windows leading to a veranda overlooking the grounds.

On either side of the nineteenth century carved marble fire-place were antique sideboards containing, on the left, Ming dynasty vases surrounding a hand-painted French mantel clock. On the right side nestled a collection of Georgian silver teapots. Watercolour paintings by nineteenth-century British artists were on show throughout the room.

Although the fireplace was intended as the focal point, my

eyes were continually drawn to the far wall. It was stacked from floor to ceiling with shelves laden with books. In front of them stood two busts on plinths – one of physicist Albert Einstein and the other of naturalist and anti-slavery campaigner Charles Darwin. They were both heroes of Gus's.

A petite waitress with blond hair and a shy smile handed us both white wine as we found ourselves standing next to a coterie of academics, scientists and diplomats from across the world.

Amid the hubbub of conversation and the clinking of glasses, my eyes eventually found Tristan, a quiet, introspective Northerner who had studied history with me.

He was speaking to another student friend, Jago Lawson, a jovial Londoner who had gained at least a stone in weight since our last encounter. His optimistic approach to life was usually uplifting, although even he had the gloomy air of an out-of-work undertaker about him.

'This is a terrible business,' he muttered as he warmly shook my hand.

'You remember Anne, don't you?' I asked.

'Yes, of course!' said my portly friend, who at thirty-eight was two years older than Tristan and me. 'The river trip at Windsor.' He lowered his head to kiss Anne, who looked prim in a charcoal-grey dress with a light-green cardigan.

'You're obviously feeling better now,' she said with a smile.

'Yes, I was a bit groggy that night, my dear, but I was as right as rhubarb the next day.' His horn-rimmed glasses slid almost to the end of his nose as he looked sombre for a moment.

'How is Claudia taking it?' I wondered.

'As well as can be expected,' Jago replied, taking a sip from his glass of wine. 'Jemima and I have been spending a lot of time over here. I think Claudia's over the initial shock, but it'll take some time.'

'You remember Jago's married to Gus's younger sister,' I mentioned to Anne in a low voice.

'Of course,' she replied. Then she asked out loud: 'How are Jemima and Lavinia coping?'

'As well as can be expected,' said Jago. He looked slightly uncomfortable in his tightly-fitting grey suit. 'The whole thing's been such a shock.'

'There were at least a hundred people at the church,' Anne continued.

'A hundred and twenty were invited,' he said as he sipped from his glass, careful to avoid spilling any wine on his jacket.

'It's a great turn-out,' remarked Tristan, glancing around the room. 'Gus would have been delighted.'

'Yes. Gus had been to four universities and was a member of dozens of societies and associations. They're all represented,' Jago admitted.

'The MP who spoke in the church – is he here?' asked Anne.

'There's two or three MPs and a Whitehall mandarin on behalf of Number Ten,' said Jago, as he glanced through the patio doors towards the tennis courts. 'And there's a few of his bosses from the MoD. One of them is that white-haired fellow by the fireplace. I think he's called Jonathan Evans.'

Anne and I peered across at the man, who returned our gaze with a smile. We both smiled back and then turned away.

'What did you think of that business in the churchyard?' Jago asked. It was question that surprised me.

'The committal?' I said.

'Yes,' Jago said. 'The old reverend's so frail and wobbly it was touch and go who'd make it into the grave first – the vicar or the coffin.'

Anne and I smiled. 'Yes, he did rather teeter on the brink,' I said.

'Of course, as you probably know, Gus wasn't much of a churchgoer,' Jago went on. 'It's doubtful he even believed in God. But funerals are for us poor souls left behind and Claudia insisted on a church service.' Anne was keen to change the subject.

'Jago, are you and Jemima still in Oxfordshire?' she asked.

'Yes, my dear,' he said to Anne while accepting the offer of a vol-au-vent from a passing waitress.

'Any time you decide to drop by,' Jago added, 'you'll probably catch me in my farmer's smock, driving a tractor and chewing a piece of straw. Hey! This food's great. D'you know? I can't remember when I last got my molars round a ham and turkey vol-au-vent.'

As Anne bit into a sausage roll, she took me aside and whispered: 'Shouldn't we ask about the accident? Jago's close to the family. He'd know what happened.'

I nodded.

'Jago?' I said, with a glance at him, 'can you tell us a bit more about what happened on the first of February?'

'You mean the accident?'

'Yes,' said Anne. 'All we've been told is it was a terrible car crash. We didn't like to probe too much when the family were grieving.'

'Terrible's the right word,' said Jago, lowering his voice. 'I'll tell you what I know, which isn't much.' Tristan, Anne and I huddled closer. Jago dipped his head and looked around like a man about to divulge a state secret.

'Gus was on his way to a conference in Surrey. He'd been advised not to go because the roads were affected by snow and ice and more snow was forecast. But you know what he's like when he's got an idea in his head.'

Jago drew a quick breath then went on: 'He sets off in his Mercedes from his flat in Bloomsbury, but police believe that, when he got onto the M25, traffic was so slow he turned off near the town of Sevenoaks and got onto the A25. That's a road that would have taken him directly to Redhill, his destination.

'But, for some unknown reason, he turned off that road as well and began travelling along a country lane just outside Westerham. His car ploughed into a tree and burst into flames. Well, fire and ambulance crews raced to the scene, but it was too late. The car was almost totally burnt out. Our old pal was pulled from the wreckage, but, of course, he'd received horrific burns and must have died quickly.'

I put my arm round Anne as I noticed she was close to tears.

'That's absolutely awful,' I said.

Tristan interrupted to say: 'It wouldn't have been the blaze that killed him. He'd have died from injuries caused by the head-on crash.'

I nodded.

'Of course. He'd have known nothing about it,' I said. 'But there'll obviously be an inquest.'

'Absolutely,' said Jago.

'Were there any witnesses?' asked Tristan, placing his empty glass down on an antique side table.

'Jemima asked Claudia about that,' Jago replied. 'Apparently no one witnessed the crash. The clock on the dashboard stopped at just after a quarter past five and the fire brigade took nearly half an hour to arrive.'

'Surely someone would have spotted a car on fire?' Anne suggested.

'You'd have thought so, my dear,' said Jago. 'But it was on the edge of a wood and the nearest house was some distance away. It was only by luck that a farm worker was cycling along the lane and made a 999 call. The rescue services came as quickly as they could, but it was all over bar the shouting. About all that was left of the car was the blackened frame and the rear number plate.'

'How dreadful,' I said, slowly shaking my head.

'So did Claudia have to go to the mortuary and identify the body?' asked Anne, who always took an interest in the practical detail, however gruesome.

'Yes. Jemima went with her,' Jago revealed. 'They went to the mortuary at Pembury in Kent. Is that near you?'

'No, that's fifty miles from us. You've been to our place. We're near Canterbury,' I exclaimed.

'Oh, yes,' said Jago. 'Well, there wasn't much to see. Bit of a wasted journey, if you ask me. It was very traumatic for them, but they insisted on going on their own.'

'That's an absolutely dreadful experience to have to go through,' said Anne.

Jago nodded. 'Yes, utterly appalling for the poor girls. Of course, the police were pretty certain from the start it was Gus. It was his car, after all, but they have to dot the i's and cross the t's. So they had to get his dental records from Tewkesbury. It took a while to get hold of them. That's why it's taken seven weeks to hold the funeral. As far as the coroner's officer was concerned, the only benefit in Claudia being there was that she was able to identify Gus's signet ring which was found in the car. She broke down in tears when she recognised it as the ring she'd bought him.'

'It's going to take us all a long time to get over this, Jago,' I remarked.

'Yes, old bean. You're right there,' he said. 'It's going to take us a very long time. Fortunately, he made a will a few months ago, so that'll make things a little easier for Claudia and the kids.'

'What on earth could have happened?' asked Anne. 'D'you think it was a heart attack?'

'Far too early to say, my dear,' said Jago. 'That may come out at the inquest, but there's no history of heart problems.'

'You know the police were here today, don't you?' said Tristan abruptly.

'How d'you know that?' I asked. Jago interrupted to say: 'Blue shirt and big feet.'

'Something like that,' said Tristan with a smile. 'You can usually spot them, but it helps if the guy next to you in the pew comes right out with it.'

'Yeah?' said Jago. 'Did he explain why he was there?'

'Just said he was keeping an eye on proceedings.'

'That's a little strange. Was he Kent Police?'

'I didn't ask. He was plain clothes.' At that moment, Anne took me aside.

'Bob,' she said. 'Just having a word with Claudia to see how she is. I'll be right back.' Then she disappeared. She said later she had found Claudia sobbing in the rustic kitchen, being comforted by Jemima and her children, Sophie and James. The youngsters were sitting quietly at the far end of the kitchen table, playing a computer game beside the Aga.

Anne told me later that she apologised for intruding and was turning away when Claudia called her back.

'I could do with a chat to take my mind off things,' the widow mumbled.

'When we offered to help in any way, we really meant it,' said Anne as Sophie broke off from her game and came to place her head on her mother's lap.

'Everyone's been so kind,' said Claudia, who was five years older than Anne. 'The police took a while to inform me, but, when they did, they were very understanding. The constable went next door to the Bartons first to make sure someone would be around if I needed support. He was very thoughtful.'

'Gus's death obviously came as a total shock,' said Anne, sitting on a wooden spindle-back chair.

'Yes. We were just getting on with our lives.'

'Do you think he... well, perhaps he had a heart attack at the wheel?' Anne asked. 'That happened to the husband of a friend of mine.'

'I'd be very surprised if it was that,' Claudia whispered. 'Just before he died, he saw the doctor about a slight back pain and the doctor said he had the heart of a lion, like his father, who lived till he was over ninety.'

'Had he had any problems? Was there anything on his mind?' Anne asked.

'There's no way he'd have taken his own life, if that's what you're wondering. In any case, it's a funny sort of suicide, knowing that he . . . ' Noticing Sophie was listening intently, she quickly added: 'Knowing what we do about what happened. Sophie and James, will you go up to your rooms? Your mum wants to talk to Aunty Anne.'

As the children departed, they left the kitchen door open. I was standing outside, waiting for a moment to ask Anne whether she wanted some more wine, and I stopped to listen to part of the conversation.

'I'll tell you something that I think's very strange, Anne,' Claudia said in a low voice, as if she feared being overheard. 'The police took four days to tell me about his death.'

'Really?' said Anne.

'Yes,' Claudia nodded.

'How peculiar,' said Anne. 'They're usually very prompt at that kind of thing – particularly when under pressure from the press to release news to the outside world. A detective sergeant who's a friend of mine said they strive to tell the family as soon as they're sure of the identity – to save them hearing the details third hand.'

'That may be the case normally, but not this time. My dear husband lost his life at a quarter past five on February the first and Kent Police didn't have the bottle to tell me about it until half past two on the afternoon of Tuesday, February the fifth.'

Anne sat open-mouthed for a few seconds. 'That's ridiculous,' she said. 'It was clearly his car. Presumably his mobile phone signal would have been tracked to the lane by the police.'

'I know,' returned Claudia, removing a paper tissue from her handbag and wiping her eyes. 'They just said the problem of identifying him led to the delay.'

'Didn't you make inquiries about him?'

'Yes, of course. Gus wasn't the best communicator, but when

he didn't phone me over the weekend, I began to get a little worried. He'd been due to take part in a private conference on weapons systems, but by Sunday night I suspected something was badly wrong. His mobile kept going to voicemail.'

'Did you call the police?'

'I called the local police headquarters in Quedgeley and they sent a constable round on the Monday. I also called the conference building and they said he hadn't shown up. The police were very good. They said they would make inquiries and might issue a press appeal. Then, on the Tuesday, an officer called round and told me what had happened.' Claudia began to cry and reached for a paper tissue from a box on the kitchen table.

'He was very good,' she sobbed. 'The policeman sat me down and explained there was nothing anyone could have done.'

Blonde-haired Jemima, who was wearing a long black dress, had been listening carefully to her sister-in-law's words. She put an arm round Claudia's shoulder to comfort her.

'Anne, you obviously haven't heard about what happened in Little Coleswood, have you?' Jemima said solemnly.

'No. What was that?' asked Anne.

'We haven't told many people but Gus was nearly struck by a lorry.'

'He might have been exaggerating,' murmured Claudia as she wiped her eyes. 'I'm sure it's irrelevant, Jem. I'm sorry, Anne. I'm just going to go upstairs and check on the children.' Clutching the box of tissues, she hurried from the room, not seeming to notice me as she passed.

'It's going to take her a long time,' said Jemima, as the two women watched her go. Then she lowered her voice.

'He was a difficult man to live with, you know,' she said. 'Of course, she doted on him, but he was dedicated to his work and was away a lot. They were always arguing. Anyway, that's by the by.' Anne sat down at the kitchen table.

'I've met Gus a few times. How was he in himself?'

'He hadn't been his normal self for a while. Anyway, I was going to tell you about this incident. My brother was riding his bicycle towards Hanley on the road from Little Coleswood when he realised a lorry was following him. He told Claudia he didn't take much notice to start with, but after a couple of minutes it didn't pass him. Gus was travelling at about ten miles an hour and the driver was a short way behind.'

'How strange,' said Anne. 'When was this?'

'Two weeks before Christmas – on December the thirteenth. Gus told us later he'd been very scared. The driver suddenly revved up his engine and his truck began accelerating towards him. Within seconds, it was upon him. He described afterwards how he'd been in fear of his life. If he hadn't glanced over his shoulder and noticed what was happening, the lorry would have ploughed straight into him. As it was, he realised in the nick of time and threw himself onto the grass verge, out of the vehicle's path.'

'Did you involve the police?' asked Anne.

'We told the constable who covers Hanley,' said Claudia. 'But, to be honest, I think he regarded it as some kind of road-rage incident. There's a lot of that round here with these narrow roads. People get held up and quickly lose their cool.'

'Was the driver ever caught?' asked Anne.

'No,' said Jemima. 'The lorry just drove off, leaving Gus on the ground.'

3

A gentle rain began to fall as a bus dropped me off in the centre of our quiet country village.

It was the evening of May the first. Nearly five hours had passed since my strange experience at Euston Square. Throughout my train journey back to Canterbury, I had tried to study details of my trade union's campaign for better pay, but I hadn't been able to concentrate. My mind was still dominated by thoughts of Gus.

I unfurled my umbrella and spent a few minutes trudging the short distance to our cottage in Hopgarden Lane.

I should have felt glad to be home – to be greeted by the red, yellow and white roses which filled our front garden with a riot of colour. But, to me, it didn't feel like a May evening at all. The month may herald the return of summer – a time of warmth and comfort. But the weather of late had been damp and dismal and I approached my front door with a feeling of uncertainty and foreboding. By now I had made my mind up. I had to make Anne aware of my experience.

After placing my folder of documents on the hall table, I found her in the living-room. She was sitting on our brown leather settee, watching a TV nature programme, while stroking Fiesta, our black cat.

'Hello, darling!' she exclaimed, jumping to her feet with a broad smile. 'How did it go?' she asked, kissing me on the cheek.

'They've decided to hold a consultation with members on future action.'

'Is that good?'

'It's roughly what I expected.' Anne, who was wearing a grey T-shirt and blue denims, sat back.

'We've had a letter from Yusuf,' she said. 'He sounds really happy since being given leave to stay in Britain. He loves Manchester and both he and his mother send their love.' Yusuf Osman was the stowaway falsely accused of murder who had been acquitted through Anne's efforts, and to a lesser extent also through mine.

'That's good. I'll have to read that in a minute,' I said. 'Darling, listen, I've got something to tell you. I'd better sit down first.'

I walked towards the dining table with the wariness of an Army engineer about to tackle an unexploded bomb. I turned a chair so I could sit down facing Anne.

'You're not going to believe what I'm about to tell you,' I said.

'Try me.'

'Well, after the meeting, I went to Euston Square so I could get the Tube to Baker Street and meet my three friends for a quick drink.'

'I believe you so far – especially the bit about having a drink.'

'Well, this is where it gets unbelievable. As I was waiting for my train – I don't know how to explain this, so I'll just come straight out with it. I saw Gus.'

'What on earth do you mean?'

'What I said. I saw Gus Morley with my own eyes – as clearly as I'm seeing you now.'

Anne looked at me in disbelief – as if I had consumed much more alcohol than the solitary drink I'd admitted to.

'We're talking about Gus Morley here, are we?' she said. 'Gus Morley, who, the police say, died in a blazing car three months ago? Gus Morley, whose funeral we attended five weeks ago?'

'Yes. I know it sounds strange.'

'Strange? Darling. have you gone mental? How could you possibly have seen Gus – unless you've started believing in ghosts? '

'No. I don't believe in ghosts,' I said. 'Nor reincarnation, come to that.'

'Well, then you're obviously talking nonsense and I'm starting to get worried for you.'

'Look,' I said. 'I know it doesn't make much sense.'

'It doesn't make any sense,' she muttered.

'But the fact remains I saw him – or someone looking extremely like him.'

Anne stood up and stepped towards me.

'OK,' she said. 'Explain more about how you came to see this man.'

'Well, I was just looking across and noticed him. I can't explain it in any other form of words.'

'He was standing on the platform?'

'No, on the train. I spotted him through the windows. He was just there in the same brown leather coat he always wore. He stood up. He walked towards the double doors of his compartment. He followed a group of people off the train. I ran out of the station to try to catch up with the man, but I just couldn't find him.'

'So you didn't get a clear look at him. You just caught glimpses.'

'Well, I suppose so.'

'What did he look like – this phantom figure?'

'Well, he looked just like Gus.'

'Describe him.'

'His face was pale with a deep forehead; not too prominent a nose; thick lips, but not puffy; and a grey goatee beard.'

'So no change from the day you last saw Gus then?'

'To be honest, I can't remember when I last saw Gus. I think it may have been the barbeque we went to at his house last summer.'

'So quite a time ago.'

'Yes, but I haven't forgotten what he looks like. I've known him since university fifteen years ago and I've seen him fairly regularly since then.'

'So the man you spotted on the train was exactly the same as Gus was at the barbeque party?'

'Well, I wouldn't say "exactly the same."'

'Ah! So how was he different?'

'The only difference I noticed was his silvery grey hair had been cut short – very short.'

'It's not the same man,' Anne declared.

'How d'you work that out?'

'Well, the laws of logic and reason,' she said, raising her voice slightly. 'They held a funeral for the man, for goodness' sake! Plus the man you saw was clearly of a different appearance. Look, you've been shaken up by his death more than you've admitted. You've obviously been dwelling too much on the loss of your friend…it's started playing tricks with your mind.'

'There's nothing wrong with my mind,' I insisted. 'I'm not making this up. I saw him as clear as day. In a way, I wish I hadn't seen him because it's been preying on my mind ever since. Just before he got off the train, he turned his face to the right. That meant I could see him more clearly.'

'Did he pay any attention to you?' asked Anne.

'I'm sure he didn't recognise me.'

'That's another sign that you must have been mistaken. If it had been your pal, he would have shown signs of recognition and he didn't.'

'It was only a casual glance,' I said. I stopped and looked at the floor.

As I had expected, Anne didn't believe me. I imagined no one else would believe me either. Perhaps the sighting of my friend would never be satisfactorily explained. Perhaps it would remain one of the mysteries of life along with spontaneous combustion, the Abominable Snowman, the Yeti, the Angels of Mons and will-'o-the-wisp.

'If I didn't find the whole idea so ludicrous, I'd say Gus Morley is still very much alive,' I announced, unsure whether I intended the words for Anne or for my own satisfaction. 'I'd say he's still alive.'

Anne returned to the settee and started stroking Fiesta, who had been roused from his slumbers by our raised voices and had been watching our verbal exchanges.

'What you're saying flies in the face of not only all that is rational and logical. It flies in the face of what we know,' she went on. 'We went to his funeral, after all. We even helped pile earth on his coffin. Who d'you think was in the coffin if it wasn't him? I grant you there's a bit of a mystery about why he turned off his main route in the car and took a side road, but it looks like a straight-forward road accident. Not only have the police confirmed he died in his burning car, we know it was his body. There's the dental records. There's the gold signet ring engraved with the initials AM. His car must have skidded in the snow and crashed into the tree. Whatever way you look at it, he's as dead as dead can be and if you carry on with your line of argument, I'm afraid we're probably going to fall out, and I don't want that to happen. Look, there's no way he could have been travelling on the Tube. You must be mistaken.'

Darling Anne spoke with the passion of a TV evangelist who had just gained a prime Sunday viewing slot.

'All right,' I said. 'I didn't mean to cause an argument. No good can come from discussing it further. We're just going round and round in circles. I'm going to make myself a sandwich and then sit down and mark some history essays.'

'Don't worry. I'll make us both a sandwich. But I just hope you get this nonsense out of your head. You're getting me worried. It concerns me when you say strange things like this.'

'I promise I'll forget about it,' I said.

But, try as I might, I simply couldn't bring myself to do so.

*

Two days later, at the end of the school day, I met Anne at the gates of New East Kent Academy in Canterbury, where I taught. She'd been shopping for shoes in the city but had so far failed to find a pair she liked.

We walked together, hand-in-hand, along the pedestrianised high street towards the bus station. The paving stones were still wet following an earlier shower. Suddenly the peace of

34

the afternoon was shattered by a shrill female voice. A smartly-dressed woman in her late thirties approached us, smiling and talking loudly.

It was Anne's friend, Prunella Ball, a tall, slim woman with long, brown hair tied closely behind her head.

'I haven't seen either of you in ages,' she hollered. 'Have you time for a coffee?' We looked at each other and nodded. Five minutes later, we were sitting on chrome chairs at a table in Cosimo's Café, which had become one of our favourite eating places. It was a small venue, tucked away in a back street, but it was well-lit, clean and usually not very busy. A short, dumpy waitress in glasses brought a menu. Anne and Prunella ordered two milky coffees while I opted for a strong coffee.

'I'm glad to have caught you,' said Prunella, a former Kent Police press officer who now worked as a freelance journalist. She draped her light-brown coat over a nearby chair revealing she was wearing a white cardigan and navy-blue jeans.

'Bob, I've been doing some background research into the death of someone called Professor Morley. I gather you were in the same cycling club at Oxford. Did you know him well?'

'How on earth did you know about that?' I asked.

'It wasn't difficult. It's on Google. He was the chairman and you were the secretary in 2004.' Anne laughed. 'Sounds like you've been doing your homework.'

Prunella nodded. 'I've been doing a lot of online research.'

'Yes. I knew him very well,' I conceded.

'Why are you looking into Gus?' asked Anne, as our coffees were served. 'He died three months ago. It was all over the papers at the start of February.'

'I know, but an inquest date's just been announced and one

of the Sunday papers wanted me to do some digging.'

As I began to sip my coffee, I immediately resolved not to mention my Euston Square experience for fear she too would doubt my strength of mind. But I was intrigued that a journalist should be interested in re-examining details of my friend's death. Prunella explained: 'Whenever there's a fatal road crash, there's always an inquest. The coroner wants to find out the cause and any factors leading up to it.' We both listened in fascination.

'I suppose the coroner wants to know if there's been any negligence,' said Anne. 'In a road accident, for example, he'll want to know if a car's been in for a service and whether work was done on the steering. If anyone apart from the driver is at fault, a family might make a compensation claim.'

'That's right,' said Prunella.

'I can't imagine this family would be seeking compensation,' I said. 'They're not poorly off and I think my friend Jago mentioned Gus had taken out life insurance. But if Claudia Morley needed a solicitor in Kent, I'd recommend Janice Carslake. She was so efficient when we used her before.' Anne appeared not to listen. She was more interested in the circumstances of the collision.

'I'd have thought the accident at Westerham was pretty cut and dried,' she declared, stirring her coffee. 'It looks like he just skidded into a tree.'

'Well, there's a variety of factors that could have led to that,' said Prunella. 'He could have had some kind of medical issue like a heart attack. He could have veered off to avoid hitting something. There could have been a fault with the car. It's not without interesting factors. I mean, did you know that, technically, the incident should have been investigated by Surrey Police? The spot where he died was just over the county border, but when the first 999 call was made, it was put through to the police and fire brigade in Maidstone, so it was treated as a Kent incident. This shouldn't have made any difference, but strangely it's made the whole event more difficult for me to investigate.'

'The old coroner's going to have his work cut out,' I remarked. 'There wasn't much left of either Gus or his car. The engine compartment of the Mercedes was just a black, tangled wreck of metal and wires.'

'That doesn't mean they can't gather any evidence. Just means the investigators have to work a little harder – that's all. They can look for skid marks and road markings. They can assess the speed of the car – all sorts of things,' said Prunella, sipping her coffee. 'Ooh that's still too hot. I think I've burnt my lip.' Anne stood up.

'I'll see if I can get some ice for you,' she declared.

'There's no need,' said Prunella, grabbing hold of her arm. 'It'll be all right.'

'When's the inquest?' Anne asked as she resumed her seat.

'It's at the Archbishop's Palace in Maidstone on June the sixth,' she replied. 'The press are still interested in the case. He was a well-respected government scientist.'

Anne leaned back on her chair. 'What are your thoughts on the case? You must have an opinion.'

'My job's to report on the facts, not hold opinions. Actually, I tend to work more on showbiz stories, but I've been promised a good fee for this one, so I've just got to see it through. If you ask me, Anne's right. He's skidded in the snow. Perhaps he swerved to miss a rabbit.'

'If you need any personal information about the professor, I'd be glad to help,' I said. 'I wouldn't want to say anything that might upset his widow, but I can talk about our times at university and what he was like as a person.'

'That would be tremendous, if you could. Do you know exactly what kind of research he was doing?'

'Well, other than that it was Government research of some kind, no. I'm afraid not.'

'I haven't got much more to do on the story for the moment,' Prunella added. 'But there's one person I need to speak to urgently who's proving a bit elusive.'

'Who's that?' asked Anne.

'It's the guy who dialled 999. He's called Tyler Buckley. Kent Police have given his address as Magpie Lane, Turner's Hatch, but it doesn't seem to exist.'

4

In eight years of marriage, Anne and I had seldom exchanged a cross word and I can honestly say I have never held any major secrets from her. But, as the second week of May arrived, I feared all that was about to change.

For, at a time when I should have been focused on getting my Year Eleven history pupils through their exams, all I could think about was the notion that Gus Morley was still alive.

Over the weekend, I had sorely wanted to raise the issue again with Anne. She was convinced the whole suggestion was nonsense and I had pledged to forget about it. But I was finding it impossible.

Anne was by now working three nights a week as an English teacher at two nearby farms. On the evening of Tuesday May the seventh, she was taking a class at Pilgrims Farm in nearby Chivingden and this gave me the opportunity to make some phone inquiries. I knew that CCTV cameras operate at all London Underground stations. I wanted to know if I could view the footage from the cameras at Euston Square at a few minutes after four pm on May the first. But I didn't want Anne to know.

Although I felt extremely guilty, I decided to avoid using the house phone and chose to call British Transport Police in London on my mobile – believing I could clear the data afterwards to remove any sign of my activity.

A gruff-voiced policeman boomed down the phone: 'How can I help you, sir?'

I said: 'This is just a general inquiry. I just wanted to know how easy it would be for me to look at some of your camera footage for the afternoon of Wednesday, May the first.'

'With what purpose, sir?'

I had to think quickly. I could hardly say I wanted proof an old friend had come back from the dead.

'Well, I'm a teacher concerned about a child playing truant. I thought I might catch the lad getting off one of your trains,' I said, hoping the tale sounded convincing.

'For us to go to the trouble of checking CCTV from the platform cameras, first of all you have to be a victim of a crime and you'd be brought into identify a criminal suspect from our cameras. It doesn't sound as though this is the case here, sir.'

'No. So a member of the public can't just call in and have a look at the camera footage?'

'No, sir. If it was an official missing person inquiry, we'd bring you into the operations room and show you the footage and invite you to identify the person. But a crime would have to be reported first. Has any crime been reported?' I had to admit it hadn't.

'Well, if that's the case, sir, I can't help. We don't let people view the footage on a whim that a child might be playing truant. We're having a very busy week.' With that, the officer hung up.

'Damn the man!' I said under my breath. It was no wonder so many disgruntled excluded children were found wandering round the capital at various times of the day and night. It was partly the fault of people like that, I decided. At least I knew now that I would get no help from the authorities. I would have to follow my own intuition and return to the scene of the incident.

It had gradually dawned on me that I might be able to contrive a second encounter with the man I had seen – the man I believed to be Gus Morley. It was possible he regularly travelled on the London Underground to Euston Square on a Wednesday afternoon. If so, I could visit the station again this coming Wednesday at around the same time - four pm – and, this time, I would be prepared. I would bring a camera and take his photograph. That way no one could argue I had taken leave of my senses. No one could claim poor old Bob Shaw was going doolally...

Two days later, at Wednesday lunchtime, I set off for London. It was a blustery, rainy afternoon, so I'd brought my umbrella. On arrival at St Pancras, I braved the elements and walked to Euston Square station, which was just a mile away along the Euston Road. I arrived at twenty past three.

It felt strange to return to the scene of my earlier sighting, but I felt compelled to see if I could meet the man again. I realised I was becoming obsessed with the incident, but felt I had to satisfy my curiosity.

The station lies hidden below the busy dual carriageway. Its southern entrance is beneath a ten-storey steel and glass edifice serving as a charity's headquarters, while a coffee shop bestrides the northern entrance.

For more than an hour, I waited beside the track, eyeing every passenger that got off. Female shoppers in summer dresses swept off each train alongside foreign tourists, office workers and noisy children. Some had remembered to bring umbrellas or raincoats. But the man in the brown leather coat was nowhere to be seen and, when the time reached a quarter to five, I decided my mission had been fruitless. I was hardly surprised not to see him, but I'd known that I really had to try.

Another idea came to me. I walked up to the concourse, swiped my travel pass and asked a member of station staff if he had seen a man in a brown leather coat with short, bristly grey hair. But the young, slim, blond-haired station assistant simply glared.

'We 'ave around forty thousand passengers passing through 'ere every day, sir,' he said. 'I imagine a fair few of them coats has passed through 'ere today an' all. In any case, I've only just started me shift.'

Defeat loomed. I walked aimlessly up the steps to the Gower Street exit, wondering if I would ever catch another glimpse of the man on the train.

After reaching the top step, I stood with my hands on my hips, gazing up and down the street. All I could see were passing taxis, the female beggar sitting on the pavement a few yards in front of me, a row of bicycles across the road, the extensively-glazed University College Hospital and other office buildings. But no sign of my quarry. I felt as lost as a flustered duck caught in a hailstorm.

As before, I hurled a one-pound coin into the woman's tin. She smiled up at me and stroked the small mongrel dog beside her.

'I remembers you, sir,' she remarked from beneath her mauve headscarf. 'As sure as I'm alive, you was 'ere last week, wasn't you? I never forgets a face.'

'You're right,' I said. 'You might think this a little strange, but I'm trying to find someone – a Tube traveller who used this station last Wednesday. I just thought he might come here every Wednesday, but I haven't seen him today.'

'Sounds important. Is it important?' asked the red-faced woman, who was bundled up in a brown coat with layers of clothing underneath. I bent down to stroke her light-brown dog, that looked like a cross between a Labrador and a Staffordshire bull terrier.

'Yes, very important.'

'What's he look like, sir?'

'Well, he's about six feet two inches tall. He's got very short grey hair and was probably wearing a medium-length brown leather coat.'

'Sounds like The Celebrity,' she muttered under her breath as if speaking to herself.

'What did you say?'

'Oh, it's just a silly joke between me and me cousin. We both do the Square. You're right. He comes on a Wednesday. He walks off down Gower Street. He's sometimes here with a minder, so we calls him The Celebrity. I asked him the other day if I'd seen him on telly, but he said No.'

'Really? You've a nickname for him?'

'Yes.'

'How interesting. So, what time does he pass through here usually?'

'Oh, you've missed him now, sir. He was a little early today. He's usually here between three thirty and four thirty of an afternoon, but it must've been nearer three today. I don't know where he goes, but he never comes back through here.'

'I'm not sure if it's the person I'm looking for,' I said.

'I understand,' she said. 'He – The Celebrity, I mean - always gives me money. There ain't so many that do, so I tend to remember them – hoping to catch 'em again, like. He's got the accent too.'

'How d'you mean?'

'He's got what you might call a BBC accent. And he often wears these glasses…'

'Tortoiseshell?'

'Yeah. A sort of a brown colour. Sometimes dark glasses. Seems like we're talking about the same fella, sir.'

'Possibly. Why d'you call him The Celebrity?'

'Oh it's just a nickname. We don't mean no harm. He's got a posh voice like an actor and he's often with a burly guy who looks like a cage fighter. You tend to think a posh fella with a bodyguard might be some kind of celebrity – that's all. Hey, I hope I don't get him into any trouble. He might not put a jingle in me tin.'

'Don't worry. He's an old friend of mine. I'm trying to track him down.'

As I left the poor woman sitting on the pavement beside the kerb, I tossed another coin into her container, a two-pound one this time.

Our conversation had left me feeling slightly reassured. We obviously didn't know whether the man she'd seen was Gus, but at least the man in the brown leather coat existed. Someone else had seen him apart from me. My first sighting was almost certainly not a figment of my imagination. Her words had the ring of truth about them and I believed her when she said the man never used Euston Square for his return journey. I walked back down the steps into the station.

*

On the following night, Anne travelled to the Finch & Davies farm in the nearby village of Sissenden to hold her regular Thursday evening English class for foreign workers.

This gave me the chance to go for a drink in our village pub, the Merry Friar. The landlord, Miles Benton, is a stout man who projects a commanding presence. His curly white hair, white moustache and straggly white beard somehow make me think of a fearsome Victorian mill owner.

As he poured me a pint of my favourite bitter, he was clearly in his usual ebullient mood. While the latest Ed Sheeran song could be heard above the hubbub of conversation, he said: 'Did you hear about the Irishman who thought patio was Italian for Patrick?'

I tried to smile out of politeness, while Miles laughed uproariously.

'Here's another. A man was visiting a hotel restaurant with his missus. The waiter says: "Excuse me, sir. Have you got reservations?" And the fella says: "Yes, the food was poor last time, but we thought we'd give you another chance." Again I only smiled weakly and sipped my ale. He knew instantly I was out of sorts.

'Oh dear, what's the matter?' he asked. 'You can tell Uncle Miles.'

'I've seen something I shouldn't have seen,' I mumbled.

'So you're a man at last.'

'Miles, I've been happily married for years. No, I've seen

someone who shouldn't have been there.'

'Why not?'

'Because he was dead.'

'You're serious?' Miles asked.

'Yes.'

Miles began reciting a poem in a low voice: 'Yesterday, upon the stair, I met a man who wasn't there. He wasn't there again today. Oh how I wish he'd go away.'

'What's that, Miles?' I asked. 'Some kind of poem?'

'It's lines written by an American called William Hughes Mearns in 1899. It's about a haunted house in Nova Scotia. Maybe you've had a similar experience?'

'D'you know? I feel like I've seen a ghost,' I said. 'But what is it with you? You're very knowledgeable all of a sudden. Have you swallowed an encyclopaedia?'

'My girlfriend's studying poetry at English classes,' said Miles. 'I get to read some of her coursework. That poem came up the other day. Anyway, about this ghost, d'you want to tell me about it? Maybe I can help. I'm a bit of an expert on ghosts, poltergeists, banshees and things that go bump in the night. Used to be a hobby. Did I tell you about the night I slept in a haunted house?'

I shook my head, hoping he wasn't going to tell me. Luckily, a customer at the far end of the bar waved a ten-pound note, which lured him away.

In truth, I was reluctant to tell my friend anything else. My mind was made up. I would go back to Euston, take a photograph of the man in the brown coat and return with the image as proof. Then perhaps my wife and friends would believe me. For the moment, I dared not discuss what I had seen for fear of everyone questioning the state of my mental health.

Later that evening, I got Miles to repeat the poem and he tried to teach me the full three verses.

'I'm sorry I've been in the doldrums this evening,' I said.

'Don't apologise, old boy.'

'I just need to sort a few things out. Then, when I'm ready, I'll tell you the whole story – don't worry. But not for the moment.'

'Take your time,' he said. 'It's just that I could see you had something on your mind.'

After my third pint, I waved goodbye to Miles and wandered out into the cool air of the night, recalling, as much as I could, the lines of the poem. As I reached the orange glow of the street-light at the bottom of Hopgarden Lane, I noticed purple buddleia swaying in the breeze and the green and white shades of cow parsley shrouded by the hedgerows. As I took my final steps home, I whispered to myself: 'I met a man who wasn't there! He wasn't there again today!'

When I walked up the drive, Fiesta was pacing about by the front door. As he brushed himself against my leg, he had the self-satisfied look of a cat who had been out hunting for field-mice. I turned the key in the lock and we staggered in together, like two wastrels fearing an unfriendly reception. Anne was sitting in the living-room, reading a magazine. She looked up as I pushed the door open.

'Prunella's just called,' she said. 'She says she's got something important to ask us.'

5

I rose at half past seven on the Saturday morning to a rich chorus of song thrushes and robins perched in trees beyond the lane. Stepping to the window, I lifted the curtain and gazed out across the open farmland.

The fields and meadows spread to the horizon like an extravagant green carpet, caressing the dips and folds of the earth. Here and there, oak and chestnut trees, thick with buds, offered their branches towards the grey, cloudy sky. They were like so many outstretched arms, entreating the sun to venture out.

Anne was lost to the world. I could just see traces of her blonde hair above the bedsheet and detected a gentle, snoring sound. I was suddenly overcome by an immense feeling of guilt. Guilt that I had, for the first time in my memory, provoked an argument with her over my experience at the Tube station. Guilt that I had broken my promise to forget all about the incident. Guilt that I was planning another trip to Euston. Guilt that my determination to uncover the truth about the man in the brown coat was developing into a mania.

An hour or so later, after we had both had breakfast, I spotted Prunella Ball striding purposefully up the drive with her notebook and pen in her hand.

'Oh, I'm glad you're here as well, Bob,' she said, as I opened the front door. 'I need to ask you some questions.'

'Always happy to help the press,' I remarked, as I took her fawn coat and hung it on the stairs. Our visitor, who was wearing a pink and white summer dress, hugged Anne and then all three of us made ourselves comfortable in the living-room.

Prunella, who was in a sombre, business-like mood, began by saying: 'You know the cops gave me the wrong address, don't you? They gave me Magpie Lane, Turner's Hatch.'

Sitting down at the dining table, she continued: 'Well, it took me several days to find out the correct address was Magpie Cottages, Plough Lane, Turner's Hatch. No matter. I've now spoken to the guy who made the emergency call.'

Anne, who had made herself comfortable on the settee, interrupted to say: 'You had something to tell us.'

'Yes, it looks as if your friend wasn't wearing a seatbelt when the crash happened.'

Anne and I were both surprised.

'How d'you know that?' asked Anne. I looked towards Prunella while I remained standing in the middle of the room.

'The guy I've spoken to, Tyler Buckley, says the man's body was in the back of the car.'

'In the back?' said Anne with a look of incredulity.

'Yes. I wanted to ask you, Bob, whether you knew if he wore a seatbelt?'

'I've known Gus for nearly 18 years. I've never known him drive without a seatbelt,' I said.

'Perhaps he'd unbuckled the belt for some reason and got thrown into the back by the force of the collision,' Anne suggested.

'Yeah. Bit of a mystery,' Prunella admitted.

'So what did this guy at Turner's Hatch have to say?' Anne asked.

'Mr Buckley? He's still shaken up about it. He first of all thought maybe some kids had set an old wreck of a car on fire. But when he got closer he realised it was a fairly new Mercedes. He ventured close to the flames and saw a man lying on the back seat. The person wasn't moving and he reckoned he was dead. He made attempts to reach him, but the heat was too intense. He then dialled 999.'

I joined Anne on the settee and put my arm round her. We were both upset to hear this first-hand account of our friend's horrific death.

'It was a terrible blaze. I've got my interview notes here if you're interested. Mr Buckley said: "It must've been around half-past five when I called 999. I'd just cycled up the lane from Yeoman's Farm where I'd been working late. The farmer let me go at quarter past five and it takes less than ten minutes to get from the farm to the place in Knights Lane where I found the car.

'It was a fireball. Tongues of flame flickered and crackled. The smoke was black and the air smelled vile. I caught glimpses of what looked like someone in the car, but I knew at once there was nothing I could do.

'When I tried to approach, I was overcome by the heat. Then I noticed, through gaps in the flames and smoke, the driver appeared to be in the back."

'Why would the body be in the back? I don't understand that at all,' I remarked. 'Unless he was alive after the collision and got into the back to try to get out.'

'Yes,' said Prunella. 'That's plausible.' Anne had been listening to the conversation intently. She suddenly said: 'Did the man notice any skid marks on the road?'

'No, funnily enough, I asked about that. He didn't see any, and he claimed there wasn't much snow around either. Anyway, Bob, I need to ask you a few things, if that's all right.'

'Go ahead. I'll help if I can.'

'The professor was a fair bit older than you, wasn't he?' she asked.

I nodded. 'Yes, he was in his early thirties when I first knew him. I was about twenty. I met him in Oxford after he'd finished courses at two other universities. He was doing a PhD in computer science when I first knew him and he went onto work for the government.'

'How did you get to know him?'

'We joined the committee of the university cycling club at about the same time. Then, when he had a problem with his accommodation, I got him a room in our student house.'

'I've been trying to contact his previous wife. You didn't know her, did you?'

'Not very well, but, in any case, all that came out in the press three months ago. His first marriage, to a woman called Jane, was short-lived and soon afterwards he met Claudia while still at Oxford. Why d'you want to know all this?'

'I can't tell you at the moment. I've been sworn to secrecy. But don't worry – it will all come out in the end.'

'So long as all this doesn't cause Claudia and the children any more pain,' Anne muttered. 'They've been upset enough already.'

*

Four days later, without telling Anne, I travelled back to Euston Square. Wednesday May the fifteenth was a mild day, but ominous grey clouds lurked in a corner of the sky, threatening rain, so this time I carried a blue plastic raincoat in a leather zip-up bag. I also brought both my mobile phones with me since one of them had been performing erratically and I wanted to be certain of obtaining a clear photograph of the man in the brown coat, if possible.

Since I now realised the man always left from the station's southern exit, I planned to keep a careful watch from across the street, trying to look as inconspicuous as I could. Bridget was sitting on the pavement with her dog as I climbed up the station steps at two forty-five pm. I threw a pound coin into her tin, patted the dog and gave him a crust of bread left over from my sandwich lunch.

'He's part Labrador, isn't he?' I suggested.

'Yes, sir. Prince is mainly Labrador with a bit of Staffordshire Bull Terrier and bit of something else – we're not sure.'

'He's a lovely dog,' I admitted, stroking the animal's head. 'We used to have a Labrador. He died of cancer a couple of years ago. Alfie would've been fourteen now.'

'Oh, I'm sorry to hear that,' she replied.

'We've got a cat now, but it's not the same.'

'No. I know what you mean. So you've come to meet your friend, have you?'

'Yes, but I'm still not sure it's him. So I'm going to wait on the other side of the road and watch for him - till I'm certain.' On saying that, I looked both ways and began to cross Gower Street.

Half an hour passed as I leaned against the silver railing

outside the hospital listening to the constant drone of traffic. I stood still, watching every person to emerge from the station exit. Fortunately, workmen in bright yellow jackets – planning to raise a manhole cover - had erected some safety barriers in the road in front of me, which helped conceal me. From time to time, a car would pass and once a red No 73 bus trundled by. I heard a pneumatic drill penetrating some distant piece of tarmac and occasionally coins clattered into Bridget's container.

But finally, just before half-past three, I saw him – the man with the brown leather coat. He appeared at the top of the station steps, smiled at Bridget, stopped to find a coin, dropped it into her tin and started to walk away.

I was more convinced than ever it was Gus as I removed one of my phones from the front pocket of my light-brown shirt – and I was determined to capture the moment. There was no mistaking his grey hair and pale skin, even though he had shaved off his beard and his nose was wrapped in a white bandage.

This time he was not dressed in the leather coat he'd worn on May the first. But he had it with him, draped over his right arm. He was wearing a short-sleeved white shirt and blue trousers with black slip-on shoes with brass buckles on his feet.

I recognised the style of his gait – confident, lengthy strides. I recognised the way he sharply turned his head while gazing around and the way he used his hands. I had paid my respects to this man at his grave. Yet he was alive.

A sudden attack of nerves caused me to struggle with my smart phone. But I jerkily pressed the shutter button. The camera whirred and clicked two or three times. I guessed I had at least a couple of images, although I feared they might be blurred.

As I lowered the phone from my face, a burly man in his late twenties with short, black, spiky hair was appearing at the top of the exit steps. He was at least six feet six inches tall and looked as tough as a Russian shot-putter. But I paid this man, dressed in dark casual clothes, little attention. My eyes were mainly focussed on Gus. Now was the time to confront him.

'Gus!' I called as I crossed the road. He peered at me, confused. Then a shocked expression spread across his face – as if he'd just learnt his entire family had been wiped out by an earthquake.

He stood still for a moment on the pavement, paralysed to the spot.

'Gus! Don't you remember me?' I cried. 'It's Bob!'

He gave no acknowledgement but strode off down the street and my words were lost in the breeze. Why the bizarre reaction? Why did he choose to ignore me?

As I watched him walk away, his broad-shouldered companion – now resembling a bare-knuckle fighter or a body builder – approached me from behind. He must have seen me use my phone as a camera. Without a word, he snatched it from me, hurled it to the ground and crushed it with the heel of his right shoe, shattering the screen. Then he thrust me against the side of the office building, knocking the wind out of me. As I turned to face him, I noticed his bare arms were embellished with tattoos of lions and scorpions.

Gus's voice, with a deep, slightly husky tone, then called out from the far distance: 'Ryan! Leave him!'

'My God!' I thought. 'The man even speaks like Gus.' My attacker had his right fist raised, ready to punch me, but he obeyed the instructions given.

The bodyguard merely snarled: 'The boss don't like no pictures!' Then he marched away, as quickly as his legs would take him, in pursuit of the professor.

Bridget looked up from her pitch. Her expression screamed disappointment. I'm sure she was thinking: 'Are you really a friend?'

I didn't care what she thought. I didn't care what anyone thought. I had to follow them both. I had to find out where they were going. I was stung by my friend's rejection. My back and left arm were bruised from the unprovoked assault, but I decided to forget that for the present. Picking up what remained of my phone and placing it in my bag, I ran off down the road after them.

Gus was by now out of sight, but his aggressive companion was just fifty metres ahead of me in Gower Street. I watched him turn right into Grafton Way.

I followed as closely as I dared deep into Fitzrovia, desperate to keep the bodyguard in my sights, despite my concern he might look back and notice me at any moment. I tried to be as inconspicuous as possible while pursuing him past a building site. As I hurried along, my undamaged phone rang, causing me to curse beneath my breath. It was Gordon Carsten, one of my school's geography teachers.

'What d'you want, Gordon?' I asked. 'This isn't a good time.'

'I've just been speaking to the headmaster,' he said in a voice that sounded as though he was down a mineshaft. 'There are curriculum changes that affect us both and he wants to see you tomorrow.'

'Thanks for the message. I'll be in school tomorrow. I'll deal with it then,' I replied. But Gordon failed to take the hint that I was busy.

'I wanted to discuss tactics with you,' he said.

'It'll have to wait, Gordon. I've very tied up,' I said, before ending the call abruptly.

As the bodyguard reached the corner of Tottenham Court Road, I caught my breath.

Gus was waiting for him outside a computer and TV shop. I ducked into a doorway, fearing they might glance over their shoulders. After a few seconds, I peered out and watched them cross the busy highway, pass a chemist shop on the corner and continue along the western side of Grafton Way. Grey, four-storey Georgian buildings and modern offices loomed above them until, finally, they turned left into Whitfield Street. After passing a university hall of residence, the pair disappeared down a narrow turning in the shadow of the six hundred and twenty-seven-foot tall BT Tower.

Breathless after running the last few metres, I reached the same turning beneath a stucco entrance arch

I found myself in a smart mews – a street where, decades ago, coachmen and grooms would have kept horses and carriages.

As I squinted at the street sign, saying: 'Hamelin Mews,' I was just in time to observe the pair entering a quaint two-storey Victorian house twenty metres ahead of me on the right.

Curiosity overcame my fears. I walked cautiously down the cobbled street until I reached the entrance. Bright mauve wisteria clambered beside the front door and curled above the ground floor windows. To the left of the black door was a shiny gold-coloured plaque proclaiming: 'Hamelin Clinic.'

There were no further details about the nature of the

enterprise conducted within. Perhaps Gus had had a hospital operation and was receiving follow-up treatment here, I thought. I went to the window and peered through one of the square panes. It looked like a small office with a reception desk.

Suddenly, Ryan's menacing face appeared behind the glass, baring his teeth like a fighting dog.

It was time to leave. I raced back towards the arch, but within seconds felt a powerful hand gripping my shoulder.

I spun round, ready to fight back, but my assailant – Ryan - struck me hard on the jaw, a blow which sent me sprawling onto the ground.

I quickly recovered, leaped to my feet and swung a punch at Ryan, directly hitting the left side of his head, but he hardly flinched and responded by jabbing me forcibly in the stomach.

Winded by the man for the second time and doubled up in pain, I must have staggered about in front of him like a stumbling hunchback. Then he pummelled my body with a series of further blows until I collapsed on the ground and passed out.

6

An electric fan was whirring somewhere nearby. I heard a rush of footsteps. Someone – I think a woman – was calling: 'Sister! Sister!'

I must have stirred from a long sleep. My face and body were aching. It felt as if I had braved several rounds with Chris Eubank Jr or Tyson Fury and I had more than a faint suspicion my opponent had had the best of the bout.

My body was racked with pain, but for the life of me I couldn't understand why. I was lying in a soft, warm bed. Perhaps I was safely at home in our cottage. I turned my sore head from left to right. At least my neck was still working, I thought, as I detected the faint smell of disinfectant.

I then felt a warm hand caressing my left arm and opened my eyes. There, in front of me, was my wonderful wife Anne, looking down. But I was mystified by my surroundings. I was in a small, well-lit room shrouded by a light-blue curtain.

'Anne!' I murmured. 'Am I dreaming?' My wife continued stroking my arm. I caught a whiff of her perfume.

'It's all right,' she assured me. 'You're in hospital.'

'Hospital?' I mumbled. 'What?' Then I remembered my encounter with Ryan. 'I'm in a bit of pain.'

'What on earth happened to you?' she asked.

'Someone took a disliking to me, darling.'

'But who?'

'It's a long story,' I said. 'I think I've been used as a human football. My face hurts a lot.'

'I'm not surprised. Have a look.' She took a make-up mirror from her handbag so I could view my face. I was shocked my light-brown hair was in disarray and my right cheek and forehead were red and swollen.

'The doctors think you were punched repeatedly,' she revealed as I turned my head from side to side to see the reflection. 'Then they believe your attacker continually kicked you while you were on the ground.'

'I was in a cobbled street,' I moaned. 'The phrase "kicked in the cobbles" springs to mind.'

'I'm glad you can joke about it,' said Anne.

'You're right. It hurts to laugh. Where are we, anyway?' I asked

'University College Hospital.'

'Am I? And what time is it?'

'It's seven o'clock.'

'Morning or evening?'

'Morning. It's Thursday morning.'

'So I've been asleep?'

'The doctor gave you a sedative.'

'How did I get here?'

'Someone found you lying on the ground in a street near Tottenham Court Road and they dialled 999. Paramedics brought you in. Bob, tell me what happened. Did you have an argument with someone? Was there a group of them?' asked Anne, who was wearing a purple cardigan.

'No, it was just the one guy,' I said as I gradually recalled the events of the previous afternoon. I quickly added: 'The coward! He took me from behind. The guy was like Tarzan on steroids. Think Arnie Schwarzenegger, circa 1970.' Anne frowned.

'We need to tell the police,' she said. 'This man needs to be charged with assault. The next person he kicks on the ground might not be so lucky.'

'I only know his first name. I don't know where he lives and I haven't any witnesses,' I muttered.

'Don't get agitated. Just tell me calmly what happened.'

'I'm really sorry, Anne. I came up here to find the man on the train.'

'You promised to forget all that nonsense about Gus still being alive.'

'I'm sorry, dear. I broke my promise. I just couldn't let it go. And now I'm glad I didn't, because I now know that Gus really is still alive. I saw him at the Tube exit, outside this very hospital.'

'You must be delirious after the attack. I'll fetch the nurse.'

'No, don't do that. Anne. I promise you I'm not making this up. I've got proof and in a minute I'll show it to you.'

'Bob Shaw, tell me right now what this is all about. Who did this to you?'

'I think it must have been a guy called Ryan.'

'Who's he, for God's sake?'

'He's a friend of Gus.'

'Don't you think we should report him to the police?'

'No. I don't want any fuss,' I said. 'Look, all I can say is that I saw Gus leaving the station and followed him to an address in Fitzrovia. I guess they took exception to being followed.' Just at that moment, a vivacious, young, dark-haired nurse drew back the curtain. I glanced at her name tag which said: 'Indira.'

'Ah, the patient's awake. Had a good sleep?' she asked, tucking me in more tightly. Then, without waiting for an answer, she added: 'Fancy a cup of tea?' I nodded and, a minute later, the two women were helping to prop me up with pillows so I could sip from a cup of hot, sweet liquid. After a few more mouthfuls, I felt revived.

Once Indira had gone, I explained to Anne I had taken photographs of Gus on my smart phone.

'Do me a favour, Anne. Can you get my phone?' I asked. 'It got smashed, but I'm sure the SIM card will be all right. As soon as I put it in my other phone, we're in business. You'll see. You'll believe me. Everyone will believe me.'

'It's probably among your belongings. I'll just check.' Anne fumbled among my clothes, which were on a nearby chair, and searched my leather bag.

'I can't see it,' she asserted.

'Oh God!' I said, sitting up in the bed. 'It's got to be there somewhere. Anne, listen to me. Anne, I've got pictures of Gus. It proves Gus is still alive.'

'Well, your phone's definitely not here.'

'It must be here unless…' I paused for a moment.

'Unless what?'

'Unless that thug Ryan stole it from me.'

*

I was considered well enough to leave hospital later that day. Anne was quietly worried about me and said little as we travelled back to Canterbury on the train. I was also silent for most of the journey. I was wondering where Gus was living now and who he was with. I was wondering if he realised I had been found unconscious on a London street after a severe beating from his companion. I was wondering why he had gone to the clinic in the mews. I was wondering what had happened to my broken mobile phone.

At least the phone mystery was quickly resolved. As soon as I arrived back at our cottage in Hopgarden Lane, I began thinking more clearly. I carefully examined my bag. In my haste, I had placed the damaged handset in an inner pocket I rarely used. The relief was indescribable. My face was wreathed in smiles.

Once I had inserted the SIM card into my second phone, I switched it on and waited impatiently to judge the quality of the camera shots taken outside the Tube station. Initially, I was concerned.

The first image was blurred and could be discounted. But I was delighted when I inspected the second one. It was a high-definition image of my friend striding, full of purpose and confidence, along the street with the charity offices in the background.

It showed the right side of his profile, including his goatee beard. His brown coat was clearly visible. I immediately transferred the photograph to my home computer and, using glossy photographic paper, printed out a full-size colour picture, which measured twenty by twenty-five centimetres.

Then, almost forgetting my injuries, I stumbled quickly down the oak stairs to the hall, calling out Anne's name repeatedly as I went. I was desperate to show her my evidence.

After a few seconds, Anne emerged from the kitchen with

an inquisitive expression, wiping her hands on a red tea towel as she walked.

'What's the matter, darling?' she asked. 'I was just putting the potatoes on.'

'Take a look at this picture,' I insisted. She held it under the light of the hall window, scrutinising it for nearly half a minute.

'It's a great likeness,' she concluded. ' But it's not Gus.' I started wishing I had made a video instead of a photograph. A video would have shown the mannerisms, the movement, the whole style of the man.

'Why d'you say that?' I demanded.

'Let's go into the living-room,' she said. She crossed the beige carpet and placed the picture on the dining table. Light was streaming through the window. I followed her across the room, peering over her shoulder.

'I know his nose is covered with a bandage,' I said. 'But all the other features point to it being him.' There was a pause. Anne was studying every detail.

'No,' she said. 'The hair's not right. It's far too short for Gus. He never had his hair like that.'

'He's obviously had it cut really short for some reason,' I insisted, finding it hard to control my temper. 'But the colour of the hair is absolutely the same.'

'This man's not the right height – Gus is several inches taller - and his chin's too prominent,' she continued.

'I wish you'd been there,' I said. 'You'd have been bowled over. It's definitely Gus. He's got the same pale skin, the same glasses and he strides along like Gus in the way a sergeant major marches onto a parade ground. He even waves his hands about in the same manner. He was carrying Gus's favourite leather coat. Look, here it is – draped over his arm.'

'There are tens of thousands of coats like that in London.'

'Not over the arm of a man who looks identical to Gus,' I hissed.

'It's an uncanny resemblance,' she agreed. 'But it must be just a coincidence.' As she continued examining the photograph at the table, I stepped over to the settee and slumped down.

'There's got to be an explanation for this,' I said. 'Whatever you think and whatever you say, there's no doubt in my mind that that man was Gus. Gus is still alive. While we were travelling home, I was considering all the possibilities.'

'I wondered why you were so quiet.'

'All I can think of is that he's faked his own death so he and Claudia can claim a gigantic insurance pay-out.'

'That's absurd, Bob. He and Claudia have got a two-million pound house set in lavish grounds. They've got their own tennis courts and swimming pool. They've got three cars. They've got both children at public school. He's a member of a London club.'

'Exactly. He's overstretched himself. He's probably on civil service pay. You know how much he used to complain about the school fees. The only recompense for a lifetime cooped up in the corridors of Whitehall is a gong in the birthday honours. They've hit money troubles and taken desperate measures.'

'Nonsense. They're not the sort of people to do that. They were pillars of society.'

'All right. Who are the sort of people to do that? You might think a former government minister would be a pillar of society but look at John Stonehouse. He dumped clothes on a Florida beach in the nineteen seventies and made himself a new life in

Australia. Two years later, he was jailed for fraud.

'And then there's the canoe man, John Darwin, who vanished in 2002 and also got jailed for fraud after reappearing in Panama five years later.'

'You think Gus Morley is about to wade into the sea? You're crazy. The hair, height and chin of this man are all wrong. I'm very worried about you, Bob. You've got a bee in your bonnet and you're just not ready to let it go.'

'Anne, one of my closest friends dies. We're heartbroken. Then he turns up again with his heart pumping, his legs walking, his hands gesturing and yelling to his chum: "Ryan, leave him!" in his cut-glass public school accent. What am I meant to think?'

'You're stupid. It defies logic. It's just someone who looks like him.' It irritated me to know my wife could not find it in her heart to believe me. I needed her support at this time of my inner turmoil.

'Anne, I know it's him. I know what I saw yesterday. And there's something else I haven't mentioned. His shoes.'

'What about his shoes?'

'Well, you see those black shoes with brass buckles at the base of the picture?'

'Yes.'

'I was with him when he bought them.'

7

The village of Hanley St Peter was bathed in sunlight as I drove our blue Ford Mondeo up the gravel drive of the former vicarage where Gus and Claudia had made their home.

I had managed the hot, tiring journey in good time after setting off from Kent alone at seven am. Most of the route consisted of motorways. My back still ached, but I was gradually recovering from the attack in Hamelin Mews three days earlier.

The daffodils that had greeted us on the day of the funeral were no longer brazenly nodding their yellow heads in the breeze. Someone – perhaps the gardener – had cut back the stems. Now, apart from the red and white rose bushes, the flower borders looked empty and forlorn.

Claudia must have heard the noise of the car. She was standing in the porch as I stepped out. In my hand, I clutched a brown envelope which contained the photograph of Gus I took outside the Tube station along with a picture of him speaking at a university graduation ceremony a few years ago.

'Good journey?' she asked as she leaned on the doorpost in a short-sleeved mauve top, black and white tweed trousers and a pair of sandals.

'Pretty good. Took me about three and a half hours,' I

replied, noticing she was holding an empty wine glass in her right hand.

'Not too bad,' she said. 'What is it – a hundred and eighty miles?'

'Something like that,' I said, reaching forward to kiss her lightly on the right cheek.

'What's happened to your face?'

'I fell down the stairs, Claudia. I'll be all right in a few days.'

'Looks like you've really been through the wars. Anyway, come on in, Bob,' she said, marching across the hall towards the drawing room. 'It's good to see you. I'm afraid you'll have to take us as you find us.' Then she stopped suddenly in her tracks.

'Why haven't you brought Anne with you?' she asked. I could hardly reveal that Anne and I had had a furious row the night before over my claims that Gus was alive and she was no longer speaking to me.

'She sends her apologies,' I said. 'She would have dearly loved to have come, but she's been working and today was her only chance to look round the department stores.'

'I can imagine it now in Marks & Spencer's: "Stand by your tills, ladies – here comes one very determined shopper!"'

'Yes, it'll be a bit like that, I expect.'

'Oh, I love Anne. She's so practical and sensible. Anyway, can I get you a glass of something?' she asked. 'I've just opened a bottle of Chablis.'

'Just a diet Coke or lemonade would be fine. I've got the long journey back to think of.'

'Of course. I'll get you a Coke,' she said as she walked towards the hall. 'Both the children are out. Sophie's gone riding with a friend and James is with his pals in Tewkesbury.'

I wandered over to the bust of Darwin and reminded myself of the inscription beneath it, which read: 'It is not the strongest of the species that survive, nor the most intelligent, but the one most responsive to change.'

Then I sat down on Claudia's green Chesterfield settee, gazing out towards the tennis courts, the swimming pool and a row of poplar trees two hundred metres away which marked the end of their grounds. Within minutes, she breezed back into the room holding my soft drink and a full glass of white wine for herself.

'It's so good to see you, Bob,' she said, sitting down in one of the chairs next to her antique mahogany dining table. 'It's taking me a while to get over Gus. We'd had our ups and downs, as you know. At one point, he even suggested a divorce, but over Christmas we managed to patch things up.

'Now he's gone. I don't mind admitting I miss him very much. I think about him all the time. But I'm getting there, slowly. Every day it gets a little easier, you know. Jemima and Jago have been my rocks. Anyway, you said you had a photograph to show me?'

'Yes,' I admitted, opening the envelope with some trepidation. 'Look, I don't want to upset you, Claudia, but I've bumped into someone who looks very much like Gus.'

'How d'you mean?'

'Have a look at this photo. I took it on Wednesday afternoon. It looks the spitting image of Gus.' I stepped across the large red Persian rug that covered the centre of the oak floor so I could hand her the image.

Then I resumed my seat and took a sip from my glass. At first came a puzzled look. Then she gazed towards me coldly as a doctor might view an Ebola patient.

'Is this some kind of joke?' she asked, glancing at the photograph, then at me and then back at the photograph.

'No, I can assure you it's not a joke. What's happened is this: earlier this month I was at Euston Square Tube station, minding my own business, when I spotted a man looking just like Gus. He'd got exactly the same brown coat Gus always wore. I tried to find him as he left the station but lost him in the crowds.

'Someone at the station has confirmed this man regularly travels there on a Wednesday afternoon, so this Wednesday just gone I was waiting for him. And this is the picture I took.' Claudia thrust her wine glass down with a thud on the highly-polished table-top. Her mouth dropped open and closed again. She looked aghast at me.

'Just what exactly are you implying?' she demanded.

'Claudia, I honestly don't understand it myself. If I didn't know he'd died and we'd all been to his funeral, I'd think he was still alive.' She sat bolt upright in her chair, returning her gaze to the picture. I quickly added: 'Of course, it all seems ridiculous now – now I'm openly talking to you about it.'

'You came all this way to show me a picture of a man who looks a bit like my dead husband?'

'Claudia, I'm sorry, but I felt I just had to see you. I was compelled to do it. I just want to solve the mystery.'

'There's no bloody mystery, Bob. It's not my husband, obviously. He's dead. This is someone who, by strange coincidence, looks slightly like him. To be honest, it's rather upsetting.'

She strolled out of the room and returned moments later with red eyes and a box of paper tissues. She took out one, wiped a tear from her right eye, and placed the box on the table, nearly knocking over the wine glass.

'Claudia, I wish it was as simple as you're thinking,' I continued. 'You seem to believe it's a man who looks a bit like Gus. I can tell you, because I was there, that he's exactly like Gus. He talks like Gus, walks like Gus and even has Gus's brown coat and brass-buckle shoes.'

'This is too much for me to take in. I think you'd better go,' she said, taking another tissue from the box.

'You can't shed any light on this mystery?' I said. 'I haven't been able to sleep very well. I've been so bewildered.'

'This man's got a bandage on his nose,' Claudia said, as she studied the picture again.

'Yes, he's obviously hurt his nose in some way,' I admitted.

'Well, you've travelled a helluva long way to show me this picture and I'm wondering why,' she said after a pause.

'I agree it looks a lot like my late husband. But he died in a car crash on February the first – three and a half months ago. I was beginning to get over his loss and now you bring me this ridiculous picture, which you claim was taken when?'

'On Wednesday afternoon – three days ago,' I repeated.

'You claim it was taken three days ago. Well, it's obvious that it's either someone trying to impersonate him or it's pure coincidence.'

'He didn't have an identical twin brother, did he?' I asked.

'No, he didn't have a bloody twin brother,' Claudia yelled. 'Look, Bob, I'm sorry. You'd better go. You've no idea how much this has upset me. Why didn't you just keep your bloody photograph to yourself? Why did you have to drive a hundred and eighty bloody miles to show this to me?'

'Claudia, I'm so sorry to have upset you, but, as you're the widow, I thought you needed to know. Someone had to be first to tell you.'

'Don't for God's sake tell me: "Don't shoot the messenger." Gus was always saying that. You didn't need to come here with your silly picture. I'm the widow, aren't I, for God's sake? Aren't the family and friends meant to protect the widow from extra grief at a time like this?'

'Claudia, I'm so sorry. I don't relish coming here today when I suspected I might upset you. But I thought that, after I met him, other people you know might meet him and tell you about him. I thought it would be better coming from me – a family friend – rather than from a stranger. Or worse still, reading it in a newspaper.'

'Reading what in a newspaper?'

'Reading that a man who was declared dead is still very much alive.'

'Are you all there? Have you had a breakdown?' I frowned at her.

'No, of course not,' I replied. 'Claudia, listen to me. This could be important. Does the Hamelin Clinic mean anything to you?'

'Why do you ask?'

'I followed this man to a London mews house. He went inside and I noticed the nameplate outside said: "Hamelin Clinic." I've checked online and I can't find anything about it. I've also drawn a blank at Companies House.'

'I don't know what you're talking about. The name means nothing to me. You and Anne were mourners, and yet you come here and add to my upset.'

'I'm really sorry, Claudia. I just thought…' I began.

'You just didn't think. You didn't think about me, Bob. You didn't think about my feelings. So I think you'd better leave – and take your bloody picture with you!' She was huddled down over the table, sobbing. I picked up the photograph and returned it to its envelope.

'I'm very sorry, Claudia,' I mumbled. 'I just felt you ought to know.' She turned her head momentarily towards me. 'Just go,' she whispered.

I saw myself out. I turned the car round and drove slowly back down the drive and out into the village street. A sea of guilt and remorse swept over me. I felt as culpable as a wayward schoolboy caught stealing silverware from the trophy cupboard.

How could I have allowed my obsessive behaviour to bring me here? I had upset my dear friend's widow to the point where she had lost her temper with me.

I had sincerely not wished to add to her suffering. I had simply wanted to untangle the mystery that was tearing me apart. But I appeared no closer to solving it.

One important issue had been settled, however. Claudia's annoyance with me appeared genuine and my claims had caused real distress. That told me that, whatever Gus was up to, it didn't involve his wife. It wasn't a joint enterprise.

*

As I drove back towards London after seeing Claudia, a new idea occurred to me. Why not obtain help from a journalist in investigating my friend's apparent return from the grave?

Seeking help from Prunella was out of the question. She was far too close to Anne. But I could approach one of the national newspapers directly, I thought. They had the staff and resources. Investigating the case would prove far easier for them.

I decided to drive to London and visit one of the newspaper offices in person. It would be Saturday afternoon by the time I reached Central London and found somewhere to park. Surely, if I showed a reporter before and after photographs of Gus, they would believe me?

It was nearly two thirty pm by the time I clambered up the steps leading to the offices of the Sunday Review, a middle-market tabloid newspaper housed in a seven-storey block close to Blackfriars Bridge in Southwark.

I found myself in a brightly-lit reception hall with a beige seating area dominated by a Lowry painting of a northern industrial scene.

'Any chance of seeing a reporter?' I asked a dark-haired girl sitting behind a long ash-effect reception desk. She smiled. 'Have you got a story?'

'I've got a story that all the papers will want, but I've decided to give it only to your paper,' I said, smiling back.

'Can I take a name?'

'Shaw,' I told her. 'Bob Shaw.'

'Take a seat. I'll see if anyone's available.' Ten minutes later, a casually-dressed man in his late twenties with scruffy dark hair emerged from a doorway and headed towards me.

'Mr Shaw?' he asked as I rose to shake his hand. 'My name's Gary. I gather you've got something for us.'

'Yes, I said,' as he joined me on the beige settee. 'Have a look at these.' I slipped both the colour photographs from the envelope and placed them on the low-level table in front of us.

'These are pictures of Professor Gus Morley who died in a

car crash,' he said at once. I was reassured. Here was someone who immediately recognised my friend and remembered his tragic end.

'This is him, isn't it?' he continued as he inspected the graduation photograph.

'Yes,' I said. 'The one you're looking at was taken two or three years ago in Manchester.' He switched his gaze to the second image.

'Now in this one he appears to be in a bit of a rush. He's got an office building in the background.'

'Yes. The second picture was taken three days ago in London,' I explained. He looked bemused.

'How can that be? He died in February.'

'That's exactly it,' I said as I turned in my seat to face him. 'That's the reason I'm here. That's the story. How can he have died in February and yet be alive in May. It just doesn't make sense.'

'I'm sorry, sir. I'm a bit confused,' said Gary, frowning and looking me up and down. 'What actually is the story you've got for us?'

'Let me explain,' I said. ' I'm a lifelong friend of the professor's. I went to university with him. I was shocked as we all were when he was found dead in February.

'But I was even more shocked – more shocked than I've ever been – when I saw him travelling on the London Underground. So I took his picture on my mobile to prove he's still alive.'

'OK, sir,' said Gary, whose surname I later found out was Toomes. 'I think the best thing will be for me to take your name and number, have a word with the news editor and get back to you.' I gave him the details.

Then he stood up. His expression told me he doubted my credibility. He was rejecting my offering as a vegan might turn down a greasy bacon sandwich.

'I'm giving you the chance to publish a story that no other papers have got,' I insisted, rather annoyed at the casual way my information was being regarded.

'Either his death has been faked or there's an impostor going round impersonating him. I'd have thought, whichever way you look at it, it's newsworthy. With all the people you've got, you could look into this.'

'I'm afraid that would be down to the news editor. He's the one who takes the decisions. Can I ask you something? Have you had any medical problems recently? I can see you've injured your face.'

'Yes, as a matter of fact. I got assaulted in Fitzrovia the other day and ended up in the UCH,' I replied at once.

'You've injured your head quite badly, haven't you?'

'Yes, I have actually,' I admitted. Then the implications of his remark hit home.

'Now look. If you're suggesting…'

'I'm not suggesting anything, sir,' said Gary. 'But perhaps you need to go home and have a good lie down. Look, the point is we'd have major problems printing a story based on what you've told me. We don't want to upset the family after they've held their funeral, do we?

'We would have to be a hundred per cent sure of the evidence before running a story along these lines. We can't just rely on a picture that may or may not have been taken on your mobile phone three days ago.'

'You're just fobbing me off,' I said, raising my voice. 'You don't believe me, do you?'

'It's not that I don't believe you, sir,' Gary insisted. He was frowning again and shrugging his shoulders. 'It's just that we would need to do a lot work on something like this and, at the end of the day, we probably wouldn't have a story our lawyers would allow us to print.

'The chances are it's just someone who looks like him. Anyway I'll have to go now. We're a bit short-staffed upstairs.'

On that note, he walked away, leaving me embittered and disheartened.

8

Fiesta was at the front door to greet me as I arrived back from London. He brushed against my trouser leg as I turned the key in the lock. It was early evening. Anne was busy in the kitchen as we both walked in. The atmosphere was colder than a deep-freeze in Yakutsk.

'Jago's been trying to call you on the landline,' she called out without emotion. 'Sounds like you've managed to upset Claudia. Hope you're proud of yourself.' Anne, who was preparing a meal, didn't turn round as I stopped by the kitchen door.

'I'm really sorry if I've upset her, but I just had to show her the picture,' I insisted. 'Someone is going to have to believe me this guy is still alive. He's walking around Central London with all his faculties in full working order and, sooner or later, someone else Claudia knows is going to recognise him – unless he changes his appearance or something.'

'There was no need for you to go straight to the widow. If you've got to carry on with your ludicrous idea, you could have mentioned it to Jago or Tristan. I'm sure they would have put you right because I'm damn sure I can't.'

'I'm sorry you still feel that way,' I said. 'How was Prunella?'

'She couldn't make it, so I went to see Gemma.' I withdrew to the living-room. I picked up a tabloid newspaper I had bought in Gloucestershire and began reading it. Moments later the phone rang. It was Jago.

'Are you out of your mind, Bob?' his voice thundered round the hallway. 'Jemima's had Claudia crying down the phone. Apparently you've told her Gus is still alive. Are you on drugs, Bob? It seems you're not only on a different planet – you're in a different bloody galaxy.

'You can't go round telling a widow their husband has risen from the grave. What've you got to say for yourself?'

'If you'd been with me on Wednesday afternoon and met this guy, you wouldn't be talking to me like this, Jago. This man wasn't just the spitting image. He's the genuine article. Gus didn't die in that car crash. He's still with us.'

'Bob, I don't understand what's happened to you. Have you fallen out of your tree? Sounds like you're a couple of clowns short of a circus.'

'If I hadn't told her, she'd have found out from a stranger, Jago. I'm sorry, but I've seen Gus and he's very much with us.'

'You can't go round saying things like that. Bob, I beseech you, don't ever contact Claudia again. If you do, I'm going to call the police, and for God's sake stop telling people Gus has risen from the dead. You need your head examined.' He then slammed the receiver down.

I looked at the newspaper, but the words weren't registering. All I could think about was the distress I was causing to people I knew and loved. Anne was more annoyed with me than she had ever been. Claudia was distraught. Jago was furious. They and Gary, one of Fleet Street's finest, were all worried that I'd lost the plot.

I lay down on the settee and closed my eyes, unable to relax and unable to stop depressing thoughts passing through my mind. Despite your best endeavours, I concluded, you are buffeted about in the swirling waters of life, never knowing where the waves will take you.

Unless blessed with a strong self-will, you may be left to drift wherever the winds of fortune and the tides of fate decide. You remain weak and powerless against the storms.

In the blink of an eye, you may be dashed against the rocks of despair or swept out to the open sea among the flotsam and jetsam, abandoned to the vicissitudes of the ocean.

I had seen what I had seen, but no one believed me. I had reached a low stage. I was close to breaking point.

*

The following morning the sun rose in a cloudless sky. Its rays streamed past the trees across the lane and burst in golden streaks through gaps in our bedroom curtains. The sunbeams roused me from my uneasy sleep and coaxed me to gaze out at the blissful sunrise. I felt slightly uplifted after managing to sleep for a few hours.

Anne had arranged to visit Prunella that day in the coastal town of Faversham, nine miles away. She had wanted to call round earlier in the week, but the journalist had been busy working. They now planned to meet for lunch at a water-side pub.

After we had eaten breakfast separately, I suspected her animosity might have diminished.

'You can come with me if you want to,' she conceded after she had slipped into a red and white off-the-shoulder summer dress with a floral pattern. 'Provided you promise not to upset me by spouting nonsense.'

Just after midday, we parked in a quiet, tree-lined back street on the edge of the town centre and walked a hundred metres to The Yacht, a quaint, weather-boarded pub overlooking the town's creek and close to the swing bridge. The slender branches of weeping willows drooped across the water's edge, partly shrouding the view of colourful yachts and sailing barges moored on the far shore.

Moments after our arrival, Anne and I were sitting in the sunshine with drinks outside the inn's main door, absorbing the waterfront panorama, when we spotted a silver car with a loud exhaust pounding across the gravel access road. We looked up to find Prunella arriving in a battered fifteen-year-old Porsche 911 Carrera.

'What a glorious day!' she proclaimed, as she locked her silver car and strode towards us in a white patterned off-the-shoulder dress and a blue wide-brimmed hat. Her long, brown hair was tumbling over her shoulders.

'I only live over there. Look!' she said, pointing to a first-floor flat with a balcony a short way along the creek, on the opposite bank. 'I suppose I should have walked. What's happened to you, Bob? Looks like someone slammed a door in your face. A common occupational hazard for us hacks, but not so common among teachers.'

'You should have seen the other guy,' I joked. 'The aches and pains are gradually going. I'll be all right in a day or two.'

After I had bought her a white wine spritzer, she launched into a long explanation as to why she had been unable to meet Anne the day before. She had been called into a Sunday newspaper office for two days running to help with an investigation into a professional footballer's affair with a model which was being held back from publication for legal reasons.

'This is my first day off in five days,' she moaned after she settled herself down on a white bistro chair. 'I'm meant to be doing a big background story on your professor friend ready for the Sunday after the inquest.

'There's so much interest in him on the newsdesk – you wouldn't believe it. He was a friend of so many establishment figures.' She took a gulp from her drink before continuing.

'I couldn't get anything out of the Gloucestershire cops about the lorry incident, so I had a word with my pal Graham. You know DS Kirwan, don't you?'

'Of course,' I said. 'He was one of the team that investigated the Lucas Sharp murder. He's a friend of ours as well.'

'Well, I've known Graham for more than ten years – since I worked in the headquarters press office. He's such an angel. He made inquiries with Gloucestershire and he came up with a few gems.'

She glanced over her shoulder to see if anyone was listening. A couple with a boy aged about ten were sitting a short distance away, but they were engrossed in a conversation of their own.

'Apparently, the lorry was registered to a man from Lithuania. There's no trace of him in the UK.'

'Maybe he's gone back to Lithuania,' I suggested.

'The Gloucestershire cops aren't taking any action. They think it was just road rage and, since the professor's now dead, there's no witness to what happened.

'Anyway, what's strange is, when they traced the lorry and checked it over, they found a piece of paper with details of the professor's Mercedes and Land Rover Discovery among the driver's documents.'

'Gus was on a bicycle when this road rage incident happened, wasn't he?' said Anne, leaning towards her friend.

'That's right. So that was a bit of a mystery. Anyway, I forgot all about the professor for a few days because I've been working on other stories. Then on Friday I had another call from Graham. He told me of another odd incident. Did you know your friend was involved in a drive-by shooting?'

'Someone shot at Gus?' I asked.

'They're not sure if the gunman was necessarily aiming at your friend,' Prunella went on. 'It looks more likely he was just caught in the crossfire. I haven't found anything about it in the newspaper library or online and it transpires the reason is his name was never given out by police.'

'That's strange, isn't it?' Anne suggested.

'Not really,' said Prunella. 'There are so many gun and knife deaths in London, the Met usually only release names after someone is actually killed – and then only after informing next of kin.

'In this case, Professor Morley wasn't badly hurt. He had a small shoulder injury. Some youths were around at the time and the thinking is that one of them was the target.'

'Where did this happen?' I asked.

'Bethnal Green in East London.'

'And when?'

'It was late evening on January the nineteenth – two weeks before his death. He went to the Royal London Hospital to have his wound treated and was then discharged.'

'How is it we've never heard about this before?' said Anne. 'Gus's widow and her sister never mentioned it. They must have known, surely?'

'It's possible they were unaware,' said Prunella. 'The wound was only slight. Perhaps he didn't consider it worth mentioning. Perhaps he didn't want to worry them.'

'He was a bit unlucky in his final months, wasn't he?' I remarked. 'He's forced to leap off his bike, gets shot and is then killed in a blazing car. They say catastrophes come in threes.'

'Graham says it's unlikely the lorry incident and the shooting are connected with his death. It's just the way life goes sometimes. Graham's always saying: "You've got to take the little potato with the big potato.'

'We say: the rough with the smooth,' I commented.

'Sorry?'

'You've got to take the rough with the smooth. It means the same as Graham's Irish expression.' Anne was silent. She was staring at the ground.

Then she turned towards me with the look of someone who has just been woken by a burst of dazzling sunlight streaking across the horizon.

'What d'you know about the shooting, Prunella?' she asked with her eyes still focussed on me.

'All I know is the professor was out walking along Bethnal Green Road when a black four-by-four with tinted windows drove past. There was a crowd of youths in hoodies sitting on a bench as the professor approached.

'Suddenly the front passenger window goes down and a guy points a pistol out of the window, according to a witness. He fires towards the youths just as the professor passes.

'The youths scatter and the professor dives to the ground, clutching his shoulder. The car just drives off and is later found abandoned.'

'So police think he was caught in the crossfire in what? A gang shooting?' I remarked. Prunella nodded.

'All this can't be just a coincidence,' said Anne after a pause.

'How d'you mean?' wondered Prunella.

'Well, we're looking at three incidents in three weeks. He survived two near-misses but in the end he succumbed.'

'How d'you mean?' said Prunella. 'You don't think… ?'

'That someone was out to kill him? Yes, I do. I think it's a strong possibility.'

'I think you're stretching things a little,' said Prunella. 'Things happen to people. Everything I've learnt about the crash at Turner's Hatch points to him having a heart attack at the wheel. The car goes out of control and hits the tree.'

'I don't buy it,' said Anne. 'He never had any heart problems. His doctor said he had the heart of a lion. There were no cardiac problems in the family.'

Prunella shook her head as Anne added: 'A picture is building up here of a man who was more than just unlucky. It's starting to look as though somebody wanted him dead.'

9

'Bob, I've something to say,' said Anne, in a gentle, soothing voice as I drove us home after our lunch with Prunella at The Yacht. 'I've changed my mind about Gus Morley. I think it's possible he could still be alive and the funeral could have been faked. I'm very sorry I doubted you.'

I was so surprised I nearly lost my grip on the steering wheel. I glanced across at her. She looked strikingly beautiful in her summer dress with her wavy blonde hair brushing against her pale shoulders.

As my gaze instantly returned to the road ahead, I asked what had caused this change of heart.

'The circumstances surrounding his death are so suspicious,' she said. 'There was the incident with the lorry. It doesn't look like road rage at all. The driver had details of Gus's four-year-old Mercedes and his old Land Rover Discovery in his cab.

'Gus was obviously targeted. He survives that and then gets shot in East London. It's too far-fetched to believe he just got in the way of a gangland shooting. The gunman was just feet away when he fired.'

'He obviously wasn't much of a shot – unless it was a warning shot,' I said.

'Gus fell to the ground, so maybe the gunman thought he'd

achieved what he wanted,' Anne continued. 'Well, put all that together with your sighting of Gus in London and you being beaten up. It's obvious to me something sinister's been going on.' I nodded.

'There's something strange about the incident with the burning car at Turner's Hatch,' I murmured. 'Gus was a careful driver and you wouldn't expect him to have a heart attack at forty-seven.'

'None of it makes any sense,' said Anne.

'I'm glad you've started believing in me at last.' I felt the dark clouds of despondency that had been overshadowing me had suddenly been swept away.

'Oh Bob,' she said. 'I'm so sorry. I can't believe I've treated you so badly. I should never have doubted you. It's just your story sounded so crazy.'

'Strange things do happen in this world,' I said, delighted by her new attitude.

'I know,' she said. She patted my arm to reassure me her animosity was over. She rested her head on my arm for the final few miles of the journey home.

Once back inside the cottage, she continued to apologise for not believing in me earlier. I turned on the television and brought the remote control over to the settee, where we sat down together. But neither of us was really interested in watching a programme.

'Your story was so unbelievable, I thought you might be going loco,' she admitted as we sat hand in hand like love-struck teenagers. 'I should have trusted you, no matter how mad it all seemed.

'It now looks as though he's faked his own death – possibly

for money. It's the only explanation I can find.' She looked down at the floor and then glanced at me.

'Bob, can you forgive me?' she asked plaintively.

'Of course!' I assured her. She leaned over to kiss me on the cheek. I turned my head until our lips met. We kissed passionately for several minutes. I wrapped her tightly in my arms as she fondled my hair and face.

I was so pleased she accepted my story and we were as one again. Then she suddenly stood up and grasped my hand.

'Come on,' she said, leading me into the hall and up the stairs to our bedroom. The sun was still bright outside as it was just a few minutes before five pm. She drew the curtains and slipped off her red dress and underwear.

I gazed across at her gorgeous body, remembering, as I stood on the opposite side of the bed, how much I adored her. We both slid beneath the duvet. Then I reached across and cuddled her warm body. She turned to face me.

'Oh Bob, I'm really sorry,' she murmured. 'I wish I'd trusted you from the start. D'you know? I was thinking. This is the first time we've argued since we found Yusuf under the motor-home and you took pity on him.'

'You soon came round to my way of thinking,' I pointed out. 'We didn't really fall out.'

'Well, I was unsure at the time if we were doing the right thing. But these last three weeks since you came back from Euston Square have been unsettling. It's been the first major disagreement in our marriage. Anyway it's over now and it'll never happen again.' I thought I'd tease Anne.

'What about that night we spent in the police cells when we broke into the house looking for clues? That caused problems as well,' I suggested.

'You've never forgiven me for putting you through that, have you?' she said, giggling. She put her arms round my naked shoulders and fondled my hair.

'From now on, I promise I will always trust you,' she said. 'And right now, Mr Shaw, I'm going to show you just how sorry I really am.'

*

Later that day, Anne cooked us both spaghetti Bolognese. Then we went into the living-room where I sat on the settee, stroking Fiesta. Anne decided we had to produce a plan of action.

'As you've proved quite successfully, no one – not even my good friend Prunella – is going to believe us when we say that Gus Morley has returned from the dead,' she said, speaking softly while sitting at the dining table.

'So, for the moment, I think we should keep what we know within these walls. I've been doing a lot of thinking, Bob. To start with, you ought to write to Claudia and Jago and apologise for upsetting them.'

'Apologise?' I exclaimed.

'Yes. For one thing, they're our friends. For another, we might need to approach them for information at a later date, so we've got to keep them on board. I suggest you couch it along the lines that Gus's death has put a huge emotional strain on you. You didn't know what you were saying. You missed him so much after the funeral and you became delusional.'

'I could phone them, I suppose.'

'No, I think you should write a letter. A letter smacks of sincerity.'

'I'll do it if you think it'll help. But I'm not happy for them to think I'm a couple of beans short of a full English breakfast.' Anne sighed and shook her head.

'Bob, darling. I'm sorry. They think that already because of what you've said. The sooner you write these letters the better.' There was a pause. I nodded.

'You're right. I'll do what you suggest.'

'Good. I also think we should try to carry on behaving as normal. I don't think we should diverge from that course until we have absolute proof Gus is still alive or until the truth comes out and everyone begins to accept he is still alive.'

'All right. But how do we get that proof?'

'I'm just coming onto that. We're going to have to pay a visit to that clinic you mentioned.'

'Why are you saying "we"? You're going to help me, are you?'

'Yes, of course – unless you don't want me to…'

'Of course I want you to,' I began. 'It's just that… I've been doing this on my own for so long. Yes, it would be cool to do this together.' I smiled across the room at my wife. The fissure in the rock of our relationship had clearly been sealed.

'Right. Well, you mentioned he goes to the Hamelin Clinic every Wednesday. What does he do afterwards?'

'We know for certain he doesn't go back to Euston Square station.'

'In that case, I think we need to follow him. Hopefully, he'll lead us to wherever he's living now. That would be a brilliant start.'

'I agree.'

'Then we can confront him and try to find out exactly what's going on.' I shook my head.

'That's not going to get us very far. I spoke to him four days ago and he didn't even have the decency to acknowledge his old pal. He totally blanked me. So he'd probably do the same if we confronted him on his own doorstep.'

'But we don't know. He may be more amenable this week – especially if we catch him on his own. There's another thing. We need to find out what they offer at the clinic and why Gus has been attending it.'

'Makes sense, but that won't be easy.'

'I know, but I think we should go up to town and try to follow him this Wednesday.'

'OK!'

'Can you write down the address of the Hamelin Clinic? I'm going to do some research on it. The chances are he hurt his nose when he crashed to the ground in East London and he's being treated for the injury, but we need to know.'

'I've already done some research into the clinic online and got nowhere.'

'Never mind. I'll have a go as well. Bob, you've been to the clinic. Can you describe the place?'

'Yes. It's just off Tottenham Court Road. It's a mews about two or three hundred metres long. You enter it through an arch and there's a clear exit at the other end. Coming from the arch, the clinic is about twenty metres along the street on the right hand side.'

'We obviously can't hang around in the mews waiting for Gus to turn up and leave. We've got to have some kind of camouflage.'

'We could use the motor-home,' I suggested. 'We could park it a short distance away. It's ideal for surveillance.'

'Bob, the motor-home would be cumbersome in London streets and absolutely no use at all if we need to follow him. No, I think we should take the car. Then at least we won't stand out too much.

'We'll also have to change our appearance a little because he'd recognise us. I'm going to suggest I follow Gus on foot when he leaves the clinic while you try and pursue him in the car. That way we get two chances of keeping up with him.'

'Sounds cool.'

'And we'll have to keep our phones on, so we can keep in touch.' She looked down at the carpet without saying anything. Then she turned her gaze to me.

'D'you know what's really strange?' she said. 'How come Claudia is so much in the dark about it? I thought they were in love.' I immediately recalled my conversation with Claudia the day before.

'Claudia admits the marriage had had its problems. Divorce was mentioned, but they patched things up at Christmas.'

'Who mentioned divorce?' asked Anne.

'Gus.'

'Really?' She looked as surprised as a vicar's wife at a fetish club.

'I'd assumed everything was fine with their marriage. I suppose you just can't tell. That seems to point to Gus arranging all this on his own - unless Claudia is a brilliant actress.'

'She was in the drama society at university,' I muttered.

'I didn't realise that. Oh, I'm also going to phone Prunella. I want to find out whether the police pathologist has made any progress with the body recovered from the burnt-out car.' I stroked the cat without speaking.

'You've gone quiet,' she said.

'I was just thinking how we might come across my old sparring partner again, Ryan, if we go to the mews.'

'You'll have to take to your toes if we see him again,' Anne agreed. I thought I detected a smile.

'He might be ready to give me another kicking,' I mumbled. 'But I'll be ready for him this time.'

'You're not backing out now, are you?'

'No, no. We'll just have to keep our wits about us and be careful. That's all.'

10

Furtively following someone through the streets of London is an extremely challenging undertaking. I know this because Prunella Ball once told us she had been assigned with a coterie of other journalists to pursue a showbiz star. The objective was to see whether their quarry would visit a lover's home.

In the event, the only member of the pack who managed to keep up had been a veteran reporter on a motorbike. Cars were often of little use in an urban pursuit, she had informed us. In many cases, you were more likely to succeed by using two-wheeled transport or even going on foot.

Anne and I realised we faced a huge number of hurdles as we set out for London on Wednesday, May the twenty-second. Our target might be driven away and I might lose him at the first set of traffic lights. My car might get stuck behind a bus.

On foot, he might get lost in a crowd. At a station, he might jump onto a moving train while Anne is held up at the barrier. He might even spot us behind him and leave us to the mercy of Ryan.

But we tried to remain optimistic and not to dwell on the potential snags and pitfalls.

Although Hamelin Mews is in a congested part of the capital, it was quiet at three fifteen pm as we drove in. It had been raining earlier and the damp cobbles glistened in the May sunlight.

Red and pink fuchsias and azaleas spilled from window boxes, while, here and there, house-proud residents had enriched the scene with bay trees and shrubs. The only other vehicle in sight, a dark-blue delivery van, was parked at the far end.

I turned the car round so that we faced the way we had come and stopped thirty metres back from the clinic.

We speculated that, since Gus previously entered through the arch, he would probably leave through it and we would have no time to turn the car round later. I turned off the engine and we prepared our disguises.

I put on a dark-blue baseball cap and dark glasses. Anne, who was wearing a white patterned T-shirt and blue jeans, had brought some old reading glasses and had tied her hair back behind her head beneath a fawn chiffon scarf. The minutes passed by slowly.

Eventually my watch showed four o'clock and there had been no sign of either Gus or Ryan.

'Maybe they're already inside and are about to leave,' I suggested to Anne.

'Or maybe they're not coming today. By the way, how did you get on with replacing your damaged phone?'

'They're sending me a new handset on Friday,' I revealed.

'They're good, aren't they?' she murmured.

Suddenly, at around four thirty pm, the two men emerged from the clinic door. Gus was not wearing his glasses or carrying his brown coat. But he was wearing a white patterned shirt and navy-blue trousers, as he had the week before, and he was still in his brass-buckle shoes.

Ryan was following closely in a grey sweatshirt and black trousers, his eyes darting continually up and down the street. For a brief second, his gaze rested on our Mondeo and then moved on.

'That's them!' I hollered.

Anne gently released the door and set off, closing it quietly behind her. Their departure was going exactly as we had predicted. They were walking out beneath the arch. Within seconds, Anne was close behind them. I turned on the engine. The car edged forward across the cobbles. The chase was on.

The two men turned left into Whitfield Street and I guessed they were heading towards Goodge Street Underground station. But, after turning left a second time and turning right when they reached Tottenham Court Road, they strode past the station and continued south for several hundred metres.

Anne was managing to keep a short distance behind them, but, unfortunately, I was forced to stop at some red traffic lights and quickly lost sight of them.

Unsure where they might be heading, I drove aimlessly for a mile or so in a vaguely south-easterly direction and then stopped in a quiet Holborn back street. Now it was nearly a quarter to five. All I could do was wait to hear from Anne.

I sat in the car in my blue, short-sleeved shirt and grey jeans, listening to a radio talk show. Then, after around forty minutes, my phone rang.

'What's happened?' I asked eagerly.

'It's been a nightmare trying to keep up with them, but they've gone into a building in Shoreditch.'

'Shoreditch? That's not far from where he was shot.'

'I know. Oh Bob, the worst moment was on the Tube. I kept

looking over at them. I think it definitely helped I was wearing trousers. Gus has always seen me in dresses in the past.'

'Where exactly are you right now? I'll try and find you.'

'I'm near a block of flats in Demerara Place, off Shoreditch High Street, but don't bring the car into the street. They might have clocked it earlier.'

'No, of course, I won't do that. I'll park nearby and come and find you.'

Although I was less than two miles from Anne's location in the heart of the old East End, I was setting out at the height of rush hour. Nearly twenty minutes passed before I reached Shoreditch by way of gridlocked roads and found a spare parking space. As I left the car, I was greeted by the rumble of constant traffic accompanied, now and then, by a blaring car horn.

Within minutes, I reached Demerara Place, where Anne was waiting for me, leaning against a wall.

The street's three and four-story glass-fronted buildings were just a few steps from fashionable Brick Lane. But there had been dramatic changes over the past two decades. Old near-derelict warehouses, workshops and abandoned Victorian institutes had been transformed into trendy, architect-designed apartments for City workers. Most of them were now light, airy, open-plan homes with floor-to-ceiling windows and laminate flooring. The district abounded with trendy bars and restaurants.

Anne kissed and hugged me as I approached just before six o'clock, no longer wearing the dark glasses and baseball cap.

'It's that building over there,' she said, indicating a four-storey grey building with balconies overlooking the street at every level from the first floor upwards. CCTV cameras kept watch from various vantage points.

'They went in about half an hour ago,' she explained.

'We don't know which flat it is, do we?'

'No. There's seven flats altogether.'

'Sounds like two on each floor and a penthouse at the top.'

'That's what I think. One flat's got no name listed – Flat Three on the first floor. The others have all got names next to the flat numbers.'

At that moment, I noticed Ryan's menacing face and shoulders appear on the first floor balcony in between a pair of dwarf cypress trees in tubs. He was scowling like a vulture.

'Don't look now,' I said, sweeping her up in my arms and kissing her passionately.

'W-what's happening?' she spluttered.

'It's all right. Ryan just showed himself. He's gone back in now.' Anne's head turned towards the building, which was called Demerara Court.

'Which balcony was he on?' she asked.

'First floor.'

'That ties in with what I thought. It must be Flat Three.'

'Or Flat Four,' I suggested.

'No, there's a woman's name listed for that one. Oh, Bob. That journey here was very stressful. They got onto a Central Line train at Tottenham Court Road and I managed to get in the same carriage. I stayed at the far end, well away from them.

'There was just one moment when I thought I might be in trouble. Ryan wandered up the carriage, looking at all the passengers. I was shocked. He came so close, I could nearly feel his breath on me. Then he abruptly turned round and went back.

'Of course, I didn't know where they were going to get off. At every stop I was on tenterhooks. D'you know we travelled five stops before they finally got off at Liverpool Street?

'Once we left the train, I had to keep fairly close to them. I could easily have lost them in the crowds of commuters. But I worried that, if I got too close, they'd spot me.

'You were absolutely right about the way our man walks. It's just like Gus. It was an effort to keep up and that Ryan kept glancing over his shoulder.'

'You were great,' I said, kissing her again. As I did so, I glimpsed the grey shirt and dark trousers of the man himself - Ryan – streaking past on the other side of the road. He paid no attention to us. He was in far too much of a hurry. He was like a great excitable, lumbering hound abruptly let off the lead.

'Come on,' I whispered. 'Now's our chance for a showdown with Gus.' It was only after crossing the road and approaching the flats I realised the main door was locked. If we spoke to him on the entry phone, he was unlikely to admit us to the building. He had flatly ignored me a week before.

Luckily a petite woman with short brown hair who knew the code for the entry system arrived as we stood peering through the glass door and she let us in.

Anne led me across the dimly-lit hallway to the concrete stairway and we climbed to the bright, spacious first floor landing. We immediately found the brown wooden door to Flat Three and she pressed the doorbell. At the same time, I turned on my mobile phone's sound recorder in my pocket so that we would at least come away with evidence of the man's voice.

A few seconds later the door sprang open and we heard a man saying: 'Did you forget your key, Ryan?' It was Gus. Or, at least, I thought the man standing there was Gus. But, seeing him directly in front of me, full on, he seemed different. The bandage had gone from his face.

All three of us stood in stunned silence for a few seconds, staring at one another. Gus – if it were he – stood motionless in his white shirt and blue trousers. He was clutching something in his hand.

'Who are you?' he said at last. 'What d'you want?' Before Anne could say anything, I blurted out: 'Gus! What's happened to you?'

'You're at the wrong flat. I'm not Gus,' said the man.

'Don't you remember me. I'm Bob Shaw?' I said. 'We were at university. I arranged for you to take a room in our student house. You must remember.'

'Sorry,' said the man. 'I don't know you. I've never seen you before.' He moved inside and shut the door. I at once thumped on the door with my fist.

'Gus, what about Claudia and the children?' I shouted. 'You can't just desert them.' There was no response.

'Leave it, Bob,' Anne implored me. 'Come away. There's nothing more we can do here.'

Slowly, reluctantly, I followed her as she descended the stairs, passed through the foyer and walked out into the street. Perhaps I'd been mistaken all along. Perhaps he was simply a man who, by mere chance, had certain facial characteristics that resembled my friend's.

I followed her along Demerara Place. Finally she stopped at the corner and we looked back towards the first floor balcony. As I switched off the voice recorder, I wondered if the man resembling Gus was there, glaring down at us. We stood talking for a few minutes, bewildered at the hostile manner in which he had sent us away.

'I'm wondering now if I've been wrong all along,' I said. 'Maybe he's just a doppelganger after all. His face looks different and he's lost a bit of weight.'

'Didn't you notice what he held in his hand?' asked Anne as we stood together in bemused silence. Her words vanished in the air as a heavy lorry thundered past. At the same time, a small black van with a noisy diesel engine turned into the road. It stopped a few metres past the flats. Two men in dark clothing got out.

'I'm sorry. I didn't catch what you were saying,' I said, moving my ear closer to her face.

'I was talking about the whisky glass he held in his hand,' she went on, struggling against the din. 'It was one of the set of four glasses that we got engraved with the words: "Happy birthday from Anne and Bob." Don't you remember? We gave them to him for his fortieth birthday seven years ago.'

11

Anne was now convinced the man in Demerara Place was Gus Morley and she discounted my minor reservations. She was determined to find out why he had pretended to be dead.

Over a fish and chip supper at the kitchen table that night, she told me: 'It's obvious the man in the flat is Gus Morley. Not only does he resemble Gus in every way ....' I quickly corrected her.

'In nearly every way,' I said. 'His nose is certainly different. It's more slender.'

'All right, in nearly every way. But the compelling evidence for me was the whisky glass. I watched you wrap all four of them. I was with you when you gave them to him and I saw him proudly remove them from the wrapping paper.'

'There are thousands of engraved glasses around.'

'Not ones that say: "Happy birthday from Anne and Bob."'

'Could you read that from where you stood on the landing?'

'He was just inches away and the light was bright.'

'All right.'

'So unless his doppelganger has stolen the glass from him, the man in the flat is definitely your old friend.'

'So why is he behaving so oddly?' I said, biting into a morsel of cod.

'That's what we need to find out.' Anne did not appear to be hungry. She put her knife and fork on the plate and leaned back on the wooden spindle-back chair.

'We're in a strange position. We appear to know something no one else knows,' she asserted 'But I've got a feeling it's all going to end badly. Eventually, Claudia and her family are bound to learn the truth and they'll be devastated – if they don't know the truth already.

'So I really want to find out what's going on. I've got some time tomorrow. Although I've got my English class in the evening, I could visit the Hamelin Clinic in the morning. It would be good to know exactly what they do.'

After supper, I wrote two grovelling letters to Claudia and Jago, apologising for upsetting them. I explained I must have been more grief-stricken over Gus's death than I had realised.

My letter to Claudia contained the lines: 'Gus's loss left a dark shadow over my life and, when I met someone who resembled him, my imagination played tricks. I began to believe for a brief time that my dear friend may have returned to us. I sincerely apologise for allowing these irrational thoughts to take hold in my mind and for adding to the enormous grief you've already suffered. I sincerely hope you and the children can find it in your hearts to forgive me.'

I then changed the words around for a similar letter to Jago. After showing both letters to Anne, I found stamps and envelopes and decided I would post them in the letterbox at the end of the lane the next morning.

*

The following day Anne was planning to set off for London on her own to investigate the mysterious Hamelin Clinic. I was unable to take any more time off because it was the summer exam period at my school. My history pupils were either sitting their GCSEs or revising heavily for them.

Fiesta was waiting in the porch when I returned just before six pm, but there was no sign of Anne. As I turned the key in the lock, a black van drove slowly past the house. The driver stopped. He appeared to be looking at me. The vehicle looked out of place among the trees and hedgerows of Hopgarden Lane.

I decided he might be lost, so I took a few steps towards him down the drive, ready to offer him directions. He immediately sped away up the lane.

Nearly half an hour later, as I was preparing supper, Anne arrived back, beaming like a baker's girl who's sold her last muffin.

'That clinic's a strange place,' she said as she stepped inside the house.

'You didn't meet the Pied Piper, did you?' I joked. Although I was peeling potatoes in a bowl of warm water, she squeezed me tightly and kissed me.

'Steady on!' I said. 'You'll have the water over.'

'Bob, d'you know the clinic's really plush? You go into this small reception area to the clickety-click sound of two women about the same age as me typing on computer keyboards behind a gleaming white desk.

'There's a luxurious grey carpet and two paintings on the wall showing French beach scenes. But, weirdly, there's only one sign up. Above a door at the right-hand side of the desk, it says: Waiting Room. There are no other notices and no leaflets.'

'So what happened?'

'The older of the women ignored me and carried on typing. I had to wait for her blonde colleague to finish a phone call. She looked up and said: "Can I help?" I said: "My doctor was thinking of referring me here. I wondered how easy it is to book an appointment?"

'"We're not open to the general public," the woman said brusquely. "This is a specialist clinic."

'So I said: "Well, I was just wondering . . . " She stopped me at once.

'"We don't take NHS referrals," she said. "You're in the wrong place. Is it a facelift or Botox you're after? There's plenty of clinics round here for that." So I said: "I've been recommended to come here. I'm told your surgeon is one of the best."

'She said : "I don't know who you've been speaking to. We can't help you. Our team do specialised work and it's closed to the general public. I'm sorry."

'Then she got up and led me to the door. As she opened it and ushered me out, she added: "I'm really sorry we couldn't help you."

'That's very strange, isn't it?' I said, as I cut the potatoes and placed them in a saucepan.

'But it wasn't a completely wasted journey,' Anne continued. 'I knocked on neighbours' doors. An old man in the next house refused to open his door. But I had more luck at the second house along.

'She was a really chatty woman with time to talk. She'd heard it was an extremely expensive clinic specialising in some branch of plastic surgery. It's reserved for military personnel, diplomats, civil servants and people like that.'

'I'm surprised if Gus matches that criteria,' I said.

'I asked her how you get referred there and she didn't know. But she said the clinic had been there for many years. She's recognised one or two of the patients as well-known figures. She's seen them turning up in Ferraris and Maseratis.'

'It's interesting that she thinks they do plastic surgery,' I said, as the potatoes began to simmer. 'That must explain the bandage on his nose. He might have had some cosmetic work done on his face.'

*

Anne was convinced we would be able to unlock some of the secrets of Gus Morley's new life if we returned to Demerara Place. She reasoned that, if we could only engage some of the neighbours in conversation, they might let slip vital clues about his transformation.

I was concerned we might encounter Ryan again. But I put that thought aside as we set off for London on the Saturday morning. It was another hot, sunny day.

After travelling by train and Tube, we reached Old Street underground station just before midday. From there, it was just a five-minute walk to our destination amid the roaring traffic.

Someone had thoughtfully left the main door of the flats open this time and we made our way to the first floor landing. There was no sign of either Gus or Ryan. I pressed my right ear to the door. No sound could be heard from within.

Anne marched to the door of Flat Four on the opposite side of the landing and pressed the doorbell.

At first, there was silence there too. Then the door was answered by the small, brown-haired woman we had met briefly at the main door three days earlier. She was slim, in her late twenties and wearing a loosely-fitting fawn jumper and blue jeans.

I feared she might feel intimidated if I appeared alongside my wife, so I strolled over to the full-length landing window and pretended to be staring down at the street below.

'So sorry to bother you,' said Anne, smiling sweetly. 'We were looking for our friend from Flat Three. It doesn't look like he's in.'

'No,' said the woman. 'He moved out two nights ago.'

'Moved out? I thought he'd only just moved in.'

'That's right. He's only been here about four months. He waved to me just before leaving with all his gear at seven o'clock.'

'He's an old friend of ours,' said Anne. 'He didn't mention us at all? You kindly let us in on Wednesday evening.'

'I'll be honest. He kept himself to himself. He only used to have a couple of visitors – the big man and a Chinese lady.'

'The big man? That must be Ryan. We know him well.'

'Very well!' I thought to myself, stroking the bruises on the side of my face.

'I didn't know that was his name,' said the woman, who had dark eyes and a pale, elfin face. 'I knew him as Mr Benjamin. He was always dashing about and always on his phone, but he didn't live there all the time.

'He sometimes brought his Chinese girlfriend along. I got the impression he was some kind of security guard – judging by his conversation.'

'Yes, we thought so,' said Anne.

'A friend's seen him working out at the Verve Fitness Club in Hoxton.'

'And Gus? Has he been going to his office?'

'I thought you were friends, but you don't seem to know that much about him.'

'It's been a long time.'

'You're talking about the man at Flat Three?'

'Yes.' The woman frowned.

'Well, his name wasn't Gus. It's Chris,' she insisted.

'Oh, that's what I meant,' said Anne, glancing over her right shoulder at me. 'They're such similar names.'

'If you'll excuse me, I've got the washing on.' Doubts were forming in the woman's mind about the purpose of our mission. She was raising the drawbridge of her defences.

'Is Chris still working for the government?'

'I don't know what he did. Most of the time, we just said Hello on the stairs.'

'Did anyone else in the building get to know him much?'

'I don't think so. Anyway I'll have to go now.'

'So you're having new neighbours now?'

'I've no idea. It's a company flat, so I'm not too worried.'

'Thank you so much for your time,' said Anne. 'Look, I haven't been able to reach Chris by phone. Have you got a number for him by any chance or a forwarding address?'

'No.'

'I suppose Ryan must have helped him move?'

'No. A bunch of guys came round in a Luton van and shifted all his gear. '

'You don't know which company?' The woman appeared impatient to get back to her washing.

'No, I don't. Look, I've really got to go.'

'You've been a treasure,' said Anne. 'Just one more thing.

D'you know if it was a hire van or removal truck?'

'Oh, God. You've got some questions, haven't you? All I know is it was a yellow van with an orange stripe round the side. It said Henderson's Removals or Harrison's Removals on the side. I can't remember exactly.

'I know that because I looked out when I heard someone hooting a car horn out in the street. Someone couldn't get past. Now I've really got to go.'

'You've been very helpful. Thank you!' said Anne as the woman closed the door.

'You've done well there,' I said after we left the building. 'We're making headway.'

'Is there any point speaking to any of the other residents?' she wondered.

'I don't think you're going to get more from anyone else. She shared the same landing and clearly saw more of the comings and goings than anyone else would have done.'

As we ventured out into the mild May air, a light drizzle was falling. We took a few steps along Demerara Place towards the main road.

Then unexpectedly I noticed a black four-by-four vehicle parked across the street. It was a Range Rover Vogue. Its occupants were, in turn, looking up at the first floor flat and towards us.

I almost instinctively crossed over and hurried towards them, sensing they might have some connection with the flats and provide us with information about Gus's whereabouts. But as soon as the driver saw me approaching, he drove off.

12

When we got home that afternoon just before four pm, we found a note on the doormat. It said: 'I urgently need you to meet me at Canterbury Police Station.'

It was signed: 'Warrant Officer Alex Lotman.' We called the phone number on the note and, although we were both tired, agreed to meet him at a quarter to five – just before the station closes for the night.

We left the car in a pay-and-display carpark a few minutes' walk from the police station. Standing by the building's entrance was a pale, broad-shouldered man with his fair hair in a crewcut and a sturdy, muscular frame.

He was at least six feet three inches tall, in his late thirties and wearing a navy-blue suit. He smiled as we approached and gave a brief wave with his left hand.

Somehow he appeared to recognise us, but I was far more curious about why he wished to see us and quickly forgot to pursue the issue.

'Mr Shaw? Mrs Shaw? I'm Warrant Officer Lotman,' said the man, shaking first Anne's hand and then my own.

He waved a grubby identity pass in front of me. I struggled to read his first name on the laminated pass card. 'I'm so sorry I had to call you in at such short notice.'

'Does that say Alexei?' I asked.

'Yes. My mother's from Eastern Europe,' he said. 'Shall we move inside the door? I'm afraid they've got the decorators in and the interview room isn't available.'

'Good idea,' I said as we moved just inside the main door. I noticed he had a small scar about an inch long on his left cheek.

'Which section of the police are you?' asked Anne.

'I'm with military intelligence,' he explained.

'So you work for the Ministry of Defence?' said Anne.

'That's right,' he said. 'Look, I'll come straight to the point. You've been seen up in Shoreditch a couple of times, visiting some flats.'

'Yes,' I replied. 'I don't think we've broken any law.'

'I'm afraid you've caused a bit of bother. Apparently, you've gone up there and upset some people. You're claiming there's a man in Demerara Court who's a friend of yours.'

'That's right,' I said. 'Gus Morley. I was at university with him fifteen years ago.'

'Mr Shaw, I want to impress on you that this man at Demerara Court is not your friend. It's an obvious case of mistaken identity. He's not Gus Morley, and I have to warn you most emphatically that you must not go there bothering him again.'

'That's ridiculous!' I said. 'We shared a house together.'

'This must be something to do with his scientific work for the military then?' said Anne. 'Silly of me to say that really. That must be the case. Otherwise why would you be involved?'

'I can't confirm anything. All I can tell you is that the man in Demerara Court is not your university friend, Mr Shaw, and if either of you go back to that flat, my information is that you will be arrested.'

'Arrested?' I exclaimed. 'What for?'

'Let me see: threatening behaviour, harassment, breach of the peace. That's just a few possibilities off the top of my head. But I can see you're sensible people. I can see it won't come to that.' Anne and I gazed at each other in shock.

'Are you serious about that?' I asked.

'Never been more serious.'

'Well, we've always upheld the law, haven't we, love?' I said turning towards Anne. She nodded.

'He's no longer in Demerara Court anyway,' she said, rather indignantly.

'It doesn't matter where the man is,' Lotman insisted. 'You are not to contact him. Is that plain?' We both nodded.

'Good,' he said, opening the door. 'I can see you've taken my advice on board and that there won't be any further problems.' All three of us stepped out of the building to be met with the dust and noise of Saturday evening traffic.

'I suppose you're going straight home now, are you?' he shouted.

'Just some shopping to do first,' Anne explained as we said goodbye and headed towards a supermarket to buy some groceries.

'What d'you make of that?' I asked Anne, when we were safely out of Lotman's earshot.

'It shows for certain that something mysterious is going on involving Gus and the Armed Forces,' she said. 'You know him better than me. What exactly was his job?'

'All I know is he worked for the government in some capacity involving weapons. Whenever I asked him, he always clammed up.'

'Must have worked for the Ministry of Defence,' Anne murmured as we reached the car park.

'That Lotman guy is a bit late telling us not to visit Demerara Court,' I replied. 'Gus isn't there now in any case.'

'Has he got the power to stop us visiting a particular place?' Anne wondered. 'He's military police – not civilian police.'

'I'm not totally sure what his powers are,' I said. 'But in any case Gus has moved and we don't know where to.'

'That's right,' she said. 'He could have gone anywhere. The thing is we don't want to get ourselves into any needless trouble, but, by the same token, we have to consider the welfare of our friends - Gus and his family.

'Someone has to question whose body was in the blazing car and find out how that person ended up there. Perhaps that person was murdered. There are dozens of questions that need answering. No one else is privy to what we know – that Gus is alive.'

'Apart from Alex Lotman and Ryan,' I said as I unlocked the car.

'That's presuming they know the truth,' Anne said. 'They may not know what we know. We may be on our own in that respect.'

Our shopping expedition was cut short. Anne was unable to find some of the food items she wanted and we decided to postpone the shopping to the next day as we were tired. As a result, we returned to the cottage earlier than expected.

As soon as the car turned into Hopgarden Lane, I knew something was wrong.

There was a black four-by-four car with tinted windows

parked a few feet from our drive, close to the home of our elderly next-door neighbour, Linda Morrison. Fiesta was not waiting in the porch.

As I drove in and parked in front of the motor-home, we noticed the front door was open. The sound of our diesel engine had no doubt alerted whoever was inside our house.

Two men, each with a scarf round his face, darted through the doorway as I switched off the ignition. The pair ran towards the car in the lane. One had a sheaf of papers in his hand while the other was carrying a white canvas bag.

I quickly got out of the Mondeo. I had been filled with indignation after Ryan's brutal attack on me. But this was worse. I was seething like a sackful of snakes and was determined that these two burglars who had plundered our home in broad daylight would not escape so lightly. Memories returned to me of the boxing classes I had attended while a young schoolboy.

'What the hell were you doing in our house?' I bellowed while the driver started the engine. As I grabbed the rear passenger door handle and banged hard on the window, I noticed a discarded beer bottle lying in the gutter. The handle failed to budge. The car door had been locked from the inside.

As the three-year-old Volkswagen Tiguan began to drive away towards the main road, I picked up the bottle and threw it with all my strength at the rear of the car.

It struck the back window, shattering the entire glass pane. The driver turned right and headed off towards Ashford.

As I watched it disappear, I thought it was a similar car to the one I had seen earlier in Shoreditch, but I could not be sure. Then I realised Anne was standing behind me.

'What was that you threw?' she asked.

'A beer bottle was lying beside the road,' I explained. 'I felt I had to do something. Maybe they'll think twice about coming back.'

'I've got most of the registration,' Anne revealed. 'It was MJ66 and then it was something like JVV or JVU.'

'Well done. Write that down quickly.' We rushed back up the drive and into the house to see what the men had stolen.

The first thing we noticed was that one of the nine bull's eye glass panes had been smashed in the front door, which explained how they had got in. The hall floor by the doorway was covered in fragments.

A rock from the garden, which had undoubtedly been used to smash the pane, was lying among the slivers of glass. One of the men must have put their hand through the gap and turned the latch from the inside.

Downstairs nothing appeared to have been touched, but upstairs it was a different story. Drawers in the main bedroom had been wrenched from Anne's dressing table and my chest of drawers. The wooden floor and bed were covered in clothes, shoes, electrical gadgets, bedding and towels.

The guest bedroom had also been ransacked with bedding and spare curtains strewn across the carpet. The study had been searched as well. My mother's writing bureau drawers had been pulled out and the contents spread across the wooden floor.

Pupils' exercise books and textbooks had been knocked off the desk, while books and papers had been swept from shelves.

'Where's Fiesta?' cried Anne. The cat usually made his presence known loudly, mewing constantly on our return in anticipation of being fed. But we had not seen him.

I ran downstairs and called his name several times. Then I

glanced through the kitchen window and spotted him skulking beneath a hedge. After a few minutes, he wandered in, looking around to make sure our uninvited guests had departed. I guessed he had been startled by the break-in.

'Hi, Fiesta!' I said. 'I'll get you some food now.' He brushed against my navy-blue trousers, purring contentedly, no doubt relieved the intruders had gone and normal service was being resumed.

'Is the cat all right?' Anne called out from the study.

'Yes, he seems fine!' I shouted back as I swept up the pieces of glass in the hall. 'Is there anything missing?'

'The desktop computer has gone and I can't find the laptop or the tablet.'

'They must have put them in the car and then come back. The bastards!'

'They've also rifled through some of my files by the look of it,' she said, approaching the top of the stairs. I walked into the hall and looked up at her.

'One of the guys had a bundle of papers in his hand,' I said.

'Yes, they've taken all the details I'd written down of Gus's appearances at the Tube station, the car crash in Turner's Hatch, the inquest and Demerara Court. They've also taken your mobile – the one with the SIM card containing Gus's picture.' I groaned.

Anne went on: 'The only good news is they don't seem to have taken my jewellery – my mother's necklace, the necklace you gave me for Christmas and my grandmother's gold rings.'

I quickly ran upstairs and searched for my old volume about the life of Henry VIII. Anne watched as I spent a few minutes wading through the jumble of books on the study floor, trying to find it. Finally, I emerged with the prized book in my hand and a feeling of triumph.

'What's so special about that book?' she asked.

'Well, apart from the fact it's one of the best recent works about the reign of Henry VIII, it contains this,' I said, removing a loose page that had been concealed inside. It was now the only print I had of Gus at Euston Square.

'At least they didn't take my photo,' I said as I brandished it in the air.

'Good,' said Anne. 'Now don't you think we should call the police? They might be able to get some forensic evidence of the two men. There may be fingerprints.'

'Yes,' I agreed. 'I'll have to try and get some glass and replace that broken pane, and maybe we should think about getting some decent security.'

Our cottage was in a quiet, rural location. Although we had neighbours on both sides – two elderly widows - acres of farmland lay behind us. That provided a good escape route if one were needed.

Anne walked thoughtfully down the stairs. I could see she was upset. Two vile strangers had invaded our haven of peace. Life in our wonderful country cottage might never feel exactly the same again.

She looked up at me. A tear slipped slowly down her right cheek. She put her arms round me and kissed me.

'Oh Bob, I feel sullied, violated,' she said.

'I know. Someone's been in our place and gone through our things. We've no idea who. We've no idea why,' I said. It had passed through my mind that the same two men might return in the future, but I thought it best not to mention this to Anne, for fear of upsetting her further.

We stood under the hall light, hugging and holding each other for several minutes. Then Anne broke the silence.

'Don't you think it's a bit of a coincidence – these men breaking in while we're at the police station with that man Lotman?' she said.

'I'd been wondering about that as well. Could easily be a connection between the two events. I think we should mention that to the police when they come.'

Anne added: 'Isn't it strange they wanted my hand-written notes? It's as if they were interested in finding out what we'd been doing.'

'It's hard to get into the minds of thieves,' I replied. 'They probably don't always act rationally. Who knows why they steal things?'

After a phone call to Kent Police, we were informed they would send an officer round when they had one available. I received the impression the earliest we could expect a visit would be on Monday morning, which suited me since it was half-term week at school and I would be at home.

We were reassured by the prospect of officers coming to visit and vowed not to disturb the scene of the crime until the police had been. We removed objects that had been dumped on the bed and, later that night, got beneath the duvet in the hope of obtaining a few hours' sleep.

I found it hard to doze off to begin with. The warning words of Alex Lotman and thoughts of the beer bottle striking the getaway car were for some time swirling through my mind. But eventually my eyes must have grown drowsy and I drifted off to sleep.

13

Two days passed. On Monday, roused by the early song of robins and song thrushes, I edged the bedroom curtain aside and peered out at the bright, new morning.

The rays of the sun glinted into the cluttered room, flickering across the clothing and bedding scattered haphazardly around.

I gazed down at the garden, where young bees had already begun their morning duties, hovering around the fragrant roses. Beyond the hedge, the foxgloves—elegant spires of dainty pink flowers - tossed their heads in the gentle breeze in time with the white daisies.

Further away, in the verdant fields and meadows past the lane, the branches of the trees swayed in rhythm with the avian chorus.

Leaving Anne to sleep on, I crept downstairs in my dressing gown, glanced through the morning paper and made us both some tea. Later Anne came down and we had a light breakfast.

At ten o'clock there was a knock on the door. I could just see the back of a tall, stout man in a dark suit standing in the porch with a notebook. I recognised him at once. I went to the kitchen door and alerted Anne.

'Darling!' I called. 'Graham Kirwan's here.' Then I opened the front door for our visitor. Kirwan is a detective sergeant with Kent Police.

We had become firm friends since Anne helped him and his superior, Detective Inspector Russell Woods, solve the Lucas Sharp murder.

'Bob! How are you now?' he asked as I beckoned him in. Anne emerged from the kitchen. He greeted her with a kiss on the left cheek.

'Now I guess you're wondering why I'm here on a Bank Holiday Monday,' he said in his faint Irish lilt. 'Well, of course, some of us still have to work today. Since we're friends now, I decided I'd better come along myself. So you've had some uninvited guests?'

'Yes, Graham,' I replied. 'They took our main computer, our laptop, our tablet and my mobile. They've also taken some of Anne's papers.' He made notes on his clipboard.

'Nothing vital like a passport or driving licence, I hope?'

'No, no. Just some hand-written notes that were only really of use to her.'

'I see. Well, can you show me the damage? There's usually damage.' I pointed to the missing pane in the front door. Then we led him upstairs and showed him the three bedrooms.

'You've been burgled all right,' he said as his eyes were transfixed by the chaotic scenes. It looked like there'd been a riot at a jumble sale.

'We were minded to clear it up, but thought you'd want to see the mess exactly as the men left it,' said Anne from behind us.

'They were certainly looking for something,' said the sergeant. 'It's normally money or jewellery.'

'But the jewellery's untouched, Graham!' said Anne.

'Shall we go downstairs and I can take down all the details.'

He followed us into the living-room, where he sat down at the dining table. I found a chair at the opposite side of the table while Anne made herself comfortable on the settee.

'Now I gather there were two men and you confronted them as you got home. D'you have any recollection of what they looked like?' he asked, jotting down notes on his clipboard.

'Well, one was quite tall. I'd say five feet ten – about the same as me.'

'I'd say slightly taller,' said Anne.

'All right, five feet eleven,' I said. 'He had light-brown hair and was a white guy. Most of his face was covered by a brown scarf.'

'What sort of age would he have been?'

'Twenty-five to thirty,' said Anne.

'And how was he dressed?'

'He had dark clothing and white trainers,' I said. 'The other guy was slightly shorter but stockier. I thought he might be from an Afro-Caribbean background.'

'Any idea of his age?'

'I'd say thirty to thirty-five.' Anne nodded in agreement.

'He had a blue top, black trousers, black trainers and a blue-and-white scarf round his face,' she said.

'Any idea on height?' the sergeant asked.

'I should think he was five feet eight or five feet nine,' I told him.

'So just to run through what happened, you got home at what time?' the sergeant said.

'It was about twenty past five on Saturday evening,' I said.

'And what did you notice?'

'There was a black Volkswagen Tiguan outside Linda Morrison's house.'

'That's Number One, Hopgarden Lane?'

'That's right. Next door here.'

Anne interrupted to explain: 'I've got the registration number.'

'That's great, Anne,' he said. After he had written the car number down, I continued our story.

'As we parked in the drive, these two men ran from the house, got in their car and drove off towards Ashford.'

'And you saw them carrying your gadgets, did you?'

'No. We think they must have loaded them in the car and then come back to pick up Anne's notes.'

'Right. Well, it seems strange behaviour – even for the young toe-rags we have to deal with these days. I mean, why take Anne's notes? I can understand the computers and phone being nicked. That's standard fare. Easy to steal; easy to sell.

'But taking someone's scrawled notes is a new one on me. Have you guys upset somebody?'

'It's strange you should say that,' said Anne. 'It's possible.' I was about to interrupt, but she stopped me.

'I'll tell him,' she said. 'Graham, we were asked to go to Canterbury police station an hour before the break-in.'

'Who asked you to do that?'

'A warrant officer from military intelligence. He gave the name Alex Lotman.'

'Military intelligence, eh?' he said with a chuckle.

'It's all right. He showed us ID,' said Anne solemnly.

'Why did he want to speak to you?'

'It's a bit involved,' she said. 'We'd been visiting someone in

121

London and he advised us not to go back to the person's address.'

'You've got me intrigued, Anne. But how d'you think this links to the raid on your house?' he asked.

'We just thought this warrant officer might have been in league with the intruders, luring us away so they could break into unoccupied premises,' I said. 'It's a bit of a coincidence.

'He arranged to meet us just before the station closed at five and that's roughly the time we think the men would've broken in.'

'I see what you mean,' said the sergeant. 'Let me take that name down and I'll make a few inquiries when I get back to CID. What was he called again?'

'Warrant Officer Alex Lotman,' I said as the sergeant began scribbling in his notebook. 'His first name might be Alexei – you know, Alex with "ei" on the end. He works for the Ministry of Defence.'

'Maybe he's bogus. I'll have to check him out,' he said. 'So who's this fella in London that's got our friend Mr Lotman hot and bothered?' I at once became hesitant, unsure of what to say and doubtful whether the sergeant would believe us.

'It's an old friend of mine,' I began. 'We have good reason to believe he's faked his own death.' I carefully watched his face for any signs he might break into laughter.

Fortunately, the policeman had a puzzled expression as he grappled to understand me.

'Now what good reason d'you have for believing your friend did that?' he asked.

'Well, for one thing, we both attended his funeral two months ago,' I replied.

'That's a heck of a good reason,' he said. 'Now you're telling me he's still around, this pal of yours, and he's living in London?'

'That's right.'

'Well, strange things happen. I'm thinking of the canoe man.'

'Not to mention Reginald Perrin,' said Anne, trying to be helpful.

'That was fiction,' I pointed out as the sergeant stroked his chin thoughtfully.

'Vanishing acts like that often turn into police matters eventually,' he conceded. 'But we'd need a lot of evidence. Have you got any proof?'

'I've got a photograph upstairs that I took earlier this month – three and a half months after he was killed,' I said.

Anne added: 'And we both saw him in Shoreditch two days ago holding a gift we gave him.' The sergeant leaned back in his chair, smiling. I wasn't sure he believed us.

'Are two trying to wind me up?' he asked. We both shook out heads, but my suspicions had been proved right.

I was annoyed with myself for even thinking he might believe us. I should have realised it would be a waste of time. I frowned. I shrugged my shoulders. Then, just as I was about to speak, Anne intervened.

'We just needed some advice. That's all,' she said. 'We weren't sure you'd believe us.'

'It's not that I don't believe you. But you have to see it from my viewpoint,' said the sergeant. 'These things are very hard to prove and, unless someone's been murdered, tricked out of money or some other major crime's been committed, we haven't the time and resources needed for a speculative venture these days.

'If you want advice, I'll tell you what my old mother would

have said: "Don't be breaking your shin on a stool that's not in your way."'

'I'm sorry?' I said. Anne looked over at me. She explained: 'The sergeant is trying to say we shouldn't put ourselves to any unnecessary trouble.'

'Correct!' said the sergeant as he lifted himself out of his chair. 'The English would say: "Leave well alone." Because, at the end of the day, you'll still arrive back with one arm as long as the other.'

'Another of your mother's phrases?' I ventured.

'Correct,' he replied. 'Look, I'll send someone round from forensics later today or tomorrow to check for fingerprints. You'll have to provide your own prints at some stage so they can be eliminated.

'I'll also check the CCTV on the Ashford road in Chasehurst and look into our Mr Lotman.' He sidled towards the hallway, eyeing us both as he moved.

'I'll keep you both posted,' he promised, opening the front door. He shook both our hands and then studied the missing pane.

'I should get that fixed pretty quickly,' he said. 'Anyone can get in right now.'

'I know,' I said. 'Graham, thanks ever so much for coming.'

'Pleasure!' he said, marching off down the drive. 'I'll be in touch.'

As the sergeant's light-blue Volkswagen Golf drew away, I turned to Anne.

'He didn't believe us,' I said.

'Well, it was asking a lot,' she admitted. 'Although I have to say in the world in which he operates he must happen upon really bizarre events from time to time.

'D'you know what? I felt he wanted to believe us. He must remember how hard we worked to find the killer of Lucas Sharp. He may have dismissed our remarks, but I've got a feeling that, if any further evidence came to light, he'd be one of the first to change his mind and support us.'

'That may be so. But right now I'd better focus on our priorities and fix this door.'

While Anne spent an hour upstairs tidying the bedrooms, I drove into the city and bought a fresh pane of glass for the door from a DIY store.

Then I came home, removed loose fragments from the empty wooden frame and slid the new pane into place. I had just finished smoothing down the putty and washing my hands when my new mobile rang. A young man's voice inquired: 'Is that Mr Shaw?'

I confirmed it was. He announced himself as Nick Casey, a reporter on the local newspaper. He had heard about the break-in and was planning to write a report about it.

'It was upsetting at the time, but we're trying to get over it now,' I informed him. 'I wouldn't have thought anyone would be interested in reading about it.'

'You'd be surprised,' he insisted. 'There's a huge interest in rural crime.' I asked him to hold on. Then I dashed upstairs to consult Anne. Like me, she felt there was no reason to keep the incident a secret.

'They smashed a pane in the front door while we were in Canterbury,' I told him. 'We disturbed them when we returned. They drove off in a black Tiguan.'

'We've been given all the details by the police, including the car registration. You never know. With a bit of publicity you might get your computers back.'

'There wasn't any damage apart from the door,' I added. 'My wife was shaken and upset, but I suppose it could've been a lot worse.'

The young journalist appeared happy with the information and I thought no more about the conversation.

The next morning, Tom the postman arrived with a letter for me. He spent a moment examining the new pane of glass.

'That's looking a lot better now,' he remarked before he headed back down the drive. The letter had a Gloucestershire postmark. It was from Claudia. It said : *Dear Bob, Thank you so much for your letter apologising for your behaviour when you visited us on May the eighteenth. I was extremely upset when you showed me the photograph of the man that slightly resembles my late husband. I was crying for a while after you left.*

'However, it was clear to see in your letter how upset you have also been over the loss of Gus. I knew he was a good friend to you. I hadn't realised quite how deeply you had missed him – so deeply that it obviously preyed on your mind and you became obsessed with the ridiculous notion that he was still with us.

'I have decided to regard your behaviour as a sign of the deep depression from which you have obviously been suffering. So, naturally, I forgive you for the way you conducted yourself.

'The sentiments in your letter came across as extremely sincere and it appears you have now returned to your senses. For that we must be grateful. It is somewhat consoling to both myself and the children to know that so many people have been affected by Gus's loss and share our grief.

'I have passed your remarks onto Jago. I'm sure that, given time,

he will also understand why you acted as you did and will no doubt find it in his heart to forgive you as well.

'Please pass on my love and best wishes to Anne. With kind affection from James, Sophie and myself, Yours sincerely, Claudia.'

14

By Thursday of that week, we were still in a partial state of shock at the way in which two strangers had infiltrated the private sanctuary of our home. But we were doing our best to forget the distressing experience and get on with our lives.

Just after eleven o'clock, while upstairs in the study preparing some revision notes for exam candidates, I heard a car with a loud exhaust roar into the lane. The sound was followed two minutes later by a loud knock on the door.

Anne, who was in the living-room, opened it and was greeted by the beaming face of Prunella Ball, dressed in the same white, patterned off-the-shoulder dress she had worn during our visit to Faversham.

Anne led her into the living-room, where they sat and talked for nearly half an hour. They left the door open, which meant I could continue writing my notes while still catching most of the conversation.

'I know you're interested in Professor Morley's death because of Bob's friendship with him,' Prunella said, as she sunk into the settee.

'Yes. Thanks for updating us about the attempts on his life,' said Anne. 'We've been carrying out our own research.'

'Anything you can share with me?'

'I will do, but not at the moment.'

'All right,' said Prunella. 'Anyway I've got some new details from Graham Kirwan that might interest you. Don't let it go outside these walls because I'm writing a big piece for the Sunday News.'

'We'll be discreet,' Anne assured her.

'The post-mortem was originally due to be carried out by Dr Theo Harryman, the main Home Office pathologist for Kent. But his wife is extremely ill and not expected to live much longer.'

'Sorry to hear that,' said Anne.

'So a senior pathologist, Dr Maxwell Griffiths, stepped into conduct the post-mortem. Of course, the body was too charred to be identified in the normal way.

'Fingerprint evidence wasn't available because the skin was burnt and it's difficult to obtain accurate DNA from burnt bone. Apparently burnt bone can be easily contaminated with external DNA.'

'I'm surprised to hear that,' said Anne. 'I learned a little about DNA while I was working at the library. I would have thought DNA testing was the best option.'

'Graham says getting DNA is a very lengthy process, whereas dental checks are fairly quick once the records are obtained from the dead person's dental practice. It's also a much cheaper process than using DNA evidence.

'Even in really bad burns cases, like this one, it's rare that they don't find at least some of the teeth. The only delay has been waiting for the professor's dental records to arrive from Gloucestershire.

'Well, these records have now arrived. Dr Griffiths says in

his report that two of the teeth recovered from the body are an exact match with teeth in the records. These are one of the professor's front incisors, which was badly chipped, and a molar restored with a gold crown.'

'So what's the pathologist's conclusion?' asked Anne, as she wrote down the details in a notebook.

'That the body in the car was Professor Morley.'

'Really?'

'Yes, of course. Why are you surprised? It's been confirmed it was the professor's car. His signet ring was also recovered and remains of his spectacles.'

Anne told me later she was dumbfounded. She knew that Gus was still alive. But a senior pathologist was convinced it was Gus's body that had perished in the car. Doubts and suspicions about the veracity of the evidence swept over her like a tidal wave.

'So the whole body was destroyed beyond recognition?' she asked.

'Yes, all except his lower limbs.'

'His legs?'

'Yes. Graham thinks that, because flames burn upwards, these limbs escaped the worst ravages of the fire.'

'What is the pathologist saying about the actual cause of death?' Anne asked after a pause.

'He's still looking into that, but the professor's head had suffered from severe trauma. It looks like the cause will go down as severe burns and head injury. But there is one really strange aspect to the case.'

'Oh? What's that?' Anne wondered.

'Well, when they measured the body in the mortuary, its

length was six feet three inches. Yet the professor's height was known to be six feet two inches. Even allowing for post-mortem expansion, that's strange.'

'It is, isn't it?' said Anne.

'I imagine Dr Griffiths will address that at the inquest next month.'

*

After Anne had gone to hold her English class at the farm at six o'clock, I left the cottage and set off for the Merry Friar. It had been a warm day. Pink-petalled dog rose sprang here and there along the hedgerows, nestling among the foaming green and white cowslips and mauve foxgloves.

Beyond the hedge, a carpet of vibrant blue bells sheltered beneath the trees. Within ten minutes, I reached the red-brick Victorian street corner pub.

'Ah, here's the famous man that fought off two burglars!' Miles declared as I walked through the door. I was unsure how he had heard about the break-in and disappointed he was proclaiming the news across the crowded bar. Voices became hushed for a moment before the conversations resumed.

'How did you know about the break-in?' I asked as he poured me a pint of bitter.

'It's on page three of today's local paper,' he revealed, grabbing a copy from beneath the bar and thrusting it towards me.

'I'm surprised they bothered ransacking the place,' he added. 'I'd have thought they'd have taken one look round and assumed someone had beaten them to it.'

'We keep our place spick and span, thank you,' I said with a smile. 'It's certainly in a better state than your other bar. You've had the same carpet there for at least seventeen years.'

'That's good quality Axminster, I'll have you know. Good for a few more years yet,' he said, leaving me to serve another customer. I seized the opportunity to glance at the newspaper.

The headline said: 'Teacher's fears as cottage ransacked by masked burglars.' I read through the first part of the report: 'An English language teacher has been left "shaken and upset" after two masked men broke into her village home.

'Anne Shaw, thirty-four, and her husband Robert left their cottage in Hopgarden Lane, Chasehurst to visit Canterbury at four thirty on Saturday afternoon.

'While they were out, the men broke in through the front door. They rummaged through the couple's possessions and stole computers and a mobile phone. When the couple returned less than an hour later, the men, whose faces were disguised with scarves, were still in the property. They ran outside and drove off.

"We obviously disturbed them when we pulled up," said thirty-six-year-old Mr Shaw, who is also a teacher. "My wife was shaken and upset."

A description of the two raiders followed, along with their car number and phone numbers for the police and Crimestoppers.

Miles collected a beermat. He slapped it on the bar in front of me and placed my beer on it.

'Hope you're insured,' he remarked.

'Yes, we're covered,' I said, handing him a five-pound note. 'Luckily, I've had this week off, so I've been able to make a few phone calls.'

'Your missus – is she all right now?' he asked as he handed me my change.

'Yes. She's tough,' I said. 'You get over these things. You've got to.'

'Are you going away this year?'

'Yes, Black Forest.'

'Oh Germany? '

'Yes. We're taking the motor-home over there in a couple of months' time.'

'That should be great. I assume you'll be cycling?'

'That's right,' I said, hoisting myself onto a bar stool. He grinned.

'Well, don't forget to bring me back a slice of that Black Forest gateau,' he said. 'My girlfriend and I were discussing holidays. You know she's a bit deaf, don't you? She fancies Spain, but I want to save money, so I suggested Eastern Europe.

'I said: "At least the idea should be mulled over." She said: "I don't want to go to Moldova." I said: "We need to book a rest." She said: "I'm not going to Bucharest either." So I said: "Maybe we'll just remain here," to which she replied: "You can totally rule out Romania!" I smiled.

'I don't know where you get them from, Miles,' I said as he went to serve another customer. A few minutes later, he returned.

'We've had a woman round from the forensic department at Kent Police,' I revealed. 'They found some prints which may or may not have been left by the two men. But I don't suppose anything will come of it.'

'No. We've been burgled a few times ourselves. They're mainly after cigarettes and spirits. The cops have stopped sending to most break-ins. There's thousands every year in Kent and last year there was a ten per cent increase. I'm afraid there's little chance of you getting your computers back.'

For the next two hours, Miles and I continued talking over the bar. During this time, he recommended a firm that installs CCTV cameras outside people's homes.

At ten o'clock, after drinking three pints, it was time to head home. I knew Anne's classes would have finished and she would now be home. I wandered back through the village and up the lane. I was surprised to find Anne waiting for me in the porch with the front door open.

'What's happened now?' I asked, as I took the final steps up the drive.

'Another Government scientist is in the news,' she revealed as she wandered into the living-room. 'It's a woman who worked with Gus. She's disappeared.'

15

I stood in the doorway for a moment beneath the waning crescent moon. Anne's words hung there in the mild summer air.

'It's on the BBC news now,' she yelled. 'If you come in quickly, you might catch some of it.' I rushed inside and joined her on the settee.

A television newsreader was explaining how a fifty-two-year-old scientist, Dr Allegra Maybourne, had vanished from her home near Andover, Hampshire on Monday of that week. Her husband Roderick at first thought she might have been called away at short notice in connection with her work.

Her mobile phone had been left at the house and he assumed, for that reason, she might have been unable to call him.

By Tuesday morning, however, he was becoming concerned as he had not heard from her and he alerted Hampshire Police. Officers had decided to release the news to the BBC that evening.

The newsreader added: 'This is the second time in three months that we have reported an event involving the Government's top-secret drone missile research department.

'Dr Maybourne's fellow-scientist, Professor Gus Morley, was killed in a road accident in February. Dr Maybourne is believed to have taken over responsibility for some of the work that was previously being carried out by the professor.

'Now with news about tonight's football we're going over to our studio in Manchester...' Anne pressed the stand-by button.

'Why didn't you tell me Gus was involved in top-secret weapons research?' she demanded. I felt a cold chill pass over me as the news gradually began to sink in.

'I didn't know,' I replied. 'I often tried to find out what it was exactly that he did. He always evaded the question.'

'We need to find out precisely what his work involved,' she said. 'There were bits and pieces in the newspapers and online in February.'

'Maybe we should've read them,' I said. 'But, to be honest, I was too upset at the time. I'd just lost one of my best mates. I didn't feel like reading about all his achievements when he'd just been killed in an accident.'

'Well, I think we need to do a bit of reading now,' she said. 'There's a good chance his fake death has got something to do with his work.'

'What d'you think the connection is?'

'Well, let's look at what we now know. He's a scientist with a top-secret job working for the government on Britain's defence. Maybe his knowledge is valuable to foreign powers.

'Then there's the lorry incident and the drive-by shooting – which could have been attempts on his life. Someone or some organisation is trying to kill him. So what does he do? He puts himself out of harm's way by faking his own death.'

'It's possible, I suppose.'

'He's then able to resume his valuable work under a new identity.'

'Drastic, but feasible.'

'But what if he's acting under duress? Maybe he's being forced to divulge what he knows to an enemy power. Maybe he's being blackmailed to act in this way.'

'Blackmailed?'

'Yes. Maybe his family are under threat and he was forced to play dead.'

'That's a heck of a lot of maybes.' Anne frowned. She was as animated as a child on Christmas morning.

'We're going to have to find out a lot more about Gus's work,' she said. 'I'm kicking myself we didn't do it before. We also need to find out more about the accident in February. Can we go over to Redhill? I want to talk to the hotel staff to see if he booked accommodation.'

'You could do that over the phone,' I suggested.

'No, the proper way to do this is to turn up in person.'

'All right, darling. We can go at eleven o'clock tomorrow, if you want.'

Early the next morning, Anne went out to buy a new laptop from a department store. I strolled into the village and brought four national newspapers back. Details about the missing scientist were splashed across them all.

One of the broadsheet newspapers revealed: 'Scientist behind new British missile research is missing.' A mid-market tabloid reported: 'Pioneering defence scientist vanishes,' while a down-market rival screamed for attention with the headline: 'Riddle of top drones boffin.'

The death of Gus Morley had been treated in a far less excitable fashion with short news reports and obituaries on inside pages. Now a second scientist had gone missing, the level of interest appeared far greater.

Although none of the headlines referred to my friend, his death was mentioned within the first few paragraphs of all the news stories, and far more information appeared about his road accident.

I spent nearly an hour reading all the reports. Gus studied physics and artificial intelligence at Oxford and Harvard universities and had then gone onto study weapons engineering at Cranfield University. He had also pursued a course on defence studies.

He was a renowned world expert on remote-controlled airborne technology who was mainly employed at the time of his death by BAMRA (the British Airborne Military Research Agency), which came under the Ministry of Defence. Like him, Dr Maybourne had studied at three universities and was an expert on drone technology.

One of the newspapers speculated that, just before his death, Gus and Dr Maybourne were believed to have stumbled on some vital new discovery which had attracted the interest of governments around the globe.

Their research was believed to be linked to the development of a new generation of remotely-piloted aircraft (Reapers). One of their projects was called Palladin. Gus had always kept his exact work secret from me. I didn't really approve of him designing weapons, but I knew they were needed to keep Britain safe and someone had to do the job.

Soon after I had finished all my reading, Graham Kirwan phoned from his CID office just outside Canterbury.

'I'm sorry, Bob, I haven't any news for you about the burglary,' he said. 'I'm afraid the trail's gone a little cold. The car was fished out of the River Medway near Cuxton and it had false number plates.

'When we checked them out, they related to a tractor driver in North Wales. He was less than happy when one of our colleagues from Denbigh called him in from the fields and accused him of nicking a computer in Kent. His tractor's never been outside Wales!

'Anyway the main reason for my call is to let you know about Warrant Officer Alexei or Alex Lotman. He doesn't exist – at least, not as far as I can ascertain.'

I said: 'You mean you can't trace him among the staff at the Ministry of Defence?'

'Correct,' said the sergeant. 'But don't take that as the final word. It's a big place, the MoD, and they're very secretive about their staff – with good reason. So I may give you another call in a few days and the information then may be different.'

After Anne returned and we learned how to operate the new laptop, I related Kirwan's news about the break-in and explained about the weapons research conducted by the two scientists.

'Have there been any strange events involving any of the other scientists engaged in the same work?' she asked, putting her shopping bags down on the floor.

'One of the newspapers has looked into that and no other incidents have been reported,' I said, remaining in my seat on the settee.

'What is Dr Maybourne's husband saying? Is he quoted in the papers?'

'Yes, he's saying that she usually calls him at least twice a day. He has phoned most of her friends and family and appealed on Facebook, as well as in the press.' Anne sat down at the table.

'Who was the last person to see her?' she wondered.

'I've been listening to the radio news. There's speculation she might have caught a train at Andover Railway Station, which is close to her house. But there've been no sightings at all.'

'I imagine British Rail Police can check CCTV at the station to see if she boarded a train,' said Anne. 'Bob, I've been thinking while I was at the shops. The same people who've given Gus a new identity could have abducted Dr Maybourne. And they could be the same people who organised the break-in to find out what we knew.'

'Yes, that's true,' I said.

'What I don't quite understand is the importance of these drone weapons,' she confessed.

'Well, nor do I. I've heard vaguely that it means someone in the relative comfort of a military control centre in London can bomb the hell out of a target in some far-away city by simply pressing a button. The unmanned drone remotely unleashes its lethal weapon of war and, within seconds, the military target can be destroyed while the controller sits back sipping his tea.'

'And which country's security services are most likely to want details of Britain's top-secret weapons research?'

'Well, the Russians for one,' I admitted.

'Exactly,' said Anne. 'While I was in the supermarket, I was thinking about that man Lotman that we met at the police station.

'He claimed they'd got the decorators in and we couldn't have use of a room, but I called in there just now. They haven't got the decorators in and there's no problem with the interview room.

'I realise now he'd asked us to meet him at the police station to lend himself an air of authenticity. Now you've told me

Graham can't find any trace of him at the MoD, it's all starting to make sense.'

'How d'you mean?'

'He and the burglars might be agents for the Kremlin.'

*

Just after eleven o'clock that day, we set off in the car for Redhill, which is nearly sixty miles away. One of Surrey's newest towns with a population of just over 18,000, it lies in the heart of the Surrey stockbroker belt.

I knew Gus had always insisted on staying at four or five-star hotels while on speaking engagements. So Anne had produced a list of the five hotels which had been awarded those ratings: the Royal Park Hotel; Springfield Hotel; Montague House; Surrey Manor Hotel; and the Stag's Head Inn.

We drove to each one in turn, asking managers, deputy managers, assistant managers and receptionists if Professor Morley had booked a room with them for the night of Friday February the first.

At four of them, we were informed they had already been asked about this by journalists or police and had been unable to find any booking for him.

Only at the Surrey Manor Hotel were the staff unhelpful. Two girls on reception said only the duty manager could provide information about guest bookings. He was away at a meeting and we would have to return another time.

In order to be thorough, Anne wrote down her name and mobile phone number on a scrap of paper and asked if they would pass it to the duty manager on his return.

An hour later, we were eating a light pasta lunch in one of

the town's cafes when her phone rang.

'Mrs Shaw?' said the male voice. 'This is Anwar Patel from the Surrey Manor Hotel. I gather you've been asking about Professor Morley?' Anne jumped up from the table and hurried out into the quiet street. I joined her outside so that I could overhear.

'Yes, that's right. How good of you to call,' she replied.

'I'm so sorry I was unavailable when you visited the hotel earlier. Professor Morley's stayed with us many times and I was extremely sorry to hear about his death.

'He always stayed with us when he'd got an early flight from Gatwick. We're only eight miles from the airport, you see. He used to check with us well in advance whenever he wanted to stay here because he particularly liked our Windsor room. Sometimes he brought Mrs Morley with him.

'However, I've checked with all our staff and he definitely hadn't arranged to stay with us on the day of his tragic death.' After she ended the call, Anne gazed at me.

'So Gus hadn't made any firm plans for accommodation that night,' she asserted. 'Strange, isn't it?'

'And he sometimes turned up at the hotel with "Mrs Morley." Was that Claudia?' I wondered.

'What d'you think?' she said. I shrugged my shoulders. It seemed as unlikely as Maidstone United winning the Premiership.

'Probably not,' I admitted.

We arrived back at the cottage in time to watch the television news at six o'clock. We thought Dr Maybourne might have been found during the day, but the programme revealed she was still missing.

Her husband Roderick, a fifty-six-year-old marketing manager, was shown on the doorstep of the family's five-bedroom detached house.

'Allegra, please come home,' he pleaded amid tears. ' I'm missing you. The boys are missing you. At least call the police and let us know you're all right. We miss you so much.'

Grey-haired Mr Maybourne, who was wearing a green check shirt and fawn trousers, wiped his eyes with a white handkerchief as he spoke to the camera.

He added: 'Her disappearance is very out of character. She normally calls me regularly. We've rarely been apart in our twenty-nine years of marriage.'

Detective Inspector Tim Perkins from Hampshire Police, who was in charge of the investigation, then appealed to the public for help.

'Obviously the whole family are devastated that Dr Maybourne has not been in contact,' he said. 'As time passes, police are becoming increasingly concerned for her welfare. If anyone has any information regarding her disappearance, they should contact the incident room here in Andover or police headquarters in Winchester.'

The BBC's South of England reporter then appeared on the screen, revealing that Mr Maybourne last saw his wife, who was born and brought up in Salisbury, on Monday morning at eight o'clock when he left their Andover home to go to work.

She told him she expected to be at home all day. But when he returned, only their two boxer dogs, Roxie and Callie, were in the house. The scientist was described by the reporter as being five feet five inches tall, of medium build and with light-brown shoulder-length hair.

She had hazel eyes and wore black-framed glasses. She is understood to have left the house without her handbag, front door keys, money, credit cards or phone.

Speaking to camera, the reporter went on: 'British Transport Police have told us they have begun examining footage from CCTV cameras at the town's railway station.

'But so far there is no evidence she left the area by train. Hampshire Police say they are not at the moment linking her disappearance with the death of her work colleague Professor Gus Morley who was killed in a road accident three months ago.

'She and the professor worked closely together in connection with airborne weaponry research. With that it's back to the studio.'

I brought my hands up to my face as the main newsreader embarked on a fresh report.

'What's the matter?' asked Anne, turning the volume down on the television.

'I've just had a thought,' I said. 'You don't suppose the pair of them have gone off together, do you? You know, left their partners to set up a love-nest of their own?'

'No,' said Anne. She waved her hands together, dismissing the idea without even considering it as a serious option.

'For all we know,' I said, 'Gus and Allegra could have planned this for weeks. They could be together right now, sipping tequilas beneath swaying palms on some remote beach or walking barefoot together across sun-kissed sands.'

16

The stunning Archbishop's Palace built from grey stone in the fourteenth and sixteenth centuries on the east bank of the River Medway in Maidstone, Kent, is a popular location for weddings. Dozens of them are held there every year with some brides arriving for their big day by boat. The sombre, doleful tone which the historic building sets also makes it a strangely fitting venue for a coroner's court.

Anne and I set out on our twenty-six-mile journey in good time for Gus Morley's inquest on Thursday June the sixth. But it took us some time to find a parking space in Maidstone town centre.

It was nearly ten fifteen by the time we approached the palace. We at once noticed vans emblazoned with the names of television companies – BBC, ITV and Sky – parked near the entrance.

As we passed the immaculately-manicured lawns and flower beds blooming with roses and peonies, we saw dozens of press reporters, photographers and television crews wandering about. Many were on their mobile phones.

We also noticed Tristan, Claudia, Jago, Jemima and Gus's older daughter Lavinia standing at the front of the building beneath stone mullioned windows. Jago was puffing on a cigarette.

'Why are we waiting here?' I asked them. 'It's due to start in a minute.'

'We're waiting for Jago to finish his cigarette,' Tristan replied in a low voice. I kissed Claudia, Jemima and Lavinia on the cheek and shook the hands of Jago and Tristan. Then Anne greeted them all.

'I think we should go on ahead,' whispered Anne, opening the heavy wooden main door and leading me through it. We climbed the oak stairs to the first floor and then followed signs along the corridor.

The courtroom, which was in the oldest part of the palace, boasted a high, oak-beamed ceiling, an open stone fireplace and a bay window overlooking the river. More than forty uphol-stered chairs had been set out in the room amid walls decorated with wood panelling and white plaster.

Anne and I found seats in the back row. As I looked round, I noticed Alex Lotman, whom we had encountered twelve days earlier, sitting a few rows in front.

Prunella Ball, dressed in pink and white, was sitting with a group of press reporters on the far side of the room. She waved. I presumed most of the other people were close friends and work colleagues of Gus.

The coroner, a dour sixty-eight-year-old Scotsman named Alastair Bonnyman, sat at the front behind a mahogany Victorian desk. He kept glancing over his shoulder at an antique clock on the wall behind him.

Dr Bonnyman, who was wearing a dark-blue suit, white shirt and blue tie, clearly believed in starting on time. Whether or not Jago had finished his cigarette, he banged his hand down twice on the desk at half-past ten and announced: 'Good morning, everybody.'

As he spoke, Claudia and the four others arrived and found chairs.

'This is an inquest into the death of Augustus Erskine Morley of The Old Rectory, Hanley St Peter, Gloucestershire. He was pronounced dead at seven pm on Friday February the first at Tunbridge Wells Hospital in Pembury, Kent, which explains why the inquest is taking place here.

'The coroner holds an inquest whenever a death is sudden, violent or unnatural; if the death takes place in custody; or where the cause of death is unknown. Mr Richardson, are the main witnesses here?'

A solemn-faced man in a white shirt with a grey tie and black trousers, who was clearly the coroner's officer, leapt up from a small table a few feet from Dr Bonnyman. He handed him a piece of paper and said: 'They're all here, sir.'

'Good!' said Dr Bonnyman with a grimace that nearly suggested a smile. 'I have to remind you all this is a public hearing and members of the press are present. Now, would the officer from Kent Police like to come forward?'

A young, fresh-faced police constable in uniform, whom we had not noticed until then, marched across the burgundy carpet to the front.

He swore the oath and announced he was PC Nigel Hartley, a constable with Kent Police, based in Westerham. Then he sat down by the table. The coroner asked him to describe how he became involved.

'I was on duty on the evening of Friday February the first, sir, and we received a 999 call at about ten minutes to six,' he said. 'May I refer to my notes, sir?'

'Yes, of course,' said Dr Bonnyman. 'These were contemporaneous notes made up at the time of the accident?'

'Yes, sir.'

'Very well.'

'Thank you, sir. I was informed of a car on fire with a person reported two miles from me at Turner's Hatch. I travelled west along the A25 and then took a left turning into Knights Lane – the first part of which is a hill.

'As soon as I reached the top at just before six pm, I saw two fire engines and a burnt-out car in a wooded area on the left. The car appeared to have crashed into a large oak tree and the front of the vehicle had become partly embedded in the trunk.

'Later examination of the vehicle confirmed it was a Mercedes, but it had received catastrophic damage and it was a smouldering wreck.'

'Were any members of the public around when you got there, constable?' Dr Bonnyman asked.

'There were two people near the vehicle – a gentleman from a nearby house and a local farmworker I know who's called Tyler Buckley. They told me there was thick smoke when they arrived.

'The fire was mostly out but the car was too hot to touch. I then spoke to the senior fire officer who informed me they had been called too late to prevent the fire taking hold. I obtained statements from the two locals.'

'Were there any witnesses to the crash itself?'

'No, sir. Despite media appeals, no one has come forward as witness to the crash.'

'Did you look inside the car yourself?' the coroner asked.

'Yes, sir. There was a blackened body in the back of the vehicle. It was terrible to see. You couldn't tell if it was a man or a woman. The clock on the dashboard was one of the few things that survived the fire. It had stopped at a quarter past five.'

Dr Bonnyman said: 'PC Hartley, what was your impression of the way the incident occurred?'

'I had the impression the driver may have been speeding as he came up the hill, although there's no evidence from CCTV cameras to back this up. It's so rural that there aren't any cameras around there.

'There's a slight right-hand bend at the top of the hill. I suspect the driver may have misjudged the bend and struck the tree. I examined the ground for skid marks but there weren't any.'

'I understand an ambulance crew then turned up and the body was conveyed to Tunbridge Wells Hospital?' said Dr Bonnyman.

'That's right, sir,' the officer replied.

'I gather a fire investigator discovered it was the professor's car from the number plate and the chassis number which survived the flames.'

'Yes sir. It was a Mercedes-Benz C Class four-door saloon manufactured in 2015.'

'You made inquiries and it was confirmed the car belonged to Professor Morley?'

'That's right, sir.'

'You later made inquiries with the garage that the professor used and found it was a petrol car that had recently been serviced and should have had no mechanical defects?'

'That's correct, sir.'

'And the lane remained closed for the following twenty-four hours to allow police and fire investigators to examine the scene?'

'Yes, sir.'

'Constable, is there a road sign on the hill warning of the approaching bend?'

'To my knowledge, no, sir.'

'Very well. Thank you. Would Mr Buckley like to come forward?'

Tyler Buckley was a tall, slim man with a sallow complexion. He was wearing a grey suit that appeared to be rather tight. After being sworn in by the coroner's officer, Dr Bonnyman indicated he should sit down by the table.

'You're Tyler Buckley of Magpie Cottages, Turner's Hatch?' the coroner asked.

'Yes, sir. But there's not much I can tell you.'

'I'll be the judge of that, thank you,' Dr Bonnyman replied. 'Mr Buckley, what time was it when you noticed the Mercedes car in the woods at Turner's Hatch?'

'It must've been just before half-past five. See, I'd done a bit of overtime at Yeoman's Farm, where I work. My boss let me go at quarter past five and, when I'm on me bike, it takes less than five minutes to get to Knights Lane.

'It looked as if the fire had been going some time when I got there. I was asked if I'd heard an explosion, but I never. As I came closer I left the bike and broke into a run. I thought there might be some poor bloke inside.

'The handle of the back door was blistering hot, so I grabbed a stick and tried to open it with that. Then a man came up the lane and asked if there were someone in the car.'

'That's the neighbour, Mr Prendergast?'

'I believe that's his name, sir. We could see a person inside but they wasn't moving. I dialled 999—it must've been half-past five - and the fire brigade come pretty quick. They took less than fifteen minutes.'

'Mr Buckley, PC Hartley says police were notified at ten minutes to six. How do you account for that delay?'

'Don't ask me. All I can tell you is that I called 999 just before half-past five. The neighbour backs up me story.'

'All right. Thank you, Mr Buckley.' The coroner read out a written statement from a fire investigator who testified the fire was so fierce flames even spread to the oak's trunk.

Fire fighters put out the fire in the tree and dampened down the car, which had been burnt out before their arrival.

The statement added: 'The evidence suggests that, after the initial collision, the fuel lines of the car must have ruptured and the leaking petrol caught fire. Flames were so fierce there was no way of telling whether the car's airbag operated or whether the deceased was wearing a seatbelt.'

The coroner then read out statements from an ambulance-woman, a hospital doctor and two members of the fire crew who attended the scene before he called senior pathologist Dr Maxwell Griffiths.

An elderly grey-haired man in a dark-blue suit with a bright blue bowtie stood up in the front row and took the seat Tyler Buckley vacated.

'Maxwell Alwyn Griffiths, consultant forensic pathologist for the Home Office,' the witness declared. He seemed as confident as a banker in a Texan oilfield.

'Dr Griffiths, do you have your report on the post-mortem

examination of Professor Morley?'

'Yes, the report's here,' Dr Griffiths replied, removing some black-framed glasses from his jacket pocket and putting them on. 'It was carried out at the mortuary in Pembury on Wednesday February the sixth.

'The deceased was Professor Augustus Erskine Morley, date of birth: twelfth of August 1971. The examination took place at two thirty pm at the request of Kent Police. I was informed life was pronounced extinct at six thirty pm on Friday February the first at Knights Lane, Turner's Hatch.

'The deceased, who worked as a Government scientist, was a Caucasian male. We know from official documents the professor's height was six feet two inches tall. At the time of the autopsy the body measured six feet three inches in length. I blame this on either post-mortem expansion or the unreliability of self-reported stature.

'The body had suffered a severe head injury as well as severe burns which had led to fragmentation of much of the body and the charring of bones. The body was virtually carbonised.

'The only parts of the body to escape the worst effects of the fire were the right and left tibia. Inside the car, we found car keys and part of his glasses - all of which had been extensively damaged.

'Family members recognised the glasses as belonging to the professor. Death was shown to have occurred shortly after the fire began from soot in the lungs and carboxyhaemoglobin in the blood.'

The coroner, who had been frenziedly writing notes, interrupted.

'For clarity, you're giving the cause of death as severe head injury as a result of a road accident?'

'That's correct. The effects of the fire upon the body occurred post-mortem.'

'And the death would have occurred almost instantaneously upon impact with the oak tree?'

'That's correct. The soot indicates the deceased would have continued breathing for a short while prior to death.'

'Thank you, doctor. Dr Griffiths, it's my understanding you had to order the professor's dental records in order to establish his identity beyond doubt. Is that correct?'

'Yes. As you know from other cases we've been involved with, the longer a fire burns, the less chance you have that there will be enough DNA left to test and DNA typing is often unsuccessful with charred bones. That's why we often fall back on the dental records.

'Once we had the records from the professor's dental practice, examination of the teeth and dental implants recovered from the fire indicated it was the professor. Of particular relevance was the badly-chipped front incisor. Family members have identified this as a tooth he damaged in an incident at home. We also recovered a gold crown which relatives have confirmed belonged to the professor.' Dr Bonnyman raised his head again.

'I gather you were subsequently able to obtain a DNA sample from Professor Morley's son, James Morley, and that this proved a positive match to DNA obtained from the body.' The pathologist nodded. Anne and I looked at each other in surprise.

'That's a bit of a bombshell,' I murmured. The coroner was now asking about toxicology tests carried out on the body.

'Did these tests show anything significant?' he asked

Dr Griffiths.

'We were unable to recover any blood or fluid to determine the level of alcohol in the body. However, in the lab, we examined the left toenails and found ethyl glucuronide – a by-product of alcohol which lingers in the body long after a person's last drink.

'The high concentration suggests a heavy alcohol user, although it cannot help us determine the level of alcohol in the system ante-mortem.'

'Thank you,' Dr Bonnyman told him. 'I'd like Mrs Morley to come forward.'

Claudia emerged from her seat near the back. She looked glamorous despite having an aura of sadness about her. Solemnly dressed in a medium-length mauve dress with a white cardigan, her neatly coiffed dark hair had been set in curls. She made herself comfortable in the witness chair after the coroner's officer had her swear the oath.

'Could I have your full name?' Dr Bonnyman asked.

'Yes. It's Claudia Imogen Morley.'

'And you live at The Old Rectory, Hanley St Peter.'

'That's right.'

'How long were you married to Professor Morley?'

'We were married in 2002.'

'Was it a happy marriage?' Her voice turned into a whisper.

'Yes. Very happy,' she said. She removed two paper tissues from her cream-coloured handbag. Lowering her voice, she added: 'He was the love of my life.'

'When did you last see your husband?'

'I hadn't seen him since Sunday, January the twenty-seventh when he left to go to London.'

'This was a regular occurrence, was it? He was home at the weekends and, to all intents and purposes, worked in London during the week?'

'Yes,' she said, wiping her eyes. Suddenly, a woman in a short-sleeved blue dress shouted out: 'Why don't you tell them about his girlfriend?'

Everyone's eyes turned to see who was interrupting. Now the heckler was standing and waving her arms about.

'Why don't you tell them about his nights away with her?' the woman shouted.

The coroner's officer acted quickly. He moved along the third row from the back on the far side of the room. He gently but firmly took her by the arm and tried to coax her away. The woman resisted him.

'I won't have any disturbance!' Dr Bonnyman declared. 'If you can't be quiet, you'll have to leave.' From what I could see, the woman told the officer she would accede with the coroner's request. He let her remain in her seat while he returned to his table beside the coroner.

Turning to Claudia, Mr Bonnyman said: 'I'm so sorry, Mrs Morley. You were explaining to me that your husband worked away during the week.'

'Yes,' Claudia said. 'It was an arrangement that worked well for us.'

'Mrs Morley, you're looking rather pale. Are you sure you're all right?' She shook her head.

'This is asking a lot of me,' she whispered.

'I know,' said Dr Bonnyman, tenderly. 'Shall we take a short break? I think we could all do with one. I'm adjourning this hearing for twenty minutes.'

As relatives and friends of Gus, witnesses and spectators filed out to gain some fresh air outside, we noticed Prunella on the other side of the room. She was trying to speak to the female heckler, but not having any luck.

I discovered later the protester was distantly related to Dr Maybourne and, without any firm evidence, had developed a theory that Gus and the missing scientist had embarked upon a close relationship. After failing to break the woman's vow of silence on the matter, Prunella headed over to our seats.

'Bob! Anne! How's it going?' she asked with a smile that could have lit up a darkened street.

'Bob's bored,' Anne complained.

'Yes, it's slow going,' the journalist agreed, taking a seat beside us. 'I'm really only here in case something sensational comes out of it. We've already got our story for Sunday. I'd love to tell you what it is, but I'm sworn to secrecy. Anyway, I'd better go. I want to have a word with my photographer.'

She hurried away to join the crowd of people who were milling around in the courtyard outside. I turned round. We were alone in the room, apart from the coroner's officer, who was tidying the coroner's desk.

'D'you want to go outside as well?' I said. 'It's a beautiful day out there.'

'Not for the moment. Can't you see how annoyed I am?' said Anne. 'This is all playing out like a set piece. We can already guess the verdict. Everyone is telling the same story - that Gus died in Turner's Hatch and it was a road accident. Bish, bosh! End of story. But we know differently.' I nodded.

'The verdict will be accidental death,' she said. 'The trouble is that it isn't.'

'How d'you mean?'

'We know it can't have been an accident. The body must have been planted in the car somehow.'

'I can't see how.'

'Nor can I for the moment. But give me time. This is a charade. There's been no mention of the attempts on Gus's life.

'Look, Bob, someone wants the world to believe Gus is dead when we know he's very much alive. But who is it? Is it Gus himself? Is it Gus and Claudia? I don't think so. This all smacks of detailed planning.

'So who's behind it? Is it some organisation? Gus has been set up with a new life, new identity and a new home like a police supergrass who's turned evidence against rival gangsters. But why?

'And what about the car accident? There was obviously a body in the burnt-out car? But whose body? In the same way there is a family pining for Gus, it stands to reason there is almost certainly a family pining for the man whose body was in the car.

'We are probably the only ones to know the truth – that Gus is still alive. So we've got to do something.'

Just then there was a creaking sound. The door behind us clicked shut. I heard footsteps scurrying away from us along the corridor outside. The coroner's officer was still tidying the desk.

'What the hell?' I exclaimed, jumping up. 'I think someone was listening to us.'

I sprinted through the doorway and along the corridor. Then I rushed downstairs and burst out of the main door, looking around me all the time for the eavesdropper.

But it was impossible to tell who had descended the stairs

just before me. Dozens of visitors were simultaneously leaving the building after an event on the ground floor.

Whoever had been paying heed to our conversation had vanished into the crowd like a magician disappearing in a puff of smoke.

17

'Are you feeling better now, Mrs Morley?' Dr Bonnyman asked as the inquest resumed at twenty minutes past eleven.

'Yes, sir,' Claudia replied. 'I'm fine now. I've had a cup of tea.'

'Always good to calm the nerves,' he said. 'So you're more composed now?' She nodded.

'Good. Now I should say, before we go any further, that I have been speaking to the lady who interrupted earlier on with a suggestion about Professor Morley's private life.

'This accusation by her has been withdrawn and I have allowed the lady in question to remain in the room, provided there are no further interruptions. As far as you were aware, the professor was a faithful husband. Is that right?' Claudia nodded.

'Yes, definitely, Dr Bonnyman,' she said.

'And, although he often worked alongside Dr Allegra Maybourne, their relationship was just platonic.'

'That's correct.'

'I'm afraid I have to ask you some more questions about the professor, if I may? I'm sorry, Mrs Morley, to have to ask this. But would you say he was a heavy drinker?'

'I'd say he was an average drinker. Just drank socially. He liked the occasional drop of whisky.'

'He was in no sense an alcoholic?'

'Definitely not.' She looked embarrassed. The coroner frowned. He stopped himself from saying something.

Then he continued: 'Now you were telling us before the break you last saw him on January the twenty-seventh. Did you speak to him or text him after he left Gloucestershire?'

'No. There was no contact. The last words I ever spoke to him, strangely enough, were: "Take care. Drive safely."' Dr Bonnyman nodded.

'He was due to attend a conference on the weekend of February the second. So when were you expecting to see him again?'

'Not until the Friday the eighth.'

'I understand you were informed of the accident on February the fifth.'

'That's right,' Claudia agreed. 'It was a terrible shock.'

'Had he told you he was travelling to the conference by car?'

'He hadn't mentioned it, but he took the car everywhere. He hated train delays in the winter.'

'We've heard the car was a Mercedes-Benz C Class built in 2015.'

'That's right.'

'Would you say your husband was a careful driver?'

'I'd say he was an average driver,' she asserted. 'He drove a little fast for my liking. Actually, I tended to travel in the back.' Ripples of half-suppressed laughter swept round the room.

'We've heard from PC Hartley your husband may've been speeding and may've misjudged the bend in Knights Lane.'

'If he was unacquainted with a road, I'd have expected him to curb his speed.'

'Well, we mustn't speculate. Mrs Morley, I don't think I've got any further questions for you. Thank you very much for taking the time to come. I appreciate it's been an ordeal for you and your family.'

Claudia returned to her seat in the back row at the far side of the room.

Dr Bonnyman then summarised all the evidence he had heard that morning. As he did so, I cast my eyes around. I noticed Alex Lotman had not returned after the break. Neither had a tall, slim man in his fifties in a fawn jacket who had been sitting behind me and reeked of an expensive American aftershave.

'There is no evidence of suicidal intent,' Dr Bonnyman said, gazing at his notes. 'So, finally, I'm drawn to the conclusion that Professor Morley was driving along an unfamiliar road.

'He misjudged the bend – possibly because he was driving too fast, although we can't be certain about that. His car left the road and collided with the tree. All the evidence is consistent with him receiving severe head injuries in the crash and then his body becoming engulfed in flames post-mortem.

'I shall be writing to the Department for Transport with a recommendation that a warning sign is erected on the hill to warn motorists of the approaching bend.

'Following my conclusions, I am recording a verdict of accidental death.' Anne gave me a knowing look and shrugged. The coroner was still speaking.

'I want to express this court's gratitude to both Mr Buckley and Mr Prendergast for the public-spirited way they acted when finding the car. They faced a traumatic situation and bravely endeavoured to rescue Professor Morley.

'I would also like to pass on my deepest sympathies to Mrs

Morley and her family. This lady's carried herself with grace and dignity at a time of great sadness. It may provide her a modicum of comfort to know the professor would have died instantly and wouldn't have suffered.

'My condolences to you and all the people who have been affected by this terrible tragedy. Thank you all very much for attending.'

As he uttered his final words, a group of press photographers who had been huddled in the corridor outside headed out to the main exit in a rush. They were eager to photograph departing witnesses on the forecourt.

But Prunella, Gary Toomes from the Sunday Review, Abdul Hussein from the Gloucestershire Echo and Richard Gardiner from the Kent Messenger were attempting to speak to Claudia. She brushed them off, saying she was too upset to talk.

'We'll be making a statement outside in a minute,' Jago announced, loudly.

Anne was annoyed at the inquest's outcome. She glowered like a surly child.

'It's all been rushed through as if Dr Bonnyman and Dr Griffiths have better things to do,' she told me in a hushed voice. 'They've jumped to all sorts of conclusions without careful examination of the evidence.'

'How d'you mean?' I said.

'They don't know for certain Gus Morley was even in the car. All they know is that he'd left London for Redhill in his Mercedes and a vehicle they've assumed to be his Mercedes from the number plate and chassis number crashed on the way. The evidence used to identify the body is very weak.'

'I agree that it's all a bit circumstantial,' I said. 'Of course, we know Gus is still alive, so that puts us at a slight advantage when it comes to weighing the evidence. I can see how, with the facts available to him, the coroner reached his verdict.'

Anne and I were the last to leave the room. By the time we emerged in the sunshine through the main door, an impromptu press conference was under way.

Jemima, in a short-sleeved floral patterned dress, was reading a prepared statement while Claudia clung to her arm. The reporters were encircling the pair, while trying to keep out of their colleagues' camera shots.

'You'll appreciate this has been a desperately sad time for our whole family,' Jemima was saying. 'We're still grieving. Gus was a kind, intelligent, generous, loving father, husband, brother and friend who was taken from us far too early.

'We're all struggling to understand how he came to die in such a cruel, horrific way. We're relieved the inquest is over and we're confident Dr Bonnyman came to the right verdict.

'We now hope members of the press, TV and radio will respect our privacy so that we can get on with our lives after our terrible loss. We would like to thank everyone who has supported us during this time of grief.'

A BBC reporter in a smart navy-blue suit asked: 'Claudia, have you any message for the family of Dr Allegra Maybourne? She was your husband's work colleague, wasn't she? She's still missing.' Jemima looked annoyed at the question.

'The family have no comment, except to say we hope Dr Maybourne is found quickly,' said Jago. Jemima was whispering to Claudia, who was still holding her sister-in-law's arm. Prunella Ball quickly asked: 'Did you know Allegra, Claudia?'

''We've got no further comment,' said an exasperated Jago.

'Now we're all leaving. Thank you for your time.'

With that, he led Jemima and Claudia away from the palace entrance. Lavinia, Tristan, Anne and I followed close behind. Every now and then, a photographer would race in front of us in an attempt to photograph Claudia. When we reached the main road, Jago asked us if we knew of anywhere suitable for lunch.

'Preferably somewhere a long way away from the press,' he added. 'Fancy asking Claudia about that woman from Andover. She only knew her vaguely.'

'There's the Maid of Kent in the High Street,' Anne suggested. After a brief discussion, our friends agreed we should at least inspect the menu at the seventeenth century coaching inn.

Anne and I led the way across the road and into the high street. Lavinia, Jago and Tristan followed. Claudia, and Jemima lagged a few paces behind. We assumed Prunella had gone to phone her news editor, but then we heard her high-pitched voice and saw a pink shape running up the street behind us.

'Anne! Bob!' she called. 'Would anyone mind if I joined you for lunch?' She clearly hoped to endear herself to our friends – particularly Claudia – for journalistic purposes. I could only admire the woman's pluck.

Anne was embarrassed, but shyly introduced Prunella to the group and vouched for her as a close and trustworthy friend. Claudia and Jago were wary of the newcomer, but their concerns were overtaken by their growing hunger and urgent need to find a place to eat.

Prunella began chatting to Lavinia and Jemima, and gradually the initial feelings of resentment faded.

As we continued walking uphill to the hotel, I noticed Jago, who was casually dressed in a checked shirt and dark trousers, was eyeing me as if we were strangers. He remarked: 'I hear you've recovered from your spell of madness.'

'I'm sorry?' I replied.

'You know, you're no longer going round telling people Gus is still alive,' he said rather loudly, nearly bumping into a passing shopper.

'That's right. I must've been more upset about Gus's passing than I'd realised.'

'You've no idea the fuss you caused,' he moaned. 'Why didn't you come to me first before upsetting the ladyfolk?' I shrugged.

'I suppose I didn't think,' I said.

'No, you bloody didn't,' he muttered, shaking his head and causing his wire-framed glasses to slip down his nose. 'Anyway I thought the verdict was about right, didn't you? I mean, the old boy could have recorded an open verdict, but everything pointed to a road accident.'

'Sorry, we don't buy it, Jago,' said Anne as we reached the double doors of the white four-star hotel. 'We feel it's all been a bit rushed.'

'I don't see it like that at all,' he retorted. 'I'd say it was an open and shut case of poor old Gus missing the bend and ploughing into the tree. Can't see the old boy could have come up with any other conclusion. I say, this is a nice place. Well done, Anne!'

The hotel was renowned for its oak beams, low ceilings and open fireplaces. There was a long varnished wood counter in the main bar. An archway led visitors through to the light, airy restaurant which nestled beneath a huge glass roof.

Within minutes, we had chosen a table for eight next to a

small blue aquarium containing tropical fish and ordered our meals. Jago went to the bar with Tristan and they returned with wooden trays laden with drinks. As we waited for the food, I turned to Prunella.

'Did anyone find out why that woman interrupted Claudia?' I asked.

'I grabbed a quick word with her. She's Ophelia Watkins, Allegra Maybourne's older sister. She'd travelled here because she suspected her sister of becoming close to Gus Morley and knew the press would be around, but she's got no evidence of an affair . I just thought she was a sad old woman.'

Tristan, who was wearing an eye-catching cream summer suit and grey tie, interrupted. He began reminiscing with me about our university days.

'D'you remember old Peter Beaumont who was in the first fifteen for rugby?' he asked. 'I saw him in London the other day. He was just propping up the bar in a pub in Chelsea.'

'That's the guy who bought a pig and kept it in his student house,' recalled Jago. 'After a couple of weeks, he nominated the poor creature for president of the union.'

'He never made it onto the ballot paper,' said Tristan, taking up the story. 'The returning officer barred him for failing to deliver a proper speech and urinating at the hustings!'

'They were good days,' Jago said. 'These days the animal rights society would probably have snatched him away to a sanctuary.'

'I expect the pig was a bit disgruntled at the ban,' I suggested. Everybody groaned.

'He'd have never lasted as president,' Tristan remarked. 'First sniff of trouble and he'd have squealed!'

'Come on. That's enough pig jokes,' said Anne. Jago must have been struck by a wave of nostalgia.

'Tristan,' said Jago. 'What do you think was the single most important thing you learned at university?' Tristan thought for a moment. Prunella appeared to be watching him with interest.

'The true impact of Pearl Harbour,' he said. 'Although the Japanese never expected to wipe out virtually the entire US fleet, their action completely changed the course of history. How about you, Bob?'

'D'you want me to be honest?' I said. 'The single most important thing I learned was, when you shop in a supermarket, always pick from the back of the shelf.' Jago laughed.

'Remind me. You studied first year history with Professor Hawkins?'

'That's right,' I said. 'But, of course, he didn't teach me that. I learnt it from one of the cleaning ladies. But it's proved sage advice that I've followed throughout my life.' Tristan smiled and then looked over at Jago.

'How about you, Jago? You asked the question. You must have something in mind yourself.' Jago smiled back. He nodded.

'Yes,' he said. 'Always take your shoes off when coming into your digs late at night after eight pints of lager - so you don't wake the landlady!' Jago, Tristan and I laughed, but Anne was unimpressed.

She glanced round the table. Prunella, Lavinia and Jemima were having a deep discussion about women's fashion. Claudia was sitting at the end of the table on her own, entirely unengaged with any of the conversations.

Anne slipped out of her chair. She moved round to where the dark-haired widow was sitting. She slid her hand over Claudia's shoulder in a comforting way. Claudia looked up at her, smiled and clasped Anne's hand.

She spoke to Anne for a few minutes until the meals arrived. Jago and Tristan were still talking about their university days. I gazed around the table, noticing that, every so often, Prunella would glance towards Tristan.

Later that day, as we were driving home, Anne revealed that Claudia had been extremely irritated by the coroner's constant questioning and was relieved when the inquest ended.

'The pathologist approached her in the corridor during the break,' Anne revealed. 'He asked Claudia whether her husband had a tattoo on his lower left calf. She said he didn't.

'But Dr Griffiths was convinced Gus had a tattoo and concluded he might have had it done recently. She told him: "For God's sake, surely I'd know if my husband had a tattoo!"'

18

Over the next few days, I found Anne and I were gradually developing divergent views about the Gus Morley affair. Of course, we had both been upset by attending the inquest. But I was now tending to take the view that, whatever stunt my friend was playing, I should no longer be too concerned about it.

He had clearly faked his death, but he must have had a good reason for doing so. Perhaps he had been extremely unhappy in his previous way of life. Eventually, his ruse would be exposed and he would have to face the consequences.

The lives of his wife and children would be torn apart on discovering he was still alive and had played a trick on them. I had tried to sound the warning bell, yet no one came running.

But Anne was now fired up. There was an air of the evangelist about her. Spurred on by what she had heard at the Archbishop's Palace, she was acting as though she was duty-bound to unearth the truth.

Perhaps her role – along with Lavinia and Jemima – as a god parent to James and Sophie influenced her thinking. But she spent the next day putting thousands of words of her notes on the new laptop. She called Kent CID, asking for Graham Kirwan to call her. She also spent hours doing research online.

On the Friday evening, when I returned from invigilating at the school exams, I came into the living-room and found her relaxing in front of the television. She got up to kiss me and turned the volume down.

'Bob, I'm expecting to hear from Graham Kirwan at any minute,' she said. 'I'm trying to get hold of a photograph of the dead man's leg.'

'Whatever for?' I asked.

'Well, it's this business of the tattoo. Dr Griffiths was convinced there was some kind of design on the lower left leg. Claudia denies Gus had one. Graham said he might be able to get hold of an image for me.'

'Where d'you think this will lead you?'

'On the trail of whose body was used for the post-mortem. Apparently, bodies can increase in length by half an inch or two thirds of an inch within the first twenty-four hours of death, but not by a whole inch.'

'Wasn't the pathologist trying to say information about people's height is unreliable?'

'That's true, but this difference of an inch suggests the corpse that they've assumed was Gus was an inch too long.'

'What about Gus's keys, glasses and signet ring? They were all there in the car?' I pointed out.

'They could have been planted,' Anne replied confidently.

'It was Gus's car. They know from the chassis number.'

'Could be a cheaper, older Mercedes and someone's forged the number. I can't imagine you'd use Gus's prized twenty-thousand pound car in a faked death crash. We could probably find the genuine one parked in some garage in London'

'Don't expect me to help you check all the private garages

in the capital,' I muttered. She shrugged.

'So I'm already finding flaws. The corpse belonged to a man who was an inch too tall and was probably a heavy drinker.'

'Gus liked a drink. He even opened the door to us with a whisky glass.'

'Yes, but these ethyl glucuronide tests on the nails were pretty damning. "A heavy alcohol user" was Griffiths' phrase, while Claudia told us what we knew - that Gus just drank socially.'

'Well, there's one part of the evidence you really can't argue with – the two teeth Griffiths came up with and the DNA they are said to have obtained from the body in the car which matched James's DNA.'

'Planted!' said Anne, defiantly.

'They've gone to a lot of trouble.'

'Of course, they've gone to a lot of trouble – whoever "they" are. They've got money. They've got resources. And somehow they've had access to a spare body. I don't understand why…'

She stopped short as her mobile started ringing. But when she answered it, it wasn't Graham Kirwan. It was Prunella.

I couldn't hear much of the conversation, but I gathered Anne's friend was in a jubilant mood. I sat back and read the newspapers. By the time Anne ended the call I had read most of them.

'Someone's full of the joys of life,' I remarked.

'Yes,' said Anne. 'After we left the Maid of Kent yesterday, Prunella got chatting to Tristan, and they found they had a lot in common.'

'I noticed she was taking an interest in him,' I said.

'They're about the same age, they're both from the North of England originally and they're both single after breaking up with their partners. They both go to the gym twice a week.'

'Well, good for them,' I muttered.

'Pru's ecstatic. She's been on her own for a few months and it's been getting her down.'

'She needs someone to fix her exhaust,' I said. 'But she won't get much help from Tristan. He's a dummy with mechanics.'

'Trust you to say that!' said Anne. 'I'm very pleased for her. She deserves a bit of happiness. She works so hard. Tristan has invited her out for a meal.'

'They live something like sixty miles apart,' I pointed out.

'He's trying to find a venue somewhere in between. I think they'd make a nice couple.'

Later that evening, I went to the Merry Friar for a couple of drinks. By the time I'd returned, Graham Kirwan had phoned Anne.

He told her he would do his best to get her a copy of the colour image showing the lower left leg of the corpse. But he explained it would be no easy task. He would have to call in some favours.

'He apologised that he'd got no news about the men behind our break-in,' she said. 'He thinks they've been very clever in covering their tracks.'

*

Summer had now arrived in its full glory in Hopgarden Lane. On the Saturday morning, you could see and sense it in the flowers – the red, white and yellow roses; the blue irises; and the orange and yellow blooms of the red hot poker.

You could hear it on the breeze as the trees beyond the hedge swayed and swished, as the bees scurried from flower to flower and as the birds sang out their carefree song.

I spent the morning writing school reports while sitting in the back garden overlooking the fields. Anne's classes had ended for the summer so she spent the time sitting in the front porch, finishing a novel she was reading.

At lunchtime, having read the last page of her book, she switched on the lunchtime news. As the orchestral opening theme music blared out, I set my reports aside and joined her in the living-room. The second news item concerned a press conference held that morning at Andover Police Station.

A tearful Roderick Maybourne was flanked on either side by his sons Peter, twenty-seven, and twenty-five-year-old Richard. Next to them sat stern-faced Detective Inspector Tim Perkins from Hampshire Police.

DI Perkins was saying: 'One line of inquiry we're pursuing is that Dr Maybourne was abducted from her home in broad daylight. We've recovered CCTV film of three people walking towards the town's railway station just after half past eleven in the morning.

'The images are hazy, but it's possible to make out a woman dressed in a light-grey skirt and jacket, which Mr Maybourne has confirmed resembles his wife.' The image appeared on the screen.

DI Perkins continued: 'The images of the men are extremely blurred but it appears they were wearing dark suits. Anyone with information about these three people should contact Hampshire Police at once.'

He said it was possible they had left the area by train. There had been several reported sightings of the missing scientist in Andover, Salisbury, Birmingham and London. He added that the charity Crimestoppers had joined with the Maybourne family in offering a five thousand pound reward for information leading to the discovery of the missing woman.

A full-length photograph of Dr Maybourne was displayed on the screen before the camera returned to the police station room crowded with journalists and photographers.

It focussed on the distressed faces of the husband and sons. Mr Maybourne read out a statement, which said : 'We have come together as a family to appeal for the public's help. Allegra and I have been married for twenty-nine years and we've never been apart for so long.

'We're appealing to the public in Andover and throughout the rest of the country to look out for her. It looks as if she might have been abducted, so, as every day passes, everyone is becoming more and more concerned.'

One of the reporters asked: 'Is it right that your wife worked in the same office as Professor Morley, who was killed four months ago?'

'She worked closely with Professor Morley,' admitted Mr Maybourne, who was casually dressed in a blue shirt and dark trousers. 'We think it's pure coincidence.'

Another voice in the crowd wondered: 'Mr Maybourne, your wife was involved in sensitive government work. D'you think that may be a factor in her disappearance?'

'We don't think so. She's never encountered any problems in the past because of her work,' he replied. DI Perkins added: 'We don't think her job is connected with this. If she's been abducted, we believe it would be for other reasons.'

'Has there been a ransom demand?' one reporter asked.

'We can't comment on anything of that nature,' the

inspector insisted.

'We just want Mum back as quickly as possible,' the younger son, Richard, called out abruptly as tears trickled down his right cheek. 'We all love her and want her home.' The news report ended with the father putting his arm round his son's shoulder to comfort him. Anne turned the volume down and looked at me.

'We've got to do something to help that poor family,' she declared. 'The police are getting nowhere. They're even discounting links with her work. But we know there's a good chance this is all about her work and that the Russians could be involved.'

'What are you suggesting we do?' I asked.

'I think we should go and see the family and look into connections with the Morley case. We might be able to help that man and those poor boys and, as a result, might be better placed to help Claudia and her family.'

'Well, I'm available to go to Andover with you for a couple of days, if you want. This is a slack time in the school calendar, but I must be back by Wednesday afternoon.'

'All right. We'll go first thing on Monday,' she said. 'It's about a hundred and twenty miles. I think we should take the car and it would be good to make an early start.'

'Sounds good to me,' I said. 'But I'm not sure what we're going to achieve.'

'Well, if we don't go, we'll never know,' she said.

*

On Sunday, Anne and I packed suitcases for our journey to Hampshire. I put three shirts in my case, suspecting we might have to spend at least two nights in a guesthouse. Anne made a note of Graham Kirwan's direct phone line at Kent CID in case she needed his assistance.

We were sitting down to a Sunday lunch of roast chicken when Anne's phone rang. It was a heartbroken Prunella.

'Tristan's called off our date,' she sobbed. 'He saw my front page story today and immediately phoned to cancel. He's decided he couldn't go out with a journalist.'

We didn't want to admit it to our close friend Prunella, but we had forgotten her major front page exclusive story was being published that day. Anne asked Prunella to hold on. Then she cupped her left hand over the mouthpiece.

'We'll have to get the Sunday News and call her back,' she whispered. Removing her hand from the phone, she said : 'Pru, I'm really sorry, but we're in the middle of a meal. Can I call you straight back?'

Half an hour later, I hurried down to the Village Stores and bought a copy of the newspaper. I could see at once why Tristan had been annoyed. The story was as welcome as an unforeseen tax demand.

Across the front page in huge letters it said: 'I WAS DRONE BOFFIN'S SECRET LOVER.' Underneath was the photograph of a blonde former model who had once appeared on the television show The X Factor dressed in skimpy clothing.

The brief front page report said: *The scientist killed in a mystery car smash had been having a secret affair, the Sunday News can reveal today.*

Further reports and photographs about the alleged dalliance appeared on the following four pages under the by-line: 'Caspar Reynolds.' At the bottom of the main story on pages two and three, it said in small letters: 'Additional research by Prunella Ball.'

I rushed home with the newspaper and slapped it down on the dining room table. For the next twenty minutes, Anne and I digested every minute detail.

The kernel of the story appeared in the first few paragraphs of the second page. The report said: *As the speculation about Russian espionage in Britain grew to a frenzy, we can disclose that Britain's top drone missile scientist was having a clandestine affair.*

'Suave Professor Gus Morley was pictured at night clubs and bars with glamorous former pop star Marina Dean – who was thirteen years younger than him. She is also a former Liberal Democrat Parliamentary candidate.

'Marina, thirty-four, said yesterday: "I don't believe his death was an accident. After the disappearance of his colleague, there needs to be a full inquiry "'

'Marina got to the bootcamp stage when she appeared on Simon Cowell's talent show eight years ago. She had limited chart success with her single When My Love Comes Home, which reached number twenty-three in the listings. She is also a former Liberal Democrat election candidate for Norfolk West...'

Anne frowned. 'I wish Prunella had warned me about this.' I was unsure what to say, so I glibly pointed out: 'Makes a change from reading about politics.' She picked up her mobile phone from the table. I thought she was going to throw it at me.

'What are you doing?' I asked.

'I'm phoning Claudia,' she said as she sat down at the table. A few seconds passed before the phone was answered.

Anne gushed: 'Oh Claudia. I'm so sorry. Prunella may be a friend of mine, but I'd no idea she would be involved in writing something like this.' I pressed my ear to the phone and managed to hear Claudia saying: 'Don't worry. The newspaper at least gave me a chance to give them a statement.'

'You mean this at the end?' said Anne. 'This bit that says : *"Mrs Morley said she was fully aware of her husband's friendship with Miss Dean. He had explained it all to her last year. They only met a couple of times and if someone wants to try to make news out of someone's death, so be it. They will be judged by the public."*'

'Yes, that's right,' Claudia admitted. Anne continued listening to Claudia. Then she praised her strength and promised we would call into see her over the summer. After ending the call, Anne called Prunella back as promised while I continued to glance over the newspaper at the table.

'Look, Pru, don't worry too much,' said Anne consolingly. 'I know, deep down, Claudia must be upset at the story. But she knew about the affair, claims it was short-lived and says this Marina Dean only went to the papers to make some quick money.' As she continued speaking she glanced at me.

'I expect I can get Bob to have a word with Tristan and smooth things over,' she said. I waved my hands in a negative gesture, unwilling to become involved, but Anne frowned. I knew when I was being overruled.

Anne informed Prunella that, despite what she told the coroner, Claudia was aware Gus had a wandering eye. 'She insisted Gus always came back to her,' Anne added.

19

Monday June the tenth promised to be a fine day as we set off by car for Andover just after seven am. There was hardly a cloud in the sky, although the forecasters were warning of the prospect of showers later in the day.

Two and a half hours and five motorways later, we reached the picturesque market town which dates back to Saxon times. Andover (population 52,000) is described in tourism brochures as being west of Basingstoke and north of Winchester.

An overspill town for Londoners in the nineteen sixties, the town's main employer is now the Ministry of Defence. An RAF station, RAF staff college and a major Army complex can all be found there.

Anne had been map reading for part of the journey. I followed her directions to the town centre and we eventually found ourselves in tree-lined Abbotts Grove, which was less than a quarter of a mile from the railway station.

Number 57, the home of the Maybourne family, was a double-fronted, red-brick detached house with a white, double-glazed front door. A silver, five-door Peugeot estate stood on the block-paved driveway.

To the right, a mauve-leaved Japanese maple tree stood in the middle of a small lawn. A policeman paced about in front of the two black metal gates to exam the credentials of any callers.

Anne had prepared for our visit by phoning Roderick Maybourne in advance the evening before, explaining our close links to the Morley family, our attendance at the coroner's court and our friendship with a detective sergeant who had been marginally involved in the car crash investigation.

She had also given him Graham Kirwan's direct phone line number in case he harboured any further doubts about our intentions.

I parked the Mondeo directly outside the house. Anne, who was smartly dressed in a dark-grey skirt with a white blouse, greeted the constable with a confident: 'Good morning!' as she stepped from the car. I was dressed more casually than her in light-brown trousers and a blue check shirt.

'Who are you?' he demanded, as we stood together on the pavement.

'We're the Shaws,' said Anne. 'Didn't Mr Maybourne mention we were coming?'

'He did say something about a couple of people from Kent. Hold on a minute!'

We waited by the gateway as he strode to the front door and rang the bell. Mr Maybourne opened it a fraction and stared out.

I was shocked by how much he had changed since the press conference. He emerged like a ghost with a pale face, straggly grey hair, sunken eyes and spindly arms. After a few words were exchanged, we were beckoned over.

'This is Mr and Mrs Shaw,' the constable explained before returning to his post.

'Please come in!' said Mr Maybourne, who was dressed in

the same green shirt and fawn trousers he had worn on his first television appearance.

He was shorter than he had appeared on screen – less than five feet eight inches tall. He led us through his spacious, light-blue hallway into a bright, modern living-room.

'We're so sorry to visit you at a time like this,' said Anne. 'Any news about Dr Maybourne?'

'No,' he said despondently, as he waved his hand towards a cream-coloured settee and invited us to sit. 'There've been more stories in the press, but it's as if she's vanished into thin air.

'The police say they're now convinced she was taken away by train, which makes sense. They're ploughing through all the CCTV film seized from the station cameras. What's your interest in all this anyway?'

'I was at university with Gus Morley,' I explained. 'We're lifelong friends. When we heard...' Anne interrupted to say: 'When we heard Dr Maybourne had gone missing, we wondered if there was a connection. Could I ask you about her job? Was she actually in the same department as Gus?'

'They both worked from time to time for the British Airborne Military Research Agency, known more commonly as BAMRA. There's the Reaper Force office in Whitehall and they both also spent some of their time at Porton Down,' he said.

'They were both highly regarded in their field of knowl-edge and expertise and, of course, their paths often crossed. But they didn't sit at desks next to each other, if that's what you're asking.'

'Were they ever involved in precisely the same projects?' Anne wondered.

'Allegra did tell me about one aspect of her work in which

Professor Morley had been particularly helpful. It involved counter-air defence dealing with swarms of drones, if I remember rightly.' Mr Maybourne made himself comfortable in an armchair.

'Did you say on the phone you were in Kent? You've come a long way,' he remarked.

'I'm a close friend of Claudia Morley,' Anne said. 'We believe the two cases are linked and we feel we owe it to the Morleys – as well as yourself - to try to find out what's going on.' Mr Maybourne nodded.

'I can understand that. The police here are privately suggesting there could be a link between Morley's death and Allegra's disappearance. But it's also possible it's just a couple of crooks out for what they can get. Maybe they think, because we live in a posh house, we've got money.'

He smiled, but it was easy to see that, behind the smile, sat an extremely worried man, concerned at the prospect of losing his wife and partner.

'Mr Maybourne,' said Anne after a pause. 'Have there been any strange incidents over the last few weeks? I mean, before Gus Morley's car crash, there were two incidents in which he was nearly killed.' He thought for a moment.

'Since you mention it, last month she thought she might have been followed by someone. Mr Perkins, the detective inspector, told me not to mention it to the press, but I don't see any harm in telling you.

'She'd just arrived back at the railway station and noticed a man reading a newspaper by the taxi rank. He was wearing a medium-length black coat, which she found strange as it was a hot day.

'As she headed home along her normal route, he began to walk in the same direction. Every now and then, she'd glance over her shoulder to see if he was still behind her. She told me she wasn't sure if he continued to follow her but thought it best to err on the side of caution.

'She didn't want to lead him directly to our front door, so she called in at a friend's house nearby for a cup of tea. Of course, she said nothing about the man to her friend.

'When she left her friend half an hour later, the man was nowhere to be seen and she returned home safely. She was worried enough to mention the event to me.'

'Did she tell you anything else about the man?' asked Anne.

'Only that he had a close-cropped military-style haircut and he walked with a slight limp.'

'Any other strange occurrences?' I wondered.

'Not really. I can't find the tablet where she stored a few of her documents, so, if she's been kidnapped, the men could have taken that as well. Or it could still be in the house somewhere. I'll have to have a thorough look.'

Anne asked: 'Anything else?'

'Well, there was the black car that stopped outside,' said Mr Maybourne. 'That was a few days before Allegra vanished. I noticed the driver peering up at the house. After a minute or so, he drove off. Could have been anyone.'

'Any idea about the make of car?' I asked. 'It wasn't a Range Rover Vogue, by any chance?'

'I'm no good with makes of cars. It was a black car. Might have been a Mercedes. That's all I can tell you. It's funny. Someone else was asking about the make as well.'

At that moment, there was a loud knock on the door. Mr

Maybourne peered through the window.

'I'm sorry. I'm afraid you'll have to go now,' he said tersely. 'It's the boys. They've been to the police station and might have some news.'

He hurried into the hall and prised the door open. Peter Maybourne could be heard muttering: 'Thanks, Dad!' as he and his younger brother, who were both casually dressed, marched straight in.

Peter began: 'You'll never guess what DI Perkins... ' Then he stopped abruptly on seeing us.

'It's all right. My guests are just leaving,' their father said, shaking our hands again. 'I'm sorry I couldn't spare any more time.' Lowering his voice, he explained: 'The boys are my priority now.' We thanked him and assured him, if we learned anything of importance to him, we would phone him immediately.

As we got back into the car, I said: 'Interesting that Allegra was followed from the station. It looks as if someone was trying to discover her address.'

'Yes.'

'Where to now, Anne?'

'I've got an idea. Let's head towards the station. We can move the car to that end of this road and then walk the rest of the way. You know how hard it is to find a parking space near a train station. You've more chance of finding a turnip in a saltmine, as old Graham would say.'

As we drove the short distance from one end of the street to the other, Anne received a text message from Prunella Ball, wanting to know if I had spoken to Tristan.

'Oh, I'm sorry, darling,' I told Anne as I found a suitable

parking space. 'I'll call Tristan now.'

On turning the ignition off, I dialled Tristan's number. His phone immediately went to voicemail. I left him a message, reassuring him that Claudia had not been upset by the Sunday News story about Marina Dean. I wasn't sure he would take any notice of my words, but I felt I had played my part.

Anne was quiet as we set off on foot in the direction of the station. As we reached the railway approach, she remarked: 'The police seem convinced she was taken away by train, but I've got another theory.

'They've got film of three people walking to the station – almost certainly along this very pavement. But what if they got a taxi from outside?'

'Surely the police would have questioned taxi drivers.'

'What if they haven't been very thorough?'

'They're always fairly thorough in a case like this that might involve national security,' I replied.

As we reached the station, we saw there were five taxis – including a minibus - parked directly in front of the red-brick station building. Anne approached each driver in turn, asking if they could recall picking up two men and a woman on Monday May the twenty-seventh at about eleven thirty in the morning.

She described their clothing. All the drivers she spoke to shook their heads. Two of them mentioned that the police and the press had already questioned them about this as part of the Maybourne investigation. One suggested we phone taxi companies in the town.

'Well, that's the end of that,' I said. 'Let's have an early lunch.' I began to walk down the slope away from the station, expecting Anne to follow me.

'I know you're straining at the leash to get to the pub,' she said. 'But let's give it a little more time.'

Ten minutes later, a white Audi taxi glided slowly up Station Approach. It crossed to our side of the road. It stopped beside Anne. The driver unwound his window. On the side of the vehicle it said: 'Abbotts Taxis.'

'You look like you could do with a lift, darling,' he observed.

'I'm very sorry,' said Anne. 'We're actually after information.'

'I'll see what I can do to help, darling, since you're on your own.' For a moment, she decided not to divulge she was with me, in case her apparent single status worked in her favour.

'Were you working here exactly two weeks ago – Monday the twenty-seventh?' she asked.

'Yes. That was my last day before I took time off. Today's my first day back. I've been in hospital for an operation.'

'Sorry to hear that. I hope you're better now.'

'Fine so far, thank you. So you don't need a taxi then?'

'No, I'm sorry. Did you by any chance pick up three people at around eleven thirty on that Monday? The woman would have been wearing grey and the men would have been in dark clothing.' The driver stroked his chin.

'No, I must be honest. It doesn't ring a bell,' he said. 'The only group of three was the sick lady and the two doctors, but they weren't dressed like that. So I don't think I can help you.'

'What d'you mean the sick lady and the doctors?' asked Anne, her face lighting up like a ray of sunshine.

'I had to take them to a clinic a few miles out of town. They said they'd had a devil of a job to get an ambulance and, in the end, they'd had to resort to a taxi.'

'Don't suppose you remember what the woman was wearing?'

'Yes, she was wearing – let me think – a sort of grey outfit. She was very subdued. The doctors sounded foreign, but they weren't in dark clothes. They had white coats on. Why are you asking anyway?'

'Haven't you been following the news? Police are looking for them. A woman's been abducted.'

'Sorry, I've been on my back in hospital. Then I was at home being nursed back to health by the missus. I've been too ill to keep up with the news.'

'It's extremely important,' exclaimed Anne amid mounting excitement. 'Where did you drop them off?'

'I took them just three miles down the road. Sorry, I can't remember the name of the place. It's on the tip of my tongue. They spoke about a clinic. In the end, I dropped them off at the centre.' A disjointed message crackled over his radio. Anne caught the words: 'Alan,' and 'pick up from the station.'

'Sorry, I've got to go,' he said, starting to wind his window up.

'Can't you recall the name of the village?' Anne shouted.

'Earlsbridge,' he replied before driving away. As I strolled back towards her, I could see her smiling to herself. I sensed that the prospect of a relaxed lunch in an Andover pub had been knocked off the agenda.

'Let's get back to the car,' she exclaimed. 'I've just found out where they took Dr Maybourne.'

20

The quaint country village of Earlsbridge lay three or four miles south of Andover. Weekend visitors were often lured there by its pretty high street where thatched cottages nestled alongside Georgian houses.

Sightseers were also attracted by scenic countryside views attained by standing on the single stone bridge which crossed the tranquil waters of the River Anton.

At the heart of the village (population six hundred and twenty) stood the twelfth century church of St Michael, a stone and flint beacon of Christian hope with a spire visible for miles around.

The only other buildings of note were a newly-built Church of England primary school, a seventeenth century inn and a shop. I formed an impression it was an affluent community and that many residents commuted to London for work.

The heavens opened as Anne and I arrived in the main street, so we found a space in the carpark behind the pub, The White Horse, and hurried inside. The main bar felt homely with its exposed wooden beams and brickwork, flag-stone flooring and open fireplaces.

'Now we're here, I suppose we'd better have some lunch,' she said. We attracted the attention of a young blonde barmaid and ordered two jacket potato meals from the menu along with two drinks.

'I suppose we've got to try and find out where our taxi driver dropped the people off?' I commented as we sat down beside the front window overlooking the street.

'He just said the centre of the village.'

'Well, that's where we are,' I said. 'I tell you what. Pubs are fantastic places to get information. We could try asking the landlord.'

'It's quite a challenge. All we know is we're looking for two men and a woman who were dropped off around midday two weeks ago. Two men in white coats and a woman in grey.'

'At least we know now why the police and everyone else have been getting nowhere,' I pointed out. 'The men must have slipped white coats over their clothing.'

'It still isn't much to go on,' she said gloomily.

'It's worth a try.'

Twenty minutes later, after we had eaten, a stocky, casually-dressed man with rolled-up sleeves came to the table to collect our plates.

'Everything all right?' he asked.

'Yes,' said Anne. 'Very nice meal.' He murmured his thanks and was about to walk away when she added: 'You wouldn't be the landlord, would you?'

'Yes, madam. How can I help?' he said.

'Just after some information,' she continued. 'Two weeks ago, some people I know came to the village. I just wondered if you might have seen them. They might have come in here.'

'What did they look like?'

'I'm a bit sketchy on how they were dressed. Two men in

dark clothes. They might have had white coats over the top. The lady would have been in a light-grey skirt and jacket.'

'Not much to go on. What sort of car did they have?'

'They arrived by taxi from Andover.'

'Where did the driver take them?'

'I'm not sure exactly. He told me he dropped them off at the centre of the village.'

'*In* the centre or *at* the centre? Because there's a community centre here called The Village Centre.' Anne sat back in her chair with a broad smile.

'I've remembered,' she said. 'The driver's words were : "At the centre." That's where he must have taken them.' Turning to the landlord, she asked: 'How d'you get there from here? Is it within walking distance?'

'Yes. You turn left when you leave the pub and take the first road on the left. It's just a short distance along there. You can't miss it,' he said, returning to the bar. Anne was delighted at this discovery, although I was more cautious, fearing we were about to face disappointment in our efforts.

Fortunately, the rain had stopped by the time we ventured outside and walked slowly along the main street. As we turned into the side road and approached the Village Centre, I felt this had simply been the dropping-off point for our taxi driver – a place where passengers could alight and he could easily turn round.

Surely, I thought, Anne wanted to find the trio's final destination. My feelings were proved right as we arrived at the car park that lay in front of the single-storey, brick-built building. Her enthusiasm waned.

'Where do we go from here?' I asked. At that moment, an

elderly lady in a brown jacket and green skirt came bustling out of the main door, heading towards one of the cars. She was smiling as if she'd just won a free ticket to the church concert.

'Excuse me!' cried Anne. 'Have you got a moment? We're looking for three people we know.'

The lady, who looked as though she was over seventy, eyed us suspiciously. Then she approached us hesitantly. Anne wondered if she had heard the question.

'We're looking for three people who might be living in a house in the village,' Anne explained.

'What are their names?' the lady asked.

'Well, we're not entirely sure, but we think they may be doctors or connected with a health clinic. Is there a health clinic round here?'

'The only clinics are in Andover. You go to the end of the lane, turn right and it's about three miles,' she said. Anne persisted.

'So there's nothing like that here?'

'No. I think there's an old folks home at the end of this lane. Maybe that's what you're looking for.' She walked off, giving a quick wave over her shoulder. Then she got into her car and drove away.

'I suppose we could try the place down the road,' I suggested. We walked for a quarter of a mile past semi-detached houses until we reached a rambling white building halfway down the lane on the right-hand side.

A five-bar entrance gate was open, so we walked across a vast concrete car park enclosed by trees until we reached the main doors.

A blue painted sign said: 'Earlsbridge Care Home.' But the whole detached building appeared to be deserted. The doors were locked and there were no curtains. We walked to one of the large front windows and peered through. No furniture was visible.

'This would be an ideal place to hide out,' I commented.

'Yes, absolutely,' she said. As we gazed through the glass, I became aware of a tall, bearded man in a dark-green raincoat striding towards us across the forecourt.

'Can I help you?' his voice boomed.

'Sorry, I think we're lost,' said Anne. 'We're looking for three people who came to Earlsbridge exactly two weeks ago today – two male doctors and a woman. We thought they might have come here.'

'This was the old folks' home,' he said. 'It closed nine months ago. Health and safety.'

'It's just that they were possibly heading for some kind of clinic and someone suggested this place. I suppose they must have had lots of doctors visiting here when it was open.'

'Yes, when it was open. But it's not open now.' I decided to try my best to help my wife.

'You obviously get visitors coming to the village all the time,' I suggested. 'You don't personally remember two men and a woman round here two weeks ago today?'

'No, I don't. Now, if I may trouble you, perhaps you'd be kind enough to leave because this is private property.' I thought the man was being unnecessarily brusque.

As we began to walk across the car park, Anne asked: 'Are there any guesthouses round here where three strangers could spend the night? Or are there any houses rented out for short-term lets?'

'The only guesthouses are in Andover,' said the man, as we

passed through the exit. He closed the gate and attached a padlock. 'There's a few people who rent out properties round here but I don't have any details.'

We watched as he walked away towards a nearby house. Then we began to stroll back up the lane towards the high street. As we neared the Village Centre, Anne suggested we knock on a few doors in the hope we could trace what had happened to Dr Maybourne and her kidnappers.

But as it was the middle of the day, many residents were at work and those householders who opened their doors had no information about a woman and two mysterious men. They also knew of no newly-tenanted flats or houses.

'I've got an idea,' I said. 'Why don't we go to the main library in Andover and look through the voters' list for this year and previous years. Maybe we can work out those properties where there isn't a settled household – you know, where people are not listed or where there are a lot of comings and goings.'

'It's worth a try,' she agreed. 'We'll also have to find ourselves a bed and breakfast place. It doesn't look as if we're going to be finished here until tomorrow or maybe even later in the week.'

*

After our early start on Monday morning, I was grateful for the chance to sleep in until nine o'clock at our guesthouse in the centre of Andover. We had only managed to find the place at the last minute. But the double room we booked at the Tudor Rose Guesthouse had surpassed expectations.

It was immaculately decorated and the bed had proved really comfortable. At half-past nine, I put on a blue check shirt and grey trousers. Then we came down the thickly-carpeted stairs to be greeted warmly by our hostess, Charlene, a slim, middle-aged lady with her black hair tied behind her head.

She welcomed us into her spacious dining room and then served us a piping-hot English breakfast of egg, bacon, sausages, mushrooms, tomatoes and beans.

'Are you in the town for long?' Charlene asked as she collected our plates.

'This is our second day,' said Anne, who was wearing a red jumper and blue jeans. 'Probably going back to Kent tonight. That was a lovely breakfast.'

'You're welcome, dear,' said Charlene, who was originally from Jamaica.

'It seems a lovely town,' I remarked. 'Is there a lot going on here?'

'We had the Johnny Cash Roadshow last week. That was tremendous,' she replied. 'You won't be here on Thursday for the market? They sell really fresh, home-made produce. There are some good prices as well.'

'Probably not,' I said.

'You're just on holiday, are you?' she asked.

'We're visiting people,' said Anne, unsure of exactly what to say.

'Well, let's hope the weather improves. It's been very stormy overnight.' Anne's phone vibrated as Charlene headed off to the kitchen.

'It's a text from Prunella,' she said. 'What shall I say?'

'Just say I've sent a message to Tristan and explained Claudia didn't seem that bothered by the story. He texted me back to say he might phone Prunella later today or tomorrow. But I don't honestly know if he will.'

'I'll just tell Prunella you've smoothed things over and he'll call her at some point.'

'Yes, that's fair,' I agreed. Anne opened her handbag and dug deeply. Somewhere, amid the myriad of cosmetics, paper tissues, keys, purse, pen, plasters, glasses, nailfiles, vouchers and receipts, lay a small notebook.

She fished it out and examined the fifteen addresses she had written in it the previous afternoon. They were houses which we judged were either likely to be unoccupied or have had occupiers moving in and out in quick succession.

She said: 'I think we should concentrate on these three, which are closest to the Village Centre: 67 Meadow Lane; 9 St Michael's Close; and 3 Priory Crescent.'

'I don't want to sound too despondent,' I said. 'But we should be realistic. There's probably more chance of the Pope riding the Grand National winner than us finding where Allegra was taken.'

'I know, but the poor woman's life's at stake. We've got to make an effort. It looks as if we've already made far more progress than the police.'

'Don't you think we should just pass on what we know to that DI Perkins and head off home? Charlene cooks a great breakfast, but one night's accommodation has cost us eighty quid.'

'Don't let's give up now,' she retorted. 'I sense we're close to finding them. I know we are.'

After settling our bill at the Tudor Rose, we set off in the car for Earlsbridge again at just before eleven am. Charlene's analysis of the weather proved accurate. It appeared as if a storm with the unbridled power of an Atlantic hurricane had swept through Hampshire.

On the way to Earlsbridge along partly-flooded roads, we noticed several trees had come crashing down. Leaves and branches had been torn from trunks. Fragments of rooftiles could be seen on pavements. Some of the heavy plastic rubbish bins had toppled over. Yet we had slept through it all.

After parking at the Village Centre, we strolled right to the bottom of the lane until we reached a dilapidated house on the edge of a wood. It appeared it had once been part of a row of terraced houses.

The others had long since been demolished, but somehow number 67 Meadow Lane had been spared from the wreckers' ball. There was no front gate. We walked a few paces down a concrete path to the door. No reply came, although we knocked several times.

We decided it must be unoccupied and walked away. As we passed, we stepped over an assortment of rubbish that had tumbled from an overturned black bin.

'Shows you what gales they must have had,' I remarked as we next called at the house in St Michael's Close. The neighbours confirmed No 9 was rented out to a group of students. Finally, we reached No 3 Priory Crescent. The lady living next-door informed us it was 'between tenancies.'

'I did warn you,' I murmured as we gloomily made our way back into Meadow Lane, pushing ourselves forward against the force of a strong gust.

As we reached the corner, an empty plastic container, buffeted by the wind, struck my left foot before colliding with a fence panel on the boundary of the first house in the crescent. A similar white container came clattering after it and came to rest in the gutter. I stooped to pick it up.

A coloured sticker on the side proclaimed: 'Mamina Kukhnya.' There was a North London address and phone number. The rest of the wording was in Russian.

'What does it say, Bob?' Anne asked as she peered at the container. The remains of a thick red liquid clung to the inside of the plastic.

'Well, luckily, my ancillary subject at university was twentieth century Russian social history, so I understand a little Russian. This phrase here, Mamina Kukhnya, means Mother's Kitchen.

'It looks like it's the name of a Russian grocery shop in North London. Someone round here has picked up some takeaway soup from there, by the look of it, and microwaved it.'

'Soup in the summer?' she asked in surprise.

'Anne,' I said. 'In the winter in Russia, temperatures fall as low as minus thirty-six Celsius. They drink soup. When the snows thaw, they go to their summer place where temperatures reach eighteen Celsius. They drink more soup. This bowl probably contained Borscht because of the beetroot-red traces.'

'You know what this means, don't you?' she said in an excited voice.

'Yes. It looks like they've come from the overturned bin outside the end house.'

21

The paint was peeling from the brown, wooden gable hanging above the upstairs windows at the end house. The panes were caked in grime. One of two glass panels in the shabby, black front door had been removed and boarded up.

Unpruned red and yellow roses languished in a small front garden overtaken by weeds and brambles. Plain fawn curtains hung loosely across a ground-floor bay window.

There was no vehicle outside and the land to the left, where neighbouring properties once stood, had returned to nature. The house, enclosed by a rickety wooden fence, looked empty and neglected.

Anne knocked twice at the solid door but there was no answer. We peered through the bay window into a living-room containing a pale green settee and matching armchair. There was an old television and a mirror on the wall – signs that, at some point, someone had lived there.

'Let's go round the back,' she suggested, pointing to a ramshackle six foot wooden fence that acted as an uncertain frontier between the property's boundary and the woods and fields beyond.

We followed the concrete path, choked with weeds, bushes and brambles, until we had nearly reached the rear of the house.

We were astonished to catch a glimpse of a swing and a slide, a sign that children had once played there. For now, the whole place seemed deserted.

'We'll have to look inside,' she said.

I frowned. 'We could be taking a hell of a chance. What if the men turn up? It's kidnappers we're dealing with here. They're not nice people.' As we stood beside a grubby side window, she turned to me.

'Bob,' she said in a soft yet determined manner I was well-acquainted with. 'We've got to inspect the house. Poor Allegra Maybourne could be locked up in here. She could be gasping for food and drink as we stand here talking.'

'All right,' I said. 'But don't forget the trouble we got into when you broke into a house in Canterbury.'

'Stop moaning,' she implored as she picked up a broken tree branch and used it to sweep the dense undergrowth in front of her aside. Just then her phone vibrated in her pocket.

'It's a text from Prunella,' she said. 'Tristan's called her and they're set for a date tomorrow night.' I shrugged as she quickly texted her friend back. Then I followed her past flowerpots, a rusty old bicycle, an old fridge and an old table and chairs until we reached a clearer area at the rear of the house.

The main kitchen window was shut, along with patio doors and two upstairs windows. We tried the back door, but it was locked. Anne peered through the keyhole and noticed the key was in the inside lock.

'Well, there's nothing else for it,' she said, thrusting the end of the branch at the door and smashing one of nine rectangular panes of glass. She threw the branch into the long grass behind her, removed the loose glass shards, inserted her hand

and unlocked it.

'What did you tell Prunella?' I asked.

'Prunella? I kept it short. Just said: "Well done but play it cool."' I chuckled.

We stepped over a few glass fragments as we entered a small kitchen with grease-stained cream walls and a ceiling tinted brown from years of cigarette smoke. Somehow I sensed tiny slivers of glass had become embedded in the sole of my right shoe, but I ignored this for now.

A cooker, kitchen cupboards and a fridge freezer stood to our right. A small table and chairs were positioned to the left, beneath the old-fashioned sash window. There were signs of recent activity.

A pan containing stewed meat rested on the hob. Two Mamina Kukhnya dishes like those found in the street – this time unopened – had been dumped on the table.

Tins and cartons of food – some newly opened and waiting to be consumed – were stacked on the kitchen worktop. We opened the fridge. Its shelves contained fresh milk and a plate of fish. Two drawers lay open. Whoever had been here had left in a tearing hurry.

Anne drew open the far door and we entered the dingy hallway where a light was shining over the dark-blue walls and casting shadows over the faded red and blue patterned carpet.

It was threadbare in places and probably to blame for the musty smell. We detected the sound of a car in the distance. Was it heading here?

We stopped still, gazing at each other, listening. The noise ceased. Perhaps the driver had entered one of the various closes that led off Meadow Lane.

Anne was now examining items of mail, free newspapers and advertising leaflets she had found lying on the floor beside the front door. At this point, I was feeling a growing unease at breaking into someone's house. What if the residents returned? What if they were violent?

It was all very well for Anne to rush in with her crusading zeal and speak about 'Poor Allegra.' But we could be assaulted or killed. If the police arrived, we faced possible arrest for trespass.

'There's lots of mail for a Mr White. They're mainly adverts for mortgages and loans, so I'm guessing he's the landlord,' she whispered. 'There's also a lot of mail for a Mr and Mrs Petrov, so I'm assuming they were the folk with the kids.'

We had seen the living-room from outside, so Anne placed the mail back where she had found it. Then, cautiously, she began to negotiate her way up the wooden stairs which were covered in the same faded carpet as the hall.

I followed close behind, continually glancing across my shoulder – half expecting the front door to burst open at any moment. My nerves were on edge. My heart was pounding like a base drum.

Every stair in the house creaked. If any enemy agent was around, our presence must surely be known. Now and then, Anne would stop still. She would listen out for any noise, but the building stayed silent.

The only sounds were birds singing in nearby trees or the throb of distant traffic. The seconds ticked by. Anne reached the gloomy landing where the walls retained the dark-blue tones of the hallway and the carpet was just as threadbare.

She tiptoed fearlessly ahead and pushed open the door to the middle room that faced us. It revealed an outdated bathroom with a pink suite that would have been fashionable fifty years before.

There were two other doors leading off the landing. I peered into the room behind the bathroom, a back bedroom designed for a girl with mauve walls and discoloured posters of pop stars from the Eighties and Nineties – Michael Jackson, Elton John, Rod Stewart and the Backstreet Boys.

'There's no one here,' I whispered. 'We've wasted twenty minutes fussing over an empty house.'

'There's one more room,' she hissed. She crept across the landing. The door of the final room brushed against the thick-pile brown carpet as she turned its handle and pushed it open.

At once I detected a faint chemical odour, reminding me of the smell that comes from our school chemistry lab. My first thought was someone had been cleaning with bleach. Then I noticed Anne had stopped in her tracks. She raised her hands to her face in horror.

'Oh my God, Bob!' she yelled. 'There's a woman in here!' She moved a few feet into the room. I peered round the door.

There, on a double bed in the centre of the dark bedroom was a pale, blonde-haired woman. She was facing us, her eyes wide open and staring. I recognised her as the person we'd been seeking.

But she looked so different from the confident, smiling woman shown in television images. Her hair was bedraggled. Her glasses were missing. Her grey skirt and jacket lay draped over a dressing table next to the undrawn curtains in the bay window.

Her body was naked except for her white bra and under-clothes. But the sight that shocked us the most was the state of her stomach, arms and legs.

They were covered in burn marks and scars – no doubt caused by her custodians torturing her with either cigarettes or hot implements.

Allegra lay writhing in pain on top of the white sheets, moaning softly. I'm afraid my immediate thoughts were for our own safety.

'Anne, don't go any further into the room. They might have used some nerve agent on her,' I shouted.

Hearing my voice, Allegra's sad, troubled eyes looked up. I will never forget that gaze, the haunted gaze of a woman in the last desperate moments of life.

'Who's done this to you, Allegra?' asked Anne as she backed into the doorway. The scientist struggled for breath. 'The eagle's claw,' she muttered. Anne looked puzzled. The words meant nothing.

'Is there any message for Roderick or anyone?' Anne went on.

'Tell Nat: hold Palladin,' Allegra murmured. She tried to raise her head. She looked at me and, in a croaky voice, added: 'Code Twenty-two.' They were the ramblings of a sick woman and they were her final words. Her head fell back onto the white pillow and she lay still.

'Oh my God!' Anne repeated.

'Come out of there!' I demanded, but my wife stood transfixed, staring at the lifeless body.

'Come on!' I urged her. 'Let's go downstairs. There's nothing we can do and we're putting ourselves at risk here.'

Anne finally overcame the trauma of the moment and followed me, closing the door behind her. We went back to the kitchen.

For a while, we sat at the table together in stunned silence. We had achieved our goal in finding her. But the triumph of her discovery was marred by her death, which we had witnessed and been powerless to prevent.

'We'll have to phone the police immediately,' she said, taking her phone from her pocket and dialling 999.

'Which service do you require?' a man's voice asked.

'Police.'

'Connecting you,' he said. Then a woman's voice stated: 'Hampshire Police.'

'We've found a woman's body,' said Anne. 'It's the missing woman, Allegra Maybourne.'

'Putting you straight through to the incident room,' the woman assured her.

'Where are you calling from, by the way?'

'We're in the village of Earlsbridge.'

'Putting you through.' Over the next few minutes, Anne explained to an officer we had been trying to help the Maybourne family. We had tracked her movements to the village and the exact house where she'd been taken.

As she related our story, she burst into tears and sobbed down the phone. She looked at me, trying to recall the address.

'Is it 67 Meadow Lane?' she whispered. I nodded and she recited the address to the officer.

'Don't worry, my dear,' I heard him assure her. 'We're on our way. Please don't touch anything and please prevent anyone else from disturbing the crime scene.' Anne ended the call and immediately phoned Graham Kirwan, but his handset was set to voicemail.

'Graham, it's Anne Shaw,' she said after the bleep sounded.

'We've found Allegra Maybourne. I'm afraid she's dead. Would you have a moment to call DI Perkins from Hampshire Police and vouch for us? Thanks.'

Less than fifteen minutes later, three police cars arrived with sirens blaring and tyres screeching. One officer thumped hard on the front door.

We hurried into the hallway. Anne turned the latch to let them in. Then a female detective sergeant demanded: 'And you are?' as she marched into the hall.

'Anne Shaw,' my wife explained. 'This is my husband, Bob.' She was followed closely by the detective we had seen on television, DI Tim Perkins. He at once took charge.

'You told our incident room you'd found Allegra Maybourne,' he said with the same stern face we remembered from the press conference. 'How d'you know it's her?' He bent down, folded up some of the leaflets and used them to prop open the door.

'We recognised her from the posters and because her grey clothes are up there in the bedroom,' I replied. 'There've been Russians staying here and we think she may've been poisoned, so I imagine you'll need to take precautions.'

'Sergeant Jones, get one of the constables to assist,' shouted the inspector, who was dressed smartly in grey. 'Stick on your hazmats and take a look upstairs.' I seemed to recall 'hazmats' were protective suits. Turning to me, he said: 'Thank you, sir, for the warning. Very sensible. I assume you both went inside the room?'

'Just hovered in the doorway,' said Anne.

The inspector stared at us. 'Can you explain how you came to be here? Is this your house?'

Anne outlined the events of the past two days – the planned

meeting with the Maybourne family; the chance encounter with the taxi driver; the research into the addresses; and the discovery of the soup containers.

'You say Dr Maybourne has died,' said the inspector, who was at least six feet two inches tall and spoke with an educated voice.

Anne sobbed: 'Poor Allegra. She died while we were talking to her in the doorway.'

'I'm not totally sure I'm buying this,' he went on. 'So you just broke in here on the trail of Russian agents and you come across the missing woman the whole of Britain has been searching for. It doesn't quite add up. I think you'll both have to come down to the station.'

We waited in the kitchen for nearly an hour with one of the constables watching over us. In that time, we were able to catch glimpses of scenes of crime officers arriving in white protective clothing and marching up and down the stairs.

At one stage, our constable was called into the hallway and questioned about something. We took this opportunity to discuss what Allegra had told us.

'She said something about telling Nat to hold Palladin,' Anne recalled. It occurred to me that Palladin sounded like the name of a headache pill.

'D'you think we should tell the inspector what she said?' I wondered.

'The message is for someone called Nat. Maybe we should wait till we find him. Maybe he works for BAMRA.'

'But it sounded urgent,' I said. 'What if we can't find this person called Nat? It might be too late.' Anne was rapt in thought. She suddenly said: 'What on earth d'you think she meant by the eagle's claw?'

'I've no idea,' I replied. 'Except I seem to remember the national symbol of Russia is a double-headed eagle.' At that point, the constable returned and we dropped the subject.

During our enforced stay, we observed a black transit van draw up outside. The male and female occupants came in and put on protective suits in the hall. I assumed they were forensic staff.

When they went up to the front bedroom, some of the other police came down, but it still sounded like a whole army tramping about upstairs. Finally, just after two pm, DI Perkins came into the kitchen.

'I've just received a call from one of our colleagues in Kent, DS Kirwan. He's explained your interest in the Gus Morley business and how you gave Kent Police valuable help with one of their murders.

'So he's accounted for your presence here. We've also had the heart-breaking task of breaking the news to the Maybourne family.

'You seem to have made a bit of an impression on Mr Maybourne, Anne. He's very grateful you found his wife, even if you weren't able to save her.' We looked at each other and nodded.

'How you came to find her in just two days when the whole of the Hampshire Constabulary have been searching for two weeks is beyond me,' he said.

'Well,' I said. 'Thanks for your kind words. We just wish we'd found her alive. Anyway it's gone two o'clock and, if it's all right, I think we'll just drop in at the White Horse up the road for some lunch.'

'I'm sorry. That won't be possible,' he said. 'You've brought me to the main reason why I needed to speak to you. Our pathologist believes you're right and that Dr Maybourne's been poisoned.

'So there's a remote chance you've been exposed to a nerve agent. I've called an ambulance. You've both got to go to hospital immediately.'

22

We were both tired and hungry after our morning's exploits. We had succeeded in finding Allegra Maybourne and all I wanted to do was have a meal and travel back to Kent.

So we were devastated to hear our health might be at risk and we were being taken to hospital. We were the only people who had entered the bedroom without protective clothing.

DI Perkins managed to convince us the threat was minimal and we were only booked in for hospital tests as a precaution. So we reluctantly climbed into the ambulance and we were soon on our way to the isolation ward at Salisbury District Hospital.

The inspector's final words were: 'They've got a lot of experience after the novichok cases. So you'll be in safe hands.'

We both remembered the case of Sergei Skripal and his daughter Yulia who were found poisoned by novichok in Salisbury.

Two other people were found poisoned afterwards, one of whom, Dawn Sturgess, died. I thought about them during the nineteen-mile journey in the back of an ambulance that rocked and lurched its way through country fields and villages before turning onto the busy A30 road and reaching the Wiltshire city.

As we travelled, I also phoned the school secretary and

explained it was unlikely I would be able to help supervise exams the next afternoon as I was undergoing hospital tests. She was rather unsympathetic.

'It would have been good to have had more than a day's notice,' she moaned. 'There are lots of other staff away and this is very inconsiderate of you.' Then she abruptly ended the call.

'When your health's at risk, I would've expected a little sympathy,' I told Anne.

'I suppose it's rather short notice,' she murmured. As soon as we reached the hospital's triage desk, we were given hospital gowns to wear and our clothes were taken away for inspection. Then various tests were carried out in the isolation ward.

We were allocated adjacent beds in a small side-room and spent an uncomfortable night there, continually interrupted by the sound of alarms, trolleys rattling past and nurses' conservations.

After a light breakfast, we discovered how to turn the television on and watched a report about the discovery of Allegra's body on Sky News.

The newsreader said: *Police searching for a missing scientist from Andover revealed today they have found a body. Allegra Maybourne, a fifty-two-year-old mother of two, went missing from her home just before midday on May the twenty-seventh.*

'Police are refusing to confirm whether the body is that of the scientist. A Hampshire Police spokesman declined to give any further information about the discovery and said that, for the moment, the search for the missing woman was continuing.

'It is believed the body was found at a house in the village of Earlsbridge, just outside Andover where residents are reporting there has been a high level of police activity.

'Hampshire Police said in a statement: "The public should not be alarmed by a police presence in the village of Earlsbridge. Officers are dealing with an ongoing investigation. This is an isolated incident and there is no risk to the public."

'During the nationwide search for Dr Maybourne, police issued an image showing a woman accompanied by two men. Police have refused to comment on whether they are still looking for the men. It's just been announced another major act has been signed for the Glastonbury Festival….'

I switched the television off with the remote.

'The police are being as secretive as ever, aren't they?' I remarked to Anne.

'I suppose they're giving the family a little time to come to terms with what's happened,' she replied.

Just before midday, we received good news. The main doctor concerned with us, a balding, middle-aged man with kind, smiling eyes, informed us we were showing none of the clinical signs of having been exposed to a nerve agent and we were free to leave.

'We've been speaking to the police,' he said. 'Although the death in Earlsbridge is being treated as a possible poisoning case, it's not believed the substance involved presents any risk to public health.'

Our clothes had been laundered on the hottest wash possible and were returned to us at lunchtime. We were finally discharged at four o'clock.

Then we had to get a taxi back to our car in Earlsbridge before we could embark on our weary one hundred and twenty-mile journey to Chasehurst.

As we travelled back that Wednesday afternoon, Anne was

silent for long periods. She appeared content simply to watch the countryside go by. But I knew, deep down, the tiny cogs inside her brain were spinning round. After a time, I asked what was on her mind.

'I've been thinking about the car crash at Turner's Hatch,' she revealed. 'Gus couldn't have set that up on his own. Staging a car crash and finding a substitute body must have involved a lot of planning.'

'If that's what happened,' I remarked.

'There must have been some organisation behind it,' she continued. 'But who were they? The Ministry of Defence, MI5, the counter-terrorism office?'

'I don't think we're ever going to find out. You know the way these people operate with their cloak and dagger methods …' I replied.

'What puzzles me is, when someone came up with this elaborate scheme to fake Gus's death, why did they leave Allegra so defenceless?'

'How d'you mean?'

'Well, those two Russian agents were able simply to saunter into her home and walk away with her. Somehow they found out where she lived and called round and snatched her in broad daylight.'

'Yes. Very worrying. But remember - there were at least two attempts on Gus's life. Perhaps that forced the hand of his security advisors and they were so tied up with him that they forgot about poor old Allegra.'

'It suggests her role in the Government research wasn't as significant.'

'Absolutely.'

'Or maybe someone misjudged the situation,' Anne added.

'Talking about Allegra reminds me,' I said. 'I think I might take a trip up to the Russian shop in Hampstead where those soup containers came from. I might get some clues as to where to find the two Russian agents.' Anne frowned.

'I don't want you doing that, Bob,' Anne said. 'That's far too dangerous. Let's leave that to the police and security services.'

On arriving home we found our next-door neighbour, Linda Morrison, had fed Fiesta and a school secretary had left a voice-mail message on our phone. I was ordered to report to the vice principal's office at half-past eight the following morning.

'While you're in Canterbury, I'm going up to the MoD head-quarters in Whitehall,' said Anne as we stood in the hallway. 'I want to find this character Nat and pass on Allegra's message. It sounds like a matter of national security.'

The next morning, I arrived at the school five minutes early and sat in the secretaries' office like a delinquent schoolboy waiting to learn his fate. After a few minutes, the grey-haired vice principal, Mrs Doreen Robinson, opened her door a fraction and summoned me in.

Her office was a bright, spacious room with tall sash windows that overlooked the playground.

'You've been having a lot of bad luck, Robert,' she began.

'I wouldn't say that,' I responded. 'I've been here most days when I've been required to be here.'

'Four weeks ago you came in badly bruised and hobbling. Then your cottage was burgled and now you've been in hospital for tests. Is everything all right?'

Mrs Robinson, who was fifty-eight, slim and renowned for her hard work and efficiency, sat down in her upholstered chair behind her antique Victorian desk and invited me to take a chair.

'I'm fine,' I replied. 'It's just that I was unexpectedly detained at a hospital yesterday and it was thought unlikely I'd be back in Kent in time to invigilate.' She looked at me sternly.

'I don't know what's been going on and I'm not sure I want to know. It's not really my business to pry into the personal affairs of our staff. But it becomes my business when it starts to affect the smooth running of the school.' I shrugged.

'I'm really sorry. I won't let you down again,' I said in a grovelling way.

'As it is, the school has been more than generous in letting you have time off for union business and it is expected, as a result, you should be meticulous about attending school at other times.'

'I understand that. I'm very sorry,' I said.

'Very well,' she said, rising to her feet. Then, before opening her study door for me, she added: 'I had your name in mind as a possible subject leader at some time in the future. I may have to reconsider that if you let us down again.'

'Once again, I'm very sorry,' I said. 'Circumstances were beyond my control. There won't be a problem again.'

When I got home after an exhausting day, Anne was giggling like a schoolgirl at a picnic. She was speaking on her mobile phone in the living-room.

'Hold on a minute, Pru,' she said in a low voice, rushing into the hall.

'Bob, I won't be long. I'm just speaking to Prunella. Your supper's under the grill. Graham Kirwan's coming round later.' On that note, she returned to the room and resumed her conversation.

Half an hour later, after my meal, I went into see Anne, kissing her on the cheek. She had just finished her call.

'Prunella had a fantastic night out with Tristan,' said Anne. 'She thinks they've got a lot in common.'

'Like what?' I asked.

'Both have got brothers in the Armed Forces. They both like Ed Sheeran and Red Hot Chilli Peppers. They like the same films and the same books.'

'A match made in heaven,' I said.

'Don't be sarcastic,' she chided me. 'I'm pleased for them. I hope it works out. They went to a restaurant in South London and afterwards she couldn't get her car started. They had to bump-start it. Poor old Tristan was totally exhausted because he had to do most of the pushing!'

'Did you go up to Whitehall today?' I asked.

'Yes. That MoD building is huge. There was a friendly woman at reception who tried to help. I told her I needed to speak to Nat in the BAMRA office, but she explained there was no one of that name working there, according to her list of personnel.

'I said: "If there isn't a Nat, maybe there's a Nathan or a Nathaniel." She shook her head. Then a sudden thought occurred to me. Maybe Nat isn't a guy at all – maybe it's a woman.

'So I said : "In your directory, is there a woman called Natalie, Natalia or Natasha?" But she shook her head again. I said: "Look, I've come a long way and I've got a message which could be important. Could I just see anyone from the BAMRA unit?"

'She phoned various phone extensions which linked to offices in Wiltshire, but no one was available. Well, by this time, I was nearly pulling my hair out. I told the receptionist: "It's a message from Allegra Maybourne!"

'I must have said it quite loudly because other people in the reception area stopped in their tracks and stared at me. I felt as awkward as a monkey in a bowler hat.'

'Well, at least you got their attention,' I remarked.

'Yes. But it didn't make any difference. I mean, who was I? I didn't have any ID. I don't look like someone from the Forces. They probably thought I was some mad woman.'

'So you left it at that and came home?'

'Yes. The receptionist said: "Sorry, dear. See if you can get a surname." So I left. No one could say I didn't try.'

'You obviously did your best.'

'Afterwards I phoned Claudia and asked the name of the man Gus worked for. She said he worked for several people, but his main contact was Jonathan Evans.

'Of course, she wanted to know why I was inquiring. I didn't want to upset her by mentioning Allegra, so I pretended I was helping Prunella with a story and she seemed to accept that.'

'How is Claudia getting on?' I wondered.

'She seems to be coping very well,' said Anne.

Soon afterwards, as she was going through her make-up drawer in our bedroom, I heard the sound of a car driving slowly up the lane. I glanced through the window as the vehicle drew up outside. It was Graham Kirwan's light-blue Volkswagen Golf. Seconds later the detective marched up the driveway and rang the bell.

'Darling! Graham's here!' I called up the stairs.

'I'll be right down,' she replied.

I invited our visitor into the living-room. His face appeared ruddier than normal, as though he had been exerting himself. He was clutching two large colour photographs, each showing a body part.

'Have you been on a run, Graham?' I asked as I shook his hand.

'Been down the gym,' he explained. After a few minutes, Anne came down. She had changed into a blue dress. Her shoulders were covered with a white cardigan and there was a slight whiff of the Coco Chanel perfume I'd bought her for Christmas.

'Hi, Anne,' he said, kissing her on the cheek. 'Well done, both of you, for finding that missing lady. Look, I've brought you photographs of Gus Morley's leg' He handed her the images, which showed the two sides of the tattooed calf. Anne peered at each in turn, holding them at arm's length.

'Not very pretty, are they?' she asserted, placing them on the table near the window so she could study them. Graham, who was wearing a brown suit, sat down next to me on the settee.

'No, they're not,' he agreed. 'Goodness knows why you want photos of your dead friend's leg, but I know you'll have a good reason. I just hope you aren't going to try to use any of the information from me to suggest police bungling. We've been scrupulous with the evidence in this case.'

'I'm just following a theory. That's all,' said Anne. 'I've no intention of trying to discredit anyone – unless it's deserved, Graham.'

Kirwan then explained the tattoo designs had initially been only faintly visible beneath the charring. Staff in the pathology lab had had to remove superficial layers of charred skin. Then they used modern photographic techniques to enhance the images.

'Sounds complicated,' Anne remarked.

'I know. It's amazing what they can do these days, isn't it?' I admitted. Anne reminded the sergeant she had also raised a question about the dead man's footwear.

'Yes, I've got the information here,' said Kirwan, removing a small black notebook from his trouser pocket. 'Dark blue cotton socks from Primark and a pair of black Adidas Gazelle trainers, size twelve.' He tore off the page from his book and handed it to Anne.

'Thanks very much, Graham,' she said. 'So could you tell me what you know about these images? This first one, about six inches long, appears to show a green man holding flowers. The other shows a bridge and some kind of Scottish symbol.'

'Yes. I can't fathom out the green man at all,' he admitted. 'Dr Griffiths' assistant printed them off from their computer. They were taken around the time of the post-mortem in early February. You wouldn't believe the efforts required to get them. Dr Griffiths says the tattoos point to a Scottish heritage.'

I frowned. 'Gus isn't Scottish. He's from Northamptonshire.'

'Then why has he got Scottish tattoos on his leg?' Graham demanded. Anne was still studying the glossy prints. She had also turned our new laptop on, ready to carry out some online research.

'Just above the ankle the first photo is a Scottish saltire – you know, the St Andrew's cross,' she said. 'It's entwined with a Scottish thistle and underneath it says: "Freedom." There's a larger tattoo just above it on the calf and I'm struggling to identify it. It looks like a bridge over a river.'

'That's right,' said Graham. 'We think it's the Erskine Bridge over the River Clyde. Don't you see? It all fits together. Morley's middle name was Erskine.'

'Look, Graham, I can assure you Gus Morley wasn't Scottish,' I said. 'He explained to me once the only reason his middle name was Erskine was because, at the time of his birth in August 1972, his father was reading Tobacco Road by Erskine Caldwell and he rather fancied the name.'

'Well, that's as maybe,' said the sergeant. 'Dr Griffiths is convinced it's the Erskine Bridge. Maybe, since his name was Erskine, he took a fancy to having the bridge on his leg. Who knows? The poor bloke's dead now, so he can't tell us.'

'And the Scottish flag and the word Freedom?' I wondered.

'Maybe it will become clear later – after your Anne has worked her magic.' A voice suddenly spoke from the table.

'There's a major fact you're missing, Graham,' said Anne. 'I've spoken to Gus Morley's widow and she insists he didn't have any tattoos at all.'

'I don't know about that,' the sergeant said. 'That's not my information. Anyway, changing the subject for a moment, that DI in Andover is full of praise for you both after you tracked down Dr Maybourne.

'He called me back to ask for more information about you. He was gob-smacked over what you did.' Anne shrugged.

'We're glad we found poor Dr Maybourne, but it was extremely upsetting,' she said.

'I'm sure.'

'Would you like a cup of tea, Graham?' I asked.

'That's kind of you, Bob, but I can't stop. I've promised the wife I wouldn't be late.' He stood up.

'Good luck with your hunting, Anne,' he said, shaking my hand.

'Thank you so much, Graham,' she said, jumping to her feet. 'This is going to prove so helpful.'

'It's a pleasure. Keep me posted, Anne.' I opened the front door for him and he walked back to his car.

As I returned to the room, Anne said: 'Bob, the pathologist and the police have made a glaring error. I'm certain that tattoo isn't the Erskine Bridge.'

23

Before being made redundant as a librarian, Anne had once spent a week in her job researching bridges around the world. She could spot the difference between a suspension bridge and a cable-stayed bridge. She could tell a cantilever from a truss.

So when she told me the police had wrongly identified the bridge tattoo on the body's lower leg, I at once accepted she might be right.

'Look at this, Bob,' she said, pointing to the photograph on the table. 'I'm fairly certain it's the Forth Road Bridge. They're often confused.'

'Does it make a lot of difference?' I asked as I stood next to her at the table. 'They're both in Scotland, and it's becoming obvious – because of the flag tattoo - the body in the car was a Scotsman.'

'It might make a difference at some point,' she insisted. 'The two bridges are fifty-five miles apart. It's important to get the facts right. The Erskine Bridge is around fourteen miles west of Glasgow, while the road bridge is around ten miles west of Edinburgh. I wonder if there's a tattoo artist who specialises in designs of the Forth Road Bridge?'

'You think it might be possible to traipse round the parlours and find the exact person who inked this poor guy's leg?'

'It might be possible,' she admitted.

'You're thinking of following the clues to Scotland, aren't you?'

'Yes. I haven't got any classes now until September. If this guy was so keen to have this particular bridge tattooed on his body, maybe he comes from South Queensferry, where the bridge is.'

I smiled to myself as I walked over to the settee and sat down. I said: 'It would be cool if you found the exact shop where the work was done and the staff told you: "You're talking about John McDonald. His family live round the corner in Murray Street."'

She laughed like an exuberant schoolgirl. 'It would be wonderful if life were that easy. Wouldn't it be great if you could link every tattoo to a particular town?'

'It works with Edinburgh. Everyone knows of the Edinburgh Tattoo.' She groaned.

'I'm going to travel to Scotland first thing Monday. I'll start calling guesthouses and train companies tomorrow. You'll be all right looking after yourself for the week, won't you?'

'I'll be fine,' I said. 'But aren't you setting yourself a really challenging task? We don't know this guy's name, address, age or anything.'

'I've got enough to make a start,' she insisted. 'He was a man with strongly patriotic feelings towards his home country of Scotland. At a height of six feet three inches, he was very tall. He was a heavy drinker, and he must have been covered in tattoos.'

'How d'you work that out? We only know about three designs on his lower leg?'

'Yes, but if someone has tattoos there, it's a fair assumption they've also had them on the rest of their anatomy.'

'Fair point.'

'We also know he's proud of the Forth Road Bridge. He was wearing size twelve black trainers and bright blue socks.

'We also know he probably died in the last few days of January. I can't think an older body would have been used because it would have started to decay and make the task very unpleasant.'

'Unless the body came out of cold storage.'

'That's possible,' she admitted.

'He might have died in England,' I pointed out.

'I know, but that's less likely. There's something like five and a quarter million Scots living in Scotland, while only 750,000 Scots live in England. So it's far more likely he died north of the border.'

'Our problem is we can't access government databases like the police and civil servants can,' I remarked. Anne glared at me.

'Government agents on the whole are only privy to the same information as the general public,' she said. 'Officials from the MoD don't have instant access to police records, for instance. So I don't feel at too much of a disadvantage. I'll spend a few days up there and see what I can find out.'

*

I thought Anne's journey to Scotland was likely to end in disappointment. But I felt it pointless to argue. Since converting to the theory that Gus's death had been faked, she had championed the cause more keenly than St Paul espousing Christianity after his trip to Damascus.

I was therefore concerned when I opened an email from her four days later. But I should have had more faith in her abilities. As I read through her letter, it was clear she had made some progress – despite the huge challenge she had set herself. She wrote:

'My darling Bob, I've had some amazing luck since arriving in Bonny Scotland. I don't know why they call it Bonny. The weather's lousy. The journey took nearly seven hours on Monday, but I've found a really nice guesthouse not far from the city centre.

'I haven't been as lucky as you were with your accommodation during your conference week in Liverpool, but I'd say the prices here are similar to those in Andover.

'Since I got here, I've been phoning the charities that help alcoholics to see if they had any deaths among their clients at the end of January. Nothing doing there.

'But, by a stroke of fortune, it turns out my landlady's husband is a former policeman. He's been calling his mates to see if anyone recalls a very tall man dying five months ago and I'm hopeful that this will take us forward. I've chatted to the night porters at three hospitals, but that proved a waste of time.

'Later on today I was thinking of calling round with the colour photographs at some of the city's tattoo parlours to see if anyone could identify the work. The saltire tattoo entwined with the thistle is very distinctive and I thought someone might recognise the style of the artist.

'You'll be interested to learn I've solved the riddle of the green man. Up here there's a folk character they call the Burry man who, following ancient tradition, appears at an annual fair only ever held in Queensferry.

'He tours the town in a costume covered in burrs from the flowerheads of the burdock... I'm sure the image of this figure on his leg points to him coming from Queensferry.

'Now to tell you something really mysterious and intriguing. I was reading through January editions of Edinburgh's evening newspaper and saw a report about a break-in at a funeral parlour run by a firm called Campbell and McKinley along the Queensferry Road.

'It happened on Tuesday, January the twenty-ninth – just three days before the car crash. I know this is all very speculative. Someone told me there are more than five thousand deaths a month in Scotland. But nothing ventured.

'Hope you're not too bored now the exams are over. Love, Anne xxx. PS. I thought you'd be interested, so here's the cutting from the Edinburgh Evening News.'

The newspaper story said: 'Police in Edinburgh are appealing for witnesses and information after raiders struck at a funeral directors.

'The burglars gained entry to the premises belonging to well-established undertakers Campbell & McKinley through a rear window. The incident in Queensferry Road happened between six pm and midnight on January the twenty-ninth.

'A spokesman for Police Scotland said: "We are conducting inquiries and are requesting the public's assistance to help determine the full circumstances surrounding the incident.

'In particular, we are appealing for members of the public who have seen or heard anything suspicious between the hours stated to come forward. Anyone with information should call Police Scotland or Crimestoppers.'

I wrote back congratulating her on her progress, but complaining I was becoming bored in her absence. I had decided to visit the Russian grocery store in North London after all. I said: '*I know you were concerned when I first suggested going up there, but I'll be very careful.*

'*We owe it to Allegra's family to find out who killed her. You can't rely on the police. It might help us solve the Gus mystery as well. I'm only going to check the place out and it's extremely unlikely I'll bump into the men who bought the soup. But, in any event, I'll be discreet.*'

Soon afterwards, Anne emailed me back, saying: *'I'm really not happy about you going there. But if you're adamant, don't park the car anywhere near the shop in case they know the vehicle and recognise it. Keep your eyes open and take the greatest care. I don't know what I'd do if I ever lost you.*'

I decided to drive to North London on Wednesday afternoon. After dressing smartly in a white shirt, blue tie and neatly-pressed grey trousers, I left just after half-past two, following the M2 and M25 motorways and the North Circular.

Altogether the seventy-five mile journey to Hampstead took me nearly two hours. The grey sky hung like a menacing canopy overhead for a while before releasing endless torrents of rain.

Mamina Kukhnya, one of only a handful of Russian stores in London, was located in a row of shops beneath some flats. It was inside a sixties building based in a side street, close to a busy crossroads.

I drove past the shop and managed to find a parking space two streets away. Then I walked back to the premises, nestled in the centre of a parade of seven businesses - mainly take-away food outlets and hair stylists.

The Russian store had a bright, welcoming exterior. In the front section was a well-lit restaurant with solid light-brown tables and seats and varnished oak floors. Four small black metal tables and chairs had been arranged outside the front for al fresco summer dining. I peered through the window. Behind the main eatery was a more dimly-lit grocery store and delicatessen.

I bought a daily newspaper from the newsagent's next door before crossing the road and walking a short distance along the opposite pavement. I waited there for nearly an hour, leaning against a lamp-post, non-chalantly watching the shop while pretending to be reading the paper.

A few customers came in. A few came out. None of them resembled the men in dark suits pictured on the posters in Andover. There was certainly no man with a close-cropped military-style haircut who walked with a limp. I decided it was time for me to venture inside. I crossed the road and walked slowly along the pavement towards Mamina Kukhnya.

After less than a minute, I pushed open the glazed door and walked into the dining area. There were two men huddled round a table drinking tea near the window, while three other men were sitting at a second table a few feet away. They were also drinking tea.

One of the men had a shaved head. He reminded me of one of the poster men, but I couldn't be certain. When I reached the long, black serving counter at the back, I found a short, stout, middle-aged woman with auburn hair who was stacking packs of food on the worktop.

She was wearing a grubby, white, patterned blouse with a brown apron covering a black skirt. On the wall behind her were shelves loaded with more packets and tins. She glanced at me as I approached. I tried to smile.

'Dobryy den!' she said, assuming I might be Russian and smiling back at me. Her teeth were like jagged yellow sticks in her mouth, jostling for position.

'Hello!' I said.

'Please, am I helping you?' she asked.

'I've heard you sell wonderful borscht,' I began.

'Yes, we're having borscht with meat or without meat.'

'I'd like to buy some with meat, please.'

'It's six pounds fifty pence. Home-made,' she said with a hint of pride.

'I've heard it's very popular,' I said, trying to make friendly conversation.

'Lots of Russians in London, they are liking this borscht. You like some?'

'Yes, please,' I said.

'Just one?'

'Yes, please. I may come back for more later.' The woman stepped through a doorway. I assumed she had gone to a kitchen. Moments later, she returned with a plastic container like those Anne and I had seen in Andover.

'You are living in Hampstead?' she asked, placing the soup on the counter. 'We can deliver.'

'No, I don't live round here,' I replied, removing a ten-pound note from the wallet in my trousers and placing it in her hand. 'Hey, I've just thought. You might be able to help me. Did two men order some borscht from you about three weeks ago? I met them in Andover – in Hampshire.'

'Russian men?' she asked.

'Yes.'

'There are lots of Russian men who come here.'

'I just thought you might remember them. Fairly tall, dark suits.' I sensed the eyes of half a dozen tea drinkers boring into my back.

She shook her head. 'Your information, it's not helping.'

'Sorry. They'd have come maybe over the weekend of May the twenty-fifth and twenty-sixth. Perhaps you delivered to them near here? They ordered a lot of food – at least four bowls of borscht,' I said.

'That's not unusual.'

'Hang on!' I said. 'They also bought tins and packets of food - and some fresh fish.'

'I'm sorry. Again, that's not unusual.' As she passed me my change, she gave me the distinct impression she was bored with the conversation and had other, more important matters to attend to.

'All right. It was just a thought,' I said, removing my borscht from the countertop. 'By the way, have you got a spare leaflet or menu I can take away?'

'I'm looking,' she replied, as she opened cupboards and peered beneath the counter.

'I'm sorry,' she said after a few minutes. 'I'm not finding. Anyway, I hope you are finding your friends,' she said. 'Do svidaniya.'

I quickly left and walked along the parade of shops towards my car. The rush hour had begun. I passed the traffic lights by the crossroads and entered quiet, tree-lined Cavendish Avenue. Drivers at the wheel of lorries, buses and cars in the next street, Hendon Park Lane, thundered off as their traffic lights turned green.

Vehicles from other directions screeched to a halt as their

lights turned against them. Office and factory workers, eager to be home, filled the air with petrol and diesel fumes as their engines hummed in the motionless queues around the intersection.

Glancing back after a few steps, I was in time to see the red lights changing. It was then I noticed a black car travelling behind me. Although on foot, I managed for several minutes to keep well ahead. I racked my brains, wondering if I had seen it before.

'Any moment now, it will drive off,' I thought. 'Or maybe they'll stop and ask me the way to the embassy.' I turned left and hurried down the gently sloping road, Orchard Gardens, where I had parked.

Rows of silent houses stood on each side with trim lawns, rhododendrons and occasional birch trees. A white car swept up the hill. Its brakes screeched as it reached the T junction before roaring off.

I looked round again. The black car had stopped a short distance behind me. It was either a BMW X5 or an Audi Q7. I was uncertain which. There were two men in the front. I couldn't see if anyone was in the back.

On reaching the Mondeo, I fumbled for the keys. I opened the door quickly and placed the newspaper and soup on the passenger seat. I started the engine. As I did so, I saw in my rear view mirror the black car had begun moving slowly towards me.

Then it was beside me – the black metal just inches away, stopping me from opening my door if I'd wished to. My heart was racing like a runaway train.

The thickset man in the passenger seat with short, cropped hair opened his window. He made a turning gesture, signifying

I should lower mine so he could talk to me. No way, I thought.

I released the brake and set off down Orchard Gardens at speed. My hands were shaking.

I turned left and then left again, believing this would bring me to the traffic lights at the crossroads, where I could find the route back to the North Circular. Thankfully, it did. I peered in my mirror. The black car was still there.

If I had to stop at the lights, I might be in trouble, I thought. One or both of them might get out and come round to my door. Anne's words about visiting the food shop came back to me over the evening air.

'That's far too dangerous,' she had warned. 'Leave it to the police and security services.' I wished now I had listened.

Luckily, the lights remained green and I shot off along the dual carriageway heading east at a rate that, I knew, was breaking the speed limit. I could not see the black car. Perhaps I'd lost them.

But moments later, as I turned onto the North Circular, I realised I was mistaken. Their driver had found sudden reserves of power.

Now they were so close the two men were almost sitting on my back bumper. My breathing quickened. Then the shooting started.

24

The bullets clattered against the back of the car like the first hailstones in a storm hammering onto a tin roof. I guessed the front-seat passenger in the black car – which I now recognised as an Audi 7 by its four-ringed logo – was firing at the nearside of the vehicle.

I just hoped the gunman's shots missed the tyres as I took the speed up to ninety miles an hour and above. My heart was pounding like a blacksmith's hammer, but all I could do was drive.

By now, I was in the far-right of the three lanes, overtaking every vehicle I came to. The road surface was slippery after the heavy rain, but I tried to forget about the dangerous conditions.

I was more concerned about the Russians than the rain. Although the gun went silent for a moment, the black Audi was still behind me. In the mirror, I could see the crazed faces of the pursuers, desperate to stop me, to punish me, to kill me.

On we sped through Edmonton, Walthamstow and South Woodford. I sensed our high-speed race across North London would be attracting shocked reactions from other drivers, but I had no time or inclination to gaze about. My focus was entirely on the road ahead, on fleeing my predators and getting back to Kent.

Then, by chance, I heard a faint noise some way behind. It was that public wail of distress that often shatters the peace of the day when you least expect it.

But today this emergency siren was a welcome sound that played in my ears like an opening symphony at a concert. The reckless way our vehicles had been travelling through the misty suburbs had attracted the attention of the police.

Now, as we approached the outskirts of Ilford in East London, several patrol cars in a row were bearing down upon us with flashing lights.

At first, I was unsure if it was their intention for me to pull over or if they simply needed to pass me so they could attend to some incident up ahead. But all quickly became clear. The men in the Audi and I were in their sights.

As I pulled into the middle lane to let the first police car pass, the driver kept behind me and continued flashing his lights. To comply, I swerved into the first lane and drew the Mondeo to a halt, partly on the grass verge.

To my surprise, the Audi driver was refusing to stop and sped on with two police cars just seconds behind him.

I glanced in my mirror to see the first of the three pursuit vehicles had stopped right behind me. An officer got out and rapped on my window.

'Would you like to get out?' he asked. I was breathless and still shaking but did as he urged me. I shuffled to the passenger side of the car, emerged from the passenger door and stepped out – straight into a puddle.

As the cold water squelched in my shoes, I moved to a drier spot and glanced around. A bleak landscape of tower blocks, electricity pylons, warehouses and factories confronted me.

Then, in shock, I spotted several bullet holes in the boot-lid and rear bumper. The burly officer pulled a small black note-book from his pocket and joined me as the traffic thundered by.

'What the hell were you playing at?' demanded the red-faced officer, who was in his early forties. 'The speed limit's fifty. You've no idea how much trouble you're in. One of our people back in Walthamstow clocked you doing over a ton.'

As a police colleague joined us on a section of hard concrete standing behind the barrier, he continued: 'Is this your car?' I confirmed it was, told him the registration and gave him my name and address – which he no doubt already had. Then he asked: 'Why were you driving like a maniac, putting yourself and other road users at risk?'

'I was being shot at. Look!' I said, pointing out the rear damage. He walked round to the back and carefully traced his fingers over the holes.

'You've really upset somebody,' his younger colleague remarked. The first officer's radio crackled into life. He moved a few feet away from me to conduct a conversation while his colleague and I exchanged looks.

'They started chasing me in Hampstead,' I told the second officer, who was about five feet eight inches tall and had a light-brown beard.

'Road rage, was it?' he asked.

'I don't know. I'd just been to a grocery store.'

'Yeah?'

'It's a long story,' I admitted. The burly officer, clearly the senior of the two, returned. The atmosphere had changed. He was smiling.

'It's all right, sir,' he announced, fixing his radio to his belt.

'We're going to overlook your driving on this occasion since it appears you were provoked.'

A feeling of relief swept over me while the two officers held a whispered conversation a few feet away. The burly officer walked back.

'Our colleagues have been in pursuit of a second vehicle and they've confirmed the presence of firearms. So you're free to go and no action will be taken.

'Our station will contact you in the near future for a statement,' he said. His colleague gazed at me sympathetically as a helicopter soared overhead.

'Are you all right, sir?' he wondered. 'Seems you've had quite an ordeal.'

'I'll be all right,' I assured him. 'So your pals have caught the Russians?'

'Russians?' said the burly constable. 'I don't know about any Russians. All I can say is that a police operation is on-going.'

'So they haven't caught them,' I concluded, suddenly aware I was speaking my thoughts out loud.

'I can't comment on active police operations, sir. I can only confirm you're free to go, but you will be receiving a follow-up call from the station. I should get some quotes for that damage. And keep within the fifty mile an hour limit in future, sir.'

The pair returned to their car and drove off. I studied the bullet holes. There were four in the boot lid and three in the bumper.

It was reassuring the car chase was over and police were taking no action against me. I looked at my watch. It was a quarter past six. The whole pursuit had lasted no more than twenty or twenty-five minutes. But at the time it had seemed an eternity. And, deep down, I knew the nightmare wasn't over.

Where were the two Russians now? Were they in the clutches of the police or had they eluded them? Were they back in Hampstead, happily tucking into their borscht – with or without meat? Or, since they almost certainly knew where Anne and I lived, were they heading to Kent to deal with their outstanding business?

I drove slowly back to Chasehurst, trying to forget the trials of the previous few hours. But it was not easy. Every time I came to a junction I wondered whether I would see a black Audi.

When I finally reached the village at just before eight pm, all I wanted to do was cook myself a meal and relax with Fiesta in front of the television.

Daylight was fading as I parked beside the cottage and found Fiesta sitting in the porch. I stroked him as I unlocked the door.

After changing my shoes and feeding the cat, I thought I'd sample the borscht. The microwave instructions were in Russian, but I took off the lid and heated the contents for two minutes before stirring and heating for a further two minutes.

The beetroot-flavoured dish had an earthy taste, but the pieces of meat were delicious. After the meal, I thought I'd take a shower. I was about to climb the stairs to the bathroom when I heard a noise outside.

I peered out across the garden at the hedge and the trees beyond. All was still, all was serene. Then a black car passed in the twilight – a black car with dimmed front lights, gliding slowly along the lane.

So it had come – the moment I had half-expected since the discovery of Allegra's body in the deserted house. The moment I would have to atone for defying the might of an enemy state.

It was too late to run, but I had a few seconds. I slipped off the back cover of my mobile phone and removed the SIM card, which I placed in a kitchen drawer along with my money, my watch, my credit cards, trade union card, keys and pocket diary. My actions were only just completed in time. Within seconds, there was a loud knock.

'Just a minute!' I called, as I replaced the cover and put the phone down on the hall table. Guardedly, I peered through the partly-glazed front door at a dark figure outside. No gun was visible. I drew it open.

Standing there, under the dim porch light, stood a broad-shouldered man with short, spiky, black hair who was more than six feet tall and slightly overweight. He was wearing a loose-fitting black sweatshirt and navy trousers. He gave a friendly smile. He looked as benign and inoffensive as a curate on his way to a tea party. But he was almost certainly the driver of the black Audi.

'Mr Shaw?' he asked. I noticed my hand was trembling. I hesitated for a moment, looking out across the garden and drive to see if he was accompanied.

'Yes,' I said.

'Sorry about this, sir, but you're coming with us,' he said, his face now solemn.

'Why? What's this about?' I demanded. He ignored my question.

'We can do this the easy way or the hard way,' he said without giving any hint of a foreign accent.

'Well, we can do it the bloody hard way!' I shouted, slamming the door in his face. Unfortunately, he had taken the precaution of placing his left foot in the way. The door struck

237

his foot and then swung open again.

'Come on, boys!' the man yelled. Two men emerged from the shadows in black masks and black gloves. They must have been hiding at the top of the drive without me seeing them.

One of them clutched a dark-brown hood in his hands. I punched him as he crossed the threshold into the hall and he fell back against the door frame, dazed. But then a second man– who was sturdier than me - wrestled me to the floor.

'Cuff him!' demanded the man with the spiky hair. The man holding the hood took some handcuffs from his belt and with difficulty, because I was struggling, he managed to fasten my wrists together in front of me. Then he placed the hood on my head and tied it securely round my neck to prevent it slipping off.

My loss of vision was complete as the two thugs led me away down the drive. I desperately tried to maintain my sense of direction, but, after we reached the lane, I lost track of exactly where I was.

At the time, I thought my new home security cameras might have captured their actions. But sadly, I found out later, the men had had the forethought to cut the wires to the cameras before knocking on the door.

'Get him in the car!' the first man ordered. It felt as if I was being pushed and jostled around to the far side of the vehicle before being bundled into a back seat. The child lock next to me was activated so I couldn't jump out at any point.

Then I heard the same voice say: 'You have the right to remain silent. If you do say anything, what you say can be used against you in a court of law. You have the right to consult with a lawyer and have that lawyer present during any questioning.

If you cannot afford a lawyer, one will be appointed for you if you so desire.'

I shook my head in disbelief. Were they Russians? Or were they British? Whoever they were, they were trying to make the whole pantomime of kidnapping me appear official by cautioning me.

'No comment,' I said bitterly. Then the voice could be heard outside the car saying: 'There's meant to be a woman as well. We'd better search the house.'

After five minutes, they must have realised there was no one else at home. I heard the front door slam shut. I discovered from their conversation later this man who barked the orders was called Stefan.

The engine started. The car roared off down the lane. Thoughts were swirling round my head. Were they taking me away to some God-forsaken hideaway in the wilds of England where they would torture me, shoot me and leave me to die? Would I ever be found alive again? Although I knew my voice would sound muffled, I tried to speak.

'Where are you taking me?' I demanded.

'You'll find out soon enough,' said Stefan, who appeared to be in the driving seat.

'Why me?' I demanded. 'What have I done to upset you?'

'There's nothing to worry about. We just need to ask you a few questions. That's all,' he said. 'Just relax. We'll soon be there. We'll find you a nice bed and you can get a good night's rest.'

'Very considerate of you, I'm sure,' I said sarcastically. 'You could have had a bright career in hospitality. Why are you Russians so interested in me? I haven't done you any harm.'

I heard Stefan ask one of the other men in a low voice:

'What's he say? Why are the Russians interested in him?' Then, in a louder voice, directed at me, he said: 'I've got no information for you. You'll have to wait till tomorrow.'

I was even more agitated than on the night of the break-in at our cottage. Where were these thugs taking me? What right did they have to barge into my home and carry me away by force? I began planning my revenge. As soon as I got home, I told myself, I would call my union's lawyer and haul them up before the highest court in the land.

We drove on. Occasionally, the car lurched to the right. I guessed the driver was swerving to avoid roadside puddles. Then I overheard one of them asking whether Stefan had paid the Dartford crossing charge.

I guessed we were on the M25 motorway, heading north. By now, I was finding it harder to breathe through the cotton material of the hood. The heat in the garment was stifling. I was sweating like a ship's stoker.

'Can you take this hood off?' I asked. 'I'm finding it hard to breathe.'

'Loosen the string, Victor, to give the man some air, ' said Stefan. 'But don't take it off.'

During the next half hour, I gathered from the men's conversations we had passed through the Dartford tunnel. After two minutes, Stefan took a detour down a slip road to a roundabout. While negotiating round it, a draught of air wafted through to me. Stefan must have opened his window.

'What did you throw that out for?' asked one of the men.

He replied: 'Now if anyone tries to trace him, they'll think he's in Thurrock!'

I realised Stefan was referring to my phone handset, which

he must have snatched from the hall table and just then thrown from the car. I was comforted by the knowledge I had foiled this cruel plan—to make my wife and friends believe I was somewhere in Thurrock - by removing the SIM card.

The car resumed its journey along the M25 motorway passing through two tunnels. I deduced these were the Bell Common Tunnel in Essex and the Holmesdale Tunnel in Hertfordshire.

Then I heard someone mention the A1, the road that leads from London to Edinburgh. Was it possible I would end up in the same city as my beloved wife?

These hopes were quickly dashed. After passing through the Hatfield Tunnel on the A1(M), we crossed several roundabouts and then began negotiating windy country roads. I was hurled from side to side in the back of the car until finally, two or three hours after leaving Chasehurst, we stopped.

We were at some kind of entrance. Stefan started speaking to an official. I listened carefully to the conversation.

Stefan said something like: 'We've got a new guest. Shall I take him to the guardroom?'

'Yes, Ivan can sort him out.' I heard the swishing sound of a barrier being raised. Then Stefan drove us along a smooth road for a short distance before we stopped again. This time he turned the engine off.

'Welcome to your new home, Mr Shaw,' yelled Stefan. All three men then guffawed.

'Shall I take the hood off?' asked Victor.

'Yes, and take off the cuffs as well,' came the reply. Moments later, as I rubbed my wrists, I found myself standing in the centre of a vast military camp. The black car had parked in front of a small, two-storey red-brick building. A sign over the yellow door at the side of it said: 'Guardroom.'

For the first time, I had a good look at the car. It wasn't an Audi. It was a Volkswagen Touareg. Perhaps the Russians who had chased me earlier had instructed a second team to abduct me, I thought.

I glanced around. It must have been about ten or eleven o'clock. The site consisted of two and three-storey red-brick office buildings, barracks, nissen huts and, in the distance, several structures that resembled aircraft hangars.

In between the buildings, I glimpsed perimeter fencing, which was about fifteen feet high; security lights; and cameras around the entrance and guardroom.

This was my first chance to observe Stefan, Victor and the third man, whose name I now learned was Anton. They were in their late twenties and casually dressed.

Victor was slim and shorter than me, while Anton was clearly the tall, hefty man who had floored me in the hall. As I watched them joking together, they could have been three seedy carpet salesmen discussing the latest Berber.

Meanwhile, I was relieved to be free of the hood. I could now breathe freely, although the cuffs had made my wrists sore.

'What's happening now, Stefan?' I said, leaving him in no doubt I knew his name.

'You're going to be searched for your own good and then we'll find you the nice bed we promised. Ah, here's Ivan.'

A man dressed in British khaki uniform emerged from the guardroom. He was of similar height to me, but stockier. Strands of ginger hair poked from beneath his cypress green beret. He also had a ginger moustache.

'Right, Mr Shaw,' he boomed. 'I'm Sergeant Jarvis. Welcome

to camp. If you'd like to follow me, we'll have you sorted out in no time.'

Seeing no easy means of escape, I followed this custody guard into the small reception area inside the guardroom. It consisted of a wooden counter with shelving beneath.

Tall, dark-green metal cupboards stood at the back of the office on either side of a doorway which, I presumed, led to the rest of the building. He lifted the counter hatch, walked through and then stood facing me. His officious manner annoyed me.

'I'm known as Ivan by most people, by the way, but you can call me Sergeant,' he said. 'Right. Turn out your pockets. I want everything on the counter. After you've done that, I want your tie and shoelaces.'

'What d'you think I'm going to do? Strangle myself with my laces?' I asked.

'It's regulations,' he said. 'What can you do?' I was angry at being abducted from my own home at night and driven to this camp. They had no authority, surely. I was a British citizen.

'Why am I here?' I demanded. 'You don't have the right to detain someone. It's the law.'

'We'll talk about that later,' said Jarvis. 'For the moment you're here and we're responsible for you.'

'Why am I here?' I insisted.

'For assessment. That's all I can tell you,' he said.

'Assessment for what? I haven't applied for anything and I haven't done anything,' I retorted.

'You're talking to the wrong person. I expect it'll all become clear tomorrow.' I urgently wanted to notify Anne about what had happened and I was about to pass on her phone number to this oaf when I suddenly thought better of it.

If they obtained her mobile number, they might use it to locate and capture her as well. So I decided to play along with my captors for the time being.

In the morning, I would demand to see someone in a position of authority. I took my stamps, comb and coins out of my pockets and placed them on the counter. My yellow tie and black laces followed.

'No mobile? Where's your mobile?' he demanded.

'Didn't bring it,' I said.

'Stefan Rogers!' the sergeant bellowed. I turned to find Stefan, Victor and Anton were all standing around the car outside. Stefan strolled casually over to the guardroom door.

'Where's his phone?' asked Jarvis.

'We disposed of it in case it was traced here,' said Stefan.

'Why did you do that? Major Thomas wanted the information on it checked out.'

'Tell her I couldn't find it.'

'You're a bloody chancer,' said the sergeant, writing out a paper receipt which listed all my items. He handed that to me before locking my belongings away in a section of the cupboard.

'Now we'd better find you somewhere to kip,' Jarvis said. 'Follow me.' With a bunch of keys rattling from his belt, he led me along a concrete path that crossed a vast floodlit expanse of grass.

As we walked, I looked again at the high wire-netting security fences surrounding the site, which I assumed covered several acres.

At last, we reached a concrete bunker which rose from the ground around a hundred metres from the entrance. Most of the accommodation appeared to be below ground with a grassy mound above.

There were no windows, but there were two huge revolving ventilators at ground level, one on either side of the entrance steps. Several small black ventilation flues for funnelling air poked through the earth at the top of the mound.

After negotiating our way down ten steps, we found ourselves in a murky corridor. Ivan unlocked a green metal door on the right and thrust it open.

As he switched on the light, he smiled like a mule and announced: 'Here we are. Home sweet home!'

25

The bullying sergeant pushed me into a drab, soulless underground chamber with a linoleum floor and concrete walls. It reminded me of rooms preserved from the time of the Second World War which I had visited on historical tours.

The walls were painted in a dull magnolia colour. There were two beds, one on either side of the room; a plain white wardrobe; a small, white bedside cabinet; an out-dated, thirty-two inch television perched on a small table; and two wooden chairs.

The room, measuring around five metres by four metres, also contained a toilet cubicle, wash basin and shower, all concealed behind a red and gold striped curtain. There was no natural light because there were no windows, but a grimy bulb hanging from a brown shade in the centre of the white ceiling cast a partial glow around the chamber.

There was a whiff of disinfectant. A double garage smelling of diesel oil would have been more welcoming.

'I think you'll find the bed comfortable,' said Jarvis. 'I'd better tell you the rules. Breakfast is at seven-thirty sharp. Lunch is one thirty. Supper is six thirty.

'I bring over all the meals, which will be consumed here. Lights out at ten thirty. There's a shaving kit and toiletries in the little cabinet by the far bed. You'll find we're fairly easy-going here and, provided you play along with us, you'll be fine.'

'You're obviously thinking I'll be here some time,' I muttered.

'That's not for me to say,' he replied. 'That's for them that's in charge. I'm just the dogsbody. What can you do? Oh, dirty laundry is collected on a Tuesday and you'll find spare clothes in the wardrobe. Judging by the look of you, some of them should fit.'

'What time does the milkman come?' I asked in a sarcastic tone. He didn't react.

'Don't worry. You'll soon get used to it,' he added.

'Am I the only prisoner?' I asked.

'We tend to use the word "detainee," he said. 'Well, I'm looking round. I can't see anyone else. Can you see anyone else?'

'It's just that I noticed a second chamber like this one on the other side of the corridor.'

'That's just a storeroom for the moment,' he said. 'But I don't know why I'm telling you this. Look, I'm going now, but if you need me urgently at any time, you press the button by the door. It goes straight through to the guardroom.

'But I'll warn you now: it's only for emergencies and if you abuse it, there'll be consequences. Sweet dreams!'

The door clanged shut and I was alone. I noticed an old railway station clock on the wall giving the time in Roman numerals as half-past ten. It was probably the only item of any value in the room, despite almost certainly being a modern replica.

A few feet away on the ceiling, above the wardrobe, there was a small ventilation grille providing a flow of air from outside. I sniffed the sheets, blanket and pillow on the bed nearest the door. At least they were freshly laundered.

I also examined the mattress, which appeared fairly new. It had been an exhausting day. I lay down and closed my eyes, but I couldn't sleep on that warm summer night. All I could think about was how unlucky I had been to have fallen into the clutches of these men.

Maybe I should have struggled more fiercely with Anton and done more to stop them overpowering me. Maybe it had been a mistake to go home that evening at all after the car chase. I wondered how Anne was faring in Scotland and whether our neighbour Linda Morrison would think to feed Fiesta.

I wondered how long I would be held in this dingy bunker room.

Above all, I was angry. Angry at myself for having gone to Hampstead. Angry at having opened my front door to strangers. And angry at being detained without proper authority. The men had failed to identify themselves, to state any reason for my detention or even to divulge where I would be held. If and when I was set free, I would use every law in the land to seek retribution. Eventually, I must have dozed off.

The next morning, the clank of keys roused me. I opened my eyes to see Jarvis lumbering into the room with a breakfast tray.

'Rise and shine!' he hollered, banging the wooden tray down in front of the television. 'Looks like it's going to be a bright, sunny day today.'

'Won't make a lot of difference to me in here,' I moaned.

'Never mind,' he said. 'Enjoy your breakfast!' As he moved towards the door, I asked: 'Any chance of a pen, some writing paper, some books and a newspaper?'

'I'll see what I can do, but no promises.' he replied as he left, locking the door behind him,

I inspected my first meal. There was a steaming cup of tea, but no sugar provided. An overcooked fried egg, two greasy sausages and some cold beans fought for space on the paper plate with a slice of buttered toast.

I was unexpectedly hungry, however, and quickly devoured my breakfast. While eating, I thought about Jarvis. He was a jovial fellow, but I realised, beneath this friendly exterior, lay a man with a ruthless streak – the kind of man who would crush a small animal that got in his way and then claim he was only acting in its best interests.

I spent the next few hours seeing how the television worked and examining the contents of my cell. There were only a few channels, but the reception and picture quality were good. I tried to shower, but the pressure seemed low and the water flowed only weakly from the spray nozzle. The toilet and wash basin were dirty.

Later, while viewing the horse racing at Royal Ascot, Jarvis arrived to collect the tray and present me with my lunch. It consisted of a ham sandwich, a bottle of spring water and an apple.

'You're a racing fan, are you?' he asked.

'No,' I said. 'Never usually watch it, but there's nothing else on.'

'I'm afraid your request for pen and paper has been turned down,' he said.

'And the books and newspaper?'

'Ditto,' he said. 'I don't know. What can you do?'

'When am I going to see someone in charge?' I demanded.

'All in good time,' he replied. He took the breakfast tray and left.

Three hours went by, during which time I flicked between various television channels and examined the clothes in the wardrobe. Surprisingly, some of the shirts and trousers fitted.

'Probably items left behind by previous inmates,' I told myself. Then, unexpectedly, a few minutes after five o'clock, I heard Jarvis unlocking the door.

'Mr Shaw!' he said with a smile. 'Meet your new room-mate, Mr Farrier.' In walked a calm middle-aged man with the quiet confidence of an ice cream seller in a heatwave. His face broke into a smile as we shook hands.

'I'm Greg,' he said with a northern accent.

'Bob,' I replied. 'Are you joining us for long?'

'I'm not sure,' said Farrier, who was slim, had short, greying hair and was a few inches shorter than me.

'I'll leave you two to get acquainted,' said Jarvis, locking the door as he left.

'This is my bed here,' I said, eager to stake my claim on the one by the door, where I had slept more snugly than I had expected the night before. To underline the point, I lay down on it. 'But I think you'll find that one just as comfortable.'

'What brings you here then?' asked Farrier, as he grabbed one of the chairs beside the table and sat down.

'Wrong time, wrong place, I suppose,' I replied.

'How long have you been here?' he asked.

'I came about ten thirty last night.'

'How long are they keeping you?'

'No idea. I've had no information. I don't know what part of the country I'm in, except it's north of London. I don't even know who I've been nabbed by or why.'

'Bloody hell. They're bastards.'

'Is it the Russians?'

'The Russians? Why would a Russian be dressed in a British uniform? No. This place is run by the British Army.'

As he spoke, it was as if curtains had parted in my mind and daylight had come flooding in. So the three men who seized me were not connected with the car chase after all. I was *not* being held by the Russians. In some way, it was the British authorities I'd upset. But how and why?

'I thought maybe Ivan was a Russian dressed in a British uniform,' I admitted. Within seconds, I realised how naïve I must have sounded.

'No. This is a British military base. You only end up here if you upset the Ministry of Defence.'

'I've no idea what they think I've done,' I said. 'But I'm sure as soon as I see someone in authority, they'll realise their mistake and arrange transport home for me.'

'Wish I had your confidence in the system, old chap.'

'Why are you here, then?'

'It's all to do with a man named Ward.' I stared blankly at him.

'And who's he?' I asked.

'I'm a relocation specialist,' said Farrier. 'I help wealthy company executives and Whitehall mandarins who've been promoted or switched to a different office.

'The clients we deal with need help finding new accommodation swiftly. I was asked to find a nice place at the start of the year for this fellow Ward – Christopher Neal Ward, to give him his full name. We gave him a 12-month contract on a flat and all was hunky-dory. Then he bolted.'

'What? He just upped sticks?'

'Yes. Really sudden, it was. He'd only been living in the place for a few months and he expected to leave with just two days' notice.'

'Two days' notice? Not two weeks' notice or two months' notice?'

'Just two days' notice. I was livid. I held onto the full deposit, of course.'

'Don't blame you.'

'So he gave me a lot of stick over it. Turns out this chap Ward had a job in the defence industry.' In a flash, I was reminded of our visits to Gus Morley in Shoreditch. I could see some surprising similarities between the tale of Farrier's tenant and Gus Morley.

But I thought it must be a coincidence. Surely every estate agent in the land had a story about tenants skipping off before the end of their contract? He was still talking.

'Well, coming from my background, I was furious at the inconsiderate behaviour of this man. My father was a founder member of a peace organisation and a conscientious objector. Some of his beliefs were passed onto me.

'I kicked up a big stink about this man Ward. I phoned the Evening Standard and some East London newspapers. The MoD obviously didn't like it and squashed the story with statements of denial. Nothing was ever printed. But someone wanted to silence me – and here I am.'

'Were you seized from your home like me?' I asked.

'I was arrested in the street by the police. At the police station, I was led out the back and these guys were waiting for me. They brought me over here and I was introduced to our mutual friend, Sergeant Jarvis.'

'Jarvis, the jolly gaoler,' I remarked.

'Exactly.'

'So what are we going to do?' I wondered.

'I've worked that out already, old chap,' he replied. 'I've got no time for the likes of Jarvis and Stefan Rogers. I'm going to demand to see someone higher up and try to get formally released.'

'And if that fails?'

'I'm going to break out of here somehow. Have you checked out the ventilation shaft?' He pointed to the corner of the room where the small rectangular grille was fixed to the ceiling.

'D'you know? I haven't taken much notice of it,' I confessed. We both walked over to examine it.

'No. It looks far too narrow for either of us to climb through,' my cellmate insisted. 'Looks like we'll have to go out through the door – if we're ever to get out of here.'

We watched television for a while. I was uninterested until the BBC News came on at six o'clock. The main story concerned the death of Allegra Maybourne.

The news reader announced: '*Police have revealed today the government scientist found dead in a house in Hampshire had been poisoned.*

'*The woman was named a week ago as mother-of-two Dr Allegra Maybourne, who lived with her husband in Andover and worked for the Ministry of Defence. A medical examination has established a noxious substance was administered to her in the days prior to her death. Further tests are being conducted on the body.*

'*Dr Maybourne was found dead nine days ago in a house in the village of Earlsbridge. Police have today appealed for help in tracing two men who may be able to assist them.*

One is six feet one inch tall, in his early forties, of medium build and with a crewcut hairstyle. A second man is five feet eight inches tall, in his middle thirties, of slim build and with short, brown hair and a beard.'

After watching the news bulletin, I recalled the devastating death of Allegra and, for a while, could not think of anything else except the brief image in my mind of her dying moments.

A feeling of desolation overcame me. The conversation with Farrier had done nothing to raise my spirits. Instead of being trapped in this dank dungeon watching television, I wished I was watching television back in Chasehurst with Anne.

At exactly six thirty, Jarvis arrived with our supper tray and we ate our meals in silence. Afterwards, I didn't care to watch any of the television programmes on offer. Instead, we spent the rest of the evening recounting our life stories.

Farrier, who was forty-five and married with three children, was brought up in Manchester. After university, he had become an estate agent and eventually moved to London with his company. He had once played for a village soccer team and supported Arsenal.

I talked about my upbringing in Kent, my time at university and my teacher-training course, my love of cycling and my teaching career. Before long, ten thirty came round. The lights went off around the camp. We both went to sleep.

It was a warm night. The heat could be stifling in the bunker – especially when the ventilation system broke down. After a few hours, I woke with beads of perspiration on my brow and removed the top blanket.

As I lay awake, recollecting the conversation of the previous evening, a sudden thought occurred to me. Gus Morley's neighbour had used the name Chris in her conversation with Anne when we visited Demerara Place at the end of May. Could Gus Morley have changed his name to Chris Ward? It was highly likely a man faking his death would choose a new name.

So did my cellmate have a connection with my scientist friend just as I did? I was uncertain how I would behave towards him in the morning. Here was a stranger I had only met a few hours before. It appeared he was, like me, in trouble with the powers that be.

But was he a fellow victim or had he been planted in the bunker in a bid to extract information from me? He was pleasant enough, but since my abduction I was loath to place trust in anyone.

As the minutes passed and I began to drift off to sleep, another thought occurred to me. Chris Neal Ward was an anagram of Gus's hero, Charles Darwin.

26

Three days passed. Farrier had coaxed Jarvis into obtaining several back copies of The Times newspaper, along with a pen and sheets of plain paper I'd been denied before.

One of us would spend a few minutes copying out the crossword grid. Then we would compete to see which of us could find the most solutions. With the first puzzle we attempted, he found twenty-six answers, while I only managed twenty-two.

However, I fared better with the second puzzle, scoring twenty-six solutions to his twenty-four. We also watched television and chose fantasy football teams for the next World Cup.

I was experiencing mixed emotions. At times, I was angry and depressed at our continued detention and missed Anne very much. It was clear there would be no Black Forest holiday this summer.

I worried about how the vice-principal would react to my long absence, fearing I might lose my job. The nights were the worst time. I wasn't sleeping very well.

However, on the positive side, Farrier was good company and it felt as though he was doing his best to keep my spirits up.

When Jarvis arrived with our breakfast on Monday, June the twenty-fourth, he bounced into the room with the cheerfulness of a Butlin's Red Coat.

'Mr Shaw, you're a lucky man,' he said with a broad smile, as he placed the breakfast tray on the table. 'One of our majors has decided she wants to have a little chat with you. Press the button by the door as soon as you've had your breakfast and I'll take you over there.'

Fifteen minutes later, Jarvis led me, blinking, out of the bunker and into the outside world for the first time in five days. It was bright outside in contrast to the sweaty, drab conditions inside our room.

He escorted me silently across the grass field to the main tarmacked access road. We then turned left under the watchful eye of two security cameras and headed towards one of the main buildings, a three-storey administration block.

As we walked, I noticed the guardroom, which stood several metres back from the roadway. Several hundred yards behind me was the entrance to the camp with two armed soldiers inspecting vehicles on their arrival.

To my left was an abandoned mechanical digger and a builder's skip filled to the brim with bricks, plaster board and timber and, behind it, three old-fashioned nissen huts lined up in a row.

Directly ahead was a block of garages with jeeps, lorries and armoured vehicles outside. In the distance I spotted a Second World War tank with its description on a plaque in front.

Jarvis, who was now trudging along beside me, remarked: 'We'll soon be there.' As he spoke, I was able to read the name on the building we were approaching – 'Wellington House,' which had probably been built in the nineteen seventies.

We passed through the glass-fronted entrance and climbed the stairs to the first floor. I had plenty of questions for the mysterious major and was full of optimism about meeting someone in authority at last. Undoubtedly, this major was going to apologise as profusely as a churchwarden caught in a vice den.

After walking more than twenty metres down a dimly-lit corridor, Jarvis whispered: 'Here we are! I'll be waiting nearby to take you back. See you shortly!'

He then knocked on the light-brown door and we waited. Almost at once an educated female voice yelled: 'Come in!'

I entered a large room to find a female officer who looked the embodiment of efficiency in a smart khaki service dress jacket and skirt. She was sitting in a black leather chair behind a maple desk clutching a silver pen. The tall, brown-eyed woman with black-framed glasses sprang up, placed the pen down and stretched out her hand to me.

'Mr Shaw,' she said. 'It's good of you to come.'

'I'm not shaking your hand,' I said solemnly 'I only shake hands as a friendly gesture or to show a spirit of peace. Neither applies here.'

'You're agitated. I quite understand. Would you like to sit down?' she asked, indicating a small black, upholstered office chair in front of her desk.

'You've got a lot of questions to answer, whoever you are,' I announced, grudgingly accepting her offer of a seat. 'What the hell am I doing here?'

'All right,' said the officer, who was in her early fifties. 'I know you're angry, but you and your wife have put us in a very awkward situation. Look, I'm Major Thomas – Natalie Thomas. This building is one of the main bases we have for the MoD's Special Surveillance Unit, part of the Intelligence Corps.'

'Where exactly are we?'

'I'm not going to tell you precisely, but we're in Bedfordshire.'

I immediately began wondering whether she was the elusive Nat of whom Allegra Maybourne had spoken. But I said nothing for the time being.

She continued: 'I'm very sorry about the manner in which you were brought here last Wednesday night, but I'm afraid it was absolutely necessary and we're currently out seeking your wife as well.'

'What the hell do you want us for?' I demanded.

'You've been interfering with operations.'

'In what way?'

She scowled at me over her glasses. 'You've been making unfounded allegations. You've really had us running around. You've just got to accept you're mistaken. Chris Ward is not Gus Morley.'

'I beg to differ,' I said.

'Look, thanks to you, you silly fool, foreign agents are beginning to think there's something suspicious about the funeral and think Morley may still be alive. You've put his widow Claudia's life at risk. We've had to give her twenty-four-hour protection in case enemy agents try to kidnap her.'

'Why would they do that?'

'Because they believe Morley may still be alive and that she might lead them to him, of course. We've got you and your wife to thank for that.

'Your loose tongues at the Kent inquest have led our enemy to believe this. Indeed, you've made our job very difficult for several weeks.

'Now I have to ask you an important question. I understand

you and your wife knew exactly where Allegra Maybourne was being kept. How exactly did you know that?'

'I'll answer your question if you answer a question from me first,' I said. 'How can you, a member of the British Army, send vicious thugs into my private home, have me handcuffed and then detain me when you've got no right to do so? I'm a British citizen, for God's sake.'

'I'm afraid all your allegations are unfounded. Cuffs are authorised by the Secretary of State. They are not considered an offensive weapon and even a member of the public could use them if need be.

'Any member of the three Armed Forces policing branches may arrest any individual they have reasonable grounds to believe is committing or has committed an indictable offence. They are allowed to use such force as is reasonable.

'In addition, we can detain individuals, if need be, under special rules introduced by Parliament in the middle of January this year.'

'Never heard of that,' I muttered.

'Well, it's in Hansard,' she sneered.

'Hang on a minute!' I said. 'The middle of January? That's around the time when the Brexit bill was heavily defeated in the House of Commons.'

'That's right. At about that time, extraordinary powers were granted to the MoD, giving us the right in certain cases to detain people like you in the interests of Queen and country. The fact is, Mr Shaw, you and your wife are regarded as a risk to this nation's security.'

'You do realise my wife, relatives and friends have no idea where I am and will start making inquiries,' I said. 'The police will become involved and possibly our Member of Parliament will ask questions in the House.'

'We're prepared for any eventuality. The nation's security interests are paramount.'

'So how long d'you plan to keep me here?'

'As long as necessary. After you've been assessed, you will be formally charged and appear in a closed court. You will be entitled to representation. But I'm afraid you seem to have adopted a rather belligerent attitude towards all this, which isn't going to help your case at all.'

'What d'you bloody expect?' I yelled.

'There's no need to shout. I might be able to make your life a lot easier, in return for a favour.'

'What sort of favour?'

'Well, to start with, you could explain how you knew where to find Allegra Maybourne.'

'It was simple. We found the taxi driver who picked her and the kidnappers up at Andover Station and, based on that information, found their safe house.'

'I don't believe that for a minute. The whole of Hampshire Constabulary were searching for them and you just happened to come across the driver that picked them up? Highly unlikely.'

'Well, it's the truth, whether you like it or not. It was mainly down to my wife.'

'We're actively trying to find her. We've got someone near your house, waiting for her, but she seems to be away.'

'No comment.'

'Look,' she said, removing her glasses and rising from her seat. 'I hope, despite everything, that you've found your accommodation more than adequate and that you'll remain comfortable there.' She moved round the desk and headed towards the door.

'Put it this way,' I replied. 'Don't expect to get five stars on TripAdvisor.' She ignored my flippant remark. Then for some reason I was reminded of Allegra Maybourne's last words again.

'By the way,' I said, standing up. 'Are you sometimes known as Nat?'

'Only by my husband. It's short for Natalie,' she snapped.

'So your work colleagues don't use it as a nickname or code name for you?'

'God dammit! I'm Major Thomas and Natalie to friends. Why are you asking such damn fool questions?'

'It doesn't matter,' I said. 'I wish I hadn't bothered.'

'The trouble with you bloody teachers is you stick your noses into all sorts of things that shouldn't concern you.' She drew back the door.

'Sergeant! Sergeant!' she yelled down the corridor. 'The interview's over!'

*

When I first arrived back in the bunker and Farrier asked about my conversation with Major Thomas, I simply said I was hopeful of an early release and tried to be positive about the experience.

But, in truth, I felt crushed. I had suffered a setback to my hopes of being allowed home and, no matter how I tried, I grew more and more despondent as the week went on. I told myself I was Bob Shaw, the teacher with a lovely wife and home. I would never let a jumped-up soldier see me plunge into the dark abyss of despair.

But, despite my best efforts, Farrier must have noticed I was a different man and, as a result, he seemed to become increasingly sympathetic towards me.

He began sharing his food with me, permitting me greater choice of television programmes and, I suspect, even pretending to be stumped by some of the crossword clues so I could beat him.

I found myself warming to him even more and decided that, if both of us were still incarcerated there the following week, I would confide in him all I knew about Gus and Allegra.

As the days passed, I tried to forget the major's diatribe. But it was impossible. There weren't enough activities in the bunker to distract me.

I was now additionally concerned about Anne. A team was out looking for her. Was she still in Scotland? Had she had any luck with her inquiries there?

Had she returned to Chasehurst, to be met by an agent from the Special Surveillance Unit? Had she been abducted like me? Would she walk through the door of the bunker at any moment?

All these questions occupied my mind. I hoped and prayed she would remain longer in Scotland, for her own good.

Of all the words spoken by the major, the ones that most stuck in my mind were: 'Foreign agents are beginning to think there's something suspicious about the funeral and think Morley may still be alive. You've put his widow Claudia's life at risk…'

Was it possible the whole business with Gus – the faked death and the creation of a new identity - had been engineered by the British secret service to protect his life? And had we put his new life at risk by our actions that summer, believing we were helping Claudia?

The major accused us of posing a security risk. Were we running with the fox when we should have been hunting with the hounds?

On Friday of that week, my spirits had risen slightly because, out of all the Times newspapers Jarvis had brought, we only had one left. By coincidence, we had both triumphed twice - Farrier on Tuesday and Wednesday, and me on Monday and Thursday. So Friday's contest would be the deciding tournament – the crunch match.

We racked our brains for nearly four hours over the clues. When we worked out the final score just before supper time on Friday evening, he had beaten me by just one answer – twenty-three to twenty-two.

'Hey, I'm surprised you didn't get two down,' he laughed. 'I'd have thought that would have been an easy one for you.'

The clue for two down was: Larkin and colleagues tease liars in bar (ten letters). I was annoyed because I had spent more than half an hour trying to figure it out.

'Look. It's simple,' he said. 'It's LIBRARIANS. You simply re-arrange the letters in the phrase "Liars in bar." The poet Philip Larkin was Hull University's chief librarian.

'I'd have thought you would have got that, old chap – seeing as your wife used to be a librarian.' My smile vanished as quickly as a candle in a gust of wind. I glared at him.

'How did you know my wife was a librarian?' I asked.

'You must have mentioned it when we talked about our lives.' The web of deceit Greg Farrier had created for my benefit was slowly unravelling.

'No, I didn't,' I said. 'I make a point of never mentioning that to anyone. She got made redundant, so it's a sore point.'

'Oh,' he said. 'I'm sure you mentioned it. You speak in your sleep sometimes, you know. I was going to tell you. Or maybe you told me and you've forgotten. Anyway, it doesn't matter. It was a good game. A close game, wasn't it?'

Shortly after that, Jarvis arrived with our supper and collected the lunch plates. Nothing more was said about the crosswords and the Larkin clue. But I was now convinced Farrier was not, as I was, an innocent man, unlawfully detained.

He was a spy, a stool pigeon, an informant. He had been briefed in advance about me and sent undercover into the bunker to find out what I knew. As a result, I took a decision never to speak to him again.

On Saturday morning, we were woken by Jarvis for our breakfast at seven thirty, but I maintained my vow of silence towards my untrustworthy cellmate.

He fired several questions at me. Would I like some of his toast? Would I like to wash first? Which television programme would I like to view?

But I remained as mute as a monk in a monastery. He must have realised his plan to wheedle information from me had backfired.

When Jarvis arrived with our lunch at one thirty, Farrier demanded to see Major Thomas. Our gaoler promised to inquire if that was possible. He returned half an hour later to say the major could see him straight away. The sergeant escorted Farrier out and he never returned.

I felt relief he had gone. Although he had at times been good company and lifted my mood during moments of gloom, he had obviously been spying on me – probably on behalf of Major Thomas.

It then occurred to me he might have been secretly recording our conversations. I spent a few minutes inspecting the light, the toilet and shower, the wardrobe and the television in the search for any hidden bug, but as far as I could tell, there was none.

As the days passed, I became engulfed again by a blanket of melancholy. I feared I could face months of detention and was uncertain whether I could cope with being apart from Anne for so long. There was only one solution. I had to escape.

27

I began preparing for my break-out. The first stage of the operation would involve fleeing the bunker. There was only one way out – through the door – and that would involve me tricking Jarvis in some way.

The second stage was to escape from the base altogether. I had a rather devious idea in mind for that. My attention had been drawn to the yellow builder's skip by the nissen huts. If it had not already been removed, it was due for collection soon.

When I had seen it the previous Monday, it was heavily filled and ready to go. If I could hide in that, I could be set on a course for freedom.

My escape bid was timed for just after ten thirty on the evening on Sunday, July the seventh. Skips are rarely removed at weekends and I was gambling it would be collected sometime between Monday the eighth and Friday the twelfth.

However, I realised, I might have to conceal myself there for several days and would need provisions. As from that Saturday morning, a week before the break-out, I vowed to conceal a certain amount of food from every meal. Each portion would be wrapped in small parcels with paper or newspaper.

From the breakfast plate, I retained sausages and baked beans. From the lunch plate, I kept apples, bananas, cheese and tomatoes. From the supper plate, I took tangerines. I pulled threads from the edge of the red and gold curtains to use as ties.

All these small packets were stored beside the shower tray, judged the coolest part of the room.

In the first stage of the operation, Jarvis would have to be immobilised in some way. He would have to be attacked or distracted. In the end, I opted for both strategies.

I had shown promise as a boxer at school. I was confident I could prove a match for him in any fight. I just hoped I wouldn't go too far and kill him. I had grown to hate the man with his ridiculous: 'What can you do?' catchphrase.

But although he deserved a good beating for the way he had connived in my confinement, my approach would have to be measured.

'The last thing I want is a murder or manslaughter charge hanging over me,' I told myself.

I had noticed over a long period that Jarvis nearly always left the cell key in the lock when entering the room at mealtimes. It was attached to a metal ring along with his other keys.

He was too lazy to remove it from the lock, for the short period of time he was inside the room. So I believed, if he was distracted and delayed inside the room, I might be able to sneak out and lock him in.

There was also a risk he might press the button to alert the guardroom. So I knew, at some point, I would have to deactivate the button.

The next few days passed slowly. On one of his visits, Jarvis informed me formally Farrier would not be returning.

'Has he been released?' I asked.

'He's not being detained any more. That's all I can tell you,' said Jarvis.

'It's a shame. I'll miss the company,' I said, feigning disappointment.

'What can you do?' said Jarvis.

I spent the rest of the week wondering where Anne was and what had happened to her. Since Farrier's departure, I felt more isolated and depressed than ever. I could not wait to go.

Finally, Sunday July the seventh dawned. I spent hours trying to watch the television, but found I was unable to concentrate. I kept going over my escape plans in my head. I kept looking impatiently at the clock.

Ten thirty could not come round soon enough. After eating my evening meal and making my last food parcel, I put on the white shirt and grey trousers I had arrived in. I also slipped on a navy blue jumper in case I got cold in the night.

All the food along with four bottles of spring water, saved from my meals, were placed in a pillow-case in the corner next to the door, together with one of the blankets.

Then I reached behind the wash basin pedestal and unscrewed the plastic U-bend. I turned on both basin taps and watched as the water gushed out onto the floor. Now I was ready.

My heart started pounding like a tribal drum. There was no guarantee I would get the better of him. Jarvis was slow, but he had some guile.

Would I succeed in tricking him? What would happen if he caught me while fleeing? Would the waste skip still be in place? What would I do if it was no longer there? I was nervous, but the adrenalin was pumping.

I pressed the button by the door. Then I loosened it by repeatedly twisting it and managed to wrench it away from the two wires it was attached to. Satisfied it could no longer raise the alarm in the guardroom, I placed the button and its holder back in their original position and waited.

Jarvis arrived in a furious temper, muttering.

'I was about to turn in, Mr Shaw,' he complained as he turned the key in the lock. By now the water, had been pouring steadily onto the floor for several minutes. It was swirling round the bed, round the wardrobe, round the table.

'Quickly, quickly!' I yelled. 'The place is flooding.' As expected, Jarvis left the key in the lock as he dashed inside.

'What the hell's been going on here?' he demanded, eyeing the pool of water covering most of the floor. He rushed over to see where the leak was coming from. It was a mystery to him because the gap in the pipework was hidden behind the pedestal.

I seized my opportunity. I grabbed the bedside cabinet – which I had emptied of soap, shampoo and toothpaste – and struck him as hard as I could on the back of his head.

How good that moment felt. It allowed me a partial release from some of the pent-up anger and frustration I felt towards him. But now I had to act swiftly.

As he lay partly concussed and moaning in pain on the flooded floor, I grabbed my items and darted through the door. After locking it behind me, I snatched the keys and sprinted up the steps.

Through the open doorway, the black expanse of the warm Bedfordshire night swept before me, studded with twinkling stars and laden with fears and uncertainty.

'Thank God it's still there!' I whispered to myself as I spotted the iron skip and raced towards it. Luckily there were no cameras or lights trained on it.

It was what builders call an eight-yard bin, measuring twelve feet by six feet. For the first time, I noticed the words "Choice Skips" on the side in faded white lettering.

After hurling Jarvis's keys into the front of the metal container, I ran round the back and searched for a suitable place to conceal myself.

Knowing I had to act quickly, I reached beneath some boarding and saw a cavity in the corner. But the skip was more than three-quarters full. Would I have the strength to lift the timber out of the way so that I could squeeze in?

After spending several minutes shifting some of the boards aside, I lowered the food, water and blanket into this empty space. Then I hoisted my left leg over the end of the skip, where the edge is lower, and hauled myself in.

I discovered it had been raining a day or so earlier. There were small pools of water at the base of the skip, but I managed to avoid them. I arranged the blanket beneath me and made myself as comfortable as I could.

It was dirty, dusty and smelled of bitumen, but I felt safe. I used metre-long lengths of wood as supports to prop up the boards and enlarge my space. I was just in time. Within seconds, a man's voice could be heard bellowing from the guardroom: 'Where's Jarvis?'

Then a woman's voice called out: 'He was going to the bunker. He said he'd only be a couple of minutes.' Another voice chimed in with : 'His mobile's here.'

It was astonishing the guard's absence had been missed already, but I felt safe for the moment in my new home. The voices stopped. I heard footsteps running past the skip and heading in the direction of the bunker.

Then the voices began again. I gathered they had found Jarvis was locked in and his keys were missing. A replacement key to the bunker cell was being sought.

I had no precise way of knowing the time, but after about five minutes, I thought I heard Jarvis's muffled shouts. He had obviously recovered quickly. The bunker's walls were as thick as those of a medieval castle, so he could well have been screaming the place down.

His voice became louder. He must have been released. He was shouting furiously: 'Search the whole damn base! He can't have gone far, the bastard!'

For what seemed an hour or more, soldiers and staff roamed around, searching for me. The worst moment came when, about half an hour after I entered my hiding place, a couple of soldiers approached it.

They made a half-hearted attempt to search through the demolition waste, removing some of the lighter timber and shining torches through the remainder.

I was petrified they would find me. I sat motionless on the blanket, my back resting on the rigid metal sidewall, my heart in my mouth.

For a few seconds, as the sound of meaningless words above drifted into my consciousness, I sensed the top board was being raised. I held my breath. I thought of Anne, of Fiesta, of the roses in our front garden. I heard the board snap back into place. Then silence. Whoever had lifted it had gone. I was safe – for the time being.

My body was tired. I rearranged the blanket so that part of it shielded me from the cool night air. Yet, for the next few hours,

I was unable to sleep. I felt tense and feared being recaptured at any moment. I dipped into the pillowcase and easily found an apple. I gnawed at it gratefully before reaching for some spring water, which I gulped down enthusiastically.

So far I had been lucky. But would my luck hold? And for how long would I be trapped in my den, waiting for the roar of the lorry that would signal the beginning of my journey back to liberty? After a few hours, exhausted, I slipped into an uneasy slumber.

*

My first full day inside the skip passed uneventfully. I ate two of the sausages and the baked beans in the morning and later enjoyed an apple and banana. I sipped some water, which I was trying to use sparingly.

My body was in a cramped position, contorted against the unyielding metal. I continually had to shift position to avoid hurting my back.

But I was far happier here than in the bunker. Here I was my own master, beholden to no one. It felt good to be out of that dispiriting place below ground. Here, though I dared not raise my head, I could see the sun flickering through gaps in the boards and breathe in fresh rural air.

Occasionally, voices would be heard, suggesting the search for me was being maintained. From disjointed overheard conversations, I learned they had searched most of the buildings and vehicles on the site and spoken at length to the sentries.

Patrols had been out, scouring the countryside in case, by some miracle, I had managed to scale the security fence unnoticed and fled. Every time a lorry drove up or down the nearby approach road, a wave of excitement would sweep over me – only to dissipate moments later as I realised it was not the skip lorry.

I had plenty of time to mull over the events of the previous weeks as I sat awkwardly in my metal hiding place, longing for the welcoming sound of the skip lorry's engine.

I thought about Greg Farrier. How much of what he told me was true, I wondered? Had he been trained in psychological techniques designed to weaken me and make me talk? It was clear now I was being held by the British, not the Russians.

But I doubted whether he was a relocation expert who had been abducted from the street. I was beginning to doubt whether Gus Morley had adopted the name Chris Ward.

I thought of Anne. It was unlikely anyone at the base had cared to reassure her I was alive. They were hunting her, for God's sake. If they did succeed in making contact with her, they might lure her to Bedfordshire on the pretext I was here and was requesting that she join me.

My captors were ruthless. They had displayed no compassion towards me. They were unlikely to show any towards her.

I suffered one small calamity. Without realising it, a corner of the blanket had become smeared in some black liquid – paint or bitumen. It spread to my trousers before I knew it.

How long could I remain in this place, I asked myself. I was confident I could sustain myself for five or six days, but what if the lorry failed to show? Could I survive two or three weeks?

I thought it wise to consider an alternative plan of escape. One option might be to sneak out of the skip at night and see if I could hide beneath one of the vehicles due to drive out the following day.

If a stowaway could cling beneath a motor-home for an hour, I was sure I could attempt a similar stunt for a short while, giving myself enough time at least to leave the base and travel a few miles.

A second option might be to scale the fence at night, I thought. As a schoolboy, I once climbed a high wall to sneak into a farmer's orchard and get some apples.

The metal fences were between twelve and fifteen feet high and topped with coiled razor wire, but if I brought the blanket with me, I could place it over the razor wire and then drop down the other side. It was probably the better of the two options.

That Monday night I slept more soundly, but I became aware of an impending crisis a few hours after dawn. I realised I had been drinking more water than I realised. There was only one bottle left. This meant I was unlikely to be able to remain in the skip for much longer.

As it was summer, I would become weak if I had no water over a period of days and be unable to either cling to a vehicle or climb over the fence. The situation was becoming desperate.

Then, unexpectedly, late on the Tuesday afternoon, came another drama. A team of squaddies approached the skip under orders to search it for a second time. On this occasion, according to the words of one of the men, they were required to delve around more rigorously.

I tried to slip further down beneath the timbers, making as little noise as I could. With bated breath, I listened out as they took turns to rummage among the waste.

A male voice moaned: 'What's the point of all this? He was out Sunday night. How could he be under all this junk without anything to eat or drink?' Then seconds later my heart pounded as a female soldier cried out: 'What's this?'

My time had come, I thought. At any moment, I would be seen, skulking in the corner like a nervous dog.

'It's someone's old shirt!' said a colleague amid laughter. 'Put it down. It's covered in plaster dust. It's nothing to do with Bob Shaw.' His words left me feeling intense relief.

'Where else are we searching?' the woman asked.

'We've got to check the huts again,' came the reply. 'Then the sergeant wants us to make up a bed in the underground storeroom. They've got a woman coming later.' The voices ceased. The sound of fading footsteps told of their departure. The search had ended as swiftly as it had begun.

But their remarks had brought fresh concern now for Anne. Perhaps she was the woman the two soldiers had referred to. Perhaps she had fallen into their clutches. In a matter of seconds, I was faced by this new fear – that my wife could be locked in the bunker.

Instead of the next morning bringing a dawn of fresh hope, perhaps it might herald a new cycle of despair.

28

I was roused from my sleep on Wednesday morning by the sound of a lorry rumbling past the sentry at the gate and up the approach road.

Judging by the amount of daylight streaming into the skip, I estimated it was somewhere between eight and nine am. I fully expected it to pass along the road towards the centre of the compound, but the roar of its engine grew louder until the vehicle stopped directly beside the container.

A wave of excitement swept over me. Was this the skip lorry? Was I about to be hoisted into the air and borne away?

The driver's feet thumped to the ground. The engine remained running. I heard a rustling sound. Darkness spread across my private corner. He was lashing a blue tarpaulin over the skip.

Moments later, as the engine continued to hum, I heard a clanking sound. He was obviously hooking up the lorry's chains to the lugs on the skip. My dream was coming true!

Within seconds, he must have pressed a lever because, slowly and jerkily, my golden chariot climbed into the air as the engine noise rose to a crescendo.

The panels and planks shook and shifted as the skip swayed from side to side like a ship in a storm. I felt a shudder as the vessel landed on the bed of the lorry – and then we were away.

I heaved a sigh of relief as I heard the driver shout his thanks to the sentry while we trundled past. We swept through the gates and began following the steady road out of the base.

One of the boards was now pressing hard upon me, but, for now, I dared not try to rearrange them nor raise my head above the metal sides.

I feared discovery by the driver. He might have been warned to look out for me, and, if he spotted me nestling among the waste, he might drive me straight back. But the further away we travelled, the more confident I became.

After five minutes of me being rocked about, the lorry slowed and I gathered we might be approaching a junction. I reached above me and carefully untied a knot in one of the cords that secured the tarpaulin.

Then I peered through a gap in the material and realised we were turning onto a major road. It was wonderful to see the blue sky and the sun's rays glinting down as we left the military camp miles behind us.

We were now travelling northwards along a country road with thick woods on the left – mainly pine trees – and open fields on the right. According to the road signs, we were heading for Bedford.

I managed to make a larger gap in the tarpaulin as we passed through two villages and a new housing development. We were on the fringes of the county town.

My mind told me to wait until we reached some traffic lights and then jump off. My remaining fruit, still in the pillowcase, would be coming with me. It looked as though we were nearing a fast-flowing bypass, which swept beneath our road at a roundabout ahead. I could see a traffic control just before the intersection.

I grabbed the pillowcase and hauled myself over the edge of the skip as nimbly as I could. Fortunately, the lights turned red and the driver braked sharply. I dropped down clumsily onto the tarmac, hurting my left foot slightly as I did so.

A driver in a blue mini who drew up behind was no doubt shocked to see me. Here was an unshaven, dishevelled man in a grubby pullover and black-stained trousers stumbling about in shoes without laces.

For all he knew, I was a tramp or itinerant worker who had scrounged a ride. And, just like a tramp, I had no money. My stamps, comb, coins, tie and laces were in the guardroom. My wallet, watch, keys and diary were in Kent. But what did that matter? I was free.

As the lorry driver continued on his way, I walked back down the road a few yards until I reached a turning on the left which led to a village signposted 'Bellington.'

On entering the lane, I passed some bushes. My presence must have disturbed a wild bird. It took me by surprise, tearing out of the thicket and squawking as it soared into the sky. Next to the bushes stood three houses which faced open fields on the opposite side of the road.

At the first two doors, when I asked to use a phone, I was turned away brusquely. But I had more luck at the third house, a white farmworker's cottage with yellow jasmine curling round the front porch.

After passing pristine yellow roses and pink clematis blooms in an immaculate garden, I noticed a middle-aged woman holding a small kitchen mop. She was peering at me through the glazed door, no doubt shocked by my demeanour.

'What d'you want?' she asked.

'I'm awfully sorry,' I began, dropping the pillow-case on the stone path. 'Could I just use a phone?' She was hard of hearing and had to open the main door to hear me.

'What d'you say?'

'I'm really sorry to trouble you, but I need to make a phone call. It's an emergency.' The woman, who was slim, about five feet four inches tall and with grey hair tied behind her head, had a kind face.

Perhaps she felt moved by my bedraggled look. Perhaps she could see in me a similarly kind, well-intentioned soul with an educated voice. But as I stood on her path, breathing in the delicate fragrance of the jasmine, she hesitated.

She said: 'I can bring my phone out to you, but I can't let you inside. We've got the builders in.'

She disappeared into the house, leaving the first door ajar but closing the internal door behind her. There were no builders' vans parked in the road or on the driveway beside the cottage.

She was obviously wary of strangers calling in her tranquil country lane. But I was jubilant that she was offering to help me.

Moments later, she returned to the porch without the mop and clutching her phone, which she handed to me.

'I'll be quick,' I pledged as she stood in the porch, watching. 'I just need to call my wife.' I dialled Anne's mobile number and waited. I yearned to speak to her, to hear her tender words.

'Please don't go to voicemail,' I murmured to myself. Then, suddenly, Anne's voice, her calm, caring voice, broke the silence of the country garden.

'Bob! Where on earth have you been?' she cried. 'Are you all right?'

'Yes, I'm all right. But how are you?'

'Don't worry about me. I'm fine. But where the hell have you been?'

'I can't talk. I'm using someone's phone, but I'm in Bedfordshire,' I said, fearing that, if I mentioned the Army camp, there was a chance the woman in the porch might want to alert them.

'Bob!' continued Anne. 'I've been at my wits' end. The police have been searching for you. We thought you were dead!'

'Well, I'm not dead, but I've had a rough time. I was abducted. Listen, Anne, you've not been home, have you?'

'No, I'm staying with Prunella. It's a long story.'

'Thank God for that. The kidnappers are out looking for you as well.'

'I know.'

'You know?'

'Yes. Where are you now?'

'I'm in a country lane just south of Bedford,' I said. Anne began crying down the phone. Tears of relief, I thought. The figure in the porch, who was listening to the conversation, gave me an anxious look like a mother learning her child is ill.

'You're in Bellington, three miles from Bedford,' the woman interjected. I nodded towards her and gave a brief gesture of thanks with a wave of my right hand.

'There's no need to cry, Anne,' I continued. 'I'm all right now.'

'We really thought you might be dead,' she sobbed. 'I thought I'd never see you again.'

'I can't wait to see you. I've missed you so much,' I said,

glancing towards the porch. 'Look, I'm at a place called Bellington. Any chance of you coming to pick me up? I know it's a long way. Hold on a minute, darling.' I turned to the woman.

'D'you know what this lane's called?'

'It's Bellington Lane,' she said. I repeated the road name for Anne's benefit.

'Pru and I will be with you as quickly as we can,' Anne assured me.

'OK. See you when you get here. Love you!'

'Love you too!' she said as I ended the call.

'You poor thing!' said the woman, as I handed her phone back to her. 'Sounds like you've had an awful time. D'you want to call the police?'

'That's very kind of you,' I said. 'But I'll be all right.'

'But you were saying you'd been abducted?'

'It's all right. The police in Kent have been searching for me. I'm sure they'll sort everything out.'

'In Kent? How long has it been – that you've been away?'

'I think it's about three weeks,' I said.

'Good God! I'm Valerie, by the way – Valerie Richards.' I shook her hand.

'Bob Shaw. I'm pleased to meet you and thank you very much for the use of your phone. By the way, what time is it?'

'Let me see, ' she said, peering at her watch. 'It's a quarter to ten.' Then she added: 'I'm just thinking. You've got a bit of a wait. Would you like a cup of tea and a little breakfast?'

'If that's not too much trouble. That's very kind. I must admit, I'm starving.'

'Not a bit. I can't ask you inside because, well… you know.'

'That's fine. I understand.'

'But if you'd like to come round the back, you can sit by the kitchen door.'

'That's terrific. Thank you!'

Picking up my food bundle, I followed her directions down the winding path along the side of the house, where there was a garage and a workshop. I passed an array of mauve asters and nodding blue clematis flowers.

Valerie found me a comfortable canvas chair on a corner of the back lawn, close to the kitchen door. The chair was so comfortable after the metal skip I was concerned I might nod off.

Ten minutes later, she brought me a plate of egg and bacon, along with two slices of hot buttered toast and a cup of tea. She placed them on a metal garden table which she dragged in front of me. It was the best breakfast I had ever tasted.

Within a short time, Valerie and I were chatting in her garden as if we had known each other for years.

As my eyes wandered occasionally across the lawn towards the apple and pear trees behind, I discovered she and her husband had lived there for the whole of their married life. He worked on a nearby farm. All their children had grown up and left home.

'So you've never had children of your own, Mr Shaw?' she asked.

'Not yet,' I replied. 'But there's still time. My wife's in her mid-thirties.' After more than an hour, Valerie returned to the subject that had brought me to her cottage - my abduction, which to me represented a dangerous territory over which I feared to tread.

'So these men who grabbed you – d'you know who they are?' she wondered.

'Oh yes,' I said. 'I know quite a lot about them.'

'And what sort of accommodation was it they kept you in? Was it a house round here?'

'I don't really want to talk about it, Valerie, if that's all right. I'm trying to put it out of my mind. It's been a terrible experience.'

'But you say they stormed into your house in Kent and brought you to Bedfordshire? It sounds extraordinary. How could they keep you prisoner for three weeks? It's just iniquitous.

'Something should be done about it. My brother may call in later. If he does, I'll talk to him about it. He might be able to offer you some advice.'

'Well, as I say, the police know all about it. They'll no doubt want to take a statement from me. I'm sure they'll have it all in hand.'

'But it might be really helpful if you speak to my brother. He works at the Army base down the road here in Hardwick.' I did my best to hide my concern at the perilous turn the conversation was taking.

'You're very kind,' I said. 'But, as I say, the police are on the case and probably wouldn't want me to discuss it with any other organisation such as the Army.' I feigned a laugh.

'I probably shouldn't even be talking to you about it!' I said.

Valerie made me a second cup of tea. She suggested I should stay in her garden to await the arrival of Anne and Prunella.

However, I was becoming reluctant to stay, concerned her brother might arrive at any time and recognise me as a fugitive. It crossed my mind Valerie's maiden name could have been

Jarvis. But, after she assured me the brother, William, only usually visited her at lunchtime, which was more than two hours away, I agreed to remain a little longer.

Valerie spoke about how she came to meet her husband. The time passed slowly. I was so eager to see Anne.

Eventually, my hostess noticed a plant that needed urgent pruning. She moved away to tend it, giving me the opportunity to glance into the kitchen through a side window. A clock on the wall gave the time as nearly twelve o'clock.

'Valerie!' I said, standing up. 'You've been so kind, but I really think I ought to be going.'

'But your wife isn't here yet,' she replied, turning towards me from the far side of the lawn.

'I know, but I mustn't overstay my welcome. You've been most kind, but she'll be expecting me to meet her out in the lane, so if it's all right with you...'

'Would you like a carrier bag to put your things in?' she asked, pointing to the pillowcase beside my feet.

'If you've got one,' I said.

'I'll just see.'

She disappeared into the kitchen. Moments later, she was back, but without any bag.

'You're in luck. Bill's just called round for a cuppa.' My heart sank as a slim, amiable man who was about five feet eight inches tall and with receding, dark-brown hair emerged from the back door.

'Bill, I want you to meet my new friend, Bob Shaw,' Valerie said. 'He's such a nice man – a teacher, but he's had the most terrible experience.'

'Oh, what's that then, mate?' he asked me. He lacked the

kind, educated voice of his sister.

'I was abducted,' I said. 'Oh, it was just a misunderstanding. The police know all about it.' He nodded as if he understood.

'Bill works in the barracks canteen,' the sister explained. 'It isn't the greatest job in the world, is it, Bill? But there isn't much employment round here, is there?'

Her brother nodded. 'It pays the wages,' he muttered. I was on tenterhooks. Surely, if he worked at the camp, he would know there was a prisoner at large? He looked at me in a puzzled way but said nothing. He touched his cheek with his fingers as his brain clicked into gear.

'So where were you held then?' he asked. Just as he spoke those words, I happened to glance along the path at the side of the cottage and spotted a blue car glide by. It was our Mondeo.

Without a word, I raced through the front garden and into the road. Anne and Prunella had gone twenty metres past the house, heading towards the village.

I ran out, waving my arms wildly above my head. Anne, who was driving, must have seen me in the wing mirror. She reversed back along the lane, stalling the engine as she reached the open driveway to the cottage.

She dashed from the car crying: 'Bob! Bob!' and rushed towards me, throwing her arms around me and kissing me as I stood in the middle of the road.

It was only after a few minutes, as we stood caressing each other, that I noticed Prunella had meanwhile introduced herself to Valerie and William. They were huddled together chatting by the front porch and smiling at us like proud parents at a school prize day.

'I thought he was dead,' Anne cried. She fondled my

face, which had a rugged, manly look after three days without shaving.

'You're a bit prickly, Mr Shaw,' she whispered.

'I just need to get back to Kent,' I whispered back.

'I think she's pleased to see him!' murmured Prunella. 'Come
on, you two! We've got a long journey. Nice to have met you!'

Prunella patted me on the back and I kissed her on the cheek.

'I'm glad you're all right, Bob, but it looks like you could do
with freshening up!' said Prunella with a laugh. She was right.
They were looking delectable – Anne in a blue, floral top and
jeans and her friend in a turquoise summer dress.

'That's true,' I admitted. 'But let's go! Thanks for
everything, Valerie.'

Bill and his sister had found a plastic carrier bag and had
placed the pillow-case and its contents inside. She came out
into the road and handed it to me, smiling.

'Have a safe journey home!' she cried.

'Thanks for taking care of him!' said Anne, getting behind
the wheel. I slipped into the front passenger seat and Prunella
got in the back. Then I reached across and kissed Anne again.

'I've missed you so much,' I said.

As she turned the car round in the lane, I gazed at the wild
roses which were entwined in the hedgerows opposite the
cottage. Their slender stems rambled without fear or limit
around the sharp-tipped hawthorn sprigs.

Their dainty white flowers seemed to dance in the breeze
around the straggly bushes, impishly shaking their delicate heads. Free, independent spirits flourishing in the
open countryside.

29

'So what on earth happened to you?' asked Anne as she drove us onto the Bedford southern bypass and we headed west towards the M1 motorway.

'It all started when I visited that Russian shop,' I said from my seat beside her. 'I asked the assistant if she remembered two men ordering takeaway soup in May. Next thing two of her customers were chasing after me in a black Audi.'

'I warned you not to go there,' Anne murmured.

'I know. They chased me for miles round the North Circular.' I glanced over my right shoulder at Prunella, who was leaning forward on her seat like an excited child.

'Prunella, I hope you haven't got your notebook out,' I declared. 'I don't want this splashed all over the Sunday News – not yet, anyway.'

'My pen's in my handbag,' said our friend.

'The bastards took pot-shots at me.'

Anne looked horrified. 'What?'

'Didn't you notice the bullet holes in our boot-lid and bumper?' I asked.

Anne shook her head. 'No.'

'I was lucky. The cops broke up the party in the nick of time.'

'So how come you ended up here?'

'Well, when I got home, I thought the guys in the black Audi might come looking for me. I'd only been back an hour when three men knocked on the door.

'But it turned out they were not Russian – they were British. They attacked me in the hall, blindfolded me and brought me to the Army base up here I've just escaped from.'

'I'm not surprised they were British,' said Anne. 'When I got back from Scotland, Mrs Morrison next door said men in a black car had been spending a lot of time outside our place. She's smart, you know. She took the registration number. Graham Kirwan at least confirmed it was an MoD vehicle, despite the last two letters being indistinct.

'We also checked our home cameras. Although the wire'd been cut, one camera had shots of some men in dark clothing as they arrived outside. I wasn't too worried about you, once we realised they were British.'

'Oh, you weren't worried? You've no idea what I've been through.'

'I didn't mean it like that. It's just that, well, you know. I was just slightly relieved, thinking that at least you wouldn't be poisoned or something.'

'So Graham suggested you stay away from Fairview?'

'Yes. Prunella very kindly agreed I could stay with her till all this blows over.'

'It's all right, Bob,' said Prunella, leaning forward and tapping me on my shoulder. 'You're both welcome to stay for as long as you like.'

'I could do with a shower.'

'Of course,' she replied. 'I've got a shower and a bath.'

'That's good.'

'Pru's got a two-bed flat,' Anne explained. 'It's great for the time being, but we can't stay there for ever.'

'What about Fiesta?' I asked.

'Mrs Morrison has kindly agreed to feed him round at her place. He's in his element, having the run of two gardens.'

'That's very good of her,' I said. 'Have the school been in touch?'

'Yes, that Mrs Robinson. She was very off-hand to start with. Then, when I explained the police were involved and you were missing, she became very supportive. They're getting a supply teacher in.'

'What sort of efforts have the police made to find me?' I asked.

'They've phoned all our relatives and friends,' Prunella explained. 'They've alerted other forces, and you've been in some of the local papers.'

'Police said they were concerned for your welfare,' said Anne.

'That's nice of them,' I remarked.

'They said you were thirty-seven, five feet ten and slightly balding with brown hair,' Prunella recalled.

'I'm thirty-six and my hair's fine,' I replied. 'We'll have to tell the police I'm no longer missing. I can't wait to report to Graham what those bastards in Bedfordshire did to me. Anyway, darling, what happened to you in Scotland?'

'I'll tell you later because we don't want to bore Pru.'

'By the way, Prunella,' I said, turning my head to the right. 'You were having a long chat with those people back in Bellington.'

'Yes,' she admitted. 'You'll laugh when I tell you this.'

Anne interrupted. 'Hold tight! We're just joining the M1,'

she said. Prunella went on: 'You had a pillow-case or something with you?'

'Yes. I've got it here. Look.'

'The woman's brother saw the label said: "MoD Hardwick."' I frowned.

'I knew I shouldn't have stayed there so long,' I remarked. 'He worked at the camp. He could have phoned his employers and they could've had me back behind bars in a heartbeat.'

'No. He didn't link you to being at the camp. He said: "Loads of people round here have got something from the barracks in their linen drawer.' He'd somehow accepted the idea you'd been holed up in a private house.'

After more than two hours, we arrived at Prunella's waterside flat at three-storey Britannia Wharf in the heart of Faversham.

Thanks partly to her parents' generosity, she owned an impressive apartment in the historic market town where around five hundred period buildings – including many Georgian properties – mingle with Victorian terraces and new-builds.

Her converted first-floor flat consisted of a large lounge with balcony views across the creek and two medium-sized bedrooms. There was garage parking for Prunella's Porsche and an outdoor parking space behind high walls for the Mondeo.

As she showed me our room, I was as delighted as a dog with a fillet steak.

'You've done well here, Prunella,' I said. Then, through the bedroom doorway, I noticed hanging on a hook in the hallway a man's grey jacket which appeared familiar to me.

'Isn't that Tristan's?' I said.

'Yes,' she replied. 'He forgot it last time he was here.'

'Oh, so Tristan's been here?' I said, thinking out loud.

'Yes. Oh, Bob. He's such a wonderful guy. He was going to be moving in here with me until I got the call from Anne.'

'Oh well, I'm glad for you both.'

'Thanks, Bob. It's all because of you we got together. I'll never forget that.'

Later, while she went to a supermarket, I had a shower and got into some fresh clothes that Anne had brought over from the cottage.

Then, while Prunella was still out, she led me to our bedroom and we made love for the first time in more than three weeks.

As I lay in my dear wife's arms, I at last felt secure from that dungeon where I had been held. I was so relieved to be back in the warm, tender arms of the woman I loved and who loved me.

We afterwards sat cuddling on Prunella's comfortable beige corner unit and I told Anne about the bunker, Ivan Jarvis, Greg Farrier, Stefan Rogers and Major Natalie Thomas. I explained how I had hidden in the skip and escaped through the gates by lorry. After ten minutes, she interrupted.

'While you've been lounging around with the Army, I've finally found whose body it was in the car crash at Turner's Hatch,' she announced.

'You have? That's brilliant. Well done!'

'It was a lot of hard work and I'm not sure it's something I want to boast about. I've added to the grief of a heartbroken Scottish widow.'

'So what did you find out?' I asked.

'I sneaked into that funeral parlour in Edinburgh late at night,' she explained.

'You did what?'

'D'you remember there was a suspicious raid at undertakers on the western side of Edinburgh? Well, I called round first in the day-time.

'They appeared extremely helpful when I called at reception. I said I'd read about the break-in and the woman chatted away freely. She said the event was shrouded in mystery because nothing had been taken, as far as they could tell.

'But when I began asking about whose funerals they had conducted in the last days of January, she suddenly changed and became guarded.'

'I suppose they, of all people, have to be discreet,' I suggested.

'I suppose so. Anyway, while I was there, I noticed hand-written lists on the wall. It looked like funeral bookings. That night, at about eleven o'clock, I called by to see if the place was open or whether I'd have to break in. Luckily, the doors were unlocked.'

'Someone was probably out the back, embalming someone,' I remarked.

'Yes. I was amazed how lax they were six months after a break-in. Anyway I crept inside and, sure enough, each sheet of paper on the wall related to a week's funerals and the sizes of coffins required.

'I found the one for the week beginning January the twenty-seventh and looked for large coffin orders. There were three. One related to a funeral booked for the end of the week – after the car crash, so that could be ruled out.

'So I took details of the other two funerals and caught a bus back to the guesthouse. I spent the next day calling on the widow of the first of the two men, but from the start I knew it was the wrong family.' I shrugged.

'No tattoos?'

'That's right,' she said. 'I was starting to despair, but I had one last person to call on – a woman called Laura McClintock, who lives above a shop in Hopetoun Road, South Queensferry.

'I spoke very sympathetically to her, saying I believed I might have some information about her husband. Could I come in? Well, when she showed me his photograph sitting on a holiday beach, I knew it was the right family.'

'Covered in tattoos?'

'None on his head, but all over his neck, hands, arms and legs. And at least six feet three inches tall.'

'Amazing!' I said.

'Yes. She invited me in and made me tea.'

' What was she like, this Laura McClintock?'

'White hair, big glasses, slightly overweight, about fifty. Quite a sweet, charming woman.'

'What was her place like?'

'Pretty basic. Just a few rooms above a betting shop. She invited me in and I straight away saw this photograph on a sideboard of her and her husband.

'He was a tanned, smiling giant of a man with a gold medallion round his neck who towered over her. He had short, grey hair, rough hands and was bare-chested with black and white checked shorts.

'His right arm was round the shoulders of his wife, who looked demure in a salmon pink floral summer dress. She told me it was taken ten years ago when they were still able to hold a conversation without it turning into a slanging match.'

'She must have been pretty mystified to find you asking questions about her dead husband,' I observed. 'What was his name?'

'Tam. He was actually known as Big Tam. He used to call her "ma bonnie wee doll." I think she might have been lonely because she was happy to talk about it.'

I frowned. 'But who did she think you were, a woman interrogating a stranger?'

'I made sure I fired all the questions in quick succession, fearing she'd clam up when she realised why I was really there. She confirmed he was a patriotic Scot, a heavy drinker and had several tattoos related to his hometown, South Queensferry.

'Then I said: "I'm really sorry, but I think your husband's body may have been snatched from the undertakers the day before his funeral on January the thirtieth."

'Well, you can imagine how shocked and angry she became. Perhaps she thought I was a crank. She demanded to know precisely who I was, so I told the whole story. I explained MI5 were the most likely culprits and probably weighed the coffin down with something because the weight had to feel correct for the pallbearers.'

'D'you remember Burke and Hare?' I asked. 'They snatched and sold bodies in Edinburgh nearly two hundred years ago.' She nodded as if she was aware of that.

'Bob, it was a very distressing experience for both of us,' she continued. 'She was truly shocked when I described the tattoos and showed her the photographs.

'She was staggered when I asked if he wore size twelve trainers with blue socks. She couldn't speak for a moment. She simply nodded.'

'You took the photos along with you?'

'Yes. They were the only tangible objects I could bring to

demonstrate I had real knowledge of the body found at Turner's Hatch. She confirmed they were Tam's tattoos.'

'So how did it end?'

'She was in tears, as you can imagine, but she thanked me for coming. She said she realised I was not getting paid and that I'd done this off my own bat. She said she would contact a lawyer.

'I explained I couldn't leave the photographs with her. They belonged to the police, but she said her advocate would want to contact us and probably apply to the police for copies.

'She's also going to speak to the church minister who conducted the funeral – which was held the day after the break-in. So I gave her our address. She was astonished when she realised I was from Kent.'

I nodded. 'I bet she was,' I said. 'Did you find out anything more about her late husband?'

'He fathered two children with her. Then he lost his job and gradually went off the rails. He became an alcoholic and, in the end, she had to throw him out.

'He mainly lived on the streets, although she sometimes let him back for a night. He was found ill in some woods in early January with a bottle of whisky beside him. He was taken to hospital, where he died.

'Natural causes, the death certificate said. When I got up to go, she became upset again. She said she'd thought Tam had been safely laid to rest and her children had been going up to the cemetery to lay flowers. She kept saying: "All the time he wasn't there."'

'What I can't fathom is why MI5 took a body more than four hundred miles from Scotland to a remote hill in Kent? Surely there are funeral parlours in Kent where they could have got a body?'

Anne glanced at my face. 'Too risky,' she said. 'Someone might have guessed a connection. Scotland is so far away no one is likely to make the link.'

'But why this particular man, d'you think?' I asked.

'They may have simply picked him from the newspaper,' said Anne. 'Laura showed me an obituary in the evening paper which paid tribute to Tam. The paper revealed he was six feet three inches tall. Or they may have made inquiries about deaths among the homeless.'

'And what about the Forth Road Bridge?' I asked. 'Why did he have that tattooed on his leg?'

'He was born a hundred metres from the bridge on the day it was officially opened, September the fourth, 1964.'

30

Anne put the kettle on and, a few minutes later, brought two steaming cups of tea into the living-room.

'I've got a lot more to tell you,' she said. 'I've found out where Gus is living.' I gave her an admiring glance.

'You've definitely been busy,' I observed.

'D'you remember that little woman in the flat next door to Gus's at Demerara Court?' she asked, sitting down beside me on the corner unit.

'Vaguely.'

'She recalled the name of the removal firm as being Henderson's or Harrison's and said the removals had been made in a yellow Luton van with an orange stripe.

'Well, I phoned all the removal firms that come under the letter H in East London and Essex and eventually discovered there was a company near Brentwood in Essex with vans like that. They're called Henson's.'

'Must be the one,' I said, stirring my tea and taking a sip.

'Yes, well, I called them and gave them a yarn about being Gus's cousin and needing to reach him urgently. I was put through to the boss and explained I'd lost his address. They were my last hope in making contact with him.

'I gave them lots of personal information which I thought

would clinch it for me, but in the end he declined. He said it was a government job and he'd been told no information was to be revealed to anyone.'

'That's a bloody nuisance.'

'Yes, but I didn't give up. I then remembered Ryan Benjamin, Gus's minder, the former bare knuckle fighter.'

'I remember him too. He left the shape of his toecap on parts of my body so I wouldn't forget him.'

'Gus's neighbour mentioned him working out at the Verve Fitness Club in Hoxton, so I bought a GPS tracking device online with a view to fixing it to his car.

'Of course, I didn't know whether or not he even had a vehicle. I waited in the street outside the club for a couple of nights and he didn't show. Then, on the third night, at about six thirty, a dark-blue BMW pulled into the entrance and I recognised him immediately.'

'He's not hard to spot.'

'No. He's a mountain of a man with spiky black hair and gold rings on one of his hands. I waited for ten minutes or so – just in case he came back to the car for anything – and then I picked up a tennis ball from the Mondeo.'

'That must be the one I confiscated from a boy who was throwing it against the wall outside the vice-principal's office.'

'Maybe. Anyway, because there were security cameras around, I rolled it along the ground in the direction of Ryan's car.

'My reasoning was that, if anyone viewed the CCTV, they would just see someone retrieving a ball. Then I pulled my hood over my head and ran past the automatic barrier into the car park.

'I fixed the tracker inside the front bumper, picked up the

ball and returned to the car.'

'And did it work? Were you able to trace Gus's new address?'

'Yes. That same evening Ryan drove to a street in Chigwell.'

'Whereabouts is that?'

'It's a town on the London-Essex borders, not far from Epping Forest.'

'What sort of place has he got?'

'I never got round there. I was going to stake the place out this morning, but then you phoned from Bellington Lane.'

'What a clever girl you are!' I said proudly.

'Oh Bob,' she said. 'I haven't told you the worst. At the weekend, I went back to the cottage to collect some clothes and pick up the post. I also found your personal items in the kitchen drawer.

'I didn't see anyone outside as I pulled into the drive, but someone must've been watching the house. As I went upstairs to our wardrobe, I thought I heard someone knocking.

'I went back down and I saw the head of a man who looked like a soldier. You know, he had a military-style haircut. He was peering through the door.'

'Sounds like the Russian man who shot at the car. Go on,' I urged her.

'Well, I shouted: "What d'you want?" He called back: "I'm wanting to talk." I said: "What about?" He said: "I believe you have a message." You can imagine how frightening it was to hear him say that. I thought straight away that maybe he was one of the Russians.

'Here I was, a hundred and twenty miles away from where we found poor Allegra and he was knocking on our door. How the hell did he find us, I thought? Anyway, there was no way

I wanted to open that door. Who knows what would have happened?' I moved next to her and took her hand in mine.

'So what did you do, darling?' I asked.

'I grabbed my handbag and tiptoed out of the back door. I locked it behind me so the house was secure. Then I hightailed it down the garden. You know the rickety fence at the bottom?'

'The one you keep asking me to sort out and I never get round to fixing?'

'Yes, that one,' she said with a nod. 'I managed to scramble over it, all the time looking towards the side of the house in case he saw me. And oh my God, Bob! He did.

'Once I failed to open the door, he must've decided to have a scout round. He raced down the garden after me and clambered over the same fence.

'I ran past Mrs Morrison's garden and dashed into the woods with him behind me. I've never been so scared. I didn't know if he was going to kill me or what.

'I ran deep into the woods for five minutes until I was close to the main road. It was only then I realised he was no longer behind me.'

'Oh darling,' I said. 'I wish I'd been there to protect you. What a horrifying experience!' I gave her a hug.

'I reckon the only thing that saved me was his limp,' she added. 'He couldn't keep up with me.'

'So you didn't go back to the cottage again, obviously.'

'Too right!' she said. 'I decided to manage for a while with the clothes I'd got.'

'I'm so glad you got away. Those Russian guys are big trouble!' I remarked. 'So you've been incredibly busy?'

'A lot of time was devoted to searching for you,' she said.

'When the police became involved in the hunt, I couldn't just sit in Pru's flat and wait.'

I kissed her on the cheek and put my arm round her. I realised how much she had suffered during my time in Bedfordshire. Once again, I cast my mind back to that stressful time in that abhorrent prison cell and felt a sense of relief that that painful experience belonged to the past.

Over the next few days, Anne and I gradually got used to sharing the second bedroom in Prunella's flat.

However, it was a challenge. The journalist normally used the room as an office. She was continually intruding like a meddlesome child, knocking on the door and asking if she could collect some book or document. It was not an ideal situation, but it was clearly not safe to return home just yet.

I urgently wanted to see Graham Kirwan and tell him about my experience in the bunker, so that he could investigate my unlawful detention.

Anne phoned him and asked him to visit me about it. She also explained about the Russian agent's appearance at our home. Graham advised her to stay away from the cottage, but said he was involved in a murder investigation in Herne Bay. He would try to visit us in Faversham on Saturday but made no promises.

I was annoyed he was not prepared to treat my case with greater urgency. How many more innocent people would have to suffer as a result of the contemptible actions of Major Thomas and her thugs?

The day after my escape from the Army base, I went into the town to obtain a new handset for the SIM card we'd saved. No sooner was my new phone working than I received a call from Tristan.

'Where've you been the past three weeks?' he demanded. 'I've left loads of messages for you.'

'I've been a guest of the Army,' I replied. Instead of asking me to explain, he at once questioned me about how long we were planning to stay with Prunella.

'It's out of our hands, old chap,' I said. 'We've been advised to stay away from home and this is the only place we feel secure.'

'What's all that about then?' he wondered.

'We're being targeted by some unpleasant people,' I replied, uncertain whether he would believe the truth if I told him. I thought it best to keep him in the dark.

'You must have upset someone then.'

'Do you want the long version or the short version?'

'Can't you stay with someone in Canterbury? Try and see it from my point of you. Prunella and I are... well, we want to spend time together, put it that way.'

'Are you on the point of moving in with her?'

'It's close to that.'

'But you've only just met her.'

'I know, but she's the most wonderful woman I've ever met. I think we're made for each other.'

'But you teach in Raynes Park, don't you?' I said. 'Your school's sixty miles away from her home.'

'She's worth it, Bob. In any case, she's in London a lot of the time with her work. She's the girl of my dreams.

'You're lucky. You found Anne nine years ago and you're happily settled, but this is the first time I've found a woman and thought this is the real thing.'

'All right. I've got the message.' I said. 'We'll move out of

Prunella's place as soon as we can.'

I was just as eager for us to leave Prunella's flat as he was. The journalist was pleasant company, but she was excitable, scatty and sometimes had her head in the clouds.

When I got back to the flat, Anne revealed Claudia Morley had just phoned. She had been informed by the Ministry of Defence she needed to be placed under twenty-four hour surveillance.

'She's complaining because she's been given a minder,' Anne explained. 'But she doesn't seem to understand why. She's been told it's connected with Gus's weapons research.

'They've said an enemy state wrongly believe he's still alive and Claudia may still be in contact with him. Claudia said something like: "It's reminded me of that nonsense Bob was spouting. There's someone here round the clock. Have you ever heard anything so crazy? They even follow me to the shops.'

I knew Claudia would have complained about the prospect of a bodyguard as bitterly as a starving woman offered a bag of cold chips. Anne told me she had tried to be sympathetic.

'I told her, if they were genuine MoD security officials, they must know what they were doing,' said Anne.

'Hold on a moment while I make a drink,' I said. After I had brought two cups of tea into the living-room and I had shown her my new handset, she told me she had had time to think.

'There's one more aspect of the Morley case I need to look into,' she informed me. 'I want to visit Turner's Hatch.'

'Whatever for?' I asked. 'There's nothing to see there now, apart from some scorched earth and a burnt tree trunk.'

'I know, but I want to see the scene for myself, imagine how the deception was managed, get into the minds of the people who pulled off this audacious stunt. I also want to talk to nearby residents – a job that wasn't done properly by the police, in my opinion.'

'You don't think PC Hartley was efficient enough?'

'No, I don't. He did enough to satisfy the coroner, but sometimes, when you scratch the surface, you find dirt underneath.'

'He that would find the kernel must first crack the nut.'

'Exactly.'

*

On the Friday morning, Anne and I set off just before ten am for the Kent hamlet of Turner's Hatch. It was a warm day and I had volunteered to drive.

The sun emerged from behind the clouds as we passed through the small town of Westerham an hour later. We eventually found Knights Lane, a turning on the left which begins with a gentle, winding, uphill slope before developing into a steep, narrow incline.

Elegant detached houses nestled behind high brick walls and black wrought-iron gates along the right-hand side of the lane as we drove to the top. On the left were open fields.

Through the gateways, we caught glimpses of extensive gardens with terraced lawns and rockeries. At one point, I had to swerve to avoid hitting an old man who was lopping overhanging tree branches half-way up the hill.

After passing the summit, the road veered to the right and the land levelled out. We at once saw on the left the burnt oak trunk and the blackened earth in front of it.

I stopped the car for a few minutes as we surveyed the scene. We had heard so much about this place. Yet to see it with our own eyes brought back memories of Gus Morley, of the inquest and all the other aspects of the affair.

Beside the tree lay a grass verge and shallow ditch and beyond that a host of bracken, bushes and trees. I found a grassy area on the right a few metres past the site of the car crash where I parked. We both got out.

'You can see why they chose this place,' she said. 'It's the back of beyond. We haven't seen a single vehicle.'

'We haven't seen a single person, apart from that old man,' I said.

Anne wanted to visit every house on the hill, asking householders if they were at home in the late afternoon on Friday February the first and whether they had any knowledge of the crash.

The first house, standing in extensive grounds at the top of the hill, was a rambling red-brick Victorian mansion. We followed a gravel drive to the entrance of the building and then climbed three stone steps to a glazed porch.

After pressing the bell, an elderly, grey-haired man in his eighties emerged at the navy-blue front door. We at once recognised him as Bert Prendergast. He was frail and supporting himself with a walking cane.

'I'm Anne. This is Bob. You were at the Morley inquest, weren't you?' said Anne. 'We're taking a fresh look at what happened.'

'What are you? Press? Insurance company?'

'No, we're friends of the Morleys,' I explained.

'Well, I've told all there is to be told,' said Prendergast, who was wearing a brown cardigan and dark-green trousers.

'I know you saw the car and tried to help,' Anne continued.

'But I wondered what first drew your attention?'

'I was in the garden and saw smoke,' he said. 'I thought some kids might have set fire to an old car. It's happened round here before.'

'Did you hear the sound of the car hitting the tree?'

'No. Come to think of it, I didn't,' he admitted. 'But we're two or three hundred yards away.'

'Is your hearing good?' I asked.

'Sound as a bell,' he insisted. 'Look, I've got to go.' On that note, he went inside and closed the door.

'At least that's something – he heard no noise,' Anne remarked as we trudged back into the lane. We visited several other houses, but at those properties where we found residents at home, no one else recalled the incident on the hill.

'I imagine some of the folk who live here go to work – possibly in London,' I reflected. 'And they were probably away at the time of the crash. Let's go home.'

'Hang on!' said Anne. 'What about that old guy who was cutting trees? What's happened to him?'

We strolled a short distance down the lane to the spot where several clipped branches were lying by the roadside. There was no sign of the gardener.

But then we heard a clicking noise from the other side of the wall. He was clearly continuing his work from within the garden. Anne pushed open one of two decorative, black metal gates and we both ventured inside.

'Excuse me!' she called. 'Could I have a word?' The man we had seen earlier with a fawn-coloured cap and blue overalls was cutting some branches a few feet away. He approached us with the wariness of an antelope in a lion enclosure.

'What is it, my dear?' he asked.

'I just wondered,' said Anne. 'Were you working round here when that car crashed into the tree in February?'

'Up the top of the hill? Yes, I was, as a matter of fact. Why?'

'We're just making a few inquiries. We think there may have been a miscarriage of justice.'

'By who?'

'Well, by the police and the coroner. They don't seem to have been very thorough.'

'No, I was surprised they didn't come and speak to me. Yes, young lady, I remember the day well. Who's this?' The gardener had suddenly noticed me lurking in the shadows.

'My husband,' said Anne.

'Bob. Pleased to meet you,' I said, quickly coming forward.

'I remember it because it was Friday, February the first and because a strange thing happened that afternoon. At about five o'clock, I was cutting the high hedge and noticed roadmen in yellow jackets closing the lane.

'I decided to go to the shed to fetch my little coat and grab a sip of tea from my flask because it was getting cold.

'As I was walking to the shed, I saw a lorry with a scrapped car on the back coming up the lane. I couldn't quite see, but it looked like it stopped just past the top of the hill.'

'Was the car a Mercedes?' asked Anne.

'It was a black car. I can't say more than that. It swept past so quick,' he said. 'Less than ten minutes later, as I was on my way back here, I saw the same lorry returning – this time without the car on the back. I thought: "That's funny. I hope they haven't dumped it." There's been a lot of car dumping because of high insurance and repair bills. My son was talking about it only the other day.'

'What happened to the men in yellow jackets?' asked Anne.

'They opened the road again and left.'

'How did you know it was the same lorry that came back?'

'From the colour of the cab. It was painted red, while the rest of the vehicle was black.'

'You didn't report this to the police then?' said Anne.

'I phoned a policewoman at Caterham. She said I must have been mistaken and that the road was closed early on the Saturday after the car caught fire – not on the Friday.

'She said a transporter was ordered to take the burnt-out car to Maidstone to be examined. I told her it was definitely Friday evening because I don't work weekends, but she didn't seem interested and couldn't see why I was complaining.'

'You wanted police to come because you feared the car had been dumped?' Anne asked.

'Precisely. There's no garage or scrapyard within ten miles of here.'

'During that afternoon, did you see any Mercedes actually drive up the lane – such as a black C-class Mercedes? About four years old?'

'No, I take an interest in cars. My son used to have a Mercedes. I would have noticed one passing me.'

'It would have been between four thirty and five thirty?'

'No, definitely not. I was out in the lane on me steps all that time, except, as I say, for when I popped into the shed.'

'You must have heard the sound when the car crashed into the tree?' I asked.

'No. Didn't hear a thing. Perhaps this place is too far down the lane.'

'Thank you,' said Anne. 'You've been very helpful indeed. By the way, I'm Anne Shaw. Could I ask your name?'

'Ken Humphreys, dear. Everyone knows me round here. Here's my card. Let me know if you need any gardening work.'

'Thank you very much,' I said as we walked back up the hill and approached the car.

'I now know most of what happened,' said Anne. 'As we thought, the whole event was staged to give the impression Gus died here five months ago. There's been a lot of organisation behind it.

'It looks like, whoever it was, smuggled the body from Scotland. Somehow - perhaps in a lab - they provided the body with skull fractures, a broken face, cerebral contusions and a subarachnoid haemorrhage.'

'You've been reading the medical dictionary again!' I quipped.

'I looked it up last night. Then they put the body in a scrapped car and battered the front of the vehicle to fit the shape of the tree. Then they brought it here, placed it in position and set fire to it.'

'That would explain how they did it,' I said. 'But how d'you account for the two teeth which the pathologist used to identify the body? And how d'you account for the signet ring?'

'I wonder if the security services used a dental expert. They could have provided Gus with new dental implants. Then they could have got this dental expert to insert the badly chipped tooth and the gold crown into the dead man's mouth.'

'Would a dentist be prepared to do that?'

'If they could find a good reason to justify it – such as the nation's security,' she suggested. As I unlocked the car and we both got inside, I turned to Anne.

'Looks like they went to a heck of a lot of trouble to make everyone, including the Kremlin, believe poor old Gus ended his days here in a terrible crash.'

'Yes,' said Anne. 'It has all the hallmarks of a road accident delivered on the back of a lorry.'

31

After Anne and I shared a late breakfast on Saturday morning, Prunella bounded into the living-room like a burst of summer sunshine, her brown hair swaying from side to side and her arms laden with shopping.

'You're up early,' Anne observed as she sipped some tea.

'I've just been to the sales at Bluewater,' said Prunella who was dressed plainly in a white patterned blouse and brown slacks. She appeared to have more baggage than EasyJet.

'I don't start work up in town till three o'clock, so this was my only chance to go. I'll change into my new dress, and you can tell me what you think.'

Five minutes later, she was pirouetting round the living-room in a bright canary yellow midi-dress like a ballerina.

'You look lovely!' gushed Anne. 'Pru, that really suits you.'

'Yes, you look cool,' I remarked, thinking I might need to fetch my sunglasses if she twirled in front of me much longer.

'D'you think Tristan would like it, Anne?'

'He'd love it,' Anne assured her. 'Where did you get it?'

'I think it was Fat Face. Or it might have been Monsoon or Diesel,' said Prunella. 'I've got the receipt somewhere. I'll check.'

'Are you sure it wasn't Butane or Wacky Wombat?' I

suggested with a straight face. 'Or Moderation. I'm told they stock everything.'

'No. Are their sales still on?' asked Prunella, standing stock-still for the first time.

'He's joking with you,' Anne murmured. 'What else did you get, Pru?'

'Oh, I've got these beige platform sandals. Look!' she gushed, pacing round the room again. 'And what d'you think about this hat? It was only twenty-seven pounds.' She swooped upon a white, wide-brimmed beach hat, embellished with an extravagant matching bow, which, moments before, she must have placed on the corner unit behind her. Now she swept it up with a flourish and wrapped it round her head.

'Do I look OK?' she wondered. I stifled a laugh.

'It's perfect. You look gorgeous, Pru,' said Anne.

'I think it quite suits me,' said Prunella.

Two hours later, she set off for her reporting shift at the Sunday News while Anne and I sat on the balcony and relaxed. We gazed down at two yachts and a sailing barge bobbing in the water below or gazed across at the pub where we had had lunch with Prunella nearly two months before.

As we chilled, I received a text message from Graham Kirwan. He had been delayed but aimed to be with us by half past two.

Finally, at a quarter to three, we noticed his light-blue Volkswagen Golf entering the car park. I went down to greet him and helped him find a visitor's space while Anne rushed about in the flat, gathering the notes, newspaper cuttings and photographs she had collected in her Morley investigation.

'This is an impressive place, isn't it?' he declared as I led the casually-dressed detective sergeant through Prunella's front door. 'Prunella's done all right for herself, hasn't she? I've met up with her at The Yacht before now, but never been to her place. Good views as well.'

After Anne made us all tea, the sergeant and I made ourselves comfortable on the corner unit while my wife sat at the table with her paperwork.

'It was a month ago when I called round at your house, wasn't it?' he said.

'Almost to the day,' I confirmed.

'Right, well, I want to start by telling you about Dr Maybourne. Hampshire CID have consulted plant toxicologists from Kew Gardens. They've confirmed traces of a poison found in the gelsemium plant were in her stomach.'

'Isn't that the plant from Asia sometimes called heartbreak grass?' asked Anne. A yacht with a crimson sail glided along the creek below.

'That's right. It was once used for pain relief, until it was found to be dangerous. It appears she was being fed the most potent form of the plant, gelsemium elegans.

'I managed to grab a word with Dr Harryman, who's back at work now. He says it leads to convulsions, paralysis of the spinal cord, muscle weakness and ultimately asphyxia.'

'So while she was being kept prisoner, her meals were laced with it?' I asked.

'The DI thinks it was given her in soup in the hours before you found her,' said the sergeant.

'God, how awful!' said Anne. 'Has her husband been told?'

'Yes. That was a sad duty the DI had to perform. Incidentally, the two Russian agents have now been identified and I can tell you a little about them, if you're interested.'

'Definitely,' said Anne. The sergeant brought a small black notebook from his pocket.

'It's going to be in the news over the next few days in any case,' he said as he sipped his tea. 'First we have Dmitry Bogdanov, aged forty-two. Six feet one inch tall. Closely-cropped hair.'

'He must be the one that walks with a limp,' I murmured.

'The guy who chased after me,' Anne whispered.

'Yes. It says here: "Walks with a slight limp following a weapons accident during training in woods near Moscow." The second guy is Sergei Petrenko, aged thirty-six. Slim with a beard.

'They are both officers in the GRU, the Russian military intelligence service. They'll be all over the papers and TV in a day or two.

'The counter-intelligence squad at the Yard and our colleagues in Hampshire have launched a joint nationwide hunt for them following their activities in Tewkesbury, Bethnal Green and Andover.

'It's going to be a major investigation and, at some point, officers might wish to speak to you, Bob. Oh, and by the way, I've finally traced Alex Lotman. He works for the Special Surveillance Unit, which is connected to the MoD.'

'They're the bastards who locked me up!' I exclaimed, before apologising for my bad language. 'Graham, I'm just back from Bedfordshire after a terrible ordeal. I was abducted and held in an underground bunker. I'd like to know if there's anything the police can do about it?'

'Anne mentioned this to me on the phone and I've made a few inquiries,' he replied. 'Unfortunately, my hands are tied.'

'Good God, man! I was assaulted, handcuffed, blindfolded

and unlawfully imprisoned for three weeks. But the police can't take any action?'

'I can sympathise with you, Bob, but our colleagues at the MoD say you were lawfully arrested and detained. According to them, you're a fugitive from justice and, by rights, I should arrest you and take you back to them.

'Of course, I'm not going to do that. I know the full circumstances so I'm going to pretend I haven't seen you. There's a chance the same people stole your computers.'

I scowled, but I could see there was little point in pursuing the issue. The police were unable to lift a finger and I had to accept it.

'You could always try taking civil action, I suppose,' added Kirwan, as he took a gulp of his tea.

'I might just do that,' I replied.

'But I'm reminded of something my mother used to say: God is good but never dance in a small boat.'

Then Anne interrupted. It was her turn to monopolise the officer's attention. She began describing in detail how she had become convinced Gus Morley was alive after seeing him at the door of his flat with the whisky glass.

She told of her conviction that British intelligence officers snatched a dead body from a funeral parlour and obtained a Mercedes from a scrapyard identical to the one Morley drove.

She claimed they must've obtained a number plate matching Morley's, forged the chassis number and placed the body inside the car at Turner's Hatch. Petrol was then used to set the car on fire.

'Graham, a gardener witnessed a black car arriving on the back of a lorry. The owner of a house just a few metres from the scene was in his garden. Neither he nor the gardener heard the sound of a car crash. Don't you find that unusual?'

'That's compelling evidence, Anne,' said the sergeant after listening to her hypothesis for nearly fifteen minutes. 'You clearly think the inquest should be reopened?'

'Yes, definitely. That inquest in Maidstone wasn't justice,' Anne declared, her voice rising like a gently howling wind. 'People have been deceived. The deceased scientist wasn't deceased.

'The burning car incident was a stunt orchestrated by British intelligence to make it appear Morley was dead.

'But, worse than that, the body of a much-loved husband and father in Scotland was stolen from a coffin and used like a theatre prop to help create the myth of the professor's death.'

Kirwan shook his head slowly. 'Those spooks had some cheek, I'll grant you. Look, it's a strong case you make, Anne, but any application to re-run the inquest would need to come from Morley's wife or the Scottish widow.'

'Don't worry, ' Anne replied. 'Laura McClintock is seeing a solicitor and has no doubt got wheels moving already. She was absolutely furious when I showed her the photographs you gave me.'

'Whoever takes up the fight, they'd need to apply to the High Court for a judicial review to challenge the coroner's conclusions,' he explained. 'Or they could apply for the inquest to be reopened under section thirteen of the Coroners' Act of 1988.

'But there's no guarantee such moves would succeed. We're living in strange times, Anne, with foreign agents operating on these shores and the threat of international conflict breaking out at any time. It's very worrying. Very worrying indeed.'

Anne leaned back in her chair and stared at the ceiling for a moment.

'Graham, poor Claudia Morley has been through an horrific time,' she said. 'A policeman at the door told her her husband had been killed in a road crash. She had to organise a funeral and face a grilling by the coroner.

'But the reality is her husband was alive all the time. His death had been stage-managed and, for some reason best known to him, he has heartlessly kept his family in the dark.'

But Kirwan appeared to think the actions of the intelligence service might be justified.

He insisted: 'If you're correct, this stage management almost certainly happened for reasons of national security and the preservation of the professor's life after two attempts to kill him that nearly succeeded.'

Anne scowled. 'I know his life was under threat, but why didn't he confide in his wife, for God's sake?' she said. 'Then there's the Scottish widow, Laura, whose husband died after battling alcoholism – although they softened the blow by dressing it up as "natural causes."

'Her happy life with her husband was shattered and blighted by drink. Then, with his corpse barely cold, it's snatched from his coffin by body thieves and taken more than four hundred miles to a remote hamlet in Kent. She and her children knew nothing of this and began regular trips to the cemetery unknowingly to pay homage to an empty coffin.

'Don't these two women deserve some amends, some redress? For surely they have been sorely wronged.'

'I'm afraid sometimes life just isn't fair,' our guest remarked, taking a final mouthful of tea. 'No doubt if you asked the perpetrators, they would try to justify their actions by saying they acted in the interests of Britain or the public good.' The officer stood up and prepared to leave.

'I'm sorry, but I don't think Kent Police can help either of you on this occasion. The main problem is this new law sneaked through Parliament six months ago.

'It gave powers to the security services so they could provide key personnel with fresh identities and, once these new identities had been established, they were to be protected from public scrutiny.

'This new set of rules was only meant to be used in extreme cases where individuals were deemed at high risk. A committee was set up following a top-level meeting between the police, Ministry of Defence, the GCHQ listening centre and MI5 to allow these individuals to be allocated new personas.

'It's a joint enterprise involving shared services, run with three representatives from each of the four bodies. The MoD is the senior body responsible. The press got to hear about it and they've been going mental, as I expect you know.'

'I hadn't realised,' I said.

'It must have hit the news while you were in Bedfordshire,' he went on.

'And while I was in Scotland,' Anne reflected.

'The press have been calling it the Anonymity Charter. But now Anne has told me about their antics in Kent and Scotland I'm thinking they could do with a better name for these new rules.

'Since they're bringing folk back from the dead, maybe they should call it the Lazarus Charter. Anyway, thanks for the tea, Anne.'

'Pleasure. You're welcome any time,' she replied. He kissed her on the cheek and waved before turning towards the door. While Anne moved into the kitchen to answer a call on her mobile, I opened the front door and shook his hand before he walked off down the stairwell.

As I closed the door and returned to the living-room, I could faintly overhear parts of Anne's phone call.

She was talking to Claudia on the Morleys' Tewkesbury landline. She had been watching a crucial tennis match taking place at Wimbledon. The pair were laughing. Suddenly there was a pause. Anne called out Claudia's name.

'Claudia?' Anne repeated. 'Are you still there?'

Anne turned to me. 'She said she heard breaking glass and now the line's gone dead.'

32

Anne stared at me in shock. ' I'd better try calling her back,' she said while pressing the numbers on her phone's keypad.

All she could hear was the engaged tone. Then she tried Claudia's mobile number. That went straight to voicemail.

'Bob, I'm worried something's happened to her. Just before she was cut off her bodyguard went to buy cigarettes and it was the first time she'd been left alone for three weeks.

'We were laughing about it. Then she told me she was frightened at the sound of breaking glass and the phone went dead. Bob, I'm really worried about her.'

Anne dialled 999. A woman's voice answered within a few seconds.

'Hello. Emergency. Which service do you require?' she asked.

'Police,' said Anne.

'I'll just connect you,' said the woman. Then a male voice broke in: 'Where are you calling from, madam?'

'I'm in Kent, but I'm worried about my friend. She's in Gloucestershire,' said Anne, sitting down on Prunella's sofa.

'What's the nature of the emergency?'

'I think someone's broken into her home. I was talking to her on the phone and the line went dead. She's got a bodyguard because her life's in danger.'

Anne passed on Claudia's name and address in Hanley St Peter as well as her own name and our current address in Faversham. Then the operator, who was in the Kent Police control room in Maidstone, promised to pass the information to force control in Gloucester. But, after ending the call, Anne remained agitated.

'Bob, I can't sit here, knowing Claudia's in trouble,' she said. 'How long would it take us to get to Hanley?'

'Around three hours,' I replied.

'Come on. Let's go,' she said. 'If we stay here, I'll just be worried sick. '

I had to drive through heavy rain on our way to Hanley. Despite claps of thunder and flashes of lightning, Anne managed to phone Jago Lawson on her mobile to alert him that Claudia might be in trouble. He and Jemima often visit Claudia and I thought, by chance, they might have been close by.

However, the pair were at their farm near the Cotswold town of Burford, a forty-minute drive from Hanley. On hearing our news, they immediately agreed to meet us there.

'Why didn't we see this coming?' Anne complained later as we turned off the M5 motorway near Tewkesbury and followed the Hanley road. 'We should have seen she was at risk. Maybe she could have stayed with us in Faversham.'

'What? In Prunella's poky flat?' I said. 'Anyway I did my best to warn Claudia weeks ago that her husband was still alive and remember what thanks I got.'

'This is different, Bob. We should have realised the Russians might target her in their search for Gus.'

The rain had eased off but the weather remained humid as we arrived in Hanley at just after six thirty pm and found a place to park.

Part of the road near the Old Rectory was cordoned off. A uniformed policeman was in the centre of the highway, advising motorists on alternative routes. Three newspaper reporters and two photographers were standing beside him.

Four police cars, a black van, a white van and a yellow South Western Ambulance Service vehicle were parked beside the gravel drive or on the roadway.

'I'm sorry, sir, madam. The road's closed,' he told us as we approached the police tape on foot.

'We're friends of Claudia Morley,' said Anne. 'We've travelled to see her from Kent. Is she all right?'

'I'm sorry. I can't give you any information. Maybe if you came back tomorrow?'

But as we waited by the cordon, wondering what to do, we heard a woman's voice crying: 'Anne! What are you doing here?'

It was Claudia. She had emerged from the house and was hurrying down the drive towards us as quickly as the brown sandals on her feet would allow.

A man in a white short-sleeved shirt and dark trousers – probably a detective – was outside the front door, making calculations with a tape measure. In the doorway stood a paramedic in green uniform, his eyes following her every movement.

'Officer, it's all right. They're close friends,' she shouted. The policeman lifted the tape so we could pass through. Claudia hugged us both. The two photographers clicked away behind us.

'We had to come,' Anne explained. 'Your phone went dead.'

'Oh Anne, it's been horrific,' said Claudia, tearfully as she led us up the drive. 'Two thugs broke in. Alex, my security guy, had only gone up the road. They must have waited for him to leave.'

'You're all right?' asked Anne.

'One of them grabbed me round the throat. Look!' Claudia, who was wearing a short-sleeved blue top and fawn jeans, showed us a red mark on her neck.

'Apart from that, it's the shock of being confronted by two complete strangers in your own home,' she said in a low voice.

'They demanded to know where Gus was. I was crying. I couldn't believe they had had the gall to break into my house. After a minute, they let me sit down. I told them my husband was dead, but they just didn't believe me.

'They were saying: "He is living. You take us to him." They were foreign – Russian, I think, or East European.'

'Claudia, that's absolutely awful, ' said Anne, putting her arm round her and comforting her like a surrogate mother.

'I must say you're remarkably calm for someone who's been threatened in their own home,' I remarked.

We stopped a short distance from the porch so the detective could finish his measuring. Raindrops from the recent shower dripped here and there from the heads of red and white roses and blue delphiniums, glistening as the sun emerged briefly from behind the clouds.

'It was all over incredibly quickly,' said Claudia. 'Alex, the security guy, came back from the village and drew his gun. He shot one of the men dead in the kitchen, but the other one knocked him to the floor and rushed past him. Nothing's been taken.'

'When you say Alex, is that Alex Lotman?' I asked.

'Yes. D'you know him?'

'We've crossed paths once before,' Anne admitted.' So how did these thugs get in?'

'They smashed a window at the side of the house. I was on the phone to you, wasn't I? I went to investigate and one of them jumped on the back of me and nearly throttled me.

'Luckily the children were out.' She added: 'God, it was so scary. They had black scarves round their faces, but one of the scarves slipped down and I saw the guy had a beard.'

The detective we'd been waiting for returned to the house and, one by one, we followed him through the porch. The paramedic, who had been hovering by the doorway, tapped Claudia gently on the arm.

'Are you sure you're all right now, Mrs Morley?' he asked.

'Yes, I'll be fine,' she replied with a smile.

'Right then. I'll be off, but the police want to talk to you again,' he said before he walked to his ambulance.

'I won't be long,' Claudia assured us as she headed off alone towards the kitchen. 'Jago and Jemima are in the lounge.'

We found our friends relaxing on the green Chesterfield settee. Jago looked uncomfortable in an ill-fitting blue shirt and beige trousers.

He was locked in an animated discussion with his wife, who was casually dressed in a pink top and blue denims.

They both stood up as we entered the drawing room. Jago shook my hand warmly and kissed Anne on the cheek, while Jemima kissed and hugged us both.

'Well done, you two – calling the emergency services so quickly!' said Jemima.

'I was on the phone to Claudia when the window was smashed,' Anne explained.

'So I've heard,' said Jemima. 'And thank you for letting us know. Poor Claudia! By the way, she says you're living away from Chasehurst. Is that right?'

'Yes,' Anne admitted. 'We've been having problems at home. I'll tell you later.'

'That bodyguard fella played a blinder, didn't he, Bob,' said Jago. 'If he hadn't turned up when he did, it could've been a totally different story.'

Jemima nodded and then whispered: 'The police seem to think they were trying to kidnap her. They had a car waiting round the corner.'

Jago raised his eyebrows. 'Kidnap her? Sounds unlikely to me,' he said.

'Are all the cops still here?' I asked.

'Yes,' said Jago. 'They're in the kitchen with the body. The pathologist is floating around somewhere as well.'

'Claudia says one of them escaped,' said Anne. The couple both nodded.

'There's a hunt going on for the one that got away,' said Jago.

'Do we know anything about them? Were they Russian?' Anne wondered.

'The cops reckon they might have been Russian agents,' said Jago. 'But that's ridiculous. Just a couple of local toe-rags from Tewkesbury, if you ask me.'

'But Claudia says nothing was stolen,' Anne pointed out.

'No, because the minder turned up with guns blazing,' Jago replied.

'Do we know what sort of car they had?'

'Some kind of black car. The cops have been knocking on doors in the next street. It's turning into quite a caper.'

'Probably won't get very far,' Anne concluded.

'I tend to think they might have been Russian agents,'

Jemima conjectured. 'Claudia says they had strong accents.

'Remember the scientist killed in Andover? She worked in the same department as Gus sometimes. So maybe it's something to do with that. She's lucky that Alex chap arrived when he did.'

She paused before she added: 'We've invited her to stay with us and she says she's going to think about it.'

'There's the children to consider, of course,' murmured Jago, resuming his seat on the Chesterfield. 'We've said they can come too, but Claudia doesn't think they'll want to leave their friends.'

'Where's her minder now anyway?' I asked. 'I haven't seen him since we arrived.'

'Helping the cops,' mumbled Jago.

'I imagine he'll be in hot water for leaving her on her own,' I said. 'If someone's given twenty-four hour protection, no British intelligence operative can afford to take a trip to the shops for cigarettes without arranging replacement cover.'

'You've got a point, Bob,' Jago agreed. Then he said something profound that I puzzled about for the next few days. He said: 'Give your enemy a chink of light and they'll have a jemmy in your door.'

*

That evening Claudia was taken to police headquarters to provide a long statement about the events of that Saturday afternoon.

While Jemima went to collect James and Sophie from their friends' houses, Jago, Anne and I walked into Hanley village and had a meal at the King's Head, overlooking the village green and the duck pond. The inn reminded me of the

White Horse in Earlsbridge as it had dark wooden beams and exposed brickwork.

Anne received a call on her mobile from Prunella, who had been working on a show business story at the Sunday News. As soon as she realised we had first-hand knowledge of the kidnap attempt, she wanted to know everything Claudia had told us.

'I don't feel I can help you on this one, Pru,' Anne told her, as diplomatically as a charm school graduate.

'My friend has spoken to me of her ordeal confidentially and I feel I would be betraying a trust if I passed on some of what she told me. I think I'll have to pass on this one.' She ended the call.

'The poor girl's only doing her job,' I remarked.

'I know and normally I would help her. But I feel an obligation towards Claudia. To be honest, I'm worried for her. She's suffered a lot. It's really not fair.'

We were later joined by Jemima, who revealed details of a conversation she'd overheard in the kitchen involving Alex Lotman. She gathered that the man he shot dead had a beard and was in this thirties.

To my mind, this fitted with the description Graham Kirwan had given us of Sergei Petrenko, the younger of the two Russian agents. This meant Dmitry Bogdanov, the agent with the limp, was the man on the run.

Jemima also disclosed that Lotman had been suspended, accused of dereliction of duty, despite his bravery in confronting the intruders. A second bodyguard had been drafted in as an interim replacement.

After the Lawsons assured us they would be spending the night at the Old Rectory with Claudia, we were happy to return to Faversham, confident she was in safe hands.

The following day, Anne received a call from Claudia while we were out shopping in Faversham.

'I'm at the Lawsons' farm in Burford,' she explained. 'Jemima convinced me I needed to get away.'

'What about the children?' Anne wondered.

'They're OK. The mother of one of Sophie's friends heard what happened. She's volunteered to look after both of them while I'm away. It won't be for long – probably just a week.'

'Be a nice break for you,' Anne agreed. 'Is your minder going with you?'

'Yes, the new guy's coming with me. I'd better go. Jemima wants me.' Then she hung up.

Later that day, we learned more about the attack on Claudia from reading online news reports. The best coverage was in Prunella's newspaper, the Sunday News, which ran a main headline saying : HUNT FOR 'DANGEROUS' FOREIGN AGENT AFTER DRONE BOFFIN MURDER.

The story beneath said: *Scotland Yard launched a nationwide hunt yesterday for a dangerous man wanted for questioning about the murder of top weapons scientist Dr Allegra Maybourne.*

'Counter terrorism officers are eager to speak to Dmitry Bogdanov, aged 42, who is described as an officer in the Russian military intelligence agency, the GRU.

'The move comes after a dramatic shooting last night at the home of a fellow-scientist, Professor Gus Morley, who died aged forty-seven in a car crash five months ago.

'Two men – one of whom is believed to be Bogdanov – broke into the home of Professor Morley's widow yesterday afternoon and attacked her. But within minutes they were disturbed by the arrival

of a passing police patrol. Bogdanov escaped, but his accomplice was shot dead at the house near Tewkesbury, Glos.

'Henry Maxwell-Brown, the Yard's assistant commissioner for counter-terrorism policing, told a press conference at the Yard: "This man is currently considered the most dangerous man in Britain and should not be approached by members of the public. If you see him, please alert the police or counter-terrorism command immediately."

'Police have refused to discuss a possible motive for the break-in, but a security expert has claimed the intruder may have been seeking the professor's research papers.

'On Saturday, detectives from Hampshire CID revealed for the first time the identities of two men of Russian extraction they wished to speak to regarding Dr Maybourne's death near Andover on June the eleventh.

'One was Bogdanov, who has cropped hair and is six feet one inch tall. A second man was described as aged thirty-six, five feet eight inches tall and sporting a brown beard. It is not known at present whether this second man was the person shot dead in Gloucestershire.

'The break-in happened at around three thirty pm yesterday at the professor's home, a former rectory. He once worked at the same weapons establishment as fifty-two-year-old Dr Maybourne.

'The professor's widow, Claudia Morley, thirty-nine and a mother of two, was in the house alone when the intruders struck, smashing a side window to gain entry. One of them savagely assaulted her from behind, choking her and injuring her neck.

'By luck, police quickly arrived at the scene after being alerted by neighbours in the picturesque village of Hanley St Peter.

'An anti-terrorism officer drew a pistol, shooting dead the unnamed man. Bogdanov wrestled the gun from the officer and *managed to flee. Forces throughout the south of England have been put on alert to watch out for him.*

'Eye-witness Dennis Newman, sixty-six, a retired window fitter from Little Coleswood, Glos said he was walking past the detached house with his dog at three thirty-five pm when he heard two loud bangs.

'"I wondered if they were gunshots," he said. "Then a man in a blue shirt and dark trousers carrying a small pistol in his hand ran out. He was tall, well-built and in his forties.

'"Then a second man in a police flak jacket and black trousers dashed out after him and pursued him down the road. It was really scary because they were shooting at each other. It was like being on a filmset."'

33

Prunella was annoyed with us after we returned to her flat in Faversham. She was like a disgruntled gazelle strutting round in stilettos.

'I do think you could have given me a few pointers about the incident in Hanley St Peter,' she complained to Anne on the Sunday morning when we got up. 'You could've at least given me an idea of how Mrs Morley reacted to the attack on her in her own home.

'You could've told me about the security guard being suspended and described the house. Doing that shouldn't have affected your friendship with the woman.'

'I faced the mother of all dilemmas, Pru,' Anne explained to her in the living-room. 'This poor woman's been suffering really badly for months. The last thing she wants is one of her friends blabbing to the press. I'm calling her every day to check how she is. It was a hell of an ordeal. She's been incredibly brave.'

'She's a real example to us all,' I said in support of Anne as Prunella left the room, slamming the door behind her. Anne shrugged and remarked: 'She'll be all right later.'

Once we were alone, Anne revealed she was experiencing pangs of guilt for keeping all her news about Gus from Claudia.

'Bob, don't you think I have a duty to tell Claudia the truth?'

she said. 'She's bound to find out sooner or later her husband is alive. Now I've got the address, we could take her to meet him. Surely she has the right at least to speak to him and confront him about what's been going on?'

I shook my head. 'Not at the moment,' I cautioned. 'Surely by now you must have realised he doesn't want to see her. He would've played his game differently and involved her if he'd wanted to. I think it's best to let matters lie – at least for the moment.'

'What? We leave her to carry on in blissful ignorance?'

'That's right. There's an important issue here you might be overlooking. If we gave her his new address, she's going to travel there and confront him. She could lead the Russians directly to him.'

'Oh, I hadn't thought of that. You're right. Perhaps we'd better leave things as they are for the time being.'

By the middle of the week, Jago and Jemima had mentioned they were going to be visiting the Royal International Air Tattoo that coming Saturday, July the twentieth.

They had three spare tickets after their neighbours were unable to attend. Claudia had claimed one. Were Anne and I interested in going?

Without my realizing it, Jago had in recent years become an aviation fanatic. According to Jemima, he spent hours studying makes and models of aircraft. He also enjoyed spotting planes land and take off at airports and visiting air shows around the country.

He persuaded me that it would be an experience I would not want to miss. After all, he boasted, two vertical-lift Spanish Navy Harriers and a Russian-built Ukrainian Air Force SU27 would be appearing.

Although Anne had misgivings, she regarded it as a chance to spend time with Claudia and find out how she was coping.

At half-past six on Saturday morning, as the sun struggled to slip from behind the clouds, we set off for the event at RAF Fairford in Gloucestershire – just fourteen miles from Jago and Jemima's home, Willow Tree Farm.

Just before nine-thirty, we found we were three or four miles from our destination. We joined a queue of cars crawling along narrow, winding country lanes, passing farms and open fields. Now and then we would enter a village, pausing amid the traffic fumes to peer inquisitively through the windows of charming cottages built from Cotswold stone.

Eventually, at around ten am, we met up with Claudia, Jemima and Jago by the entrance and entered the showground.

'Glad you could make it, old bean,' said Jago, clasping my hand warmly as he greeted us in a brown tweed jacket and black corduroy trousers. 'They've got some magnificent machines here. Got to support the old RAF.'

The highlight of the day for me were the aerobatics performed by teams in the skies above while Jago preferred examining the cockpits of various aircraft, taking photographs as he went.

After a picnic lunch, I could tell the women were becoming bored with gazing into the sky. Anne gave me a hug. Jemima was going to drive her and Claudia into Burford to visit the shops. They would meet Jago and me back at the farm in the evening.

Two hours later, just before four o'clock, Jago, suggested: 'Bob, if we want to miss the queues going home, I think we should make tracks now.' I nodded. We headed towards the car park and set off for Willow Tree Farm.

Jago's home, set in an acre of grounds, was an imposing eighteenth century period farmhouse built from Cotswold stone which I had visited four or five times before.

Opened gates led up a winding driveway to a small turning area around an ornamental pond in front of the house. Despite its name, there was a solitary willow among a host of silver birch trees.

The living-room, containing an inglenook fireplace and exposed oak beams, had leaded light windows and patio doors overlooking landscaped gardens, mainly laid to lawn. The kitchen was arranged in traditional style with an Aga, while the four bedrooms and a study upstairs were served by a grand oak staircase.

'Would you like a scotch, Bob?' he asked as we wandered into the living room.

'Just a small one with ice. I'll be driving later, Jago,' I replied, taking a seat on his grey sofa.

'You can both stay the night if you want,' he said.

'Well, that's kind of you, but I think we'll head back. It's been a long day.'

'Please yourselves. The offer's there.' Despite my request, Jago, who had inherited the farm from his father, poured me a double whisky.

Then he sat down in an armchair opposite and started telling me about all the improvements he had made to the farm and the problems he had had recruiting trustworthy employees. Watching rain splatter onto a pile of bricks would have been more engrossing.

'Sorry to interrupt,' I said after a few minutes. 'D'you

know? I feel very guilty. I haven't asked you how Claudia's been getting on? That was a terrible experience she went through last weekend.'

'She's holding it together well, but she's been fed a lot of nonsense by people and she's starting to believe it.'

'How d'you mean?'

'Well, she's got it into her head her life's at risk and she's got to have minders wherever she goes. It's making her delusional.'

'Delusional?'

'Yes. Some days she is haunted by the thought her husband might still be alive. Jemima has to reason with her and bring her down to earth.

'The trouble is the two men taking it in turns to mind her. They keep feeding her this ridiculous line that the Russians believe Gus has falsified his death and that's why she needs protecting. The whole world's gone crazy.

'We have to put up with these guys hanging around. Jem's had to make up a bed in the spare room for the one staying overnight. I know she's had a tough time, but I'll be glad in a way when Claudia goes back to Hanley. It's a bloody panto-mime, old bean!'

'I didn't realise you felt like that.'

'Oh, Jem doesn't mind. She'll put up with all the hassle. Claudia's like a sister to her.'

'The authorities obviously believe Claudia's life's at risk. I mean, that Russian guy Bogdanov is still on the loose.'

'Who?'

'It's been in all the papers.'

'I don't read the papers. If you ask me, it was just a couple of low-lifes from the local town, out to make a quick buck.'

Just then my mobile phone rang. It was Anne.

'Bob, where are you?' she asked in an excited voice as I looked across at my friend.

'At the farm with Jago.'

'Listen. I was talking to Claudia over tea in Huffkins and she was rattling off a list of people who've given her some amazing support – Jemima, Jago, Jonathan Evans and the vicar.

'I asked her to remind me who Jonathan was and d'you know what she said? She said Gus worked for him and some people knew him as Nat!'

'I don't follow you,' I replied. 'Are you saying that this Jonathan Evans is the man Allegra intended the message for?'

'Yes,' said Anne. 'Nat can be a shortened form of Jonathan. What's that, Claudia?' She broke off to speak to Claudia and then told me 'He's head of the military research agency, BAMRA. Don't you remember? He was the white-haired man we ... '

'I'm sorry ,' I said. 'The line keep's breaking up. I think you were saying he was the white-haired man at the funeral that Jago pointed out to us. Is that what you said?'

'Yes.' Jago had just poured himself another whisky. He glanced at me.

'What's this?' he wondered. I raised my finger, urging him to wait a moment.

'Bob, can you phone him straight away? I haven't got a very good signal.' I took a pen and my diary out of my trouser pocket, ready to write down the number.

'Don't worry. I'll call him now. Just give me the number,' I said. She dictated it and then I repeated it to ensure I had taken it down correctly. Jago had downed his whisky in a single mouthful.

'All right. I've got that, I'll ring him from here. Don't worry. Remind me the code number Allegra gave us'

'Code twenty-two.'

'OK, Code twenty-two. I've got that. See you later, darling.'

'Bye, love!' I rose to my feet.

'Jago, is it all right if I use your main phone?' I asked. 'I've got an important call to make and I'd prefer to use a landline. I don't mind paying for it.'

'Don't be silly, Bob. It's no trouble at all. Follow me up to my study.'

He led me up the varnished wooden stairs and then along the landing to the smallest of the five bedrooms, which had been converted into Jago's office. There was a small desk by the door with a personal computer.

On the left was a large leaded light window while, at the far end of the room, stood a light-brown executive-style desk with a black leather high-back chair behind it.

As soon as I passed through the doorway, my attention was drawn to the computer, which had been left on.

The screen had a background consisting of three horizontal stripes - white, blue and red. In the centre was a golden claw with red talons holding a golden orb or globe, which I recognised as part of Russia's double-headed eagle coat of arms.

I immediately thought back to that chilling moment as we were gathered near Allegra's bedside. The very first words she had uttered had been: 'The eagle's claw.' I was puzzled but suspected the symbol must have some connection with Putin's Russia and the men behind Allegra's poisoning.

Jago must have noticed me glancing at the screen. I sensed

he had left his computer on by mistake. His screen-saver had not been intended for my eyes. He was grappling about in the left-hand drawer of his desk for something.

I lifted the receiver of his phone, which was on the edge of his desk, and took my diary from my pocket, preparing to dial Jonathan Evans' mobile number.

Jago's fingers reached over and pressed down on the phone's hook switch, cutting the connection. I looked up.

He was standing motionless behind the desk. He was holding a gun. He was pointing it at me. I froze like a cornered animal.

'What the hell's going on, Jago?' I demanded.

'I can't let you make that call,' he said.

'Two minutes ago you said I could.'

'I never intended to let you make that call,' he said. 'I just wanted to bring you up here where I keep my Beretta.'

'Why shouldn't I make the call?'

'Because we don't want Evans to receive any message from Allegra.'

'Why the hell not?' As soon as the words left my lips, I began to realise the frightening truth of the situation. Jago was in league with the Russians. I stared directly into his eyes.

'You're a Russian agent,' I declared, backing away towards the door.

'Agent is perhaps too strong a word,' he said. 'I prefer peace advocate. I always have been – since university. And they've looked after me rather well.

'The West mustn't be allowed to become too powerful or it will destabilise the world. Bob, I couldn't let you make that phone call. Our plan to disrupt Britain's defence programme would be frustrated.'

'You want to wreck Britain's drone missile system?'

'I suppose there's no reason why I can't tell you now. A code twenty-two warning means – for the people who work for BAMRA – that there is a saboteur working on the inside.

'In eleven days' time, Britain is due to carry out a major test of the Palladin prototype with a launch in Wales. But it's not a new drone. It's a laser used for defence against drones. It's the world's most powerful computer-controlled laser which can track and destroy swarms of enemy drones within minutes. But, as soon as the test begins, an explosion will wreck the entire laser launch base. So the billions of pounds that Britain has spent on the laser and radio frequency technology will go up in smoke. I can't allow you to thwart that by warning Evans.'

'You're demented, Jago. Everything you've achieved in your life has come about because of our great country. Your education, your farming career, all your hopes and dreams.'

'That's where you're wrong,' he insisted. 'All my life I've been frustrated by the inequalities and injustices in the world. I've never felt safe and secure in this country – what with all the money spent on conventional, nuclear and drone weapons.

'Anyway, I'm afraid we're now in a rather unfortunate situation, old bean. I'm afraid I'm going to have to kill you.'

'Don't be ridiculous, Jago. What on earth are you going to tell the women when they come back?'

'I'll just have to say you asked me to show you my pistol and it went off. A desperately sad accident.'

'They'll call the police and your evidence will unravel,' I said. 'They'll start checking you out and your story will crumble.'

'I'm sorry, Bob. You've been a good friend, but you've pushed me into a corner. I've got no choice.' As he spoke, we heard the distant roar of approaching cars. Anne, Jemima, Claudia and the security guard had taken two cars into the town. They were both arriving back simultaneously.

The noise seemed to set off a reaction in Jago's brain. He stared into my face intently. He pulled the trigger. I heard a loud bang.

34

I was in a daze. Someone was talking to me, but I couldn't understand what they were saying. There was a sharp pain in my chest.

The aroma of malt whisky hung in the air as if I'd been locked in a Scottish distillery. Someone – I think it was Anne - was calling out: 'Can someone fetch a glass of water? I think he's coming round.'

I opened my eyes. Beside me on Jago's living-room sofa, caressing my hand, sat Anne - my sweet, darling wife. I summoned up the strength to speak.

'What happened?' I asked.

'You were shot with a blank cartridge,' said a voice. But this time it wasn't Anne. It was a man whose tones I recognised.

'You're in a state of shock,' said the voice again. I glanced down at my green checked shirt and grey cardigan. There was a bullet-hole in both, surrounded by scorch marks. Then I remembered. I'd been shot.

I looked up. Standing at the far side of the room in a black, short-sleeved shirt and grey trousers and waving a whisky glass was a figure I'd last seen in the Bedfordshire bunker. It was that two-faced weasel, Greg Farrier. He was eyeing me like a doctor observing a troublesome patient.

'What the hell are you doing here?' I asked. 'Have you come to take me back to that hell-hole?'

'Oh, you're speaking to me now, are you?' he replied.

'D'you know him, Bob?' asked a shocked Anne.

'Yes, I know him,' I conceded. 'He's the crafty bastard who shared a cell with me in an effort to make me say something prejudicial. I expect he wants to take me back to Bedfordshire.'

'Actually you're wrong,' he said. 'Major Thomas doesn't require you now. The world's moved on.'

'That's very benevolent of her,' I sneered. I couldn't believe this despicable man was standing just a few feet from me. What further shocks were in store, I wondered.

'I know you're still bitter,' said Farrier, who must have been helping himself to Jago's whisky. 'And I can understand why. But you're very lucky I was around this weekend, old chap. I've just saved your life.'

'How d'you work that out?' I wondered. Farrier sat down in the armchair where, shortly before, Jago had been sitting, describing life on the farm.

'I'm on protection duty, taking care of Mrs Morley,' he said. 'While our friend Mr Lawson was out in the fields on Friday evening with one of his farmhands, I made a point of searching the house.

'It's what any good operative should do when their client is staying over in a strange building. I found Lawson had a Beretta in his desk drawer and, for safety reasons, replaced live rounds with blanks.

'Mind you, I never thought for a minute he'd be pulling the trigger so soon. After he used the gun, I confronted him. He tried to make a run for it out of the building, but I was too quick for him. I rugby-tackled him outside and handcuffed him. The cops arrived soon after and he was driven away.'

'You see,' said Anne. 'You should be grateful to Mr Farrier. You'd be dead if he hadn't acted as he did.' I clutched my chest and moaned.

'I can see you're still suffering from shock,' she added.

'Something came out of the muzzle of that pistol. I'm sure it did,' I muttered.

'You've been struck by a jet of hot gas – that's all. You're lucky you weren't standing any nearer to our treacherous friend,' Farrier observed. 'Blanks can kill if you're too close.'

'How did I get down here?' I asked Anne.

'We carried you down,' she said. 'You've been a little disorientated for a while. A lot has happened. The police have been and taken Jago away.'

'That was a helluva shock, finding out he was a Russian sympathiser,' I commented.

'A Russian sympathiser? D'you mean a spy?' Anne wondered.

'I suppose so. All those years I've known him too. If I hadn't tried to make that phone call to Nat, I doubt whether he'd have been unmasked.'

'Don't you believe it,' said Farrier. 'We've had him under observation for some time.'

'Where've they taken Jago?' I asked him. Anne replied on Farrier's behalf.

'Oxford Police Station,' she said. 'Jemima's gone over there in the hope she'll get a chance to see him.'

'She won't,' said Farrier curtly. 'He's expected to be charged with attempted murder and possession of an illegal firearm under the Firearms Act of 1968.

'He's also likely to face a charge of conspiracy to violate the Official Secrets Act. So he won't be allowed visitors and it'll be a long time before he's mucking out the cows again.'

'So he's been on the government's radar for a while?' I asked.

'Can't comment on security issues,' he said. 'All I'll say is we're bloody glad we've got him. By the way, you'll have to give a statement later.'

I turned to Anne. 'And where's Claudia?'

'She's upstairs, having a lie-down,' she replied.

'Poor Claudia!' I said. 'It's been one thing after another.'

'Poor Jemima!' said Anne. 'I don't suppose she had any idea her husband was a spy. It was a tremendous shock for her.'

'I don't expect she can believe it. How long have they been married?'

'Fifteen or sixteen years.'

'Well, I'm sorry if my presence here has come as a bit of a surprise,' said Farrier. 'And I hope eventually there'll be no hard feelings. I was only doing my job when I joined you in the bunker.'

'Look, thank you for replacing the bullets with blanks,' I said. 'You did me a favour there, but it'll be a long time before I can forgive you for the way you behaved in the bunker.'

Farrier left the room to check on Claudia. I remained on the sofa, still feeling dazed. First I'd had to contend with the shock of finding Jago was a spy; then Farrier had popped up, reminding me of my terrible experience in the Bedfordshire bunker. I felt I could never trust anyone again – apart from my darling wife.

Maybe I'd found a new meaning for the phrase 'bunker mentality.' Once I was sure Farrier was out of earshot, I turned to Anne.

'Jago had an eagle's claw image on his computer!' I whispered. 'I should have been more discreet. I discussed Allegra's message in front of him and we went to his study to use his phone. Then he pulled out his gun!'

'He was meant to be our friend,' said Anne. She then reminded me we still had a vital task to perform – to make that call to Jonathan Evans.

Jago's study was closed off as a team of forensic experts were examining the scene of the shooting. So Anne walked over to a small table by the fireplace where the Lawsons kept their downstairs phone extension.

She sat down on a small chair and dialled the number for Evans. I stood by the front window, watching police and forensic staff coming and going.

Finally a male voice answered. Anne turned the loudspeaker on so I could overhear the conversation.

'Jonathan, it's Anne Shaw,' my wife announced. 'Claudia Morley's just given me your number. I'm a friend of hers.'

'Hi, Anne,' he replied. 'I remember you and your husband Bob from the funeral in March. How are you?'

'We're both fine,' she said. 'Well, that's not strictly true. Bob's just been shot, but it turned out to be a blank cartridge.'

'I'm all right now!' I bellowed from my place by the window.

'He says he's all right now. I'll come to the point. We've been trying to find you because it was we who found Dr Maybourne just before she died. She gave us an important message to pass on.'

'To pass onto me?' he said in a surprised tone.

'Well, she said to tell Nat. I tried finding you at the MoD, but no one knew anyone called Nat. It was only when Claudia blurted out your nickname we realised the message was intended for you.'

'I'm known as Nat at BAMRA. There's a lot of Johns working here. Nat was a name my family used to call me, so I started using it after a few weeks in my current post.

'I knew the part you'd both played in tracing Dr Maybourne. I heard from various contacts of mine. But no one mentioned anything about a message. What did she say?'

Anne explained: 'You have to bear in mind she was weak and frail. She'd been poisoned and was gasping for breath. I asked who'd done this. She said: "The eagle's claw."

'Of course, that meant nothing to us. I asked if she had any message for her husband or anyone else. These are her exact words: "Tell Nat: hold Palladin."'

She looked at me for confirmation. I nodded.

'Then her last words to us were: "Code Twenty-two."'

'Are you sure she said twenty-two and not thirty-two?'

'Definitely twenty-two, wasn't it, Bob?' I nodded again.

'Right. Well, that's extremely important. Thank God you were both there. Is this your number that you're calling from?'

Anne explained she was using the main phone at the farmhouse where Jago Lawson lived and that he had just been arrested for spying. Evans appeared to know all about that and was unconcerned. After she passed onto him her personal mobile number, he said he would have to end the call and act on Allegra's message.

'Thanks, Anne. I believe we may still be in time,' he said. 'I'm really extremely grateful to both of you.' Then he hung up.

I walked over to my wife and took hold of both her hands.

'That's it,' I said. 'We're done our duty now.'

'Yes. I just wish I knew what it all meant.'

'Jago told me the Russians have got someone working with the research team on the Palladin project,' I said. 'It's a laser which Britain plans to use for defence against drones. There's a test taking place in eleven days' time and the saboteur is aiming to do something to stop it happening.'

'No wonder Nat Evans was grateful,' said Anne.

'He's probably searching for the saboteur as we speak,' I added.

Later, Claudia came downstairs wearing the same dark-green dress she had worn earlier. She was red eyed. Her cheeks were stained with tears.

'Gus is alive, isn't he?' she said.

'I think we'd better all sit down,' said Anne, gently touching Claudia's arm. The women seated themselves on the grey sofa while I settled in the armchair.

'I've just discovered Gus sold our Bloomsbury flat in the spring for three million pounds,' Claudia explained. 'I've also been talking to Greg Farrier.'

'Gus is alive,' said Anne. 'But he's changed his appearance. It looks like he's been forced to take a new identity to survive.'

'If he's changed his appearance, how can you be so sure it's my husband?' she asked.

'I didn't believe it was him to start with,' said Anne. 'So we followed him to an address where he was staying and he came to the door with the whisky glass we gave him for his fortieth.'

'I see,' said Claudia, although she still appeared confused. She paused. Then she said: 'This has obviously involved a lot of planning. Why didn't he involve me? Why is the wife the last to know?'

'Bob and I don't know. All I can tell you is he's had some plastic surgery on his face ...'

'Plastic surgery?'

'He's changed his name and, like you, he's got a bodyguard.'

'What about the burning car? Was that all an act?'

'British intelligence arranged it to look as though Gus died in the car.'

'But why? That's what I don't understand. Why?' I interrupted to say: 'There were at least two attempts on his life.'

'We think they orchestrated the whole thing so that Gus could begin a new life,' Anne went on. 'MI5 must've thought they knew what they were doing,'

'You've no idea how bad this has made me feel,' Claudia sobbed. 'First I'm told he's dead. So we hold the funeral. Then he's alive again – but he's a different person. What about me? What about the kids?'

'Maybe it was thought impracticable to seek new identities for all four of you,' Anne suggested. Claudia was drying her eyes with a paper tissue. Her sorrow was gradually turning to anger and bitterness.

She suddenly blurted out: 'Maybe he wanted to dump his family and set up home with someone else!' Anne remained as calm as a windless sea.

'There's no suggestion of another woman,' she asserted. 'Look, Bob and I don't really know why Gus acted in the way he did.'

'D'you know where he's living now?'

'I do, but ...' I interrupted to say: 'Claudia, if you go round to Gus's new place, the chances are you'll lure the Russian agents there like cats to a canary.'

'Sod the Russians! He's my bloody husband. How am I meant to move on if I don't see him and talk to him? I need to know how I stand with him. Are we still husband and wife? If we're not, I want a bloody divorce so I can get on with the rest of my life.

'I'm in some kind of halfway house – unsure whether I'm a widow or an abandoned wife. This is all too much for me. On top of everything else, I come back from Burford to find Jago has pulled a gun on you, Bob, and stands accused of working for the Russians. Seems like the world's gone crazy.'

'I know it's hard,' said Anne. 'I know you're in pain, but I really don't think it's a good idea for you to visit Gus at the moment.'

'You've got to remember there's a Russian agent with a gun out there somewhere,' I muttered. 'He might be watching us even now.'

'Bob's right, Claudia,' Anne assured her. 'We need to take advice before you make any attempt to approach your husband. You don't want to put his life in further danger.'

'Advice? From whom?'

'I don't know yet,' said Anne. 'We'll have to bide our time. But make no mistake. When the time is right, I'll happily give you the current address I have for him. In fact, I'd be happy to take you there myself.'

35

Peals of laughter echoed round Prunella Ball's flat as we climbed the stairs late on Saturday night. As Anne turned her key in the lock, we realised the merriment was coming from Prunella's bedroom.

As we went into the kitchen to prepare some hot drinks, Tristan Barnes, wearing a frilly mauve ladies' dressing gown and brown slippers, walked non-chalantly into the living-room with a broad grin across his face.

Then he saw us and the smile vanished as swiftly as a candle in the wind.

'Bob, what a lovely surprise!' he said nervously, slurring his words slightly. 'And Anne! Great to see you both.' Anne was pouring boiling water into a teapot at the time, but I shook his hand warmly.

'I'm a little surprised to see you,' I said. 'Particularly in that dressing gown. I'm not sure if it's your colour.'

'Yes, well, it's all Prunella had. Bob, this wasn't planned. Oh no. It's just that I had a little bit too much to drink. You know how it is. One drink leads to another.

'Prunella kindly asked me if I wanted to stay over. I didn't want to lose my licence, so I expect she'll make me a bed up on the settee. Oh, that doesn't sound right, does it? I mean she'll make up a bed on the settee, although that doesn't sound right either.'

'One way or another, you'll get to bed,' I replied, solemnly. 'Tristan, you haven't heard what's happened today, have you?'

'No, what? You haven't won the lottery?'

'Jago Lawson is a Russian spy.'

'What? Jago? Are you joking?' he said with a look of disbelief.

'Here, I've just made you a cup of tea, Tristan,' said Anne. 'You'd better sit down.'

'Thanks, Anne. I think I better had.' As he slumped down on the corner unit, Prunella, alerted by the commotion, sprang out of her room in a white negligee beneath a black satin dressing gown.

'Hi, you two! What's going on?' she asked.

'We've had a bit of a dramatic day!' Anne explained, handing steaming cups of tea to Prunella and me.

'Yes,' I said. 'We've found out Jago is working for the Russians and always has done, apparently. Even when he was at university. By the way, this is all off-the-record for the moment.'

'Absolutely,' said Prunella with a nod of her head.

'He took a pistol out of his desk and shot Bob,' said Anne.

'What?' exclaimed Tristan.

'Bob's all right, as you can see. It was loaded with blanks,' she added. Tristan shook his head.

'I was only talking to him on the phone the other day,' he said. 'You know, he always refused to talk politics.'

'Now we can understand why,' said Anne. 'Listen, d'you remember a month ago we found the body of the dead scientist near Andover?' They both nodded.

'Well, she gave us a cryptic message to pass on about a

Russian saboteur to one of her colleagues.'

I interrupted her. 'By sheer fluke, we found out the colleague's proper name just as we were visiting Jago,' I said. 'I'm afraid Jago must have overheard us discussing things and, when I began calling the guy concerned, I found I was staring down the muzzle of his gun.'

'Bloody hell!' said Tristan. 'He didn't want you to make that call, obviously.'

'That's right, and then it all came out about how he backed the Russians because he's concerned about world peace.' Tristan stared at the floor.

Then he said: 'If it wasn't you and Anne telling me this, I'd find this extremely hard to believe. I've known Jago most of my life. He never seemed to take much interest in current affairs or the news. He only ever talked about farming.'

'You can never tell with people,' said Anne as Tristan shook his head. 'Maybe that's how be blended in. But behind the scenes there was much more to the man. For instance, he was avidly interested in aviation.'

'Especially British and American warplanes,' I added.

'Anyway, what's happened to him?' Tristan asked.

'He's been arrested and taken to a police station,' Anne explained.

'You'll eventually have to let me do a story,' said Prunella.

'Well, I've had to make a statement to a policewoman from Oxford,' I told her. 'They warned me I might be needed as a witness and to keep schtum, so I'm not sure I can help you. It's all a bit cloak and dagger. He's probably going to appear in a closed court on Monday.'

'But when the case is all over, can I have it as an exclusive?'

asked Prunella. I smiled. She was as tenacious as a terrier tracking a fox.

'Yes, of course,' I said. 'When it's all over.' Anne interrupted to say: 'The tea's going cold. I'd better make some more.'

'Hold on a moment, Anne,' said Prunella, grinning broadly. 'Maybe we should have something stronger than tea because we've got some news as well, haven't we, Tristan? We're getting engaged!'

'Oh, Pru!' said Anne. 'That's brilliant!'

'Hang on!' Prunella added, dashing back into her bedroom. She returned seconds later with a small navy-blue box.

'Look at this wonderful ring Tristan's given me!' she exclaimed as she opened it, disclosing a nine-carat white gold diamond solitaire ring.

Anne walked to the doorway where Prunella was standing and gave her a hug. I strode over to Tristan, after a glance at the ring, and shook his hand warmly.

'Well done, mate!' I said. 'I'm sure you'll both be very happy.'

'She's the most wonderful woman,' he replied. 'I really believe we're made for each other.' I could not resist adding: 'They must be paying you well in Raynes Park. Have they got any vacancies?'

Prunella had meanwhile fetched a bottle from the kitchen fridge and a set of glasses. Although it was nearly midnight, we were soon toasting their future happiness with champagne at the end of an extremely eventful day.

*

All four of us got up late on the Sunday morning. It was a bright, sunny day and we were still in a mood for celebrating.

We crossed the Creek Bridge and walked round to The Yacht, the quaint, weather-boarded pub on the opposite side of the water from the flat.

I bought lunch for us all and we sat in the shade beneath one of the willow trees, enjoying two bottles of wine. Although we were marking his engagement, Tristan only had two glasses because he had to drive back to London that evening.

During lunch, Anne suddenly asked her friend: 'Tell us about the proposal.' Prunella had a mouthful of food at the time, so Tristan answered for her.

'I knew Prunella was the one for me – almost from the moment I first met her in Maidstone,' Tristan confessed.

'There was a small hiccup after my front page story appeared three days later!' Prunella admitted. She laughed out loud.

'Yes, just a small glitch,' Tristan continued. 'Then we had a few dates and I sensed our future lives would become entwined. Then last night I proposed.'

'Did he get down on one knee?' asked Anne.

'Yes, he did!' said Prunella. 'He took me back to the Maid of Kent.'

'The place where I first set eyes on her,' Tristan recalled.

'Halfway through the candlelit meal, he said he couldn't wait any longer,' Prunella explained 'I didn't know what he meant.

'Then he went down on one knee and said: "Prunella, you're the most wonderful person I've ever met. Would you do me the honour of becoming my wife?"

'I couldn't believe it. I burst into tears and somehow, in the middle of all the weeping and laughing, I found the energy to say: "Yes." Well, you can imagine all the other diners must have wondered what was going on.'

'Maybe they thought Tristan had dropped something and was stooping to pick it up,' I suggested.

'Maybe they did. But once he brought the ring out and slipped it on my finger, the place went mad. All the diners applauded and the waiters brought us free drinks!'

'That's brilliant, Pru. We're so happy for you both,' said Anne, giving her friend another hug.

'Yes. That's cool,' I said.

'As soon as we can, we'll be moving out and letting you two lovebirds have a bit of privacy,' Anne added.

'Don't worry,' said Prunella. 'You're welcome to stay on a bit longer. I know you two have had a difficult summer. I'm sure you'll be back in Chasehurst as soon as it becomes safe for you.'

I wasn't sure Tristan felt as equanimous as his fiancée. He was no doubt eager to pursue his new relationship unencumbered by strangers. However, he nodded and mumbled: 'That's right. We know you'll be moving on soon.'

'I'm sure it won't be long now,' said Anne. I wasn't so confident. I took a sip of wine. I said nothing.

The next day, Monday July the twenty-second, was forecast to be an even hotter day. Over breakfast, Anne revealed she was becoming homesick.

'D'you think we'd be safe to go home now?' she asked as I tucked into my fried egg and bacon.

'I don't know. I miss the place too,' I admitted. 'I particularly miss Fiesta. I didn't think I would, but I do. I wonder how he's getting on?

'Farrier mentioned the Special Surveillance Unit aren't interested in us anymore. What was it he said? "The world has moved on." Not that I necessarily trust a word he says – after what happened in Bedfordshire.'

'The trouble is there's that Russian agent at large as well,' she muttered.

'I know. For all we know, he may be parked outside the cottage right now.'

While we were washing up the cups and plates, Anne's mobile phone rang from an undisclosed number. As she answered it, a male voice asked: 'Anne, are you and your husband free tomorrow?'

It was Nat Evans, sounding as amiable as a politician on election day. 'I'd very much like to see you both, if that's possible.'

'Well, we're both available,' she replied. 'What did you have in mind?'

'I was wondering if you could come over to Salisbury? If you came by train, I could send a car to the station to pick you up. Naturally, we'll cover your travel costs.'

'I'll just have a word with my husband,' she said. Placing the handset on the table, she walked over to where I was wiping my hands.

'We're both free to go to see Nat Evans in Wiltshire tomorrow, aren't we? I was thinking we could go by train.' I nodded in agreement.

'Yes, Mr Evans,' she said, picking up the handset. 'We'd be delighted to see you. You say it's the BAMRA building at Porton Science Park? What time did you have in mind? Midday? Yes, that should suit us fine. We'll have a look at the train times and I'll let you know later today what time we're likely to arrive.'

36

The sun's rays speared through the curtains as we rose from our bed the following morning. Anne's silver wristwatch and mobile phone glinted in the beams of light on the dressing table.

I peered out across the creek. Barges and yachts were swaying in the gentle breeze.

This was officially the last day of term at my school, a day when the pupils are always in high spirits, looking forward to their long summer break. It was a day I enjoyed because there was often banter between teachers and pupils. We could chat in a relaxed away about their plans for the summer.

But this year, for the first time, I was missing all that. Instead, Anne and I were heading for Salisbury and our meeting with Nat Evans.

We caught the London train at Faversham Station just before half-past eight. After taking the Underground to Waterloo, we boarded the Salisbury train and arrived in the cathedral city, where six weeks before we had received hospital treatment, at twenty minutes to twelve.

As promised, Evans had sent a car to collect us from the station. It was a dark-blue Ford Galaxy which whisked us into the city suburbs and then through rolling English countryside.

Eventually, after nearly twenty minutes, we passed between two rows of magnificent horse chestnut trees and arrived at our destination.

High-security Porton Down, which covers a 7,000-acre site, was first opened in 1916 in response to Germany's development of chemical weapons. Since then it has acquired a reputation for carrying out biological and chemical warfare experiments.

The British Airborne Military Research Agency were based in a wing of a huge grey building which mainly houses the MoD's Defence Science and Technology Laboratory. There were several older buildings nearby which reminded me of the Bedfordshire Army camp. The whole site was protected by mile upon mile of chain-link fencing.

We immediately became aware of a host of warning notices and security signs as the car approached the redbrick gatehouse. Anne and I had to sign the visitors' book and were issued with identity passes.

We also had to hand over our mobile phones under the scrutiny of CCTV cameras. There was tension in the air. I was as jumpy as a dog being inspected at Cruft's.

Then, as unseen staff watched, our driver accompanied us on foot to the reception desk in the main building. There a dark-haired woman in a green uniform led us to the lifts and we were escorted to Evans' office at the far end of the second floor.

All I had remembered about Evans from our brief sighting at the funeral wake in Hanley St Peter was his white hair. As we shook his hand in turn, he appeared to be aged about sixty-four.

He was tall, slim, wore gold-rimmed glasses and had enhanced white teeth – which, to me, suggested affluence. He had a friendly manner.

'Anne! Bob! So glad you could make it,' he said. 'Nat Evans. Please come in. How was your journey?' He led us into his plush office with a fawn-coloured carpet, grey walls and a floor-to ceiling window overlooking open fields.

'Not too bad,' said Anne. 'I'm glad we didn't take the car.'

'How long was it?'

'About three and a half hours,' I said.

He found us both grey upholstered chairs. Then he stepped behind his bow-fronted walnut veneer desk and made himself comfortable in a high-backed, black leather chair.

'You've had a tiring journey. Can I get you tea or coffee?' asked Evans, who was smartly dressed in a grey suit, white shirt and bright blue tie.

'Two teas would be very nice – both with one sugar,' said Anne. The head of the research agency lifted his desk phone and asked a secretary to bring three cups.

'Before we go any further,' he said, 'I have to state quite clearly there is only so much I can tell you because of the Official Secrets Act.

'However, the Secretary of State wants me to thank both of you most sincerely for your sterling work in finding our missing scientist, Dr Maybourne. I'm not sure how you did it but thank God you did – despite you only having a few minutes with her before she died.'

'It grieves us we couldn't prevent her death, but we were glad to be of help. We did it partly for our friend Claudia,' said Anne.

She explained how we had located Allegra in Earlsbridge, how two Russian agents had pursued me after I visited Hampstead and how I'd been detained by MI5 for three weeks. She also explained how she herself had travelled to Scotland and found the family of the man whose corpse was used in the fake crash.

'I can't comment on any of those last details, but what I can say is that the message you passed to me from Dr Maybourne was of vital importance.

'We've had our suspicions for some time about one of the key members of our research team who was engaged on the Palladin project, the fastest and most powerful anti-drone laser system ever invented.'

Anne interrupted. 'Can I ask why it's so important?' she asked

'Defence chiefs are concerned about enemy nations attacking Britain with "drone swarms" in future combat operations,' he said.

'But Professor Morley has devised a laser powerful enough to shoot them out of the sky. The lasers are still not fully developed, but the aim is that they will eventually be launched from ships and submarines. They will be able to wipe out enemy drones within minutes of launch time.

'The Yanks have something similar, but their technology is not so suitable for the UK. Of course, the Russians are desperate to find out all they can about the professor's work.' Evans paused. He glanced down at a small laptop opened in front of him.

'I can't tell you how grateful we were to receive the intelligence from Dr Maybourne,' he said. 'I had personally asked her to let me know if she uncovered conclusive proof this person was aiming to sabotage the launch at the end of this month.

'Her code twenty-two message was confirming our suspicions. It was devastating news to us because the suspect performed a significant role in the enterprise. However, of course, we had to act. She was arrested. Her home was searched and it became clear she was part of the Eagle's Claw gang.'

Anne at once said: 'The Eagle's Claw? Those were Allegra's first words to us.'

'And I found an eagle's claw symbol on Jago Lawson's computer screen,' I pointed out.

'The Eagle's Claw, or Korot Orla to use the Russian phrase, is the name of the team of agents sent here by the Kremlin to learn as much as they could about this British project. They were then tasked with destroying the prototype which was scheduled to be tested in Wales.

'Because of the vital information we received from you, we carried out a thorough search and, yesterday afternoon, found an explosive device. It had been set to go off at the time of the launch.

'Of course, an Army bomb disposal team were alerted. The device was defused and removed. We've now aborted the launch. The trials will not recommence until we are completely certain the threat from enemy agents has passed.'

'But why Eagle's Claw?' asked Anne.

'It's simply a name the Russian agents used. Russia's coat of arms is a golden, double-headed eagle. At the base are two claws – one holding an imperial sceptre symbolising power and the other an imperial orb representing the world.

'This team of agents used the symbol of the claw holding the orb to recognise one another. I can't emphasise enough how grateful everyone is you passed on Dr Maybourne's final words.

'You can't imagine the time, ingenuity and plain hard work that went into building Palladin. It's so far cost Britain billions. So the nation owes you a huge debt of gratitude, both of you.

Have any of the newspapers contacted you?'

'No, but then we're not staying at our normal address at the moment,' Anne explained.

'Well, there was a reward for information leading to the discovery of Dr Maybourne. It was raised from five thousand pounds to ten thousand pounds and I'm going to recommend this money should be paid to yourselves.' We glanced at each other and smiled.

'That's very kind of you,' said Anne. 'But if the money were to be awarded to us, we would want it to go to Roderick Maybourne and his sons. They've suffered a terrible loss and deserve the money more than us.'

'A very noble gesture,' Evans said. 'I imagine the Government or the Palace may also find a way to reward you both. The two of you, on your own, have saved Palladin. By the way, I take it you haven't had lunch?'

'No, we haven't,' I replied.

'Well, later on I'm going to treat you both to a slap-up meal as a token of our deep gratitude.'

'If it weren't for Claudia, we probably wouldn't have known your name and phone number,' said Anne.

'How is Claudia?' he asked. 'I feel so sorry about the way she's been treated.'

'She's bearing up,' said Anne.

'The foreign agent behind that outrageous attempt to kidnap her has fled the country.'

'Dmitry Bogdanov?' said Anne.

'Yes, Bogdanov. That's not his real name. His real name is Ivan Volkov, which translates into English as "The Wolf." He's a colonel in the Russian military intelligence agency, the GRU.

'I'm afraid the British didn't act quickly enough after he was unmasked. A European arrest warrant was issued, but it was too late. He'd gone.

'We've found CCTV images of him flying out from Gatwick Airport. As a result, the Foreign Office are going to send some Russian diplomats home. It'll be all over the news in the next few days.'

'It's a shame Volkov wasn't caught, but that does suggest their game might be over for the moment,' I murmured.

'We think so. Their activities usually die down for a while after one of their agents has been exposed. You say you're not living at home at the moment. Is that because of Russian threats to yourselves?'

'Well, there were threats from the Russians. I was shot at after visiting the Russian shop in Hampstead,' I conceded. 'And Anne was chased by Volkov. But, to be honest, I'm more wary of the British. The Special Surveillance Unit burgled our home and then I got illegally detained.'

'I wasn't fully aware of that,' he said, stroking his chin. 'Maybe the Charter Committee were behind that.'

'What's that?' asked Anne.

'Well, I think I'm able to talk about this now – now that the risk of danger has abated. I don't know how much you both keep up with the news, but last year 10 Downing Street was forced to reveal the powers by which MI5 operate in this country.

'It was admitted agents are, on occasion and according to certain rules, permitted to engage in criminal activity under a secret order known as the "Third Direction."'

'I'd heard something about that,' I admitted, although Anne's face was blank.

Evans went on: 'Then in January this year the position changed again. The law was updated so that the MoD could better protect key personnel in the face of renewed threats from Russia.

'You might have heard about it – the Anonymity Charter, it's sometimes referred to. A top-level meeting was held between the ministry, counter-intelligence, GCHQ and MI5. They created a charter of new rules to assist individuals in securing new identities.

'They called themselves the Charter Committee and it was recommended that Professor Morley should be the first to benefit.'

'What were these rules?' I asked.

'I won't bore you, but they cover things like relocation of targeted individuals to a safe house, cosmetic surgery, birth re-registration, personal security, securing identities against accidental disclosure, monitoring communications – that sort of thing.

'We won Parliamentary approval and a provisional budget of seven hundred million pounds has been set aside for it.'

'And the new law gave them a mandate to do all that? I've heard there's a campaign being mounted against it on the grounds that this charter threatens civil liberties,' I said.

'Yes, some misguided people are trying to overturn the charter. They may succeed. But I'm afraid the threat from abroad is too great now. If it's overturned, the authorities will just have to find a way round it.

'We need these tougher protection measures to ensure the country's future is kept secure.' My temper began to rise like steam in a sauna.

'It's thanks to those draconian measures that I was snatched from my own home,' I said in a raised voice. 'I was blindfolded and abducted. Then I was deprived of my liberty for three weeks - locked up in an underground bunker.

'Admittedly, I had to bash the gaoler on the head, which I suppose I shouldn't have done, but I was desperate to escape.' Anne was shocked by my sudden burst of annoyance but sympathised with my feelings.

'You think the actions of this Charter Committee are justified, do you, Mr Evans?' she asked.

'We know that sometimes the needs of the individual have to become secondary to the needs of the community as a whole.

'I'm sorry to hear you were locked up for three weeks, Mr Shaw. But taking action like this to preserve and protect the identity of our leading scientists and government personnel is, in my view, a price worth paying.'

Now it was Anne's turn to raise her voice.

'You seem to think this charter gives the authorities a mandate to wield unlimited powers as they wish. They used those powers to steal a body from a heartbroken Scottish family to fake a death.

'You seem doubtful from the expression on your face, but I have looked into the eyes of the widow whose husband's body was snatched from a funeral parlour and used in the fake car crash.

'I have seen myself the personal anguish the charter people can cause. Is it a price worth paying?'

'Listen, I regret to hear about all the hurt that's been caused. None of this was known to me. I'm hearing about it for the first time.

'I'm sorry, Bob, you weren't treated in a more dignified way and I'm sorry about the upset caused to the family in Scotland, if that was the case. I will make personal inquiries about both these issues later today. All I can say is exceptional measures have to be taken in exceptional times.'

'Why was our friend Professor Morley chosen as the candidate for these protection measures?' Anne asked.

'There had been at least two attempts on his life and his work was vital to the future of Britain's security,' Evans replied.

'I've been a lifelong friend of the professor,' I said. 'Obviously he was based here at Porton Down.'

'No, he wasn't – not all the time. This was part of the problem. He sometimes worked here. He worked at the MoD in London. He worked in Cambridge. Sometimes he worked at his Gloucestershire home. Sometimes he worked at his London flat. For the security people, he presented a logistical nightmare.'

'So far he's the only person in Britain to be covered by this protection scheme?' I asked.

'No, we wanted to protect several key personnel involved in Britain's drone missile projects because we're so much in advance of the Russians – or so we believe at the moment – and the Kremlin has responded by encouraging them to defect or, if they won't do that, by eliminating them.

'I'm afraid Dr Maybourne was a special case. She refused to have anything to do with Charter. She insisted she was safe, living with her family. Of course, we argued with her, but we couldn't get her to change her mind and we all know how it turned out for her.'

'We were nearly stopped from passing on Dr Maybourne's dying words to you,' said Anne.

'Yes, I heard. A Russian sympathiser, a man named Lawson whom I knew vaguely, tried to kill you, Bob, didn't he?'

'That's right,' I said. 'He tried to shoot me when I tried to dial your number. Luckily, it was a blank round.'

'Lawson's been a thorn in our side for years,' he said. We looked at each other, shaking our heads. It had been three days since the incident at Willow Tree Farm.

Yet it was still astonishing to be sitting here, in these offices of the research agency, and be reminded that such a close friend of ours had a secret side to his life.

'We couldn't believe it when we found out what he'd done,' Anne observed.

Evans frowned. 'Lawson had a close pro-Russian contact working within the RAF's drone missile division and together they were sending secrets to Moscow. We also believe he may have been behind the incident in Little Coleswood in which Professor Morley was nearly killed.

'It was through Lawson the agents were able to rent the house in Andover where poor Dr Maybourne was discovered. He probably gave your description to the agents who then chased you from Hampstead.

'We think Lawson delved into documents kept at the professor's house and thereby discovered precisely where work on the Palladin project was taking place.'

'I always wondered why he kept so close to Gus and Claudia,' I muttered, thinking aloud.

'The only thing I can say in his defence is he always tried to look after Claudia,' Evans admitted. 'We understand he remonstrated with the Russians, pointing out to them she was oblivious as to her husband's whereabouts and making a point that they shouldn't harm her.

'But it seems his words may have fallen on stony ground.'

As I glanced past Evans' head at the green countryside beyond his window, I momentarily thought of the fields opposite our home in Hopgarden Lane.

'Mr Evans, d'you have any idea when it might be safe for us to return home?' I said. 'We've been forced to stay with a friend in a small two-bedroom flat and we're desperate to return to a normal life.'

'There's no reason why you shouldn't return home,' he replied. 'I'm sure the authorities can overlook the fact you left your gaoler with a bump on the head, in the circumstances.

'There should no longer be any reason for the Special Surveillance Unit to be seeking you out. What's more the Russians who targeted you are either dead or back in their motherland. It should be safe for you to go home.' We smiled at each other and linked hands.

'Anyway,' he said, 'd'you think it's time for lunch?'

37

White daisies and pink foxgloves tossed their heads in the light wind as we drove slowly up the lane towards our cottage on the following Thursday morning. Blood-red poppies had sprung up here and there in the fields on the far side of the hedge.

Every summer they reminded me of the lives lost in two world wars. I wound down my driver's window, soaking in the bright sunshine and the warm morning air. The oak and birch trees around us swayed in the breeze.

As the car drew up outside, we were greeted by an array of red, white and yellow roses in the flower borders next to the unmown lawn. Flourishing proudly by the fence stood purple asters and nodding blue clematis flowers.

'It's good to be back,' I murmured to Anne as we walked together to the front door just before midday. For a brief, chilling moment, the memory flashed across my mind of how, five weeks earlier, I was attacked in the hallway and frog-marched away.

I noticed the bare CCTV wires dangling on the wall and vowed to get the cable repaired as soon as possible. Anne unlocked the front door and pushed it gently forward.

'I wonder where Fiesta is?' I said, stooping to pick up two

letters lying on the mat. We didn't have to wait long. He must have heard our car pull up. I glanced round to recognise his black form pass gingerly up the drive, his upright tail twitching behind him.

He strolled up and brushed against my legs as if to say: 'Where on earth have you been?'

'Sorry, old boy,' I said, bending down to stroke him in the hall. 'We're back now.' I looked up to see Anne gazing down at us.

'Oh, Bob!' she sighed, stepping towards me and throwing her arms around me. Time stood still for a precious moment as we remained, hugging each other, by the foot of the stairs. The grass needed cutting. The hedge needed trimming. The roses needed pruning. But I felt as happy as a child on Easter morning.

We were back in the home we loved and, despite the dramas of the previous weeks, we had surmounted them and emerged relatively unscathed.

Neither of us spoke. We both seemed to know instinctively what each other was thinking and feeling. We were home and we could start to rebuild our lives again.

Anne made some tea while I put some food and water down on the kitchen floor for Fiesta. Then we opened the post together.

The first letter came from Allegra Maybourne's husband, Roderick. I wasn't sure how he had obtained our address. It was a long, rambling letter, thanking us again for finding his wife – even though we had been unable to save her.

Part of the letter said: '*Here, where I live with my sons, all of us very much alive, some of the flowers that have grown in our garden are dying off in the heat of the summer. But in the cemetery up* the road where my poor wife lies, along with the rest of the dead, grieving families have adorned the graves with the most beautiful living blooms in the most vibrant colours.'

Anne then picked up a second letter. It was from an assistant private secretary at 10 Downing Street and had the previous day's postmark. She opened it with rising excitement.

It said: '*Dear Mr and Mrs Shaw, The Prime Minister has asked me to write and thank you for the sterling efforts you have made over recent weeks on behalf of our country. The Chief of the Defence Staff has today confirmed it was largely through your efforts the missing scientist Dr Allegra Maybourne was located, albeit, sadly, in the closing moments of her life.*

'*He was full of praise for the way you passed on details of her final words to the ministry. As a consequence of your prompt action, the department was able to set measures in place to prevent a defence project that is vital for our nation's future from being sabotaged.*

'*While we have no wish to attract the glare of publicity to these matters, we wish to inform you personally of our gratitude for the admirable work you have carried out as private individuals in the interests of Britain.*

'*It is clear you took certain risks and made personal sacrifices to ensure the appropriate authorities were notified. Your actions have shown great social responsibility and initiative. It is the Prime Minister's intention, when events allow, to invite you to 10 Downing Street in order to express our gratitude in person.*'

'Who'd have thought we'd get a letter like that?' said Anne. 'We'll have to frame it and hang it on the wall.'

I nodded. 'It's great to be recognised for something after all the challenges of the past few weeks,' I agreed.

Ten minutes later, there was a loud knock on the front door.

I peered through the living-room blinds to recognise our neighbour, Linda Morrison, standing outside with a smile on her face. Although she was eighty-seven and walked with a stick, she was still alert and sprightly.

'Good to see you back,' she said, her green eyes twinkling as I opened the door.

'It's good to see you too,' I said.

'Do come in,' Anne yelled from the kitchen before emerging in the hall. 'Thank you so much for caring for Fiesta. Here's some money to cover the cost of the cat food.' She handed grey-haired Mrs Morrison a twenty-pound note.

'Oh, it wasn't as much as that,' said the old lady, who was wearing a long, pink and blue patterned dress and carrying a small grey handbag.

'No, I insist,' said Anne. 'You've been so kind looking after Fiesta at short notice. Come and sit down for a moment.' She led her to a chair beside the kitchen table. The old lady sat down with difficulty and placed the money in her bag.

'He's been no trouble,' she said. 'Except on one occasion I caught him with a small bird in his mouth.'

'That's strange,' I said. 'He hasn't chased birds for a while.'

'He's either been sleeping in the kitchen or creeping upstairs and sleeping on top of my bed,' she continued. 'But he's been restless. He's obviously missed you both. Anyway, it's good to see you back.'

'By the way, I don't know what's been going on, but we've had some strange cars driving slowly up the lane these last few weeks. I hope you're not in any trouble.'

'I'm afraid I haven't been paying for my drugs' I told her with a straight face. For a moment, she looked shocked. Then she realised I was joking and began to laugh.

'You're quite a comedian!' she declared as I smiled down at her. 'I also had a strange visitor a few days ago. It was a man looking for you, Bob.' My smile vanished as quickly as a teenager's first wage packet.

'It was a foreigner with a limp,' she said. 'I had a laugh and a joke with him because we've both got leg problems.'

'Did he have close-cropped hair?'

'Yes. That's right. What they used to call a crew-cut.' I nodded towards Anne. We both knew who the man was.

Mrs Morrison continued: 'He was asking if I knew where you were and I just said you'd both gone to stay with a friend. He wanted to know where, but of course you hadn't told me where and I couldn't advise him.' Mrs Morrison searched her handbag.

'Here you are, Bob,' she said. 'He asked me to give you this.' She removed a colourful leaflet and handed it to me.

'What's that, Bob?' Anne wondered.

'It's a leaflet from the food shop, Mamina Kukhnya. The woman at the counter couldn't find one when I called in,' I explained. 'How kind of him. Did the man say anything else?'

'You know the funny way foreigners sometimes speak,' she said. 'He said something like: "Tell Mr Shaw I hope to see him very soon. We have the business unfinished."'

'What on earth does that mean?' asked Anne.

'I think you can work it out,' I replied. 'He thought I knew how to find Gus.'

After Mrs Morrison had gone, I switched on the television and we settled down on the settee to watch the lunchtime news. Bizarrely, the thoughtful man with the restaurant leaflet featured in the first news item.

As Jonathan Evans had predicted, Britain was taking reprisals against Russia. The newsreader announced: *'Britain is to kick out twelve Russian diplomats after confirmation that a murdered government scientist was poisoned with a substance imported from Moscow. Senior Government scientist Dr Allegra Maybourne was found dead in an isolated house near Andover last month.*

'A post-mortem revealed she had been poisoned. Now further tests have indicated a Russian-sourced toxin was involved. The National Security Council in London was told foreign intelligence agents operating within the UK were believed to be behind the murder of the fifty-two-year-old mother-of-two.

'A visitor from Moscow, Dmitry Bogdanov was named by police earlier this week as a suspect. He went on the run and is now believed to have fled the country.

'His real name has been disclosed by a journalism website as Ivan Volkov, aged forty-two, who was a colonel in the Russian intelligence agency, the GRU. He was also being sought after a bungled kidnap attempt on a British citizen at a house in Gloucestershire.

'Today it can also be revealed for the first time that a suspected foreign agent has attempted to sabotage Britain's top-secret laser defence project, named Palladin.

'A woman alleged to have been working for the Russian government was arrested in Wiltshire over the past few days. She is accused of attempting to infiltrate a UK weapons research centre.

'Government sources say relations between the two countries broke down after discussions in Whitehall.

'A Foreign Office spokesman said today: "We gave the Russian government until midnight on Wednesday to explain their senior operative's involvement in the death of a British scientist found

dying from a Russian-sourced poison. The Kremlin has refused to treat our inquiries with respect and has been encouraging its agents to operate freely in this country without regard for the rule of law."

'A spokesman for the Russian Embassy said: "We can't understand why the Foreign Office is making such spurious claims. No Russian citizen has been involved in any illegal activity in Britain. We are meanwhile continuing to demand details from the Home Office relating to the suspicious death of an innocent Russian tourist in Gloucestershire on July the thirteenth."

'On Monday, a thirty-eight-year-old British citizen, Jago Anthony Lawson, from Burford, Oxfordshire, appeared before a special court in Oxford charged with offences under the Official Secrets Act and attempted murder. He was remanded in custody for one week.'

Anne and I looked at each other.

'You don't think there's any mistake, do you?' I asked her.

'Mistake? How d'you mean?'

'That Dmitry Bogdanov character – he really has left Britain, has he?'

'Well, Evans spoke about him being caught on CCTV flying out of Gatwick.'

'Yes, you're right – plus it's on the news. He must be back in Moscow by now.'

'Listen, Bob. On Saturday, I'm going shopping in Canterbury. While there, I'll call in at the travel agents. It might still be possible for us to go to the Black Forest. And next week I want to visit Jemima and give her a bit of support. She's in a hell of a state.'

'It must have been a shock,' I admitted. 'Yes, two weeks in Germany would be great! I was thinking about magical woodlands and green hills of the Black Forest when I first saw Gus on the train. But you know what August is like. Our only chance might be finding a last-minute cancellation.'

'While in Canterbury, I also want to get Pru and Tristan an engagement present,' Anne explained. I leaned over and kissed her on the cheek. When it comes to largesse, Anne could be as kind as a summer morning.

'We gave Prunella flowers and wine before we left,' I pointed out.

'I know, but that was for putting us up. We still need to get them an engagement gift. I was thinking of buying a coffee machine. Pru loves coffee and she'd really appreciate one.'

'That sounds cool,' I said.

38

When Saturday morning came, Anne set off for the shops promptly at nine o'clock. After a late breakfast, I collected my toolbox from the garden shed, in between light showers, and began repairing the CCTV lead at the front of the house with a cable connector I'd bought the day before.

Just before nine thirty, the phone rang. I put my screwdriver down and hurried to the hallway table to grab the receiver.

'Hello, Bob?' said a voice. It was a cultured voice with a deep, slightly husky tone. I recognised it straight away.

'You've got a nerve after all this time,' I exclaimed.

'You sound angry, Bob. Are you angry?'

'Yes, I am. I'm bloody angry,' I admitted. 'You can't imagine what we've been through, Gus. Or should I call you Chris?'

'It doesn't matter now,' the professor replied. 'You can use either. I've been toying with the idea of calling you for a few days. In the end, I thought I'd leave it till today, when you're not in school.'

'School broke up on Tuesday, but, in any case, you're lucky to find me here. We've been away for the best part of two months.'

'Another of your cycling holidays? Where did you go?'

'No, it wasn't a holiday – mainly thanks to you.'

'How d'you mean?'

'We've spent weeks trying to work out whether you're dead or alive, and it's got us into a lot of trouble.'

'I've heard about the first-rate work you both did in finding Allegra and passing on her message.' There was a pause while my friend had a short coughing fit.

'It's all right,' he said. 'I'm still with you.'

'Did you also hear about your brother-in-law?' I asked.

'I know. Spying for Russia. I saw it in Tuesday morning's papers. He was in court on Monday, wasn't he? I couldn't believe it. I had to read it several times. I feel so sorry for Jem. That's when I started thinking about calling you.'

'It didn't say much, did it?' I said. 'Reporting restrictions.'

'It mentioned an offence of attempted murder. D'you know what that was?'

'Yes. He tried to shoot me. I was at his farm when Anne found out Allegra's message was meant for Jonathan Evans. I tried to use his landline and he pulled a pistol on me. Thankfully, someone had replaced the live round with a blank and I recovered pretty quickly.'

'God. I'll have to ask Nat about that.'

'Yes, you do that. Gus, we've had quite a time this summer. Your pal Ryan set on me when I followed you both from the Tube station. I ended up in the UCH.'

'I'm really sorry about that. I gave him a hell of a rollicking.'

"We've upset the Kremlin,' I went on. 'I've got Russian bullets in the back of the car to prove it and then Anne was chased through the woods. And we've also upset the British. I got locked up for asking too many questions. All because of you.'

'I can't apologise enough, but you have to try to see it from my point of view. The Russian Eagle Claw cell had orders to eliminate me. A decision was taken at the highest level for me to change my identity. They warned me it wouldn't be easy – and it wasn't.'

'Why at least didn't you acknowledge me when I spoke to you at Euston and then at your flat?'

'Don't you see? I'd consented to take part in their protection scheme. Once I'd done that, I had to play it by their rules. I couldn't tell them: "A very good friend of mine has recognised me, so I stopped on a street corner and we had a catch-up."

'They were paying for me to change my facial features with plastic surgery. They were paying for me to have a bodyguard. They were arranging my accommodation in a safe house. They were arranging a new name and identity. I was part of a programme.'

'You were part of a charade,' I said. 'So the whole business of faking your death was carried out totally with your consent?'

'Yes. I didn't really have any choice.'

'So you had your face rebuilt from scratch?'

'Yes. You wouldn't recognise me now, Bob. Since January, I've been on a programme conducted by a brilliant oral and maxillofacial surgeon at the Hamelin Clinic. He's one of the world's top experts on treating the entire cranio-maxillofacial complex.

'He and his team have altered everything. I've been having my skull reshaped. I had a whole new set of dental implants and the old ones, for some reason, were wrapped up and taken away.

'They also took away my signet ring, which had my old initials on, and took a sample of my DNA. I don't really know why. They said it was best I didn't ask too many questions.

'As well as the implants, I've had rhinoplasty and jaw

reconstruction. My face has been like a miniature building site. But strangely enough, I enjoyed the whole experience. I received a new name and they even concocted an entire back story for Christopher Neal Ward.'

'Your voice is still the same,' I remarked.

'It's the only thing that wasn't changed. Listen, this isn't the way I've wanted to lead my life,' he insisted. He broke off to cough again. Then he went on: 'The Russians approached me and asked me to work for them. They knew I was involved in Palladin and wanted it for themselves.

'It's the most sophisticated anti-drone laser system ever invented – even though I say so myself. If the full details ever became public knowledge, all the major world powers would want it. I won't bore you with the technical stuff, but, of course, I refused to work for the Russians and that's when the trouble started.

'They thought they could persuade me. I was nearly mown down by a lorry and nearly killed in the street in East London. That's when the MoD decided to set up the Charter Unit and devised a plan to make the world believe I was dead. Everyone fell for it.'

'Except me.'

'Yes, except you. Although I'm not sure how you rumbled me.'

'I saw you on the Tube at Euston Square at the start of May.'

'Oh, I see.' He went quiet for a moment. He was panting like a terrier.

'If you were meant to be assuming a new identity,' I said, 'I'd have thought you wouldn't take the risk of travelling on the Tube where you could be seen.'

'It must've been just a million-to-one chance you were there,

Bob,' he said. 'At that point, I'd only been given an initial assessment at the clinic and I was mostly wearing dark glasses. A week later, my appearance had completely altered.'

'You weren't wearing dark glasses when I first saw you. Only your hair looked different. I don't know why you didn't go to the clinic by cab.'

'I love trains. Always have done. One of my pals helped design the latest engines. Anyway, what's happened has happened. You saw me and you were like a dog with a bone. You didn't give up, did you? Nor Anne.'

'We felt an obligation to your family. Anne spent weeks searching for the truth of what happened. She even went to the trouble of finding your up-to-date address. She put a tracker on Ryan's car.'

'Always was a damn clever woman, your Anne.'

'Gus, we couldn't understand what was going on with you. After all, we'd been to your funeral.'

'I hear there was an excellent turn-out.'

'Yes, there were some good hymns and we all laughed when the vicar called you Nigel by mistake.' I thought back to the lonely lychgate, the hillside path, the daffodils, the fluttering flag, the coffin decked in flowers and the tearful mourners.

'You know I was very sorry to hear about Allegra's death,' he continued, speaking hesitantly. 'She was a brilliant scientist and a lovely, warm human being. She was offered the same protection deal as I was, but she declined. She was a family woman and didn't feel under threat in the same way as me.'

He stopped for breath. Then he went on: 'I imagine the Russkies tried to recruit her as well, but I've no way of knowing. She didn't have quite as much knowledge of drones as I did, but she would still have been of great use to them. She insisted there was no way she would change her identity and, as a result, fell victim to the Eagle's Claw.'

'Gus, it's clear Anne and I are not the only ones to have suffered through your decision to change your identity. Claudia and the children have suffered as well – as I'm sure you're aware.'

'Yes, Bob, it grieves me to admit it, but I've treated Claudia very badly. But, you know, we'd been drifting apart for a long time. We were making each other unhappy. I can say this to you because I've always regarded you as a friend.'

I smiled. 'Well, I suppose we still are. And, if we're still friends, I have to ask you this. Was it just in order to save your skin that you agreed to pretend to be dead? Or was there a woman on the scene – such as a well-known pop singer?' The line went silent for a moment.

Then the professor said: 'I can see there's no hiding the truth from you, my old friend. You're right. There was another woman.'

'I thought so!' I muttered.

'But it's not Marina Dean, as the press suggested. The new woman in my life was called Lisa. She's Chinese.' My eyes lit up.

'We heard a Chinese woman was seen at your flat, but we thought she was your bodyguard's girlfriend,' I said with an amused expression.

'Who told you about her?'

'A neighbour at Demerara Place.'

'No. She was my girlfriend. Bob, I realise now I've behaved very stupidly. I feel I can tell you all this now because you've been a lifelong friend. I know I've let my family down. I was just swayed by her captivating looks, her flirtatious smile, her shapely legs. But now she's left me.'

'I suppose she couldn't put up with the subterfuge anymore,' I suggested.

'Partly that,' he agreed.

'Why on earth didn't you just get a quickie divorce and take her to China while you had the chance? It would've been a lot simpler. No one would've found you there.'

'No, I'm afraid that would never have worked. They'd have still found me. In any case, I was determined to try to carry on with my work in Britain.'

'You've given up a lot – your country house and your children, for example.'

'I'd tired of playing the country squire. Material things have never meant much to me and the Government promised to pay me compensation in any case.

'But you're right about the children. I've missed them terribly and sometimes I lie in bed at night wondering if giving them up was a sacrifice too far.' The line went silent for a moment. All I could hear was my friend's heavy breathing.

'Are you all right?' I asked.

'No,' he said. 'Bob, there's something else I need to tell you. I'm dying.'

'You're dying?'

'Yes, this time it's for real. I'm calling you from an isolation ward. I don't suppose it matters now if I tell you. I'm in the Royal London. Obviously, I'm not allowed visitors.'

'Oh, God, Gus. What's happened?'

'Poisoned,' he muttered. 'You know all the business in the

news about Dmitry Bogdanov? I was his target and he found me in the end.'

'Oh my God, Gus! That's terrible!' I said. 'How on earth did that happen?'

'They weren't as cute as your Anne using a tracker. They did it the hard way, following Ryan's car over several days.'

'Was it a black Audi Q7 by any chance?'

'Yes, it was! How did you know?'

'I was once followed by the same car.'

'Bogdanov must've followed me on foot once he'd discovered where I'm now living. He put something in my drink when I was in a café. I haven't got long to go.'

'Gus, I don't know what to say.'

'They haven't told me what poison it is yet. Novichok's been ruled out. The lab are still carrying out tests, but I'm getting weaker by the day. I just phoned to talk to you while I'm still coherent – you know, before I'm completely gaga.'

'You know, of course, if there's anything at all I can do,' I said. It occurred to me that, when Farrier told me the world had moved on, this might have been what he was referring to. It was no longer so vital to safeguard Gus's new identity as if it were a state secret.

'Well, you could say sorry to Anne and Claudia, and anyone else I've offended,' Gus said. 'I've made a will, leaving everything to Claudia and the children.'

I lost the power of speech for a moment. At the beginning of the conversation, I'd been furious at my friend's gall in calling me. Now I was full of remorse at my initial comments and full of pity at his plight.

He continued: 'The British did the best they could to protect me with a new identity but somehow they found a chink in the armour. However, the British research programme will carry on. Britain will carry on.

'Palladin will eventually be trialled and, I believe, prove successful. There will be other advances in weapons technology. It's just that they won't be designed by me. It'll be someone else.'

As he was speaking, a shocking thought occurred to me. In his twenties, Morley had studied Russian. Had he worked for them himself – like Lawson - at some point in his past and then turned against them? Was that the issue that had enraged the Kremlin?

After all, oligarchs, double agents and disgraced former servants of the motherland are their normal prey in Britain – not scientists. I had no proof and it was a question I decided to leave for the moment.

'It's bad luck that agent found you,' I observed.

'There's a lot of foreign agents out there,' he replied. 'They're in every town, every city. They look like you and me. It might be the man at the next table in the restaurant or the woman sitting behind you in the pub.

'It might be the old man sitting two rows back on the bus or the old lady sitting opposite you on the train. Sometimes they're inactive for years and mingle with ordinary members of the community. Then the word comes and they act.'

'Isn't there anything doctors can do for you?' I wondered.

'There may be some treatment they can devise if they discover exactly what it is that's killing me. But they would probably be too late. They've already consulted the best brains in the medical world. I sense I'm on the way out and nothing can be done.'

'I'm most terribly sorry, Gus. I'll make a point of explaining everything to Anne and Claudia. Don't you think it might be an idea for you to call Claudia yourself? She and the children would love to speak to you. Maybe, for one last time … '

'I don't want to put the family through any more trauma. I haven't got long. I'd prefer to remember them as I knew them. I understood what I was doing when I signed the consent forms to make a fresh start. I think, in the circumstances, my words of apology and regret might sound better coming from you, my old friend.'

*

Of course, when Anne returned from Canterbury, I told her all about my unexpected phone call. Some of the information was already known to her, but she gasped in surprise at most of my revelations.

She was devastated to hear Gus Morley was slowly dying. He told me at the end of the call he would be unlikely to last out the end of the summer.

We called in on Prunella the following morning to present her and Tristan with their engagement present – a black pod coffee machine. The journalist, who was flaunting her new yellow midi-dress, tried it out at once and we were the first guests to be served with steaming hot cups of beautifully-blended coffee.

Later, as we drank wine outside The Yacht pub beside the rippling waters of the creek, I related details of my conversation with the professor to Tristan and Prunella.

They both laughed when I mentioned Gus's fling with the Chinese woman, but Anne, wearing a blue off-the-shoulder dress, didn't share their hilarity. She frowned and suggested Lisa might have been a Chinese government agent. She had never mentioned this before.

I at once felt as though a bright sun had risen from amid the cloudy skies. Shadows had fallen away. A new day had brought a new vision.

Could Anne's words be true? Could Gus have been pursued by the forces of one enemy power, only for them to be outwitted by a representative of a rival - a woman who had managed to inveigle her way into his inner sanctum and even share his bed?

It's a tactic that's been commonly employed by intelligence chiefs for centuries – using a seductive 'femme fatale' to wheedle confidential information from an influential figure. It's a tactic the Russians themselves are extremely familiar with.

A voice in my head reminded me the woman who wins a man's heart is often the one who wins his secrets.

Our friends' smiles gradually faded. They could see we had suspicions about Gus's latest liaison. Prunella immediately tried to move the conversation on. She clutched Tristan's hand tightly as she topped up all our glasses.

Then she declared: 'I don't understand why Gus was considered such a prize to the Russians anyway. It's just the information they crave. Scientists are two a penny. One dies and another springs up in their place. I'm sure, even as we speak, other senior scientists are filling the shoes of Gus and Dr Maybourne.'

'I'm not certain I agree with you,' I said. 'Not in this case. It's the person who's invaluable. His brain, his personal thoughts can't be replicated by another brain or by a computer.'

'I don't know about that,' Tristan interjected. 'I've heard that computers will one day be more advanced than humans – if that hasn't happened already.'

'No,' I insisted. 'There's something unique about the human brain. The minds of men like Gus are of vital importance for the future. I've been thinking about this a great deal since my phone conversation with him.

'It was Albert Einstein who said something like: "Imagination is more important than knowledge. For knowledge is limited, whereas imagination embraces the entire world, stimulating progress, giving birth to evolution." You can replace one scientist with another and they will work with the same information and knowledge.

'But every now and then a man comes along whose work transcends that of others and whose abilities are so great, their role becomes vital to the nation and their contribution to society becomes the envy of other states.' Prunella frowned.

'That's too profound for me,' she remarked, draining her glass.

'I'll get more wine,' I announced, rising from my chair and heading in the direction of the bar. I felt a warm hand on my arm as I reached the pub door.

'I'll help you, darling,' said Anne, as we stepped inside. She stopped me from proceeding further towards the bar counter.

'You're upset, aren't you?' she whispered, gazing fondly into my eyes.

'Yes,' I admitted. 'I've lost my friend once. Now I'm set to lose him again. Life's tough. After all the problems he's caused, you'd think I'd be more in control of my emotions.'

'You'll move on, darling,' Anne assured me. 'We'll all move

on. We have to.'

'Yes, you're right. I know you're right. But it'll take time. It'll take a lot of time.'

'You've got time,' she said. 'Come on. Let's go and get that wine.'

THE END

ACKNOWLEDGEMENTS

My sincere thanks go to the following:

My friends Richard Brooks, Bob Ellis, Geoff Verney and Chris and Roseann Ellis for reviewing the initial drafts of my manuscript and for their support and encouragement.

TV journalist John Cookson for his friendship and advice; Simon Dormer for assistance with my website; graphic artist Charlotte Mouncey for the cover design; and to my publisher James Essinger for his unfailing hard work, patience and support.

My understanding partner Lin for her support at all times.

Caroline and Stan Sturgess, the parents of Dawn Sturgess, who graciously agreed that the book could be dedicated to their daughter. Caroline was kind enough to say: 'We hope the book is well received.'

Marina Litvinenko, the widow of Alexander Litvinenko, for agreeing the book could be dedicated to her late husband and for her help and support.

BY THE SAME AUTHOR

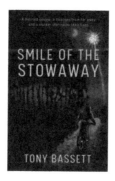

Desperate to reach England, a bedraggled immigrant clings precariously beneath a couple's motor home as they cross the Channel. Once holidaymakers Bob and Anne overcome their shock at his discovery and their initial reservations, they welcome the friendly stranger into their home in defiance of the law.

But their trust is stretched to the limit when the police accuse the smiling twenty-three-year-old of a gruesome murder. Could this man from six thousand miles away be guilty? Or is the real killer still out there?

Former national newspaper journalist Tony Bassett tells how Anne turns detective, battling against a mountain of circumstantial evidence and police bungling to discover the truth.

This gripping first novel concerning a death in a remote Kentish country cottage is packed with mystery, suspense and occasional touches of humour.

ISBN 978-1-911546-45-0
Available from www.amazon.co.uk
www.theconradpress.com and all good bookshops